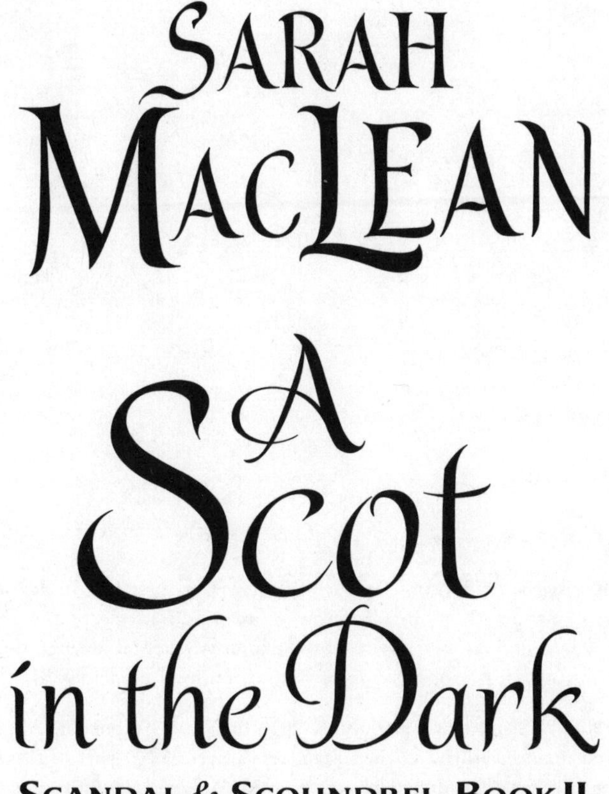

SCANDAL & SCOUNDREL, BOOK II

AVONBOOKS

An Imprint of HarperCollins*Publishers*

This is a work of fiction. Names, characters, places, and incidents are products of the author's imagination or are used fictitiously and are not to be construed as real. Any resemblance to actual events, locales, organizations, or persons, living or dead, is entirely coincidental.

First Avon Books mass market printing: September 2016
First Avon Books hardcover printing: August 2016

ISBN 978-0-06-246584-9

16 17 18 19 20 QGM 10 9 8 7 6 5 4 3 2 1

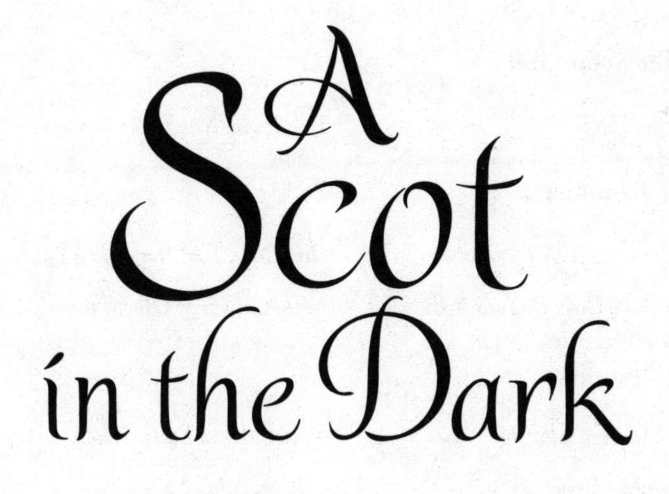
A Scot
in the Dark

Romances by Sarah MacLean

Scandal & Scoundrel

A Scot in the Dark

The Rogue Not Taken

Rules of Scoundrels

Never Judge a Lady by Her Cover

No Good Duke Goes Unpunished

One Good Earl Deserves a Lover

A Rogue by Any Other Name

Love by Numbers

Eleven Scandals to Start to Win a Duke's Heart

Ten Ways to Be Adored When Landing a Lord

Nine Rules to Break When Romancing a Rake

The Season

For the scandalous girls

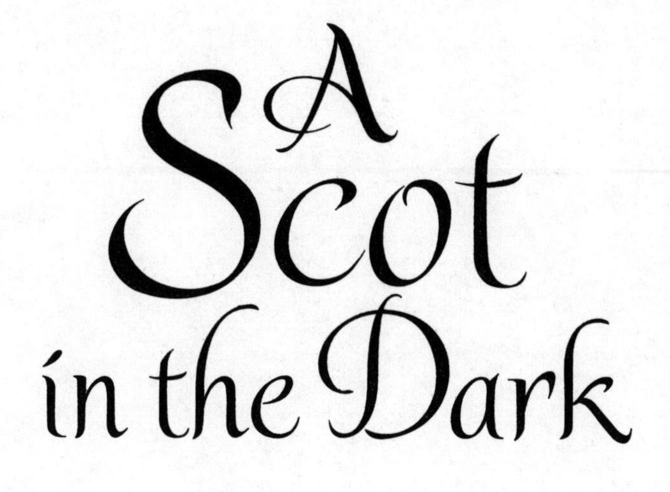
A Scot in the Dark

Scandal & SCOUNDREL

Vol 2 / Iss 1 Sunday, 9 May 1834

WARNICK'S WILD WARD

WE HAVE IT on excellent authority that the oddsmakers on St. James's are wagering that a certain duke has returned to London to remind his not-so-young ward that her gossip is not his gain. In the brisk spring air, the Duke of Warnick dons the mantle of matchmaker for Miss Lillian Hargrove, now known as MISS MUSE to those who have heard of (or, better, seen!) the promiscuous painting that has scandalized Society and summoned the SCOTTISH SCOUNDREL south! Excitement is expected with the arrival of the Highland Devil (and Halfhearted Duke). All that can be assured is that spring will bring more tartan to town . . . and *ton*.

MORE TO COME.

Prologue

DUCAL DEVASTATION!
ONE DOZEN DAYS OF DARKNESS AND DEMISE

March 1829

Bernard Settlesworth, Esquire, believed that name was destiny.

Indeed, as the third in a familial line of solicitors to the aristocracy, it was difficult not to believe such a thing. Bernard took immense pride in his work, which he performed with precision on nearly every day of the year. After all, he would tell himself, the British aristocracy was built on the hard work of men such as he. Without the Bernard Settlesworths of the world expertly calculating ledgers and deftly managing enormous estates, the House of Lords would crumble, leaving nothing but the dust of ancient lines and fortunes.

He did the Lord's work, ensuring the aristocracy remained standing. And solvent.

And though he took pride in all aspects of his work, there was nothing Bernard enjoyed quite so much as meeting with new inheritors, for it was in those moments that the Settlesworth name was best put to work—settling worth.

Bernard enjoyed this part best, that is, until tragedy struck the Dukedom of Warnick.

Two marquesses. Six different earls and baronets. A landed gentleman and his three sons. A vicar. A ship's captain. A hatter. A horse breeder. And one duke.

Lost to a spate of tragedies that included, but was not limited to, a carriage accident, a hunting mishap, a robbery gone wrong, a drowning in the Thames, an unfortunate incident with influenza, and a truly unsettling incident with a cormorant.

Seventeen dukes, if he were honest, Bernard supposed—all dead. All within the span of a fortnight.

It was a turn of events—seventeen turns of events—unheard of in British history. But Bernard was nothing if not dedicated, even more so when it fell to him to play protector to such an old and venerable title, to its vast lands (made vaster by the rapid, successive death of seventeen men, several of whom died without issue), and large fortunes (made larger by the same).

And so it was that he stood in the great stone entryway of Dunworthy Castle in the cold, windy, wild of Scotland, face-to-face with Alec Stuart, once seventeenth in line for the Dukedom of Warnick, now the last known heir to the title.

Face-to-face wasn't quite accurate. After being greeted by a pretty young woman, Bernard had been left to wait, surrounded by massive tapestries and a handful of ancient weaponry which appeared to have been haphazardly affixed to the wall.

And so he waited.

And waited.

After three quarters of an hour, two large dogs appeared, bigger than any he'd ever seen, grey and wild. They approached, the movements deceptively lazy. Bernard pressed himself to the stone wall, hoping they would decide to find another, more appetizing victim. Instead, they sat at his feet, wire-haired heads reaching nearly to his chest, grinning up at him, no doubt thinking him quite tasty.

Bernard did not care for it. Indeed, for the first time in his career, he considered the possibility that soliciting was a less than enjoyable profession.

And then the man arrived, looking wilder than the dogs. He was dark-haired and big as a house—Bernard had never seen a man so big—well past six and a half feet, he imagined, with what might have been twenty stone on his broad, muscled frame, and none of it fat. Bernard could tell that bit, because the man wasn't wearing a shirt.

Indeed, he wasn't wearing trousers, either.

He was wearing a kilt. And carrying a broadsword.

For a moment, Bernard wondered if he'd traveled through time as well as space on the journey to Scotland. It was, after all, 1829, despite the Scotsman appearing as though he'd arrived via three centuries earlier.

The enormous man ignored him, tossing the sword up onto the wall where it stuck as though by sheer force of its owner's will. That same owner who then turned his back on Bernard and made to leave.

Bernard cleared his throat, the sound louder than he'd intended in the massive stone space, loud enough for the man to turn and cast a lingering look over the solicitor's diminutive-in-comparison frame. After a long silence, he said, "Who are you?"

At least, that's what Bernard thought he said. The words were thick on the man's tongue, wrapped in brogue.

"I—I—" Bernard collected himself and willed the stutter away despite being surrounded by beasts both human and canine. "I am waiting for an audience with the master of the house."

The man rumbled, and Bernard imagined the deep sound was amusement. "Careful. These stones shan't like hearin' that ye think they've a master."

Bernard blinked. He'd heard tales of mad Scots, but he hadn't expected to meet one. Perhaps he'd misunderstood in the confusion of rolling Rs and missing syllables. "I beg your pardon."

The man studied him for a long moment. "Mine or the keep's?"

"For . . ." Bernard wasn't sure what to say. He wasn't apologizing to the castle, was he? He tilted his head. "Is Mr. Stuart here?"

The enormous man rocked back on his heels, and Bernard had the distinct impression that his obvious discomfort was pleasing to the great brute. As though he shouldn't be the one who was uncomfortable, what with traipsing around the castle half nude. "Aye."

"I've been waiting nearly an hour for him."

The dogs sensed his irritation and stood, clearly offended by it. Bernard swallowed.

"Angus. Hardy." Instantly, they retreated to their master's side.

And it was then that Bernard knew. He looked to the half-naked man across the entryway and said, "You are he."

"Aye, but we still have nae established who you are."

"Alec!" A young woman's voice echoed through the castle. "There's a man here. Says he's a solicitor from London!"

The new Duke of Warnick didn't look away from Bernard as he raised his voice in reply. "He also says he's been waiting for me for an hour."

"Seemed nothing good could come of a fancy London solicitor," the voice sang down. "Why bother you while you were having a spar?"

"Why, indeed," the Scot replied. "Apologies. My sister does nae care for the English."

Bernard nodded. "Is there a place we might speak more privately?"

"As I care even less for the English than my sister does," the duke said, "we needn't stand on ceremony. You are welcome to state your purpose here and now. And then you may leave."

Bernard imagined the man's view of England would change quite a bit once he discovered he'd become a peer of the realm. An exceedingly wealthy one. "Of course. It's my very great pleasure to tell you that, as of twelve days ago, you are the Duke of Warnick."

Throughout his career, Bernard had witnessed all manner of

response to the reality of inheritance. He'd stood by in the face of devastation of those who had lost beloved fathers, and recognized the eagerness on the face of those with not-so-beloved sires. He'd witnessed the shock of distant inheritors, and the joy of those whose fortunes had changed in the blink of an eye. And, on the least pleasurable of his days, he'd witnessed the devastating burden of inheritance—when a newly minted aristocrat discovered that his title had come with nothing but incapacitating debt.

But in the more than twenty years that he had served the upper echelons of the aristocracy, Bernard had never once met with apathy.

Until now, when the Scotsman he'd crossed a country to find calmly said, "Nae," turned on his heel, and made for the exit, dogs on his heels.

Settlesworth sputtered his confusion. "Your . . . Your Grace?"

A long bout of laughter came at the honorific. "I've no interest in an English title. And I certainly have no interest in being anyone's grace."

With that, the twenty-first Duke of Warnick, last of a venerable line and rich as a king, disappeared.

Bernard waited another hour in the stone keep and a full three days at the only inn in the nearby town, but the duke had no interest in speaking with him again.

And so it was that for the next five years, the duke rarely showed face in London and, when he did, he eschewed all things aristocratic. Within months, London society had discerned his disdain and decided that it was they, in fact, who disdained him, and not the other way around.

The Diluted Duke, they contended, was worth neither time, nor energy. After all, seventeenth in line for a dukedom was virtually no duke at all.

Such a view suited Alec Stuart, proud Scotsman, more than well, and he resumed his life without a second thought for the trappings of his title. As he was no monster, he managed his now vast estates with meticulous care, ensuring that those who relied upon Warnick lands were well and prosperous, but he avoided London, believing that as long as England ignored him, he could ignore England.

And England did ignore him, right up until it didn't.

Right up until a missive arrived, revealing that alongside the estates and servants and paintings and carpets he had inherited, alongside the title he had no interest in using, the Duke of Warnick had inherited something else entirely.

A woman.

Chapter 1

LOVELY LILY TURNED MISS MUSE!

April 1834
Royal Academy Exhibition
Somerset House, London

Miss Lillian Hargrove was the most beautiful woman in England.

It was an empirical fact, requiring absolutely no confirmation from experts on the subject. One had only to set eyes upon her, noting her porcelain skin, precisely symmetrical features, high cheekbones, full lips, curving ears, and a pretty, straight nose that evoked the very best of classical sculpture, and one simply knew.

Add to it her red hair, somehow not at all brash but a rich, golden hue that evoked the most heavenly of sunsets, and her grey eyes like a summer storm, and there was no question at all.

Lillian Hargrove was perfect.

So perfect, that the fact she had come from nothing—that she lacked title, social standing, and dowry, that she had been plucked from Lord knew where by London's finest artist, to whom she was not married—was somehow rendered irrelevant when she entered a room. After all, nothing blinded gentlemen (titled or otherwise) quite like beauty, a fact that was enough to set any matchmaking mama with an invitation to Almack's on edge.

Which was why the female half of the aristocracy took exceeding pleasure in the events of the twenty-fourth of April, 1834, the opening day of the Royal Academy Exhibition of Contemporary Art, and the day Lillian Hargrove—current favored beauty of the scandal sheets—was made a proper scandal.

And ruined. Thoroughly.

Later, when that same subsection of the *ton* whispered fervently about the events of the day, white gloves hiding fingertips stained black with ink from the gossip rags they swore they never read, the conversation would always end with a horrified, gleeful "The poor thing never saw it coming."

And she hadn't.

Indeed, Lily had thought it would be the best day of her life.

It was the day she had been waiting for her entire life—all twenty-three years, forty-eight weeks. It was the day Derek Hawkins was to propose.

Not that she had known Derek for her entire life. She hadn't. She'd known him for six months, three weeks, and five days—since he'd approached her on the afternoon of Michaelmas as she lingered in the Hyde Park sun on one of the last warm days of the year, and told her, in no uncertain terms, that he was going to marry her.

"You are a revelation," he'd said in his cool, crisp voice, surprising her from her book.

Another might have considered his unexpected arrival the reason for her breathlessness, but Lily had known better. He had taken her breath away because he had found her, ignored in her place in the margins. Despite her beauty, she was alone and unnoticed by the world, thrice-orphaned—first by her land steward father; then by a string of ducal guardians, each meeting a quick end; and, finally, in full, by the neglect of the current duke.

In her loneliness, she'd become very adept at being unseen, so, when Derek Hawkins noticed her—when he saw her with the full, blinding force of his gaze—she'd fallen quite in love. Quite instantly.

Lily had done her best to seem unaffected by his words. After all, she had not read every London ladies' magazine published in the last five years for nothing. Looking up at him, she tried her best, softest smile and said, "We have not met, sir."

He'd crouched next to her at that, removing the book from her lap—charming her with his blinding white teeth and even more blinding impertinence. "A beauty such as you should not have time for books."

She blinked, drawn to his cool blue eyes, trained upon her as though they were the only two people in all London. In all the world. "But I like books."

He'd shaken his head. "Not as much as you shall like me."

She'd laughed at the boast. "You seem very certain of yourself."

"I am very certain of you," he'd said, lifting her hand from her lap and pressing a warm kiss to her gloved knuckles. "I am Derek Hawkins. And you are the muse for which I have been searching. I intend to keep you. For all eternity."

She'd caught her breath at the vow. At the way it evoked other, more formal ones.

Certainly, meeting Derek Hawkins was a shock. She'd been reading about him for years—he was a legend, an artist and star of the stage, renowned throughout London and beyond as one of the most skilled theatrical minds of a generation. News of his talent and good looks preceded him—and while Lily could not in the moment confirm the former, the latter appeared quite accurate.

But it was not his celebrity that won Lily over. She had more than fluff between her ears, after all. She did not dream of a famous suitor.

She dreamed of a suitor who would ensure she was never alone again.

After all, Lily had been alone for her entire life.

In the days and weeks that followed, Derek had courted her, playing the part of the perfect gentleman, escorting her to autumn festivals and winter events, even hiring an older female servant to chaperone them on public outings.

And then, on a cold, snowy afternoon in January, he'd sent a carriage for her, and she'd been ferreted to his studio—the inner sanctum of his artist's world.

Alone.

There, in the sun-soaked room, surrounded by dozens of canvases, he'd honored her with his words and promises, worshipped her beauty and her perfection and vowed to keep her with him. Forever.

The words—so pretty and tempting and precisely what she'd always dreamed of hearing from a man so handsome and skilled and valued beyond measure—had filled her with more happiness and hope than she'd ever imagined possible.

For two months and five days, she'd returned to the studio again and again, sitting with more than a little pride in the room, warm with winter sunlight and Derek's gaze. She'd given him everything he asked. Because that was what one did when one was in love.

And they were in love—a fact that was proven by this moment, as they stood in the great hall of the Royal Exhibition, surrounded by the brightest and most renowned of London's populace. Lily was a half step behind Derek's right shoulder (where he preferred her), wearing a pale yellow frock (slightly lower than Lily would have liked, but which he'd selected himself), her hair up in a tight, unyielding twist (precisely the way he liked).

As they'd ridden to the exhibition, the rain forcing them inside his carriage, where it tapped its rhythm on the roof and shut out the world beyond, he'd taken her hand in his and whispered, "Today is the day that changes everything. For all time. After today, all will be different. My name will be whispered throughout the world. And yours, as well."

She'd blinked up at him, heart bursting, knowing that he could mean only one thing. Marriage. She'd smiled and whispered back, "Together."

The carriage had slowed in that moment, and they'd arrived at the exhibition, but she'd heard his agreement in the thunder of the rainstorm beyond.

Together.

And now they were here, and she was feeling prouder than she'd ever been in her life, for this man who would soon be her husband, and for herself as well. After all, it was not every day that the orphaned daughter of a land steward was so privileged to stand before all of London with the man she loved.

The room was massive, the walls reaching twenty feet high and every inch of them covered in artwork. Every inch, that was, but one central spot behind a dais on the far end of the space, this one covered instead with a curtain of sorts, as though what was there was due a magnificent reveal.

Derek turned back to give her a wink. "That one's for us."

Lily smiled. *Us.* What a lovely, lovely word.

How long had she wished to be part of an *us*?

"Mr. Hawkins," the secretary of the academy met them at the midpoint of the room with a firm handshake and a fervent whisper in Derek's ear. "Thank goodness you've arrived. We are ready for the announcement immediately, if you are, sir."

Derek nodded, his lips curving into a wide smile that marked his triumph. "I am always ready for announcements such as this."

Lily looked about the room, taking in the crush of people, all waiting for the exhibition to begin. She recognized a handful of London's brightest, and was immediately unnerved by the idea that she was surrounded by titles and funds. She stiffened, suddenly wishing that Derek had proposed yesterday, so she might be allowed to reach for him—to steady herself in the force of London's combined gaze.

"He's brought that Hargrove girl with him." Lily resisted the urge to turn at the sound of her name, whispered, but too loud not to be heard. She assumed that had been the speaker's plan all along.

"Of course he has," came the scathing reply. "He delights in dotage. And look at the way she stares after him. Like a pup after a bone."

The first speaker tutted her distaste. "As if it weren't enough that she looks *the way she does.*"

Lily willed herself not to listen and fixed her eyes on the back of Derek's head, where his black hair curled in perfect whorls.

They did not matter.

Only Derek mattered.

Only their future. Together.

Us.

"Everyone knows anyone who looks the way she does is a complete scandal. I cannot believe he'd bring her here. Today of all days. There are *dukes* in attendance."

"I heard the *Queen* might appear."

"If that is true, it's even more disgusting that he would bring her."

"His own consort!" The words came on a chortle, as though they were clever.

They weren't.

Lily resisted the suggestion that she might be something other than Derek's betrothed. As though she were a scandal. And even though she wasn't—even though there was nothing scandalous about love—her cheeks flamed and the room grew warmer.

She turned to Derek, willing him to hear the women. To turn and tell them that not only were they speaking out of turn, but that they were speaking out of turn about his future wife.

But he didn't hear. He was already moving away from her, bounding up the stairs to the place where the curtain hung, hiding his masterpiece. He hadn't let her see it, of course. Hadn't wanted to tempt fate. But she knew his skill, and knew that whatever he had selected for the exhibition would take London by storm.

He'd told her as much only minutes earlier.

And when it did take London by storm, the women behind her would eat their words.

Derek had reached the center of the dais, made a show of peeking behind the curtain before turning toward the assembled crowd as Sir Martin Archer Shee, the president of the Royal Academy, welcomed London to the exhibition. The speech was impressive, delivered in the distinguished man's booming Irish brogue, noting the venerable history of the academy and its exhibitions.

Indeed, the art on the walls was very good indeed. It was not the quality of Derek's, of course, but it was fine art. There were several very nice landscapes.

And then it was time.

"Each year, the academy prides itself on a special piece—a first exhibition from one of Britain's most skilled contemporary artists. In the past, we've revealed unparalleled works from Thomas Gainsborough and Joseph Turner and John Constable, each to more acclaim than the last. This year, we are most proud to showcase renowned artist of stage and canvas, Derek Hawkins."

Derek's chest puffed with pride. "It is my masterwork."

Sir Martin turned toward the unexpected interjection. "Would you like to speak to it now?"

Derek stepped forward. "I shall say more once it is revealed, but for now I shall offer only this. It is the greatest nude of our time." He paused. "The greatest nude of *all* time."

A hush went over the room. Not that Lily could hear it over the loud rushing in her ears.

Nude.

To her knowledge, Derek had only ever painted one nude.

It bests Rubens, he'd said as she'd lain in repose on the cobalt settee in his studio, surrounded by satin pillows and lush fabrics. *It is more glorious than Titian.*

The words were not a memory, however. He was speaking them again, now, casting his arrogant gaze across the crowd. "It makes Ingres look like he should return to school." He turned to the president of the academy. "The Royal Academy, of course."

The boast—an insult to one of the greatest artists of the day—unlocked the assembly, and the collective whispers rose in a cacophony, adding sound to the wild heat that consumed Lily.

"Outrageous," someone said nearby.

He'd sworn it was for his eyes alone.

"I've never heard such conceit."

He'd promised her no one would ever see it.

The women behind her spoke again, snide and unpleasant. "Of course. That's why he brought *her*."

It couldn't be she.

It couldn't be.

"No doubt," came the agreement. "She's low enough to be the model."

"*Model* is too kind. It implies value. She is too cheap for such a word. Only allowed inside the door because of the goodwill of—"

She turned to stare at them, halting the words in the speaker's throat, the truth of the moment bringing unwanted tears to her eyes. They didn't care. The two women stared right at her. As though she were a roach in the gutter.

"Her guardian clearly understands that beauty has no bearing on worth."

Lily turned away, the cruel words setting her in motion. At first, simply to escape the horrid women, and then, to escape her own fear.

And then, to stop Derek from baring her to the world.

She pushed her way through the crowd, which was already crushing closer and closer to the stage and the painting, still hidden. Thankfully. Sir Martin had resumed speaking, but Lily did not hear the words, too focused on getting to the dais.

On getting to the painting.

She climbed the stairs, driven by something far more powerful than embarrassment.

Shame.

Shame for what she had done. For trusting him. For believing him.

For believing she'd ever be more than herself. Alone.

For believing in the promise of *us*.

And then she was on the stage, and he was turning toward her, the room going silent once more, in utter shock at her presence. At her intrusion. The president of the academy turned wide eyes on her.

Derek moved with perfect ease, however, waving one arm toward her. "Ah! My muse arrives."

It was time for Lily's eyes to go wide. He'd ruined her. As though she'd removed her clothes in front of all of London. And still, he smiled at her, as though he didn't see it. "My lovely Lily! The conduit of my genius. Smile, darling."

She would never have imagined that the words would have made her so very furious. She didn't stop moving. And she did not smile. "You swore no one would see it."

The room gasped. As though the walls themselves could draw breath.

He blinked. "I did no such thing."

Liar.

"You said it was for you alone."

He smiled, as though it would explain everything. "Darling. My genius is too vast for me not to share it. It is for the world. For all time."

She looked to the crowd, to the hundreds of eyes assembled, the force of their combined gaze setting her back on her feet. Making her knees weak. Making her heart pound.

Making her furious.

She turned back to him. "You said you loved me."

He tilted his head. "Did I?"

She was out of space. Of time. Her body no longer hers. The moment no longer hers. She shook her head. "You did. You said it. We said it. We were to be married."

He laughed. *Laughed.* The sound echoed in the gasps and whispers of the crowd beyond, but Lily didn't care. His laugh was enough to slay on its own. "Dear girl," he mocked. "A man of my caliber does not *marry* a woman of yours."

He said it in front of all London.

Before these people, whom she'd always dreamed of becoming. Before this world, in which she'd always dreamed of living. Before this man, whom she'd always dreamed of loving.

But who had never loved her.

Who, instead, had shamed her.

She turned to the curtain, her purpose singular. To destroy his masterwork the way he'd destroyed her. Without care that those assembled would see the painting.

She tore at the curtain, the thick red velour coming from its moorings with virtually no pressure—or perhaps with the strength of her fury—revealing . . .

Bare wall.

There was nothing there.

She turned back to the room, surprised laughter and scandalized gasps and whispers as loud as cannon fire rioting through her.

The painting wasn't there.

Relief came, hot and overpowering. She whirled to face the man she'd loved. The man who had betrayed her. "Where is it?"

Teeth flashed, blinding white. "It is in a safe space," he replied, his voice booming, placing them both on show as he turned back to the room. "Look at her, London! Witness her passion! Her emotion! Her beauty! And return here, in one month's time, on the final day of the exhibition, to witness all that into something more beautiful. More passionate. I shall set grown men to weeping with my work. As though they have seen the face of God."

A collective gasp of delight thundered through the room. They thought it a play. Her a performer.

They did not realize her life was ruined. Her heart crushed beneath his perfectly shined boot.

They did not realize she was cleaved in two before them.

Or perhaps they did.

And perhaps it was the realization that gave them such glee.

CHAPTER 2

SCOT SUMMONED SOUTH BY WILD WARD

Two weeks & four days later
Berkeley Square

A ward. Worse, an *English* ward.

One would think Settlesworth would have told him about that bit.

One would think that among the dozens of homes and scores of vehicles and hundreds of staff and thousands of tenants and tens of thousands of livestock, Settlesworth would have thought it valuable to mention the existence of a single young female.

A young female who, despite her utter lack of propriety on paper, would no doubt swoon when she came face-to-face with her Scottish guardian.

Englishwomen were consummate swooners.

In four and thirty years, he'd never met one who didn't widely, loudly, and ridiculously threaten the behavior.

But Settlesworth hadn't mentioned the girl, not even in passing, with a "By the way, there's a ward, and a significantly troublesome one at that." At least, he hadn't mentioned it until she'd been so troublesome as to require Alec's presence in London. And then, it was *Your Grace* this, and *scandal* that, and *you must come as quickly as possible to repair her reputation* in conclusion.

So much for Settlesworth being the best solicitor in history. If Alec had any interest in aiding the peerage, he'd take out an advertisement in the *News of London* to alert them to the man's complete ineptitude.

A ward seemed the kind of thing a man should know about from the start of his guardianship, rather than the moment the damn woman did something supremely stupid and ended up in desperate need of rescue.

If he had any sense, he'd have ignored the summons.

But apparently he lacked sense, all told, and Alec Stuart, proud Scotsman and unwilling twenty-first Duke of Warnick, was here—on the steps of number 45 Berkeley Square, waiting for someone to answer the damn door.

He considered his watch for the third time in as many minutes before he set to knocking once more, letting all his irritation fall against the great slab of mahogany. When he completed the action, he turned his back to the door and surveyed the square, perfectly manicured, gated and just blooming green, designed for the residents of this impeccable part of London and no one else. The place was so damn British, it made his skin crawl.

Curse his sister.

"A ward!" Catherine had crowed when she'd heard. "How exciting! Do you think she is very glamorous and beautiful?"

When he'd told Catherine that, in his experience, beauty was the reason for most scandals, and he wasn't interested in dealing with this particular one, his sister had insisted he immediately pack his bags, playing him like a fine fiddle, the baggage. "But what if she's been greatly maligned? What if she's all alone? What if she requires a friend? Or a *champion*?" She'd paused, blinking her enormous blue eyes up at him, and added, "What if *I* were in her place?"

Younger sisters were clearly a punishment for ill deeds in former lives.

And current ones.

He crossed his arms over his chest, the wool of his jacket pulling tight across his shoulders, constricting him just as the architecture did, all ironwork and stone façade. He hated it here.

England will be your ruin.

Next door, a gaggle of women exited number 44 Berkeley Square, making their way down the steps to a waiting carriage. A young lady saw him, her eyes going wide before she recoiled in shock and snapped her gaze away to hiss a whisper at the rest of the group, which instantly turned in unison to gawk at him.

He felt their stares like a blazing heat, made hotter when the oldest of the group—mother or aunt, if he had to guess—said loudly, "Of course *she* would have such a man waiting for an audience."

"He looks veritably *animalistic.*"

Alec went instantly cold as the group tittered its amusement. Ignoring the wash of fury that came over him at the assessment, he returned his attention to the door.

Where in hell were the servants?

"She's probably renting rooms in there," one of the girls said.

"And other things as well," came a snide reply. "She's outrageous enough for it."

What on earth kind of scandal had the girl gotten herself into?

Settlesworth's letter had been perfunctory in the extreme, apologizing for not apprising him of the existence of the ward and laying the girl at Alec's feet. *She is at the heart of a scandal. A quite unsurvivable one, if you do not arrive. Posthaste.*

He might hate all things English, but Alec wasn't a monster. He wasn't about to leave the girl to the damn wolves. And, if the she-wolves next door were any indication, it was a good thing he was here, as the poor girl was already their meal.

He knew what it was to be at the hands of Englishwomen.

Resisting the urge to tell the women they could pile into their carriage and drive straight to hell, he raised his fist to pound once more.

The door opened in an instant and, after impressively recovering from his shock, Alec glowered down at the woman standing before him, wearing the drabbest grey dress he'd ever seen.

He imagined she was no more than five and twenty, with high cheekbones and porcelain skin and full lips and red hair that somehow gleamed like gold despite the fact that she was inside a dimly lit foyer. It was as though the woman traveled with her own sun.

Drab frock or no, it was not beyond hyperbole to say she was easily the most beautiful woman in Britain.

Of course she was.

Nothing made a bad day worse like a beautiful Englishwoman.

"It's about bloody time," he growled.

It took the maid several seconds to recover from her own shock and lift her eyes from where they had focused at his chest up to his face, her eyebrows rising with every inch of her gaze.

Alec was transfixed. Her eyes were grey—not slate and not steel, but the color of the darkest rainclouds, shot through with silver. He stiffened, the too-small coat pulling tight across his shoulders, reminding him that he was in England, and whoever this woman was, she was irrelevant to his interests. With the exception of the fact that she was standing between him and his immediate return to Scotland.

"I suggest ye let me in, lass."

One red brow rose. "I shall do no such thing."

She closed the door.

Alec blinked, surprise and disbelief warring for a fleeting moment before they were both overcome by a supreme loss of patience. He stepped back, sized up the door, and, with a heave, broke the thing down.

It crashed to the foyer floor with a mighty thud.

He could not resist turning to the women next door, now frozen in collective, wide-eyed shock. "Animal enough for you, ladies?"

The question spurred them into action, sending them fairly

climbing over each other to enter their carriage. Satisfied, Alec returned his attention to his own house and, ignoring the pain in his shoulder, crossed the threshold.

The maid stood just inside, staring down at the great oak slab. "You could have killed me."

"Doubtful," he said. "The door is'nae heavy enough to kill a person."

Her gaze narrowed on him. "Number Eighteen, I presume."

The words could not have held more disdain. Ignoring them, Alec lifted the door from its resting place and turned to lean it against the open doorway. He deliberately thickened his accent. "Then ye ken who I am."

"I'm not certain there's a person in London who wouldn't easily ken you. Though you might learn the word *know* if you wish them to understand you."

He raised a brow at her smart mouth. "I don't care for being left waiting at the door of my own home."

Her gaze moved pointedly to the door, removed from its hinges. "You make a habit of destroying things when they displease you?"

Alec resisted the urge to deny the words. He had spent the majority of his adult life proving that he was not coarse. Not rough. Not a brute.

But he would not defend himself to this woman. "I pay handsomely for the privilege."

She rolled her eyes. "Charming."

He refused to reveal his shock. While he had little to no experience with aristocratic servants, he was fairly certain that they did not make a habit of sniping at their masters. Nevertheless, he did not rise to the bait, instead taking in the impeccable home with its broad, sweeping center staircase, stunning and massive oil landscapes on the walls, a touch of gilt here and there, indicating modernity rather than garishness. He turned in a slow circle, considering the high ceilings, the massive mirrors that captured and reflected light from the windows high above, casting the whole space in natural light, and offering a glimpse of a wide, colorful carpet and a roaring fireplace through a nearby open door.

It was the kind of house that should belong to a duke with impressive pedigree, no doubt decorated by some previous duchess.

He stilled.

Was there a previous duchess? With seventeen dead dukes, Alec would bet there was more than one previous duchess.

He growled at the thought. All he needed was a widow to deal with on top of the scandalous ward and the petulant staff.

The staff in question heard the sound of displeasure. "I knew they called you the diluted duke, but I did not think you would be so . . ."

The impertinence trailed off, but Alec heard the unspoken worlds. *Beastly. Coarse. Unrefined.* He lost his patience. "I suggest you fetch Lady Lillian. Immediately."

"It's Miss Hargrove. She's not highborn."

He raised a brow. "This is England, is it not? Have they changed the rules, then? You gleefully correct dukes now?"

"I do when the duke in question is wrong," she said, "Though you should be fine, as few will understand enough of your monstrous accent to know if you are right or wrong."

"You seem to understand me well enough."

She smiled too sweetly. "My vast good fortune, I suppose."

He resisted the urge to laugh at the quick retort. The woman was not amusing. She was moments from being sacked. "And what of the respect that comes with the title?"

"It comes from people who are impressed by said title, I imagine."

"And you are not?"

She crossed her arms. "Not particularly."

"May I ask why?"

"There have been eighteen of you in five years. Or, to be more precise, seventeen in two weeks, followed by you for five years. And despite this being the first time you've set foot in this house, it—and all its contents—belong to you. Are cared for. For *you.* In absentia. If that's not evidence that titles are ridiculous, I'm not sure what is."

She wasn't saying anything he didn't believe. But that did not mean she was not maddening—likely just as mad as the other woman in the house. "While your insubordination is impressive and I do not entirely disagree with your logic, I've had enough," he said. "I intend to speak with Miss Lillian, and your task, whether you like it or not, is to fetch her."

"Why are you here?"

He let stony silence stretch between them for a long minute, attempting to intimidate her into doing as he asked. "Fetch your mistress."

She was not intimidated in the slightest. "I think it amusing that you refer to her as mistress of the house. As though she isn't a prisoner of it."

That's when he knew.

His ward was not the swooning type, after all.

Before he could speak, however, she continued. "As though she were not a belonging just like the door you summarily destroyed like a great Scottish brute."

He didn't mean to hear the word.

But somehow, standing here, with this impeccable Englishwoman in this impeccable English town house in this impeccable English square, wearing an uncomfortable suit, barely fitting in the open doorway, feeling big and out of place, he couldn't help but hear it.

Couldn't help but feel it, close and unsettling, like the tight cravat around his neck.

How often had he heard it from beautiful women? Whispered in awe, as though they were too busy imagining the fine, deep notch he would make in their bedposts to keep their innermost thoughts to themselves. When one came in the size he did, women tended to desire it, like a prize. A bull at the county fair.

Massive and beastly.

The word honored their desire even as it demeaned his own.

Just as it had demeaned him on his mother's lips, marking her regret as she'd spat it at him—always too large to be fine enough for her. Too big to be worthy of her. Too coarse. Too Scottish.

Too much a reminder of her disappointing life.

She'd loathed his size. His strength. His inheritance from his father. Loathed it so much that she'd left, that single word her parting gift to her only son.

Brute.

And so, when he heard it here, in this place, on the lips of another beautiful Englishwoman, with such thorough disdain, he was unable to avoid it.

Just as he was unable to resist retaliating. "I had hoped you wouldn't be beautiful."

She narrowed her gaze. "The descriptor does not seem a compliment on your lips."

A vision flashed, this stunning woman laid across a bed, hair spread like fire and gold across white linen, long limbs beckoning, pink lips parted. Desire shot through him like pain, and he forced himself to remember his place.

He was her guardian. She was his ward.

And English at that.

She was not for him.

"It's not," he said. "It makes it far more likely you did it."

Her eyes were glorious, more expressive than he would ever have imagined, and filled instantly with challenge. "Did what?"

"Ruined yourself."

The anger changed to something else, gone so quickly that he might not have recognized it if it were not so unbearably familiar to him.

Shame.

And in her shame, in the way it bore the shadow of his own, he instantly regretted his words. And he wished them gone. "I should not have—"

"Why not? It is true."

He watched her for a long moment—taking in her straight

spine, her square shoulders, her high head. The strength she should not have, but carried like honor, nonetheless.

"We should begin again," he said.

"I would prefer we not begin at all," she said, and turned away from him, leaving him in the hallway, with nothing to keep his company but the sounds from the square beyond floating through the permanently open doorway.

SHE NEEDED THE Diluted Duke like she needed a hole in the head.

She closed the door to the sitting room off the foyer, pressing her back to it and releasing a long breath, willing him gone from the house. Gone from her life. After all, it was not as though he'd taken an interest in her for the last five years.

But, of course, he was here now, literally banging down the door of her home, as though he could barge in like an avenging guardian king, as though he had ownership over her and her scandal.

Which, of course, he did.

Damn Settlesworth and his copious letter writing.

And damn the duke for turning up, uninvited. Unwanted.

Lily had a plan, and it did not require the duke. She should not have incited him. She should not have insulted him. Indeed, one did not catch flies with vinegar, and the duke was a rather fat fly.

She crossed the room to the sideboard on the far end.

Not fat.

Poured herself a glass of the amber liquid there.

He was all strength. Lily did not think she would forget the image of the great oak door bursting from its hinges, as though made of paper. And she did not think she would ever not lose her breath at the vision of the enormous man, big as a house and handsome beyond measure, standing in the wake of his destruction, framed by sunlight as though the heavens themselves had sent him down.

She stopped.

What utter rubbish. Being housebound for the past two weeks

and four days, hiding from the rest of London, she must have been addled by the onset of fresh air that had arrived when the man had beat the door down.

That alone was enough to set any woman on edge.

Particularly one who had been fooled by handsome men before.

Lily had no interest in his broad shoulders or his brown eyes or his full lips that seemed at once soft and firm and terribly tempting. And she hadn't even noticed the cheeks and nose and jaw, strong enough to have been hewn in iron by the most talented Scottish blacksmiths.

She sipped at the whisky in her glass.

No, the only interest she had in the Duke of Warnick was in getting him gone.

"Lillian." She whirled around to find the object of her lack of interest in the now-open doorway. His brown gaze fell to the glass in her hand. "It's half-ten in the morning."

She drank again, purposefully. If ever there were a time for drink, it was now. "I see you are aware of how doors properly function."

He raised a brow and watched her for a long moment before saying, "If we are imbibing, I'll have one, as well."

She gave him her back as she poured a second glass, and when she turned to deliver it to him, it was to find that he'd already crossed the room without sound. She resisted the urge to move away from him. He was too large. Too commanding.

Too compelling.

He took the glass. "Thank you."

She nodded. "It's your drink. You're welcome to it."

He did not drink. Instead he moved away, to the fireplace, where he inspected a large classical oil painting of a nude man, sleeping under a willow tree beneath the gaze of a beautiful woman, dawn crawling across the sky. Lily gritted her teeth as she, too, considered the painting. A nude. Unsettling in its reminder of—

"Shall we discuss the scandal?"

No.

Her cheeks burned. She didn't like it. "Is there a scandal?"

He turned to look at her. "You tell me."

"Well, I imagine the news that you broke down the door in broad daylight will get around."

Something flashed in his eyes. Something like amusement. She didn't like that, either. "Is it true, lass?"

And, in that moment, in the four, simple words, spoken in his rolling Scottish brogue, warm and rough and almost kinder than she could bear, she wished herself anywhere but there. Because it was the first time anyone had asked the question.

And it was the millionth time that she'd wished the answer were different. "I think you should go."

He was still for a long moment, and then he said, "I'm here to help."

She laughed at that, the sound without humor. "It is impressive, Your Grace, how well you sound the caring guardian."

"I came as soon as I heard of your predicament."

She was a legend, evidently. "It reached you all the way in Scotland, did it?"

"In my experience, rumor travels like lightning."

"And you've much experience with rumors?"

"More than I would care to admit."

Lily heard the truth in the words. "And were your rumors true?"

He was silent long enough for her to think he might not reply, so it was a particular shock when he said, simply, "Yes."

She'd never in her life been so curious about a single word. Of course, it was nonsense. Whatever his scandal, it was not like this. It had not destroyed him.

It had not forced him to flee.

She met his gaze. "And now, what? You arrive to tend your reputation?"

"I don't care a fig for my reputation. I am here to tend yours."

It was a lie. No one had ever cared for Lily's reputation—not since her father had died. She'd never had a patroness, never a friend.

Never a love.

The thought came with hot tears, stinging with the threat of their appearance, unwelcome and infuriating. She inhaled sharply and turned back to the sideboard, refusing to reveal them to him. "Why?"

His brow furrowed. "Why?"

"You don't even know me."

He hesitated. Then, "You are my responsibility."

She laughed. She couldn't help looking back. "You've never once taken interest in me. You did not even know I existed, did you?" She saw the guilt in his eyes. The truth there. "I suppose that is better than the alternative."

"Which is?"

"That you've known about me for years and simply ignored my existence."

He would not have been the only one.

"Had I known . . ." He trailed off.

"What? You would have returned to London years ago? Immediately taken up the banner of guardian and savior?"

He shifted on his massive feet, and she felt a twinge of regret, knowing that he did not deserve her accusations. She bit her tongue, refusing to apologize. Wishing he would leave. Wishing he had never come.

If wishes were horses.

"I am not a monster," he answered, finally. "I did not ask for the responsibility, but I would have made certain you were provided for, without hesitation."

'Twas always thus. A promise of funds. Of room and board. A promise of all the bits that came easily.

And a dearth of everything that had value.

She waved her hand to indicate the beautiful house. "I am perfectly provided for. Look at the beautiful cage in which I perch." She did not wait for him to reply. "It is no matter, either way. I am afraid you are rather too late." She pushed past him, saying, "I am in the market for neither guardian nor savior. Indeed, if the last few years have taught me anything, it is that I would do well to save myself. Play my own guardian."

He did not reply until she reached the door to the sitting room. "You're older than I expected."

She stopped. Looked back. "I beg your pardon?"

He did not move. "How old are you?"

She matched the impertinent question. "How old are *you*?"

"I am old enough to know that you're older than any ward should be."

"If only you hadn't had such a longstanding disinterest in your guardianship, you might know the answer to your question."

"Do not take it personally."

"Your longstanding disinterest?"

"Now that I know you exist, I find myself quite interested."

"I suppose you would be, now that I'm a creature under glass to watch and point to as a warning to all others."

He raised a black brow and crossed his arms over his massive chest. "Seconds ago, you were a bird in a cage."

"It is the mixed metaphors you are interested in?" she retorted.

He did not hesitate. "No, it's you."

The words warmed her. Not that they should have. "A pity, that, as I am not interested in you."

"You should be. As I understand it, guardians have quite a bit of control over wards."

"I'm a ward of the Warnick estate. I would not get too possessive, if I were you."

"Am I not Warnick?"

"Perhaps not for long. You dukes do have a habit of dying."

"I suppose you'd like that?"

"A woman can dream." His lips twitched at the words, and if she were to tell the truth, she would have admitted that she enjoyed the fact that she'd amused him. She was not interested in the truth, however.

"Well, I am not dead yet, Lillian, so you are landed with me for the time being. You'd do best to answer my questions." He paused, then repeated himself. "You're rather old for a ward, nae?"

Of course she was. She'd been lost in the fray. Her father had died and left her in the care of the duke, and all had been well for several years, until the duke had died. And sixteen more, as well. And then this man—this legendary Scot who had eschewed all things English and never even turned up in Parliament to receive his letters of patent—had been in charge.

And Lily had been forgotten.

No dowry. No season. No friends.

She looked to him, wishing there were a way to tell him all of that, to make him understand his part in the mad play of her life, without rewatching the play herself. As there wasn't, she settled upon, "I am, rather."

She sat in a pretty little Chippendale chair, watching him as he watched her. As he tried to understand her. As though if he looked long enough, she would unlock herself.

The irony was, if he'd done the same a year earlier, she might have unlocked herself. She might have opened to him, and answered all his questions, laid herself bare to him.

Her lips twisted in a sad smile at the thought. Laid herself bare in all ways, likely. Thankfully, he was a year too late, and she was a lifetime different.

"I am ward of the estate, until such time as I marry."

"Why haven't you married?"

She blinked. "Many would find that inquiry inappropriate."

He raised a brow and indicated the door to the house. "Do I seem a man who cares for propriety?"

He did not.

There were a dozen reasons why she was unmarried. Reasons that had to do with being orphaned and ignored and alone and then desperately smitten with the wrong man. But she was not going to share them. So she settled on a simpler, no less honest, truth. "I have never been asked."

"That seems impossible."

"Why?"

"Because men are a ha'penny a dozen when it comes to women like you."

Women like her. She stiffened. This man made her beauty sound as it felt. "Have a care. Your flattery will spoil me, Your Grace."

He sat then, folding himself into a matching chair, his enormous frame making it seem minuscule. "Alec."

"I beg your pardon?"

"You may call me Alec."

"While that may be done in the wilds of Scotland, Your Grace, it is thoroughly inappropriate here."

"Again with the invocation of propriety," he said. "Fine. Call me Stuart then. Or any number of the other invectives you've no doubt been thinking," he said. "I'll take them all before duke."

"But you *are* a duke."

"Not by choice." He drank then, finally, grimacing after he swallowed the amber liquid. "Christ. That's swill." He threw the rest of the liquid into the fire.

She raised a brow at the action. "You disdain the title and the scotch it buys."

"First, that should not be called scotch. It is rot-gut at best." He paused. "And second, I do not disdain the title. I dislike it."

"Yes, you poor, put-upon man. Having one of the wealthiest and most venerable dukedoms in history simply land in your lap. How difficult it must be to live your horrid, entitled existence." He had no idea the power he had. The privilege. What she would do to have the same.

He leaned back in the small chair. "I spend my own money, earned honestly in Scotland. I have ensured the tenants and staff who rely upon the dukedom continue to prosper, but as I did not ask for the title, I do not interact with its spoils."

"Myself included." She could not resist the words.

"I'm here, am I not? Summoned south by my ward. Surely that counts for something."

"I didn't summon you."

"You might not have set pen to paper, lass, but you summoned me as simply as if you'd shouted my name across the border."

"As I said, I've no need for you."

"I'm told the world disagrees."

"Hang the world," she said, turning her attention to the fire as she added, "and hang you with it."

"As I am here to save you, I would think you would be much more grateful."

The man's arrogance was quite remarkable. "However did I come to be so very lucky?"

He sighed, hearing the sarcasm in her words. "Despite your petulance, I am here to rectify your alleged . . ." He cast about for an appropriate word. ". . . *situation*."

Her brows shot together. "My *petulance*."

"Do you deny it?"

She most certainly did. "Petulance is what a child feels when she is denied sweets."

"How would you describe yourself if not petulant?"

Furious. Foolish. Irritated. Desperate.

Ashamed.

Finally, she spoke. "It is no matter. It's all too little, too late." After a pause, she added, pointedly, "I've a plan, and you are not a part of it, *Duke*."

He cut her a look. "I suppose I shouldn't have told you I don't like the title."

"Never reveal your weakness to your enemy."

"We are enemies, then?"

"We certainly aren't friends."

She could see his frustration. "I've had enough of this. Why don't we begin here. Settlesworth tells me you have ruined yourself in front of all London."

The words, no matter how often she thought them herself, still stung on another's tongue. Shame flooded her, and she did everything she could not to reveal it.

She failed. "How is it that the ruination is mine and not—"

She stopped.

He heard the rest of the sentence nonetheless. "Then there was a man."

She met his gaze. "You needn't pretend you don't know."

"It is not pretending," he said. "Settlesworth gave me very little information. But I am not an idiot, and looking at you, it's clear that there was a man."

"Looking at me." He had no idea how the words stung.

He ignored her. "So. You did not ruin yourself. You were ruined."

"Six of one, half a dozen of the other," she mumbled.

"No," he said, firmly. "They are different."

"Not to anyone who matters."

A pause. "What happened?"

He did not know. It was remarkable. He did not know what she had done. How she had embarrassed herself. He had only the vagaries of a solicitor's summons and the boundaries of his imagination. And in those vagaries she remained, somehow, free of the past.

And, though she knew it was simply a matter of time before he heard about the scandal of Lovely Lily, Lonesome Lily, Lovelorn Lily, or whatever nickname the scandal sheets thought clever today, she did not wish him to know now.

And so she did not tell him.

"Does it matter?"

He looked at her as though she was mad. "Of course it matters."

She shook her head. "It doesn't, though. Not really. It only matters what they believe. That is how scandal works."

"Facts matter, Lillian. Tell me what happened. If they make it worse than it is, I will paper London with truth."

"How lucky I am to have a guardian and a champion all in one," she said, injecting the words with sarcasm in the hopes she could irritate him into leaving his line of questioning.

He whispered something in Gaelic then, something that she did not understand but that she immediately identified as a curse. He tugged at the cravat, tied too tight around his neck, just as the coat he wore was too tight at the shoulders. The trousers too tight at the thighs. Everything about this man was larger than it should be. Perhaps that was why he knew, instantly, her truth. That he saw her flaws so clearly.

Flaws saw flaws.

He returned to English. "We cannot solve the situation if I do not know its particulars."

"There is no *we*, Your Grace." The words were firm and full of conviction. "Until today, you did not know me."

"I will know soon enough, girl."

But not from her, and somehow, ridiculously, that was important. Somehow, it meant that she could be something with him she was not with others. "You needn't concern yourself with it," she said. "In ten days, my *situation* will be resolved."

One way or another.

If she said it enough, it might be believed. She might believe it herself.

"What happens in ten days?"

The painting is revealed.

Not just that. "I turn twenty-four."

"And?" Alec leaned forward in his chair, elbows on his knees, fingers laced together.

And the painting is revealed. In front of all London.

She looked to him, ignoring the thought. It wouldn't matter. She had a plan. "And according to the rules of my guardianship, I receive the funds necessary to leave London—and my scandal—behind."

His brows rose. "That must be a great deal of blunt, lass, if it can erase you from memory."

"Oh, it is," she said. "I can leave London and never return. So, you see, Your Grace," she said, allowing triumph into her voice. "I have a plan to save myself. No guardian required. I plan to run."

She hated the plan. Hated the way it ended with Derek winning. With London winning. With the life she'd desired out of reach. But she had no choice. There was no other way to survive the scandal that would mark her forever.

Alec watched her for a long moment before nodding once and leaning back in his chair, dwarfing the furniture with his sheer size. "That's one way of saving yourself."

She did not like the phrasing. "One way."

"Do you love him?"

She went pale at the words. "What?"

"The man. Do you love him?"

"I have not acknowledged that there is a man."

"There's always a man, lass."

We were to be married. The tears again. Hot and angry and instant and unwelcome. She willed them away. "I don't see how it is your concern."

I wish I hadn't. I wish I'd never met him.

I wish—

I wish I weren't so ashamed.

He nodded, as though she'd answered him. As though a decision had been made. "That is enough, then."

And a decision, somehow, had been. She tilted her head. "Enough?"

He stood, enormous and somehow suddenly far more imposing—even more than he had been when he'd sent the door flying from its hinge. As though he were her king, and not simply a man she'd just met. And when he spoke, it was with a firm certainty that made her—for a heartbeat—believe his words.

"You shan't run."

Chapter 3

***FALLEN ANGEL FISTICUFFS:
SCOTTISH BRUTE SERVES BRUMMELLIAN
BRAGGART SCATHING SETDOWN***

Alec took to the one place in London that had furniture built to accommodate a grown man. That the place also came with scotch imported from his own distillery, a ring ready for a fight if he felt so inclined, card and carom tables, and a handful of men he did not loathe was an added bonus.

"Warnick returns." The Marquess of Eversley—known to all the world as King—dropped into a large chair across from Alec. "Alert the news."

"I am off the clock," Duncan West, newspaper magnate, said dryly from his own seat next to Alec. "Though I admit curiosity, having been summoned by the Diluted Duke."

Membership in The Fallen Angel—Britain's most exclusive gaming hell—was by invitation only and had little to do with fortune or title. Indeed, the nobs who frequented White's and Brook's and Boodles's were most often not invited to join the Angel.

King was a member, as was West—despite the newspaperman having had a series of public disputes with the owners. As he called the two men friends, Alec found himself welcome at the club without membership, a fact for which he was grateful. Even he had to admit that they didn't make gaming hells quite the same way in Scotland. Or anywhere else for that matter.

Alec looked to King. "My thanks for the invitation."

His friend raised a brow. "As you virtually demanded it, there's no thanks necessary."

"I required a good drink."

"You could land yourself an invitation for membership, considering the Angel is the only place in London a man can get Stuart scotch." King's gaze settled on Alec's coat. "Assuming you found a better tailor, for God's sake. Where did you get that coat?"

Alec shrugged one tight shoulder. "Mossband."

Eversley barked a laugh at the answer—a barely there town on the English side of the Scottish border. "It shows."

Alec ignored the retort. "Neither London clothing nor London clubs are necessary in Scotland."

"You enjoy London clubs in London, however," West interjected.

"I'm not addled," Alec said, drinking deep before he leaned back in a massive leather chair and leveled West with a serious look. The man was owner of five of the most profitable publications in Britain, three of which were widely believed to be the pinnacle of modern journalism.

But it was not the legitimate publications that interested Alec. It was *The Scandal Sheet*.

"You're not off the clock tonight," he said to the newspaperman.

West sat back. "No, I assumed not."

"It seems I have a ward."

One of West's blond brows rose. "Seems?"

"My solicitor failed to inform me of such."

"That's a rather terrible solicitor, if you ask me."

"He took me at my word when I told him I was not interested in the London trappings of the dukedom."

King chuckled. "He thought the girl a trapping? Christ. Don't tell her that. In my experience, women don't enjoy being thought of as such."

No. Alec didn't imagine Lily would enjoy that. "I know about her now, however."

"Everyone knows about her now," West said.

"Because of the scandal," Alec replied.

"Because of her," West clarified. "She's widely believed to be the most beautiful woman in London—"

"She might well be," Alec said. He'd never seen one so beautiful.

"She's not," King and West spoke in unison.

Alec rolled his eyes. "Your wives excepted, of course."

His friends smiled broadly and West continued. "Miss Hargrove is also a curiosity. A beautiful woman attached to a dukedom, not officially out in Society, but regularly seen on the arm of one of Society's most venerated peacocks."

Alec resisted the distaste that came at the idea. "The source of the scandal, I assume?"

"You don't wish to ask her for the particulars?" West said.

A memory of Lily's obvious shame flashed. "I don't think she is interested in telling me."

"Mmm."

Alec frowned. "What does that mean?"

"Only that they are never interested in telling us." The newspaperman was married to a woman who had been something of a scandal herself—sister to a duke, unwed mother to a daughter who was now as much a source of paternal pride to West as his own children.

"Luckily, this one isn't to be my problem," Alec said.

"They're always our problem," King interjected.

"Not Lillian Hargrove. Unlike the rest of London, I did not know of her two weeks ago, and I have no intention of knowing of her two weeks hence. She's to be the problem of the man who disgraced her." He looked to West. "I simply need to know who that is."

West's gaze flickered to a faro table nearby, and he watched the game for a long moment. Alec followed suit. A man dressed all in white joined a threesome there, flashing a broad smile at the dealer and setting a massive amount of money on the table.

Alec looked back to his friends. "Who is that?"

King raised a brow at West, who sat back in his chair. "Shall I tell you what I know of your ward's circumstance?"

Alec nodded, the faro table gone from his mind.

"There is a painting."

Alec's brow furrowed. "What kind of painting?"

A pause. Then King said, "Allegedly? A nude."

Alec froze, the words summoning a great roar in his ears. Not words. Word. *Nude.* Long limbs. Full lips. High breasts. Round hips. Skin as soft as silk. And eyes like a silver storm.

No.

"A nude of whom?"

West's hands went wide, as if to say, *Isn't it obvious?*

Of course, it was.

Alec shot forward in his chair. "Allegedly. King said allegedly."

West replied. "It's not alleged."

He turned on the newspaperman. "You have seen it?"

"I have not, but my wife has." He paused. "Georgiana is on the Selection Committee of the Royal Academy."

Alec's heart pounded. "And it is Lillian." West remained still and Alec grasped for another solution. "How do we know she honestly sat for it? You and I both know that scandal is rarely truth."

"It's true in this case," West said.

"How do you know that?"

West cut him a look. "Because I'm exceedingly good at my job, and I know the difference between gossip and fact."

Alec considered the woman he'd met hours earlier. Yes, she was beautiful, but she was not an idiot. He shook his head. "Not in this case," he said. "I've met the girl. There's no way she posed for a nude."

"Love makes us do strange things." King's words were simple and direct, and Alec hated the ring of truth in them.

He did not want to acknowledge the truth. He did not want to imagine her nude for a man. He had enough trouble not imagining her nude, full stop.

Nevertheless. "So the girl is in love."

It was the question he'd asked earlier—the one she'd answered without words. She hadn't needed words. He'd seen the sadness in her eyes. The wistfulness. As though she wished the man in question to appear there, in her sitting room.

He knew about wishing. And he knew, better than most, how false emotion could lead to some mediocre artist manipulating and mistreating her. He met West's eyes. "Where is the painting?"

"No one knows. It is set to be the final piece exhibited as part of the Royal Exhibition in ten days' time," West said. "They select the best, Warnick. And this one—Georgiana says it is unmatched."

"The most beautiful portrait ever painted," King interjected.

"We don't know it is her."

"She admitted it, Warnick."

Alec stilled again. "She did what?"

"She stormed the stage. Caused a scene. Professed her love. Was rebuffed. In front of all London," West said. "That alone was enough to destroy her in their eyes, but there are those who believe she is a part of it. That she and her artist worked together to ensure that the painting's reputation will precede it when it travels the country. The world."

Alec cursed and shook his head. "Why would she do that? Why ruin herself? The girl is locked away in my house, waiting for the funds to run."

Not that she would get them from him.

He'd seen women run. He'd run himself. And he knew what happened when the running stopped.

Lillian Hargrove would not run.

"She wants the funds from you?" It was King who spoke this time.

Alec shook his head. "In ten days' time, she inherits pin money."

West swirled the scotch in his glass. "Fine timing, as the painting is revealed in ten days' time."

Alec met his gaze. "What are you saying?"

One lean shoulder lifted and fell. "Only, imagine the *Mona Lisa*."

Alec huffed his irritation at the exercise. "Who cares a fig about the damn *Mona Lisa*?"

"A great many people, I imagine."

Alec cut him a look. "I grow weary of your obvious self-made brilliance, West."

The newspaperman smirked. "You're self-made, are you not? You only lack the brilliance."

"A pity, considering the size of you," King needled. "I suppose it is true what they say. We can't have everything."

Alec cursed them both. "Fine. The *Mona Lisa*. What of it?"

"Imagine how renowned the model would be if we knew her name."

Shock flared. "You think Lillian wishes for fame?" Memory flashed. Those grey eyes, storm clouds of sorrow. "No."

King raised a brow. "I am married to a Dangerous Daughter. Living proof that some revel in fame." Not six months earlier, the Marquess of Eversley had found a stowaway from one of London's most notorious families in his carriage. That stowaway had become an unexpected traveling companion and, after the story broke, the most scandalous member of the family. And Marchioness of Eversley.

"You would have never married if not for me."

King cut him a look. "Oh, yes. Your part in the play was most definitely welcome. I didn't have to make amends for it at all."

"You're lucky you had amends to make," Alec said. "Someone had to knock some sense into you."

"And for that, I will be forever grateful." The words rang with a remarkable honesty.

"Och," Alec said, looking away. "There's nothing worse than a nob who loves his wife."

"Watch it, Duke. Halfhearted or no, you are a nob now—all you need is the wife."

It would never happen. He'd learned his lesson every time he'd considered it. Every time he'd been passed over for money, for title, for refinement. Every time he'd been desired for his body and nothing else. The Scottish Brute.

He shook his head. "I've enough trouble with women, thank you."

"It's because you scare the wee things," King said, mocking Alec's brogue.

"This one isn't scared of me." If anything, Lillian Hargrove was willing to battle him without hesitation. "She could do with a little more apprehension, honestly."

"Another reason to believe she might be party to the scandal," West said. "Lovely Lily, immortalized for all ages."

He loathed the moniker, not that he would show it. "I didn't know she called herself Lily," he replied, drinking again, disliking the fact that these two knew more about her than he did.

And he did not like that they might be right. That Lily might have destroyed herself for a man, without hesitation. He thought back on the girl, on their meeting earlier. She didn't seem to be proud of her scandal. Did not wear it as a badge of honor. He had seen the regret in her gaze. The shame there.

Recognized it as keenly as he knew his own.

He shook his head. "She was not part of it."

"Then the performance at the exhibition . . ." King began.

West finished the thought. "Was not a performance at all." He looked to Alec. "Poor girl. What now?"

I plan to run.

She wouldn't run. If he had to tear London apart brick by

brick to ensure it, she would stay here and have her reputation restored. England would not chase her away or destroy her, the way it so easily destroyed those who did not suit it.

One solution remained—safe and swift and utterly acceptable. Swiftness was most certainly a boon. Swiftness ended in Alec returning home, to Scotland, far from London and Lillian Hargrove, who was turning out to be more trouble than expected.

"You could marry her." King's words startled Alec from his thoughts.

"Marry whom?"

West smirked. "The London air is clouding your thoughts, Scot. The girl. Miss Hargrove. King is suggesting you marry her."

A vision flashed, Lily beautiful and perfect in her simple grey dress, skin like porcelain and eyes flashing fire. There was a time when he would have proposed on the spot, blinded by her beauty and desperate to win her heart. To claim her for himself.

Despite his size. Despite his hulk. Despite his lack of grace.

He knew better now. He was for baser acts than marrying.

"Even if I weren't her guardian—"

King interrupted. "What nonsense. If I had a pound for every guardian who married his ward, I'd be rich as sin."

"You are already rich as sin," Alec replied. "Either way, she wouldn't have me." It took a moment for him to realize that West and King were staring at him. "What is it?"

West found his tongue first. "I think I speak for us both when I say the girl would get down on her knees and thank her maker you proposed."

The Scottish Brute.

So big. So beastly. Only for working days.

The memories burned. How many Englishwomen had denied him anything more than sex? Held themselves for another when it came to marriage? Even if he were interested in the girl. Even if she were more than a troublesome beauty keeping him from home . . . He shook his head. "I am not the husband in question."

King watched him, he knew. But he did not look to the man who had known him since their days in school. Not even when the marquess said, "What then?"

"I am a duke, am I not?"

King lingered over the last of his scotch. "With the patent to prove it."

"And dukes are allowed to do their will."

West smirked. "It is a perk of the title, I am told."

Alec nodded. "The man who ruined her. He marries her."

A wild cheer from the faro table nearby punctuated the words. Alec looked toward the noise, noting the man in the white coat and trousers once more. It appeared that the peacock had lost a massive round, if the shock on his face were any indication.

So it was in gaming hells. One moment up, the next, down.

So, too, it was when it came to women, Lily's scoundrel would soon discover.

Alec turned back to his friends. "He marries her if I have to put a pistol to his head and force him to do it."

King blinked. "You might have to."

"Well, being a brutish Scot will help with that. The plan is impenetrable." He turned to West. "A name, if you please."

"I shall do one better," West said, finishing his drink and indicating the card table. "Name and location. You seek Derek Hawkins, artist and theatrical genius. The vision in white currently nursing his loss."

It was not possible.

Alec could not imagine this man conversing with Lillian, let alone . . . No. There was no way that too-honest woman would be caught dead with such an obvious peacock. He looked to King for confirmation. "No."

King nodded. "Indeed. Artist, theatrical genius, and proper ass."

He didn't know what he'd imagined. Someone stronger. Less of a dandy. Alec wouldn't have been surprised by someone devastatingly handsome, or someone with incredible wealth, or a man who oozed disgusting charm. But this man—this pompous peacock—this man didn't seem fit to cloak a puddle and aid Lily's walk through town.

Do you love him?

Alec had expected someone deserving of her.

Suddenly, his plan did not seem so perfect.

He looked to his friends and asked the only question that came to mind. "*Why?*"

Before they could answer, the card table erupted in another commotion. From what Alec could see, the Hawkins character was attempting to negotiate a loan with the casino. The majordomo had been summoned, and Hawkins was saying, "My name will soon be known throughout the world! How dare you refuse me?"

The casino employee adjusted his spectacles and shook his head.

"I assure you," Hawkins blustered. "Your employers will be livid if they discover that you've denied me funds. I shall be the most famous Englishman there ever was! Newton? Milton? *Shakespeare?* They will pale in comparison to Hawkins. They will beg to honor me here in this place, and I will decline because of your"—he waved a hand at the majordomo's eyewear—"obvious shortsightedness."

"Good Lord. He's worse than I imagined," Alec said.

"He's only warming up," West said, calling for more drink.

"If you don't have the blunt, you don't play, Hawkins," one of the other men said, obviously eager to return to the game.

"I have the blunt. I simply don't carry it with me." He turned to the majordomo again. "Are you deaf, as well as blind? Do you not understand that I am the greatest artist of all time?"

The table erupted in jeering hoots, and Alec could not stop himself from laughing at the insufferable man. He looked to his friends. "You've the story wrong," he said. "No way in hell is this man her scandal." Lillian wouldn't be able to stomach more than a minute with this pompous ass. She would see the truth of him immediately.

The ass continued, entirely sure of himself. "I'm Derek Hawkins! I do not exaggerate the quality of my work! My genius is more than any the world has ever seen!"

Alec looked to King. "Is he always this way?"

"If by 'this way' you mean a pompous prick, yes," came the dry reply. "He courted my sister-in-law for a time. I cannot imagine why she refused his suit."

"I can't force Lillian to marry him."

"I thought she loved him?"

"I don't care," Alec said. And he didn't. There was no possible way he was wedding her to this clown.

He was going to have to deal with the situation in a different way.

"I demand an audience with an owner," Hawkins insisted.

And as though he had been willed into being, one of the owners of the casino appeared. The tall, ginger-haired financier of the club spoke with utter calm. "Hawkins, how many times must we tell you, you are too unlucky for us to bank you without collateral."

"You haven't any understanding of art, Cross," Hawkins declared. "Bring me someone with an eye." He fairly begged for another owner. "Bourne. Or Chase. He'll see reason. My collateral is my name. My work. I am the star of this year's Exhibition. Did you not know that?"

"You have mistaken me for one who cares about this year's Exhibition." The man called Cross was unimpressed. "You leave and return with funds, and we'll discuss a seat at the table. For now, the game resumes without you." He turned to indicate that the dealer should deal the cards.

"Your mistake. I shan't grace you with my presence once the painting shows. It's the greatest nude since Rubens." Alec gritted his teeth, the word *nude* ricocheting through him. "Better than Rubens. I am Leonardo. I am Michelangelo. I'm *better.* You could have enjoyed the profits yourself. And now, you will *beg* me to return."

"No one has even seen this legendary painting, Hawkins!"

someone said. "Come back in ten days when we've a chance to decide for ourselves precisely what kind of *genius* you are."

Hawkins turned on the man. "You know it will be revealed in ten days, which tells me you're planning to have a look."

"At Lovely Lily in the flesh? You're damn right I do."

Alec was on his feet, fists clenched, before he could think.

"Warnick." King was beside him in an instant. "Careful. You shall make it worse."

West did not move from his chair to warn, "Mine is not the only rag you need worry about, Duke."

Later, Alec would be proud of himself that he did not tear the men limb from limb as originally intended. Instead, he spoke, the solution coming even as he spoke the words, thick with angry brogue. "I shall spot the artist."

The room seemed to still, as every person in attendance turned to face him.

"Who are you?" Hawkins asked, confusion and relief warring in the face of Alec's appearance.

Alec spread his hands wide, in innocent affectation. "You look your gift horse in the mouth?"

"No," Hawkins said. "Not necessarily. But I like to know to whom I am indebted."

Alec nodded. "Does it matter? Mine is the only offer of blunt there is for you tonight."

Hawkins's gaze narrowed, his head tilting as he considered Alec, his gaze settling on wide shoulders in a too-tight jacket, the ill-fitting sleeves of the garment. His thick burr. "And if I say yes? What comes next?"

"Then you play your game."

Hawkins tilted his head. "And?"

"And if you win, you win."

"And if I lose?"

"Then I take back my money. With interest."

Hawkins's gaze narrowed. "What interest?"

"The painting."

Hawkins blinked. "The painting for the Exhibition?"

"The very one."

Hawkins's gaze flickered to King and West where they watched the interaction. Recognition flared and he returned his attention to Alec. The man was less of a fool than Alec had given him credit for. "The Duke of Warnick? Lily's disappeared guardian!"

Lily. He loathed the name on this dandy's lips. "Miss Hargrove, to you," Alec snapped.

Hawkins was already beyond the name. "I never would have recognized you. They say you're big, but I would have thought you could have found a tailor with your fortune. The cut of that coat—it's abominable." Hawkins shrugged and straightened his sleeve with a disdainful laugh.

"Do you wish the money or not?"

"You think spotting me the funds for cards will buy you a masterpiece?" Hawkins's chest puffed out with pride and misplaced certainty. "It's a work of *genius*. Not that I expect a man cut from your cloth to understand what that means." He paused, somehow looking up at Alec and also down his nose. "It will steal breath for the rest of time."

Alec took a step toward him. "I shall show you what it is like to lose your breath."

"Warnick." King again. Alec heard the rest of the warning.

Don't make it worse.

The men nearby had tripled in number, smelling a fight in the air.

He took a deep breath. "Ten thousand."

The number was outrageous. More than the painting could possibly be worth.

Something flashed in Hawkins's eyes. Something like greed. "It is not for sale."

"Everything is for sale," Alec said. He knew it better than anything. "Twenty thousand."

A collective gasp rose from the men assembled. Twenty thousand pounds would keep Hawkins for years. For the rest of his life.

But the offer was a mistake. It revealed too much of Alec's desire. Too much of his willingness to save the girl. It put Hawkins in power, dammit.

The artist smirked. "If only you had been here a year earlier, think of what your misplaced sense of responsibility might have prevented."

Alec did not move. Refused to rise to the bait. Refused to pluck the dandy's head from his shoulders as he deserved.

Hawkins continued. "If only you were different, Duke. You might have saved her."

Hawkins couldn't have known the words would set Alec off. Couldn't have predicted their power. His fists clenched, every muscle tightening, threatening to attack. Desperate to do so. "From your actions, you mean."

Light came into Hawkins's eyes. "I assure you, Your Grace, she was party to it," he said, the words filled with foul suggestion. "She was desperate for it."

The men surrounding them hooted and jeered at the words, at their summary destruction of Lillian. The chortles and shouts turning into gasps when Alec moved, a dog loosed from his chain.

He lifted Hawkins from his feet by the collar of his elaborate topcoat as though he weighed nothing. "That was a mistake."

"Put me down," Hawkins squeaked, his hands clawing at Alec's fist.

West rose. "Not here, Warnick. Not in front of the world."

Alec tossed the vermin to the ground. Looming over Hawkins, he said, once more, "How much?"

Hawkins scrambled to his feet. "You can't just manhandle me. I am—"

"I don't care one bit who you are. How much for the picture?"

"You'll never get it," Hawkins spat, high-pitched and terrified, filled with false bravado. "I wouldn't take your money if you offered ten times as much, you Scottish thug. You're a perfect match. As cheap as she is. Just luckier."

The words reminded Alec of his intentions, that there had

been a time when he'd actually planned to force this bastard to marry Lily.

As though he'd ever let him near her again.

As though he'd ever allow him to breathe the same air as her.

"I have been more than polite," he said, stalking Hawkins back as the men assembled chattered and grumbled.

A voice rose over the crowd. "Twenty pounds on the Scot!"

Alec ignored it. "I was willing to pay you for the painting. A fair price. More than fair."

"No one will take that wager. Look at him! Fists the size of hams!"

Those fists clenched and unclenched.

"I'd pay just to see the fight!"

"I don't put it past him to force Hawkins to the altar!"

"Ten quid on that!"

Hawkins could not keep his mouth shut. "As though I'd take lowborn, lonely, sad Lillian Hargrove. As though a genius marries a muse. I could have anyone. I could have *royalty*."

"Take 'im to the ring, Warnick! Show 'im your displeasure!"

"I don't need the ring." Alec wasn't displeased. He was murderous. "Listen to me and listen well," he said, low and barely discernible through his angry brogue. "Commit my words to memory. Because I want you to spend the next two weeks wondering how I'm going to do it."

"Do what?" Hawkins was terrified.

"Destroy you."

Hawkins blinked, and Alec saw his throat working, as though he was considering a reply. Finally, he shook his head, turned on his heel, and ran—straight through the curtain that marked the doorway to the club, and out into the London night, chased by the laughter and jeers of the rest of the membership of the gaming hell.

After several long seconds, King appeared at Alec's shoulder. "It seems he is not an imbecile after all. Running was a good choice."

I plan to run.

Lily's words echoed through him, full of desolation, reminding him of another who had run and been destroyed.

He shook his head. "That man drives her from London over my decaying corpse."

West joined them. "Then you no longer intend him to wed the girl?"

The words summoned an image of Lily in Hawkins's arms, her hair spilling down her back, tangled in his fingers. Her lips on his. And Alec wanted to upend the nearest card table.

He settled on, "Not for all the blunt in London."

"What then?"

"It is no matter who she marries. Only that she does."

King and West looked to each other, then back to Alec, now firmly resolved in his modified plan. He waited for one of them to speak. When they did not, he said, "What of it?"

After a long moment, West replied. "Nothing. It sounds an excellent plan."

King raised a brow. "I cannot imagine how it could possibly go wrong."

Alec heard the sarcasm in the other man's tone, and in scathing Gaelic, told him precisely what he could do with himself, before turning on his heel and heading for the club's boxing ring.

He could do with a fight.

Chapter 4

DILUTED DUKE AND DOGS RESUME RESIDENCE

Lily should have known when she saw the maid scurrying past the foot of the stairs at eight o'clock in the morning that something was amiss.

She should have sensed it from the quivering silence of the house, as though someone of import was present. But she didn't.

Not until she smelled the ham.

For five years, Lily had descended the same stairs at the same time to take tea and toast in the breakfast room. It was not that she preferred tea and toast for breakfast—simply that it was the food that was offered. And even then, there were days when the cook forgot her, and she had to go looking for breakfast. Those were the better days, honestly, because they allowed her to enter the kitchens and be in the company of others.

Lily lived in the margins of life at 45 Berkeley Square. She was neither nobility nor servant—too highborn to be welcome in the lives of the staff, not highborn enough to be honored by them. For the first year, she'd ached for their friendship, but by the second, she'd simply become a part of this dance, weaving through them, not unwelcome, but more . . . invisible.

Though she had disliked the disinterest for years, recently, she had become comforted by it.

After all, Lily was no longer invisible beyond this house.

She was altogether *too* visible beyond this house.

The fact remained, however, that the invisible did not receive ham for breakfast. And so it was that, as the maid disappeared down the long hallway and the salty scent of cured meat beckoned to Lily from the breakfast room, she realized that she was not alone in the house.

That the duke had decided to take up residence.

She pushed open the door to find him behind a newspaper, a plate piled high in front of him, nothing but shirtsleeves visible.

Shirtsleeves. The man didn't even have the courtesy to dress for dining.

Therefore, Lily did not have the patience for courtesy. "You slept here?"

Alec Stuart did not lower the newsprint when she crossed the threshold. "Good morning, Lillian."

The words rumbled through her, thick with a Scots brogue that she told herself she did not care for, as it was too low. Too languid. *Far too familiar.*

Of course, it had to be familiar, as the man was sitting at her dining table, as though he owned the place. Which he did, of course.

She stopped halfway down the large dining table and repeated herself. "You're not staying." That's when she noticed the dogs seated on either side of him, two enormous grey wolfhounds, all wiry fur and lolling tongues, one with several inches of slobber hanging from his jowl. "And they are *certainly* not staying."

"You don't care for dogs?" He did not lower his paper.

She did, actually. She'd always rather wished she had one. "They are dogs? I thought they were small horses."

"This is Angus," he said, one hand peeking out from behind the paper to stroke the massive head on his left. "And this is Hardy." He delivered similar care to the other. "They're kittens. You'll like them."

"I shan't have a chance to, as you are not staying. There are eight other residences in London, *Your Grace*, not to mention wherever you've laid your head the other times you've been to town—I'm sure you can find another that will suit."

He lowered one corner of his paper. "How do you know I've been to town before now?"

"Good God," she said. "What happened to your face?"

"A lady wouldn't notice."

His right eye was swollen shut, black and a wicked shade of green. "Is the lady in question blind?"

One side of his swollen lip lifted in a barely there smile. "You should see the other man." He returned to his paper.

She should be grateful for the beating. For the way it took away from those supremely distracting lips. She'd never in her life even noticed a man's lips before, and now all she could think was how she hoped the swelling was not permanent. It would be a tragedy to ruin such a mouth.

Not that she was interested in his mouth.

Not at all.

She cleared her throat. "What did he do to you?"

"Nothing," he said, as though the entire morning were perfectly ordinary. "I went looking for a spar."

Men would forever perplex her. "Whatever for?"

"I found myself irritated." He set the paper aside.

Her eyes went wide. "You are wearing tartan."

A deep red plaid cut a diagonal swath up his torso, over his shoulder, where it was met with another drape of wool and fastened with a pewter pin. The garment only underscored how ill-fitting he was here, in this house—in this world he'd inherited so unwillingly.

In this world that she had so desperately wanted before she'd so desperately wanted to be rid of it.

He lifted his paper again. "I find it more comfortable."

"Are you wearing trousers?" The words were out before she could rein them in.

His good eye met hers with a piercing brown gaze. "No."

She'd never in her life been so embarrassed as in the wake of that single, simple word. She wished to crawl beneath the table. She might have done, if doing so wouldn't have brought her entirely too close to the source of her embarrassment.

Thank heavens, he changed the topic. "You did not answer me."

She couldn't remember the question. She couldn't remember any question in the entirety of her life but her last. She was mortified.

"How do you know I've come to town before now?" he repeated.

"I read the papers, just as you do," she said. "You're a particular favorite when you arrive in town."

"Oh?" he said, as though he did not know it already.

"Oh, yes," she said, recalling the way the scandal sheets described him, *the ladies' dark dream*. She supposed he was a particular specimen, if one liked the tall, broad, and brutish sort of thing. Lily did not like it. Not at all. "The whole of London is warned to put out the sturdy furniture, in the event you happen along for tea."

A muscle in his cheek tightened slightly, and Lily was surprised that the triumph she expected to feel knowing that she'd struck true did not come. Instead, she felt slightly guilty.

She should apologize, she knew, but instead bit her tongue in the long, uncomfortable moment that followed, during which he remained still as stone, coolly regarding her. They might have stood there for an age, in a battle of will, if not for the long strand of drool that dropped from one dog's jowl to the carpet below.

Lily looked to the spot before saying, "That carpet cost three hundred pounds."

"What did you say?"

She smirked at his shock. "And now it has been christened with your beast's saliva."

"Why in hell did you spend three hundred pounds on a carpet? For people to walk on?"

"You gave me leave to decorate the house as I saw fit."

"I did no such thing."

"Ah, of course," she replied. "Your solicitor did. And, if I am to live in such a cage, my lord, it may as well be gilded, don't you think?"

"We return to the bird metaphor?"

"Clipped wings and all," she said.

He lifted his paper once more, his reply dry as sand. "It seems to me that your wings work very well, little wren."

She stilled, not liking the unsettling knowledge in the words. Returned to the original topic. "You took no interest in the house, Your Grace, so I see no need for you to live in it."

He replied from behind his newspaper. "I find I have an interest in it now."

The cool statement reminded her of why she had entered the breakfast room to begin with. She took a deep breath. "You are not—"

"Staying. Yes. I am not without ability to hear."

She didn't doubt his sense of hearing. She doubted his sense, full stop. But it did not matter. The house was large enough for her to avoid him until her funds arrived, and she was free of him. And London.

Before she could say as much, however, they were interrupted by the arrival of the butler, Hudgins. "Your Grace," the ancient man croaked as he doddered into the room leaning heavily on a cane, a slim parcel under his arm. "A missive has arrived for you."

Lily turned to assist the butler—always half doubting his ability to get from one location to the next without hurting himself—removing the parcel from his hands. "Hudgins, you mustn't overtax yourself."

The butler looked to her, clearly insulted, and snatched the parcel back. "Miss Hargrove, I am one of London's best butlers. I can certainly carry a parcel to the *master* of the house."

The haughty words sent heat rushing through her—embarrassment of her own. His quick retort did not simply reveal that he'd been insulted, but also served to remind her of her place, neither above nor belowstairs. And certainly not permitted to instruct the staff in front of the duke.

She immediately searched for a way to make amends as he doddered toward the duke, setting the envelope on the table.

"Thank you, Hudgins," Alec said quietly, the low burr rumbling across the room. "Before you leave, there is another matter with which you might assist me."

Lily was forgotten. The butler straightened as much as his aging bones would allow, obviously eager to prove he was more than able to help. "Of course, Your Grace. Whatever you require. The entire staff is here for your aid."

"As this is a matter of serious import, I would not wish for any but you to aid me."

Lily turned to the duke with a frown—wanting to underscore Hudgins's frailty. To make the point that the butler no longer served in the traditional sense. That despite his rising and dressing the part each day, he did little more than answer the door when he was able to hear it, which was becoming less and less frequent. Hudgins had earned a retirement of sorts, comfortable and quiet. Could the Scotsman not see it?

"I require a complete accounting of the items of value in several rooms of the house," Warnick said. "Paintings, furniture, sculpture, silver . . ." He trailed off, then added, "Carpets."

What on earth? Why? Lily's brow furrowed.

"Of course, Your Grace," the butler replied.

"Not all the rooms, you understand. Only the critical locations. The main receiving rooms, the sitting rooms, the library, the conservatory, and this one."

"Of course, Your Grace."

"I should think it would take you no longer than a month to produce such an accounting. I should like it to be as thorough as possible."

It should not take the man more than a week, honestly, but Lily did not say as much.

"That should be a fine amount of time," Hudgins replied.

"Excellent. That is all."

"Your Grace." Hudgins bowed ever so slightly, and doddered out of the room, Lily watching, waiting for him to finally, finally close the door behind him before she turned on the duke.

"For a man who is so keen to eschew a title, you certainly enjoy ordering the staff about," she said, approaching him once more. "What an inane request! A full accounting of the contents of the house. You've estates valued at literally millions of pounds, Your Grace. And ham."

She hadn't meant to say the last bit.

He tilted his head. "Did you say ham?"

She shook her head. "It's irrelevant. What do you care what is on the walls of the sitting room in a home you did not know existed last week?"

"I don't," he said.

She went on, barely hearing the reply. "Not to mention the tedium of such a task—he'll be occupying each of those rooms for days, considering his unwillingness to end his servitude and live out his life in—" She stopped.

He tossed a piece of ham to the dog on his left.

"Oh," she said.

And a crust of bread to the one on his right.

"The sitting rooms. The receiving rooms. The library. Here." He did not reply. "All rooms with comfortable furniture. A month to catalogue the contents."

"He is a proud man. There's no need for him to know he's been pastured."

She blinked. "That was kind of you."

"Don't worry. I shall continue to play the beast with you." One large hand stroked over a dog's head, and Lily found herself transfixed by it—by its sun weathered skin and the long white scar that began an inch below his first knuckle. She stared at it for a long moment, wondering if it was warm. Knowing it was. "Tell me, is it just the old man? Or do all the servants overlook you?"

She lifted her chin, hating that he'd noticed. "I don't know what you mean."

He watched her for a long moment before lifting the parcel from the table. She watched as he slid one long finger beneath the wax seal and opened it, extracting a sheaf of papers.

"I thought you did not read your correspondence."

"Be careful, Lillian," he said. "You do not wish for me to ignore this particular missive."

Her heart began to pound. "Why?"

He set it aside, far enough away that she could not see it. "I wrote to Settlesworth after you apprised me of your plans."

She caught her breath. "My funds."

"*My funds*, if we're being honest."

She cut him a look. "For nine days."

He sat back in his chair. "Have you never heard of catching more flies with honey?"

"I've never understood why one need catch a fly," she said, deliberately pasting a wide, winning smile on her face. "But it is done, then. I shall hereafter think of you as a very large insect." She pointed to the papers. "Why are my funds of interest?"

He set a hand on the stack. "At first, it was just that. Interest."

Her gaze lingered on that great, bronzed hand on the document that somehow seemed to feel more important than anything in the world. That document that clarified her plans for freedom. She was so distracted by the promise of that paper that she nearly didn't hear it. The past tense.

Her attention snapped to him, to his brown eyes, watching her carefully, unsettlingly. "And then what?"

He made a show of feeding a piece of toast to one of the dogs. Hardy, she thought. No. Angus. It didn't matter. "I met a man last evening. Pompous and arrogant and obnoxious beyond words."

Her heart pounded with devastating speed. "Are you certain you were not looking into a mirror?"

He cut her a look. "No, I was looking at Derek Hawkins."

Her heart stopped.

Luckily, she did not have to speak, because he continued, "I went looking for him."

Which meant he knew. About everything. About her idiocy. About her desperation. About her willingness to do whatever a man asked of her. About her naiveté.

She went hot with shame, hating herself.

Hating him for resurrecting it.

She swallowed. "Why?"

"Believe it or not," he said, and she could hear the surprise in his tone, "I intended to force him to marry you."

What had he said?

She was certain she'd misheard him. Panic rose. Was he mad? "You didn't!"

"I did not, as a matter of fact," he said. "Once I met the man, I realized that there was no way on green earth that I would allow you to cleave yourself to him."

Cleave. She hated the word. Hated the roughness of it. The way it seemed rife with desperation. With obsession. With unpleasant, simpering longing.

You said you loved me.

The shame came again, flooding in on the memory of the words, high and nasal and desperate. In front of all London, punctuated by their mocking laughter. With his.

And now Alec Stuart, twenty-first Duke of Warnick, the only man in London who had not known the circumstances of her shame, knew them. And worse, thought to save her.

Panic rose. "I never asked to be cleaved to him."

"I am told you did, lass. Quite publicly."

She closed her eyes at the words, as though if she could not see him, she could not hear the truth. He knew. Knew everything about what had happened with Derek. But somehow, he couldn't see the truth of it. That everything she'd ever desired, everything for which she'd ever dreamed . . . it was all impossible now.

She'd made it so.

Her fists clenched at her side and she opened her eyes to find him staring at her, as though he could see right into her soul. She looked away, immediately. "You would be surprised what ruination in front of all of London will do to one's desires."

There was a long moment as he waited for her to look at him again.

She could not do it.

Finally, he let out a long breath and said, "For what it is worth, Lillian, Hawkins is possibly the most loathsome man I've ever had the misfortune to meet."

She looked to him, willing him to believe her. "I do not wish Hawkins. Nor do I wish your help. Indeed, all I wish is to have a life that is my own. And free of—"

Scandal. Shame.

She shook her head, unwilling to say the words aloud. "All of it."

She would run. She would start fresh. And someday, she would forget that for which she'd always dreamed. The marriage, the family, the belonging.

Thankfully, she did not have to explain it to the Duke of Warnick, who lifted the papers from the table and said, "I intend to give you that life, Lillian."

Relief flooded, deep and nearly unbearable. He had put the idea of marrying her off from his head. She smiled, unable to contain her joy at the words. She could begin anew. She could forget Derek Hawkins and his manipulation. His pretty lies. "Alec Stuart, you are the world's greatest guardian."

It seemed she could catch flies, after all.

He stood then, his chair balancing on two legs before returning to the floor with a thud, punctuated by the sudden sensation of sawdust in her mouth, as she witnessed the plaid in all its glory, falling in perfect pleats to his knees, below which perfect, muscled calves, the likes she had never before seen, curved and tightened.

Good God. The man was Herculean.

No wonder the ladies adored him.

Her gaze traveled to the edge of the fabric, drinking in the curves and dips of his knees. She swallowed, the act a challenge, wondering how it was she'd never noticed the precise shape of a knee.

She shook her head. How ridiculous. She didn't care about knees. Not when her freedom was on the table.

"My money."

He leaned against the table and looked down at his papers. "From what I understand, you receive five thousand pounds on your twenty-fourth birthday."

Blood rushed through her, making it difficult to think, and she let out a long breath, and laughed, relief coming light and beautiful, making her happier than she'd been in a long time.

Happier than she'd ever been.

Bless his great Scots heart.

It was enough to leave London. To buy a cottage somewhere. To start anew. "In nine days."

"The same day the painting shall be revealed," he said.

"At once, a welcome birthday gift and a wicked one," she replied with a little self-deprecating laugh. "An irony, as I cannot remember the last birthday I received a present at all."

"There is something you should know, Lily."

And through the happiness, she heard the name he'd never called her. The name she called herself—the one she'd shared with Derek. The one he'd shared with the scandal sheets he enjoyed so much.

The one that had become Lovely Lily. Lonely Lily.

Her gaze snapped to his.

There was a catch.

"As you remain unmarried, you receive the money at my discretion." He paused, and she loathed him in the moment, hearing the words before he said them. "And I require you to marry."

Chapter 5

LOVELY LILY LIVID . . . DEFIES DUKE! DISAPPEARS!

"You cannot force me to marry."

It was the sixth time she'd said it. It seemed Lily had a knack for repeating herself when she was frustrated. What was more, it seemed that she had a knack for ignoring him when she was frustrated.

Which was likely for the best, because the fury on her face when he'd presented her with the terms of his guardianship and his plan to get her married made it very clear that she would have happily knocked him to the ground if she'd thought she could.

She might still try to do just that, which was why he was keeping his distance, watching her pace the room. He'd taken enough of a beating in the ring the night before.

She hesitated at the far edge of the room, staring out the large window that opened onto the house's handsome back gardens. Angus and Hardy had taken up watch by the fireplace, lying with their large grey heads on their paws, eyes following the hem of her skirts. Alec watched as her hand worked the fabric of those skirts before she turned back to him, her anger returned. "You—" She stopped herself. Took a deep breath.

Alec would have wagered his entire fortune that she wanted to say something utterly unladylike. In fact, he wasn't sure if he was impressed or disappointed when she looked back to the gardens and said, "You can't."

He didn't even know the woman. He shouldn't care how this situation made her feel. Indeed, it shouldn't matter how she felt. It should only matter that he was one step closer to being gone from England.

Damn England.

The only place in the world where this kind of idiocy mattered.

He took pity on her nonetheless. "According to Settlesworth, you're right. I cannot make you marry."

She spun around to look at him. "I knew it!"

She would marry, nevertheless. He crossed his arms and leaning back against the hearth. "How old were you when your parents died?"

She came toward him, as though she could force him to return to the topic at hand, but seemed to collect herself once more. "My mother died when I was barely one year of age. In childbirth with a babe who did not survive."

He saw the sadness in her eyes. The regret. The desire for something that would never be. He was drawn to that familiar emotion like a pup on a string. He stepped toward her. "I am sorry. I know what it is to spend a childhood alone."

"Your parents?"

He shook his head. "Barely present. Better absent."

"I thought you had a sister?"

He could not hide his smile as he thought of Cate. "Half sister, sixteen years younger, born while I was . . ." He hesitated on the memory. Cleared his throat. "While I was at school. We did not know each other until I was eighteen and my father died and I returned home to care for her."

"I am sorry. For your father," she said.

He replied with the truth. "I am not."

She blinked at the honest answer, and he immediately moved to change the topic. "Cate is as troublesome as if we shared full blood."

Her eyes were grey as the North Sea when she replied, "I wouldn't know how troublesome that is, as it has always been me, alone." Before he could find a reply, she said, "At least, since I lost my father. I was eleven."

The words reminded him of the purpose of his question. He nodded. "Well, he took good care of you."

Better care of her than his father had cared for him. He'd always been a memory of his mother. And, for his mother, he'd always been a reminder of what she might have had.

She laughed, the sound void of humor. "He left me in the care of a family that was not my own. That was so far above me in station that . . ."

She trailed off, but Alec did not need to hear the words. "How did he know the duke?"

"He worked for him. As land steward. Apparently he was quite good at it, as the then duke agreed to assume my care. A pity that the now duke does not feel similarly." She looked away, the grey morning casting her in ethereal light. Christ, she was beautiful. Alec had no doubt that Hawkins's painting was the masterpiece he claimed it to be.

The thought of the painting shook him from his reverie. He tried his best to sound kind. Comforting. Like a guardian. "I am, you know. Caring for you. Taking responsibility for you. I am attempting to give you the life you wish, Lily."

"Don't call me that."

"Why not?"

"Because it's not for you," she said.

It was not for Hawkins, either, and still he used it.

He resisted the urge to say the words. She was not wrong. The name was all too familiar. She was at best Lillian to him, even as she should be Miss Hargrove. She shouldn't be Lily.

It didn't matter that he wanted her to be.

And he certainly had no right to want her to be anything. She was his ward, and in that capacity, responsibility and problems and nothing else.

Fine. He could play the English guardian, cold and callous and lacking in feeling. God knew he loathed it enough to be familiar with the part. He began anew. "The terms of your guardianship include the factors of which you are aware. You are not allowed to marry without the express approval of the dukedom and, though you receive funds on your twenty-fourth birthday, it was clearly assumed that you would be married, because the terms indicate that I am able to hold those funds in trust until such time as you do marry, should I think you . . ."

It was his turn to trail off.

She wouldn't allow it. "Should you think me what?"

"Irresponsible."

A wash of red came over her cheeks. "Which, of course, you do."

"No," he said, without entirely thinking the response through.

"You do, though. After all, what guardian wouldn't after his ward experienced such a disastrous scandal?" There it was again, in her tone. The humiliation.

He should have murdered Derek Hawkins when he had the chance.

"I don't think you irresponsible. But I think your desire to run unreasonable."

She cast him a withering look. "But marriage to a man I do not know seems more reasonable?"

He lifted one shoulder. "Choose a man you know. Choose anyone you like."

She lost her temper. "I don't know any other men. Believe it or not, I do not make a practice of knowing men. I know Derek. And now I know you. And excuse me, Your Grace, but you're rather much of a muchness when it comes to desirability in a husband, with the singular difference that he covers his legs when he dresses."

Singular difference. Alec could not resist responding to the madwoman. "Ah, but he dresses like an albino peacock, in my experience, so in that, I'd say you're best off with the tartan, lass."

She scowled her irritation at him, and he pressed on, unable to stop himself. "Shall I enumerate the other ways in which we differ?"

"I do not pretend to believe I can stop you, *Your Grace.*"

She was not simply mad. She was also maddening. "Well, I might begin with the obvious. I did not make your acquaintance with the goal of ruining you in front of all London."

"Did you not?"

The question came quick and simple and utterly unsettling, "What does that mean?"

She did not reply, instead setting her jaw determinedly, as though she might remain silent forevermore.

He huffed his frustration. "Either way, Lillian, I have not proposed."

"And thank heavens for that," she said.

He bit his tongue at the words. She meant them to sting, but could not know how much they did, coming on a wave of memory. Of shame. Of desire for women for whom he would never be high enough. Never proper enough. Never good enough.

Lily would have a man good enough. "We go in circles," he said. "You marry."

"And if I don't wish to marry the man you choose?"

"I cannot force you."

She shook her head. "That might be the law, but everyone knows that forced marriages—"

"You don't understand. I cannot force it because it is a separate condition of your guardianship that you are able to choose your husband for yourself, and that you remain under the care of the dukedom until such time as you marry."

Her mouth opened, then closed.

"You see, Lillian? Your father did care for you." Her eyes went liquid at the words, and he was struck with a keen desire to pull her close and care for her himself. Which would not do. And so, instead, he said, "That, I might add, is why you are the oldest ward in Christendom and somehow, remain my problem."

The words worked. The tears disappeared, unshed, replaced by a narrow gaze. "I would happily become my own problem if you would give me my freedom, Duke. I did not ask to be a burden any more than you asked to shoulder me."

And the irony of it was that if he did that—gave the girl the money and sent her away, he'd be on the road back to Scotland at that precise moment.

Except he couldn't. Because it wouldn't be enough.

"Why?" she interrupted his thoughts, the question making him wonder if he'd spoken aloud.

He looked to her. "Why?"

"Why do you insist I marry?"

Because she was ruined if she did not. Because he had a sister six years younger than she, and just as impetuous, whom he could easily imagine falling victim to a bastard like Hawkins. Because he would lay down his life for Catherine in the same situation. And, though he found himself more than able to turn his back on the rest of the London bits of the dukedom, he would not turn his back on Lillian.

"Marriage—it's what women do."

Her brows rose. "It's what men do, as well, and I don't see you rushing to the altar."

"It's not what men do," he replied.

"No? So all these women marching down the aisle, whom are they marrying?"

She was irritating. "It's not the same."

That laugh again, the one without humor. "It never is."

He didn't like it. Didn't like the way it set him back. The way it made him feel that he was losing in whatever battle they fought.

"Alec," she said, his name another blow of sorts—soft and quiet and tempting as hell on her pretty lips. "Let me go. Let me leave London. Let them have the damn painting and let me go."

She might have convinced him. It was not an impossibility, until she said, soft and desperate, "It's the only way I'll survive it."

It's the only way I'll survive.

He inhaled sharply at the words—words he'd heard before. Spoken by a different woman but with the same unbearable conviction.

I must go, his mother had said, his narrow shoulders in her hands. *I hate it here. It will kill me.*

She'd left. And died anyway.

Alec couldn't stop it from happening.

But he could stop it from happening again, dammit.

"There is no outrunning it, Lillian." Her brow furrowed in confusion, and he pressed on. "The painting—it is to be the centerpiece of the Royal Exhibition's traveling show."

She tilted her head. "What does that mean?"

"It will travel throughout Britain, and then onto the rest of the world. Paris. Rome. New York. Boston. You'll never escape it. You think you are known now? Just wait. Wherever you go, if they've access to news and interest in salacious gossip—which is everywhere I have ever been, I might add—you shall be recognized."

"No one will care." She stood straight as an arrow, but her tone betrayed her. She knew it wasn't true.

"Everyone will care."

"No one will recognize me." He could hear the desperation in the words.

Christ, she was beautiful. Tall and lithe and utterly perfect, as though the heavens had opened and the Creator himself had set her down here, in this place, doomed to be soiled. The idea that no one would notice her, that no one would recognize her, it was preposterous. He softened his reply. "Everyone will recognize you, lass." He shook his head. "Even if I doubled the funds. If I gave you ten times as much, the damn painting would follow you."

Those straight shoulders fell, just enough for him to see her weakening. "It is to be my shame."

"It is your error in judgment," he corrected.

She smirked. "A pretty euphemism."

"We have all made them," he said, wishing for some idiot reason that he could make her feel better.

She met his gaze. "You? Have you made such an error?"

More than he could count.

"I am king of them," he said.

She watched him for a long moment. "But men don't carry the shame forever."

Alec did not look away from her, from the words that so many believed true. He lied. "No. We don't."

She nodded, and he saw the tears threaten. He resisted the urge to reach for her, knowing instinctively that touching her would change everything.

He hated himself for not reaching for her when she turned away, for the door. "And you think you shall find a man who will choose to marry me. What nonsense that is."

"I've given you a dowry, Lillian."

She paused, putting her hand to the door handle, but not turning it.

He took the stillness as indication that she was listening. "There was none attached to you. Presumably because you were so young when you became ward to the estate. Also, presumably why you've never been asked for. But now there is. Twenty-five thousand pounds."

She spoke to the closed door. "That is a massive amount of money."

More than she needed to catch a husband.

She could catch a husband with nothing.

"We shall find a man," he said, suddenly consumed with distaste at having to buy her a future. It had seemed such an easy solution the night before. But now, in the room with her, he felt the whole thing slipping away from him. "We shall find a man," he repeated. "A good one."

Alec would carry him to the altar if necessary.

"We have nine days," he said.

"To convince a man to take a risk on my scandal before all the world has truly witnessed it."

"To convince a man that you are prize enough to ignore it."

Lily turned, grey eyes flashing. "Prize."

"Beauty and money. Things that make the world go round." Not just those things, he wanted to say. *More.*

She nodded. "Before the painting is revealed. Not after."

He opened his mouth to reply, but did not have a good answer. Of course before. Once she was nude in front of the world, she would be—

"Before my shame is thoroughly public," she said, softly. With conviction. "Not after."

He ignored the topic, instead saying, "Marriage gives you everything you wish for, lass."

"How do you know that for which I wish?"

"I know what a woman wants out of life." He found himself unable to meet her gaze. "It is marriage. Not money."

She gave a little huff of laughter. "Well, any woman worth her salt wants both."

He had her. "You'll get both. Just as you wanted."

"I *wanted* to marry for love."

He recoiled from the very idea. Love was a ridiculous goal—one that was not only implausible but nonexistent. He knew that better than anyone. But Alec had a sister, and so he knew a thing or two about women—and knew, without question, that they believed in the great fallacy of the heart. So he lied to her. "Then we shall find you someone to love."

She faced him then, tilting her head and watching him as though he were a creature under glass, fascinating and disgusting all at once. "That's impossible."

"Why?"

She lifted one shoulder and lowered it. "Because love is for the lucky among us."

"What does that mean?" he said, her words rioting through him, unwelcome in their eerie truth.

"Only that I am not counted among the lucky. Everyone I have ever loved has left."

He did not have time to reply, because she was through the door and gone, leaving him with his dogs, the words echoing in the empty room.

ENGLISHWOMEN WERE SUPPOSED to be meek and biddable.

No one had told Lillian Hargrove such a thing, apparently.

When Alec had told her he was willing to give her a dowry that would get her married to any man she chose, it had occurred to him that she might embarrass him with thanks. After all, twenty-five thousand pounds was a king's fortune. Several kings' fortunes. Enough to buy her and the man of her choosing—whoever that was—the life she wanted. An approximation of the love she'd desired.

Granted, Lillian Hargrove was not the swooning type, but the woman would not have been out of bounds to be grateful. A tear or two would not have been unexpected.

Instead, she'd declined the offer.

He'd left her alone for the day, giving her time to change her mind—to come to terms with the idea and realize that his decision had been benevolent if nothing else. After all, she'd wanted marriage once—albeit with an utter ass—and if she considered his solution, Alec was certain she would agree it was best.

These disastrous events could end with marriage and children and the kind of security of which women dreamed.

I am not counted among the lucky.

Bollocks. Luck changed.

If the woman wanted love, she would get it, dammit. He might not believe in it, but he'd will it into being if need be.

He was her guardian and he would play the role, dammit. He would repair her reputation, and he would return to Scotland. And she would be another's problem. And that would be that.

They had no choice. There was no way to run from the painting, unless she was willing to live life as a hermit. She certainly couldn't spend the rest of her life rattling around number 45 Berkeley Square, a ward of the dukedom. She was too old to be a ward now—what would it look like when she was forty? Sixty?

It was ridiculous. She would no doubt see that.

Alec had arrived early to the afternoon meal with plans to read his correspondence until she arrived, preferably with an apology and sense on her lips.

After a quarter of an hour, he called for his luncheon. After a half an hour, he finished his letters, but remained with them, pretending to read, not wanting her to think he was waiting for her. After three quarters of an hour, he called for a second meal, as the first had grown cold in the waiting.

And after an hour, he'd called for Hudgins, who took another ten minutes to arrive at a virtual crawl.

"Is Miss Hargrove ill?" he asked the moment the man entered the room.

"Not to my knowledge," Hudgins replied. "Shall I fetch her?"

Alec imagined that it would take the old man the same amount of time to reach Lily's rooms as it would take Alec to search the entire house. And so he declined the offer and did just that.

She was not in the kitchens or the library, the conservatory or any of the sitting rooms. He climbed the stairs and began to search the bedchambers, beginning with the floor where he slept in the suite that had been described to him as "the duke's rooms." Sharing the corridor were door after door of perfectly neat, beautifully appointed, large, airy, clearly unused spaces. How many people were supposed to live in this damn house?

And where was Lily's chamber if it was not among these?

He climbed to the third floor, imagining that he would find rooms similar in size to his own, massive and filled with her things. It occurred to him that there was nothing in the common areas of the house that indicated that she lived here at all. In the two days that he had shared the space, he hadn't seen a single thing out of place. A book left on a side table. A teacup. A shawl.

Hell, Cate produced trails of items throughout the Scottish keep, as though she were leaving breadcrumbs in the forest. He'd just assumed all women did the same.

The third floor was darker than the second, the hallway narrower. He opened the first door to discover what must have been a nursery or a schoolroom at some point, a large room with a lingering scent of wood and slate, golden shafts of afternoon light revealing dust dancing in the space. He closed the door and headed down the dim corridor, where a young maid replaced candles in a nearby sconce.

"Pardon me," he said, and whether it was the Scots burr or the polite words or the fact that he was nearly two feet taller than she was, he shocked the hell out of the girl, who nearly came off the floor at the sound.

"Your—Your Grace?" she stammered, dropping into a curtsy worthy of a meeting with the Queen.

He smiled down at her, hoping to put her at ease. She shrank back toward the wall. He did the same, to the opposite side, suddenly deeply conscious of the fact that he was so out of place in the narrow space. Wishing he were smaller, as he always did in this godforsaken country, where he threatened to crush furniture like matchsticks.

Pushing the thoughts to the side, Alec returned to the matter at hand. "Which is Miss Lillian's chamber?"

The girl's eyes went even wider, and Alec immediately understood. "I am not planning anything nefarious, lass. I'm simply looking for her."

The girl shook her head. "She's gone."

At first, the words did not make sense. "She's what?"

"Gone," the girl blurted. "She's left."

"When did she leave?"

"This morning, sir." After their disastrous breakfast.

"When will she be back?"

Those wide eyes gleamed white. "Never, Your Grace."

Well. He did not like the idea of that. "Show me her chamber."

She immediately obeyed, walked him down the turning hallway, all the way to the back corner of the house—to the place where the servants' stairs climbed in narrow twists to their chambers on the upper levels of the house. To such a strange location in the home that he nearly stopped her to repeat his original request, certain he'd terrified the young woman into miscomprehension.

But he hadn't. She knocked on a barely there door and opened it a crack, immediately leaping back to allow him entry.

"Thank you."

"You—you're welcome," she stuttered, the surprise in her voice leaving Alec hating this country anew, with its ridiculous rules about gratitude and the servant class. A man thanked those who helped him, no matter their station. Hell. *Because* of their station.

"You are free to go," he said softly, pushing the door open, revealing Lillian's quarters, tiny and tucked away, so small that the door did not open all the way, instead catching on the foot of the little bed.

One side of the room shrank beneath a deeply sloped ceiling, beyond which the servants' stairs climbed, threatening the entire space with a sense of deep, abiding claustrophobia. The sunlight that had streamed into the nursery made the tiny room warm, but that could also have been the result of its contents.

Here were all of Lillian's things, the breadcrumbs that were missing from the forest of the rest of the house: books piled everywhere; several baskets of needlepoint, filled with threads in a rainbow of colors; a little wooden hammock overflowing with old newspapers; an easel with a half-painted view of tile rooftops and trees in spring—the view that lived beyond the narrow little window that dwarfed the opposite wall.

The bed was covered in blankets and pillows, more than Alec had ever seen on much larger beds, each coverlet in a bright color that seemed to run at odds with the others.

That was, perhaps the most shocking thing about this room—not the size, nor the clutter, nor the fact that it was as far away from the rest of the house as possible, though certainly all those things surprised—but the color. There was so much of it.

It was so different from everything he'd seen of her before.

So opposite the rest of the house she'd decorated according to the latest styles and the demands of myriad ladies' magazines. Here, in this wild, wonderful space filled with clutter and color and . . .

Stockings.

Alec's gaze fell to the foot of the bed, where a pair of pretty silk stockings was draped over the plain wood frame, so carelessly that he imagined Lillian had removed the long sheaths of silk with distracted speed.

He would be lying if he said he did not pause for a moment to consider such an action, Lily one foot up on that colorful bed, untying the little white ribbons at the tops of the stockings and rolling them down her legs, tossing them over the rail before tossing herself into the pillows to rest.

Not that *rest* was the first thing he imagined her doing in that bed after removing the stockings. He imagined her there, spread across that little bed, hair wild over her pillow, eyes half-closed, lips parted, beckoning.

To him.

He was instantly hard, and entirely furious with himself. He cleared his throat. He was her guardian. And she was his ward. His *missing* ward.

And he was in this room to locate her, with or without her stockings.

He shifted at the discomfort of the thought. *With.* With her stockings.

He turned away from the offending garments, ignoring his body, instead looking to the rest of the room, so clearly Lillian's sanctuary, so much so that he felt like the worst kind of criminal entering the space. A burglar with the crown jewels. A layman in a sacristy. Later, it would occur to him that even if he'd attempted to stop himself from entering that strange little room, he would not have been able to do so.

Alec stepped in, leaving the door as open as it could be left, his attention falling to the little wooden desk tucked under the low ceiling, where a pile of paper sat in organized chaos, a pen atop it, having left a blotch of ink on the pristine sheet. He ducked into the space and ran his fingers across the ecru, thinking on other letters—the ones that had summoned him south to this woman, who could drive him mad if he allowed it.

Certainly, standing in this room, she seemed the madwoman. She had a half-dozen bedchambers to choose from and a dozen more rooms in which to live, and still she chose this little hole.

There was a large hinged trunk against the wall next to the desk, left unlatched. Alec leaned down to open it. It was filled with letters, it seemed, a collection of well-worn envelopes that had obviously been opened and reopened, each with a letter that had been read and reread.

He lifted one, knowing that he shouldn't, knowing it made him a scoundrel, but too riveted to Lily's name and the bold, black direction scrawled across the envelope to stop himself. He opened it, his eyes immediately falling to the signature.

Hawkins.

It was remarkable how quickly one man could loathe another.

His gaze scanned the words . . . a mountain of pretty gibberish.

The loveliest lady in London.

My muse.

Someone had sketched a flower in the margins of the letter, a beautiful, bold lily, fluted and perfect. Alec supposed it was Hawkins who had done so, even as he wished the man's talent was less than purported.

My Lily.

Alec balked at the nickname, scrawled in that bold, confident hand, and her words from the previous day echoed through him. *Don't call me that. It's not for you.*

Well, it certainly wasn't for this Hawkins imbecile, either. And she sure as hell didn't belong to Hawkins.

She belonged to him.

Alec shot straight up at the thought, cracking his head powerfully against the ceiling, so hard that he swore in a loud, long, utterly inappropriate string of Gaelic.

One hand to his head, Alec stood, continuing his colorful invectives. As the sting subsided, it occurred to him that he should be grateful for the blow to the head, however, as it had literally knocked sense back into him.

Lillian Hargrove did not belong to him.

Indeed, he was working quite hard to ensure that she was firmly in his past.

What if he did give her the money? Not the five thousand she was due—the twenty-five? Fifty? Enough to take herself from Britain. To the Continent, to the Americas, to somewhere else entirely. She would have a fortune large enough to secure a future as a queen anywhere she liked.

He imagined her in silks and satins in Paris, in a wig that fairly touched the sky, the world at her feet, and no one there caring a bit that she had once been in London, living beneath the servants' stairs.

She *wasn't* his sister, after all. Cate was a child, barely eighteen, with no sense of the world beyond. Lily had the knowledge that came with age and womanhood. She'd sat for a damn nude, hadn't she?

She'd gotten herself into this particular situation, hadn't she? And while she was old enough to know better. She had to have known what might have come of it.

The shame would still follow her.

He knew better than most how it would, burrowing beneath the skin and never leaving. Whispering in the night. She'd never escape it, even if she escaped those who would cloak her in it.

Just as he never had.

He leaned down to replace the letter, noting the place where the paper had once been, and what it had revealed. He crouched, collecting the layer of correspondence that hid a mountain of white fabric. Of white clothes.

Tiny, white, child's clothes, all embroidered linen and lace collars, gowns and caps and blankets. Instinctively, Alec reached out to touch them—to hold them up, these pristine, clearly unused clothes. The little dress in his hand had a row of pretty blue flowers embroidered along the hem. Another had a row of brown rocking horses, with golden saddles and halters. A third, the moon and stars in fine yellow.

He knew without hesitation that these clothes had been made by Lily. For her children. Likely for those she expected to share with that imbecile Hawkins.

Without thought, Alec continued to dig through the trunk, finding little caps and socks and soft cotton boots with red leather bottoms. In a state of utter madness, he tipped the boots up and put the soles to his nose, breathing in the scent of fine leather, feeling the softness against his skin. Like a madman.

He dropped them like they were aflame, and yet, somehow, remained unable to look away from them when they landed on a layer of satin and lace that did not look like it was for a child at all.

He looked over his shoulder to the open door, fleetingly imagining what he would say if a servant happened by, but not entirely caring if he were discovered. He was too far down this particular road at this point.

He lifted the dress from the trunk and knew immediately what it was—pristine and white, as untouched as the children's clothes he'd found above and somehow, oddly, far more precious. Far more important.

This was Lillian's wedding dress. No doubt sewn with dreams of happiness and a future filled with love and family.

She wanted to marry.

She dreamed of it, and of the family that would come with it.

As he held this garment in his hands—proof of her desire, of the fact that she did not wish to be alone, that she had not spent her life dreaming of being alone with none but herself for companion, he found his commitment to his plan renewed.

She was his to protect. To care for. And he would do it. He would get her married. He'd fulfill her dreams.

Of course, to do that, he had to get the girl found, which wasn't going to happen as long as he stood around in what would kindly be referred to as a cupboard beneath the servants' stairs. She'd likely gone to visit friends.

A noise punctuated the thought, a little bang, followed by several thuds and a peal of muffled laughter, and Alec realized that the room wasn't just minuscule. It was loud. He could hear the servants on the other side of the wall.

Why on earth did she sleep here?

He did not have time to consider the question, as it occurred that the proximity to the servants was a boon in this particular moment. He left the room and poked his head out into the servants' stairwell, catching a footman and two maids descending. "You there."

They went stone still, and one of the young women squeaked.

The footman spoke first. "Your Grace?"

"Who are Miss Hargrove's most frequent visitors?"

Silence.

Alec tried again. "Her friends. Who visits her?"

One of the girls shook her head. "No one."

His brow furrowed. "No one?"

The other shook her head. "No one. She does not have friends."

The words came heavy in the dark stairwell, and surprising enough for Alec to have to work to hold back his instinctive *How is that possible?* Lillian was beautiful and clever and had the power of a dukedom behind her. How could she possibly lack friends? Perhaps they simply did not come to the house.

He nodded once. "Thank you."

"Your Grace?" the footman asked, confusion in his voice.

"Och," Alec replied. "In Scotland we're more grateful than they are in England, apparently. You needn't peer at me like a lion in a cage."

The servants blinked in unison. "Yes, Your Grace."

Alec returned to the landing as the trio passed. "Oh!" one

of the girls cried a split second later before she popped her head around the door frame. "She sees the solicitor."

It was Alec's turn to blink. "I beg your pardon?"

"Older man. Wiv spectacles. Starswood or somefin'," she said.

"Settlesworth?"

The girl smiled. "That's it! Comes once a month. One of the other girls says it's 'ow Lillian—" She corrected herself. "*Miss Hargrove*—gets her blunt." Another pause. "Her money."

Of course it was.

She couldn't leave home without funds. And Settlesworth held the purse strings. Alec turned to leave the girl before another thought occurred. He turned back to find her watching him. "Why does she sleep here?" he asked, indicating the room.

She blinked, considering the little room as though she'd never thought to look at it before. Shook her head. "Don't know, rightly," she said, finally. " 'Twas ever thus."

Alec nodded at the unsatisfying answer, thanked the girl, and headed for his solicitor's offices.

Chapter 6

DUKE GOES TO THE DOGS!

If he wished to marry her off, he'd have to find her, first.

The Dukedom of Warnick boasted eight London residences. There were four town houses scattered throughout Westminster and Mayfair, a house east of the city on the banks of the River Thames, a lodging house off Fleet Street that she'd been told was "for income" (though it didn't seem that the dukedom lacked such a thing), a sprawling home with extensive gardens in Kensington, and a little house east of Temple Bar that was supposedly quite drafty.

Lily had always preferred number 45 Berkeley Square the best, likely out of comfort, as the house had belonged to the Duke of Warnick she'd known best—the one who had died five years earlier, beginning the spate of ill luck that had subsequently taken the lives of sixteen other Dukes of Warnick, leaving the dukedom several residences richer, thanks to those interim dukes who had died without heirs, wives or family. Bernard Settlesworth, taxed with managing the London bits of the dukedom, had purchased the properties in the months and years following the deaths. As a result, Alec Stuart, Number Eighteen, now claimed them as his own, despite very likely not knowing that they existed.

Which was his problem.

Lily, on the other hand, did know they existed. And she was not afraid to use them.

Not that Lily had ever actually *seen* the other houses. She'd never had much interest in them. Certainly, she'd had interest from the outside, but as they'd been subsumed into the dukedom, their staffs reduced to skeletons, Lily had always imagined that the devil one knew was the devil with which one stayed—and at least number 45 Berkeley Square had killed a duke who'd held the title for longer than a quarter of an hour.

Nevertheless, Lily was not one to look a gift horse in the mouth, and the fact that there were seven other places to lay her head beyond Berkeley Square was a fine gift indeed.

So it was that the previous evening, she'd arrived at number 38 Grosvenor Square and been warmly greeted by Mr. and Mrs. Thrushwill, the gardener and his happy housekeeper wife. The two had shared their ploughman's supper with her and opened a room—one they proudly kept clean and aired for just such an occasion.

Lily had tucked herself into bed, filled with thoughts of how she intended to avoid the Duke of Warnick's mad scheme to put her on the marriage mart.

Step one, avoid the Duke of Warnick.

Certainly, 38 Grosvenor Square would be an excellent start, as he'd have to go searching for her. This house would buy her time. Two days. Possibly more.

And in the darkness, surrounded by crisp, clean linen, she'd felt relief for the first time in two weeks, five days. For the first time, she felt as though she were captain of her own ship.

That feeling lasted all too briefly, soon replaced with the thoughts that had consumed her since the opening of the Royal Exhibition. Thoughts of Derek. And of her own stupidity.

If only she'd seen the truth about him. That he'd never honored her. That he'd never intended to. That every promise he'd ever made, every pretty word he'd ever spoken, had been a lie.

Lily lay there in the dark, quiet house, turning those lies over and over in her mind, remembering the way they'd made her ache, filled with desire and something far more dangerous. *Hope.*

How many times had she dreamed of being seen? Of being loved? Of being honored?

And how well had she destroyed every possibility for that?

She'd seen the truth in Alec's gaze over his breakfast in Berkeley Square. The sympathy there. No. Not sympathy.

Pity.

It was out of pity that he had come. Out of pity that he stayed, with his ridiculous promises of a massive dowry and a husband—though how she was to get it in eight days . . . it was a fool's errand.

But the other option . . .

The painting will follow you.

Her shame would follow her.

Your error in judgment.

She hated the words, the tacit agreement that she had, in fact, shamed herself. That she would never be able to move beyond it. She didn't want to believe it, even if it rang true. After all, even if she did marry, Society would never accept her. And they certainly wouldn't accept a man willing to have her. No matter the funds.

Once again, a man fortified her scandal. The fact that her once-absent guardian did it with too-noble intentions mattered not a bit.

If only he would see that.

It was not the only thing he would never see, she vowed in the darkness. He would never see the tears that dampened her pillow long into the night as the darkness cloaked her in regret.

She didn't think of the house at all until she woke, eyes on stalks, exhausted from her fitful night, to discover that the housekeeper had risen much earlier and removed myriad coverings to reveal a domicile filled with dogs.

There were more dogs than she could imagine—paintings and statues and tapestries of hounds, gilded dogs threaded into the silk wall coverings, ornate sheepdogs carved into the wooden baseboards, dogs sitting watch on either side of the front door to the town house, and elaborate spaniels wrought into the wall sconces.

Lily slowed her descent on the stairs, taking in the madness of the decor, coming to the bottom step and letting her fingers trace the intricate curves of the mahogany bulldog's head at the start of the banister. This figure was perhaps the most unsettling of all—mouth open, teeth sharp, even a little tongue threatening to loll.

Eyes wide, she turned in a slow circle, considering the sheer quantities of hounds and decided that it was very possible that she had made a mistake in choosing number 38 Grosvenor Square to hide from the duke.

And then she heard his voice, coming from the back of the house, and she was certain of it. As she had resolved to hide from Alec Stuart for as long as possible, however, Lily headed for the exit.

Another of the ducal holdings would have to do.

"We only heard last night that you were opening the house, Your Grace," the housekeeper said in a high pitch. "We've done as much as we can to prepare, but we will need to add staff." She paused, then quickly added, "Or, if you plan to take residence here, we can summon staff from Berkeley Square."

Lily had seconds to make her escape.

"Oh! Miss Hargrove! Good morning!" called Mrs. Thrushwill.

She froze halfway to the door.

"Going somewhere, lass?"

She blushed, turning, captured by Alec's brown gaze and those perfect lips, one side raised in arrogant amusement. Pasting a bright smile on her face, she said, "I was going to take a walk in the square." She turned to the housekeeper. "Good morning, Mrs. Thrushwill."

The older woman returned the smile. "I trust the room was comfortable?"

"Quite," Lily said.

Mrs. Thrushwill looked to the duke. "We shall air another room for you promptly, Your Grace."

What? *No.* "He's not staying."

"Oh," the housekeeper replied, obviously crestfallen. "I thought—"

"I am staying, in fact," said the duke. "Thank you."

"Oh," the housekeeper said once more. "Of course. Of course." And then she dropped a curtsy and hurried off, no doubt to tell all the world about the kind, gracious, handsome duke.

Not handsome.

Giants were not handsome. Certainly not giants who were attempting to ruin Lily's life.

"Your eye is turning colors," she said. "Purple. And yellow."

"A walk?" he prompted.

In for a penny, in for a pound. "I quite enjoy nature."

"Nature."

She nodded. "Quite."

"Grosvenor Square is not *nature.*"

"It is green, is it not? There are trees."

"It's surrounded on all sides by fence and buildings."

"If you think about it, all of nature is surrounded by buildings," she pointed out. "Perhaps you are simply incorrectly identifying the boundaries."

He was unable to concoct an exasperated answer as, in that exact moment, he seemed to realize that the house was decorated in canine glory. "What in . . ." He trailed off, his gaze falling to a particularly garish portrait of a greyhound on one wall. In it, the dog lay in impressive repose, long, spindly legs tangled together, long, sleek head on a red satin pillow, "Is that a *crown*?"

Lily approached the portrait to investigate the headwear and considered the title, embossed into the gilded frame beneath. "*The Jewel in the Crown,*" she read aloud. "Do you think the dog is named Jewel?"

"I think the dog is being mistreated abominably."

She turned back to him. "Perhaps Angus and Hardy would like crowns."

He looked scandalized by the very idea. "This house is hideous."

"I quite like it," she said. "It feels like a home." There was something valuable in that, dogs or no.

"I thought you did not like dogs."

"I thought you *did* like them, Your Grace."

He ignored the taunt. "We are not taking up residence here."

"You are correct. *We* are doing no such thing. I have ceded Berkeley Square to you. With pleasure. I find I prefer houses with working doors."

"You fled."

"It was not fleeing."

"Not very skilled fleeing, as here we are," he said. "Settlesworth sends his regards, by the way."

Her gaze narrowed. "Settlesworth is a traitor."

"Settlesworth is attempting to save his position, and was happy to be able to provide me with information of import."

"Now my location is of import?"

She thought she heard him sigh before he said, "Of course it is."

"Ah, right," she snapped, not wanting to believe he meant well. "Because it is best you know the location of your problems."

"You cannot escape me," he said. "So, why not work with me? We could get the situation rectified and I can return to Scotland. I know we'd both like that."

"As lovely as that bit sounds, your scenario results in my marrying a man I do not know."

"I told you, you may choose any man you like. I've no intention of standing in your way."

"I choose myself," she said. "I'd rather rely upon myself than you. Or any other. I find myself more reliable."

He sighed again, and she heard it filled with frustration and something more. Something she loathed. "Don't you dare," she said, turning on him in fury. "Don't you dare pity me. I don't want it."

He had the grace to look surprised. "It's not pity I feel."

"What then?"

One side of his mouth turned up in a smile she would have called sad if she'd believed for a moment he cared. "Regret."

For heeding his summons, no doubt. For landing himself with her. "We all do things we regret, Duke." She knew that better than anyone.

There was a long moment of silence before he changed the subject. "Which one owned this odious place?"

She didn't hesitate. "Number Thirteen."

"Ah. The one killed by a sheep, allegedly."

"Precisely."

"What happened to him, really?"

She blinked. "That is what happened to him. He was killed by a sheep."

His brow furrowed. "You are joking."

"I am not. He fell off a cliff."

"Number Thirteen?"

"The sheep. The duke was out for his daily constitutional. Below." She clapped her hands together. "Quite smashed."

His lips twitched. "No."

She raised one hand. "I swear it is true."

He looked around the garish room. "You'd think the dogs would have warned him."

She laughed, unable to contain it. "As the hounds survived, it is possible the animal kingdom was working together on the matter."

He laughed, then, deep and rumbling and more comforting than she would like to admit. More tempting.

At the thought, she collected herself. "We should not laugh at his misfortune."

He did the same, coming closer. "We all have misfortune. If we cannot laugh at it, what is there?"

She cut him a look. "Once again, you remind me of your own terrible sufferings, having to be rich and powerful beyond measure, and all because seventeen other poor, put-upon men were hit by falling sheep."

He continued to advance. "I thought it was only one falling sheep?"

"A sheep with a ducal vendetta. You should be careful in the wilderness."

"The wilderness of Grosvenor Square, you mean?"

"It does not hurt to be vigilant."

He laughed again. "And Lady Thirteen? What of her?"

"Number Thirteen was a widower. Childless. No family to inherit."

"No family but the dogs, you mean?"

"I'm told the dogs did not care for the décor."

He chuckled, and she warmed at the response, reveling in the low growl of humor that she might not have heard if he weren't so close. When did he get so close? And why did he smell so wonderfully crisp and clean? Couldn't he smell like other men? All perfume and stench?

If she weren't careful, she might begin to like him.

He might begin to like her.

"Why run from me, Lillian?" he asked softly, deep enough for the words to roll through her. "Why run here?"

Because there was nowhere else.

Well. She couldn't tell him that.

Before she could find an appropriate answer, however, he added, "Why are you alone?"

She stilled at the question, going cold, then hot. *Alone.* What a horrible word. What a horrible, honest, devastatingly apt word. She stepped back, coming up against the wall and the painting. A crowned dog on a silk pillow.

A dog better loved than she'd ever been.

He shook his head and backed away. "I'm sorry. I shouldn't have asked that. It's just that—" he stopped. Changed tack. "What I meant was, why haven't you had a season?"

"I haven't wanted one," she lied.

"Every woman wants a season," he said.

She tried again. "I'm not an aristocrat."

"You are ward to one of the richest dukedoms in England," he said. "You could not find a sponsor?"

"Sadly, Your Grace, money is not enough to secure a girl a sponsor."

He raised a brow. "A girl? Or a girl like you?"

Relief flooded through her at the question, returning them to solid, adversarial ground. She narrowed her gaze. "What's that to mean?"

"A girl who sits for a nude."

Anger flared. Anger, and a hurt she'd tucked away and sworn never to consider again. "Any girl," she said, tartly. "You need connections for a season."

"You're connected. I'm a goddamn duke."

"You forgot me," she said finally. "I had no sponsor because none would have me. A shadow of a duke is not enough to win over the attention of London, it seems. Shocking as it is."

"I am here now."

She raised a brow. "Yes, well, surprisingly, your dukedom has lost some of its . . . cachet."

"Why in hell is that?"

She made a show of tracking the swath of tartan from his shoulder, over his torso, and down to the place where it hung in pleats just above his knees. "I cannot imagine."

He scowled at her. "You're having a season now. This year."

She laughed around the flare of panic that came at the words. "I don't want one." She had already been too much on show. The gossip pages already knew enough of her. And that was before Derek became involved.

"I'm afraid I don't care. It's the way we get you married."

"There is no *we*, Duke. There is no getting me married. I told you. I wish my freedom."

"If you want freedom from me, lass, it comes in the form of marriage. Nothing else."

"Couldn't you imagine me marrying myself? Give me the dowry for taking responsibility for myself?"

He smirked. "Marriage to a man."

"You ask me to trade one master for another."

He raised a brow. "I'm offering you your pick of men. Any man in London."

"And I'm to get down on my knees and thank you."

"Gratitude for such an exorbitant dowry would not be out of line," he pointed out.

She offered a long-suffering sigh. "And if I don't agree to a marriage?"

He opened his mouth as though he had something very serious to say, before thinking twice of it and closing it once more. He took a deep breath and exhaled, all frustration, before meeting her gaze. "You want your funds? You get yourself married."

"And my husband gets my money." And a ruined wife.

He watched her for a long, serious moment before he repeated himself. "Where would you go, lass?"

She lifted one shoulder. "Anywhere but here."

"What does the future look like?"

It had looked like love and marriage and children. It had looked like quiet idyll and the happiness that came with contentment. With security. With the keen knowledge that one's life was well tended.

She'd only ever wanted a family.

A man of my caliber does not marry a woman of yours.

She closed her eyes at the words, spoken by a man who had once lauded her beauty, whispered it in awe, claimed her his muse.

She shook her head, eradicating the thought, returning herself to the moment at hand. To Alec's question. "The future looks like anywhere but London," she said, hearing the irritation in her voice.

He shook his head. "No. That's *where* it looks like. I asked *what* it looks like."

It looked like a life without shame.

The thought came unbidden and painful, packed with the

truth, that she'd ruined her life. That she'd risked everything for what she had believed was love.

She hated him then. Hated the way he saw too much, this great, unexpected, unwilling duke. But she would not tell him the answer. As much as he thought she was his problem to manage, he was wrong. She was her own problem.

And she would manage herself. Without him.

"It looks like happiness."

He didn't believe her.

He shouldn't believe her.

He huffed his frustration. "Happiness isn't so easily found, Lily. It is not as simple as giving you funds and setting you free."

There was such truth in the words that she couldn't help herself. "How do you know that?"

"Because I do," he said. And she waited for him to elaborate, desperate for him to continue. They stood there for long moments before he finally said, "I've had enough of this. Your season begins tonight."

"My season."

"Eversley is hosting a ball. You are invited."

A ball. Her stomach twisted at the words. She could not think of anything she wished to do less. "No, thank you."

"You are laboring under the misapprehension that you have a choice."

The words raised her ire. "You know there are seven other residences in London where I could hide."

"You are unconvinced that I would find you?"

"You wouldn't find me in time for my season to begin tonight."

He leaned in, and when he spoke, the words were low and graveled with Scots burr, sending a shiver of something unnamable down her spine. "I will find you, lass. Always."

Her lips fell open at the words. At the promise in them.

At the idea that she might be worth seeking.

He straightened, and the moment was gone. "Find yourself a gown, Lillian. We leave at half-nine."

"And if I don't?" she asked, the words softer than she intended. She cleared her throat, tried for taunt. "What then, Your Grace?"

He considered her then, his brown eyes beautiful and glittering in spite of the shiner he sported. He watched her until she grew uncomfortable, shifting beneath his attention.

"Find yourself a gown," he repeated. "You won't like it if I have to find one for you."

He left the room, leaving Lily alone in an explosion of canine decor, flooded with unsettling warmth at his words.

She resisted the sensation.

She would not be unsettled by him.

Instead, she would find herself a gown, and she would do the unsettling.

Chapter 7

"LOVELY" LILY STARTS SEASON WITH SPECIOUS STYLE

At half-nine that evening, Alec stood at the foot of the main staircase, trying to avoid the gaze of Jewel. The bejeweled hound appeared to see everything from her position and, as she lay in repose on her inane silk pillow, she most certainly mocked him.

Nearly as much as his own dogs did from their position across the foyer, standing sentry.

The overwhelming canine judgment seemed entirely reasonable, however, as Alec was certain he looked ridiculous.

The tailor he'd found on Savile Row earlier in the day had sworn to be in possession of formalwear that would "perfectly accommodate His Grace," when, in fact, the formalwear accommodated no part of him, least of all any grace he might summon. When Alec had told the simpering man such, he'd been assured that "the fit was de rigueur."

Alec was not an imbecile, however. His coat was too tight. As were his trousers, if he were honest.

So big. A great, Scottish brute.

Nothing about you fits, you beast.

He hated England.

But time was of the essence and he could not wait for a better-fitting garment. Tonight, he began the hopefully blissfully brief end to his sojourn in England. He'd asked West to put it out that Lillian was now in possession of a massive dowry, and he felt confident that young pups across London would happily throw their hats in the ring upon their immediate arrival at Eversley House that evening. The woman was, after all, wealthy and beautiful and ward to a duke.

She'd be smitten by sunup.

All she had to do was turn up. He looked up the stairs. No Lillian. He looked to the large clock at one end of the room, where a pendulum wrought with dogs swung back and forth. Twenty to ten. She was late.

She was here, he knew. He had hired two boys to watch the exits of the house, ensuring that if she attempted an escape, they would follow and he would find her. But presence in the house did not mean that she planned to attend the ball willingly. He was about to climb the stairs and seek her out when she appeared.

To be fair, Alec did not notice her first. Hardy did, the hound immediately coming to the foot of the stairs, staring up at her, and—to Alec's utter surprise—barking excitedly.

"What in—" he began, following the direction of the hound's gaze, the remainder of the question cut off by utter shock.

As best as he could tell, she was dressed as a dog.

He should have known she would have a better plan than either escape or avoidance. Of course, her plan involved doing her best to counter *his* plans for the evening. It was to be a battle of wills—and her first shot was an impressive one.

He was not a man who noticed fashion, but this particular dress would not be unnoticed. It was a gold and bronze monstrosity, with skirts that filled the staircase and sleeves that dwarfed her. That would have dwarfed him, he'd wager. As though that weren't enough, gold and bronze seed pearls were sewn into the skirts, arranged in little echoes of the canine form, and the bodice—

impressively fitted despite Lily having had mere hours to adjust it to her form—was covered in ornate gold fastenings, each a different dog—spaniels and terriers and bulldogs and dachshunds.

His gaze fell to her waist, where a large gold belt accentuated her shape in a garish display—a greyhound in full, extended motion, spanning the width of her.

Jewel, no doubt.

And all this before he considered her headwear, an elaborate pile of auburn curls, fastened with an array of hound-shaped pins, and shot through with a golden rod topped with a hound on the hunt, in mid-leap, heading to catch a hare, which somehow dangled high above, on a spring of sorts.

"Good God," Alec said, as there was no other possible response to the display.

She did not hesitate in her descent, all grace, posture that would make a queen proud. It almost made one believe that she was not aware that she wore a garment that was best described as an abomination.

She was remarkable.

She stilled on the third stair from the foyer, standing eye-to-eye with him, broad, false smile on her face. "Is there something amiss, Your Grace?"

"So many things, Miss Hargrove."

She made a show of fluffing the massive skirts. "I realize this frock is a touch out of season, what with it having been unworn for more than five years, but you did insist I find a dress."

"Yes. The fact that the gown is out of season is precisely the problem." His gaze went to her reticule, a small terrier-shaped satchel dangling from her wrist. "Is that fur?"

She looked to it. "Surely not dog's."

"I cannot imagine Lady Thirteen was the type to wear her obsession." She snickered a laugh and he enjoyed the sound a touch too much. He cleared his throat. "Well then. Onward, Miss Hargrove."

She hesitated.

He had her. "You did not think a little thing like that dress would dissuade me from my plans?"

"There is nothing little about this dress," she said.

"It will be a miracle if it fits inside the carriage," he agreed, turning away from her, heading for the door, keenly aware of the fact that she was not following. Turning back, he met her grey gaze from across the foyer. "Come now, Lillian, surely you did not think I would give up so easily?"

"I did think that you would be smart enough to recognize that if I am seen in public in this dress, no man will ever have me."

"You misjudged."

"Your sense of fashion?"

He did not rise to the bait. "Your own beauty."

The words set her back. "I—" she started, then trailed off.

"That is what they call you, nae? The most beautiful woman in London?"

"Nae," she mocked in an extreme Scottish accent. "Not in this."

He wished it were true. He wished there were a way to look at her and not see her beauty. But some things were empirical truths, and Lillian Hargrove's beauty was just that. Even now, dressed as a canine clown.

Not that Alec intended to do anything about her beauty. He'd learned his lesson about beautiful women, and it was one he did not intend to learn again.

He opened the door, baiting her. "To the coach, Miss Hargrove . . . or are you too much a coward? Would you like to find a less garish ensemble?"

Her shoulders straightened. "Not at all. I am quite comfortable."

She sailed past him, spine straight, rabbit waving to and fro above her head, and climbed up into the waiting carriage without hesitation. Alec followed, filled with curiosity and no small amount of respect.

Once he had arranged himself on the seat opposite her, avoiding her diaphanous skirts and contorting his long legs into the little free space she had left, his too-tight trousers threatening to inhibit blood flow to his legs, she said, "Are *you* quite comfortable?"

"Does it matter?" he asked, knowing that the repetition of the question she'd asked so often in their acquaintance would annoy her.

Enjoying the feeling of annoying her, because it made it easier to ignore the sensation of admiring her.

He did not admire her.

"I suppose not," she said, surprising him. "But I was making polite conversation."

He did not wish to make conversation, so he grunted a nonverbal reply and watched the buildings beyond the window as they passed.

She did not look out the window. She looked at him.

Alec felt more constricted with every moment that passed, until he did his best to get the upper hand. "I imagine you wish you'd changed gowns."

She did not waver. "Nonsense. I've simply taken pity on you, my lord. We will make a fine pair, considering that coat does not fit you."

He shifted at the mention of the clothing, the movement underscoring the truth in her statement. "No?"

She shook her head and moved forward, taking hold of the outer edge of one sleeve and giving it a little tug, as though testing its strength. "No." He resisted the urge to move at the light brush of her gloved hand against his. For a moment, he entertained a wild thought of capturing that hand, of pressing it to his own. And then her gaze fell to his lap, and he imagined pressing her hand to the straining fabric at his thighs. Before he could embarrass himself, she added, "Nor do those trousers. You should find yourself a better tailor." She paused, then added, teasing in her tone, "Someone English, perhaps."

He remained transfixed by her hand, disliking the way it felt on him.

Liking the way it felt on him.

Before he could decide, she removed it from his person, and—madly—he wondered if he could convince her to return it so he could make a thoroughly informed decision on the matter.

Instead, he cleared his throat and pressed himself back against the seat. "This *was* an English tailor. I'm told he's very good."

"He's not. *I* could have made you a better suit."

"Yes, well, considering what you are currently wearing, I shall remain with the poor tailor."

She was affronted. "I beg your pardon. This dress did not simply fit itself to me." She slid a hand over the seam at her side, where the bodice fit like skin. Alec could not help but follow that hand. It would have been rude not to.

More rude than what you imagine doing with that particular seam?

He did not have to respond to the thought, as Lily continued. "I am an excellent seamstress."

The words unlocked the memory of her chamber in Berkeley Square. Of the trunk there, filled with wedding dresses and children's clothing. And those boots.

Those damn boots, he could still smell them.

"Apologies," he said, shifting at the thought, suddenly uncomfortable. "Your skilled craftsmanship is overshadowed by the rest of the qualities of that gown."

She smiled at that, white teeth flashing in the dimly lit carriage, and he disliked the thread of pleasure that came with the response. "Trust me, Duke. This gown is impeccably crafted. It's simply hideous. *You* require another tailor."

The tailor had been scared to death of him. Too terrified to tell him that he was too big for the ready-made clothing that he had in stock. Too terrified to send him somewhere else.

After all, Alec was a duke. One did not turn down a duke.

Not even one who was so monstrously large and so ill-fitting in manicured, cold, perfect England.

What a beast.

Barely tamed.

Brute . . .

Discomfort shot through him, having nothing to do with the clothing, and everything to do with something that the right tailor could not repair. "I shan't be staying long enough to need another. We shall get you betrothed and I shall return to Scotland for the summer, where summer is not filled with putrid stench and steaming cobblestones. Where we have real nature."

"Unfettered by fences."

"Certainly not iron ones."

"You do not like London."

"London should not take it personally. I don't like England."

"Or the English."

"Not many of them."

"Why not?"

Because England had given him nothing but pain.

He did not reply.

She frowned at him. "We have some lovely things."

His brows rose. "Name three."

"Tea."

"That is from the Orient, but it was an excellent try."

She sighed. "Fine. Shakespeare."

"Shakespeare has nothing on Robbie Burns."

Lily looked to him. "You're being ridiculous."

He spread his hands wide. "Go on, then. Give me your best Shakespeare."

"It's all the best," she said, smartly. "It's *Shakespeare.*"

"It seems you cannot think of anything worthy of competition."

She looked away, as though she could not imagine how he couldn't see the truth of her argument. "Fine. *My bounty is as boundless as the sea, my love as deep; the more I give to thee, the more I have, for both are infinite.*"

He raised a brow. "A children's love story."

She gaped at him. "It's *Romeo and Juliet.*"

"Babes without any sense. Killing themselves over infatuation."

"It's considered one of the greatest love stories of all time."

He lifted one shoulder. Let it drop. "Unless you know better."

"And I suppose that your Burns is the better in question?" she scoffed.

He leaned forward in the darkness, allowing his brogue to thicken. "Infinitely so. You want romance, you ask a Scot."

She leaned forward as well, bridging the space between them, competitive and beautiful, insane dog dress be damned. And when she spoke, she had a matching brogue. "Prove it."

Later, he would wonder how the night would have proceeded if the carriage hadn't taken that moment to slow, heralding their arrival at Eversley House, where half the *ton* waited beyond the carriage.

He would wonder if he would have made good on his instincts, and pulled this bold, brave, teasing Lillian into his lap and given her all the proof he could muster.

Luckily, he'd never know.

Because the carriage did slow. And they did arrive.

And he was reminded that kissing Lillian Hargrove was out of the question.

SHE HAD MISJUDGED the depths of his desire to get her married.

She'd also misjudged the depths of embarrassment that would consume her if she wore the dog dress in public. Suddenly, as she stood at the base of the steps to Eversley House, windows blazing above with golden light, noise from the revelry spilling out onto Park Lane, Lily was consumed by dread.

It was not an unfamiliar emotion, considering her general nervousness when near the aristocracy—utterly out of place, not noble enough to be welcome into their ranks, and somehow too close to their world to be ignored. Even without a season.

If only she'd never met Derek, perhaps she could have been ignored.

But Derek Hawkins made a point of being seen, and the

moment he'd set eyes on Lily eight months prior, as she dawdled on the banks of the Serpentine, she'd been doomed to be seen as well. She pushed the memories of that afternoon aside, and took a deep breath, as though doing so could drive her forward, with courage.

"You are certain you do not regret your sartorial choices?" Alec asked dryly in her ear.

She ignored the thread of pleasure the low whisper sent through her. "I confess, *Your Grace,* I am surprised you are familiar with the word *sartorial.* What with your own problematic clothing situation."

He chuckled, guiding her forward, hand on her arm, and she at once loved and hated the security she felt in it. "We have books in Scotland, Miss Hargrove."

"So you said. Better than Shakespeare."

"Aye," he murmured, low and private as they approached the footman standing sentry at the door.

"You still haven't proven it," she said, panicked at what might come when she stepped inside the house. Into this world he was forcing upon her, even as she was desperate to flee it.

This world she'd always secretly wished to be a part of.

No. She refused to give credence to the thought.

She stiffened, and he felt the movement. Must have, because he kept talking, as though they were in the sitting room in Berkeley Square. "*To see her was to love her, love but her, and love for ever . . .*"

She stilled on the top step, the words shocking her. She turned to look at him. "What did you say?"

He continued. "*Had we never lov'd sae kindly, had we never lov'd sae blindly . . .*" he recited, and the low burr, its wicked rumble, loud enough for her ears alone, made her forget where they were, and what she was wearing, and what awaited them inside. "*Never met—or never parted . . .*"

She shook her head as if to clear it. They did not even know each other. She was simply drawn to the poetry. This Robbie Burns was exceedingly talented.

"*We had ne'er been broken-hearted.*"

He fairly whispered the last, low and dark and wonderful, and the promise of a broken heart filled her with aching sorrow. Without warning, her eyes filled with tears, and she looked away from him, to those dancing nearby, a whirlwind of enormous sleeves and vibrant silks.

"Lass?" His hand tightened at her elbow, strong and steel, meant to comfort but only reminding her that comfort was fleeting. That sorrow was the most honest of all the emotions. Sorrow and regret.

Thankfully, they were inside the house then, and she was able to pull away from his touch, relinquishing her cloak to a footman who could barely hide his shock at her horrible dress. She took the moment to dash a rogue tear from her cheek before turning back to the duke and saying, "Perhaps your Burns isn't terrible."

He did not reply, searching her face for an answer she'd never be willing to give him. "Lily . . ." he said, and for a moment, she wondered what he might say if they were alone. What he might do.

"The Highland Devil graces us with his presence!"

And then the Marquess of Eversley was there, and she was saved, if one could be saved in this situation.

"I don't even live in the Highlands," Alec grumbled.

The marquess clapped his shoulder with a strong hand and said, "The first rule of London, friend. No one cares about the truth. You've a distillery there, and so Highland Devil it is. Good God, that eye is ghastly." He turned to Lily with a smile, his dark brows rising high with surprise as he took in her clothing. She had to give the marquess his due, however; he masked his shock nearly instantly and bowed low over her hand. "Miss Hargrove. The truth, in your case, is precisely what they say. As lovely as your legend suggests."

"You needn't lay it on so thick," Alec growled from behind her. "She's wearing a dog dress."

"I think it's perfect," Eversley said, not looking away from Lily. "I'd like to purchase one of the same for my wife."

She couldn't help but match his winning smile. The scandal sheets called the Marquess of Eversley the Royal Rogue, and Lily could easily see why. He could charm any woman present. Of course, he'd traded the moniker for a new one—the Harnessed Husband—and he was now known throughout London as being thoroughly smitten with his marchioness.

"Only because you don't want anyone noticing that your wife is as beautiful as Miss Hargrove."

Lily attempted to ignore the qualifier and its casual reference to his opinion of her. Of course, she'd heard it before, that she was beautiful. She'd read it in the gossip pages. She had eyes and a looking glass. But when Alec acknowledged her beauty, it seemed somehow different.

Somehow both more true and less important than ever before.

Eversley was growling at him now. "You'd do best to remember that I don't want anyone noticing her beauty, Duke. Especially not you."

Alec rolled his eyes, extracting a piece of paper from his coat pocket. "Can we get this done?"

"Christ, Warnick, you brought the damn list?"

Lily's brow furrowed. "What list?"

The men spoke at the same time.

"It's nothing," Eversley said.

"No list," from Alec, even as he looked down at the paper.

"You're both terrible liars." Two sets of wide, handsome eyes met hers. Lily reached for the paper, and Alec held it out of reach, the fabric of his coat pulling tighter across his muscled frame. She pulled her hand back. "You are behaving like a small child."

He lowered his arm. "It's nothing."

"It's most certainly not nothing. Not if you're playing games with me while at a ball."

His gaze slid to the hound and hare protruding from her coif. "I'm not the only one playing games tonight, lass."

She took advantage of his moment of distraction to snatch the list from his grasp, turning her back on him instantly to look at it.

There were five names scrawled on it. An earl, two viscounts, a baron, and a duke.

She looked to him. "What is this?"

Alec did not reply, but his cheeks went slightly ruddy, as though he had been caught in a particularly damning act. And perhaps he had. She scanned the list again, looking for the unifying theme of the names.

They were all titled. All with extensive lands.

All decent men, if gossip was to be believed.

And all poor as church mice.

They were potential suitors. Lily looked up at Alec. "Why does the Duke of Chapin have a question mark next to his name?"

Alec looked to Eversley, who was suddenly riveted by the carpet beneath his feet.

Lily would not be ignored. "Your Grace?" she prompted, enjoying the way his jaw set at the honorific.

He returned his attention to her. "We are not certain that he is interested in marriage."

She narrowed her gaze. "You intend to sell me like cattle in the marketplace."

"Don't be dramatic, Lillian. This is how it's done."

He hadn't even begun to see dramatic. "How you marry off your scandalous ward, you mean?"

He did look at her then. "Well, it's not as though you've made it easy. Name the man you want, and I'll get him for you."

"I told you, I don't want to marry."

"Then the list it is."

She looked down at the list. "I *certainly* won't marry the Duke of Chapin."

"Cross the damn duke off the list. Replace it with a butcher, a baker, or a goddamn candlestick maker. But you're going to marry if it kills me."

"Warnick," Eversley warned. "Language."

Lily didn't hesitate. "Killing you might be the only benefit to marrying."

He leaned in then, close enough that the marquess would not hear them. Close enough for Lillian to note that his eyes were not simply brown. They were brown flecked with gold and green and grey. She'd think them beautiful if she didn't loathe the very sight of their owner, who thought himself a hero despite presenting himself every kind of villain.

"You like your Shakespeare so much, how about this," he said. "*Sell when you can*, Lillian Hargrove. *You are not for all markets.*"

She snapped to attention. "What's that supposed to mean?"

"Only that time is of the essence."

Shame flooded her, hot and unpleasant. Her heart threatened to pound out of her chest and, in that moment, she hated him. She pulled herself straight, pushing her shoulders back and holding herself with all the poise of a royal. "You, sir, are a bastard."

"Sadly not, love. But I can see how you would wish it so; after all, it's my legitimacy that's landed us in this particular situation."

She didn't reply, instead pushing past him and following the throngs of people up into the ballroom, suddenly caring little for what she must look like in the ridiculous dog dress—too distracted by the blood rushing in her ears to hear the whispers around her as the *ton* became aware of her.

And yet, somehow, she heard him perfectly, the whispered curse as she walked away, followed by the Marquess of Eversley's, "That was off-sides, Warnick."

Good. Let his friend scold him. He'd acted abominably.

Lily had had enough of the man and his coarseness. He could wither and die in the doorway to Eversley House if he wished. Hang him, his offensive list, and his pretty Scottish poetry.

She was more than happy for them to part now.

Lily stepped into the Eversley ballroom, immediately drawn to the wash of bright golden light, the field of candles throughout the room, hanging from the chandeliers high above and ablaze in sconces and candelabra everywhere she turned. But it was not the candles that glittered most brightly. It was the people. All of London seemed to have turned out for the Eversley ball in bright silks and satins to match bright eyes and cheeks, the excitement of the season flooding through them.

Lily came to a stop just inside the room, stunned into panicked stillness. What was to come next? She was at a ball, dressed thoroughly inappropriately, angry and frustrated and hurt and desperate for some exit from this current, disastrous situation.

She could feel London's eyes upon her, hot and scathing, chatter becoming silence as she straightened her shoulders and lifted her chin, willing herself to remain strong. As she looked out at the assembly, she saw the gazes slide away, like silk on fur, unable to stick. Fans raised, heads turned, and whispers began.

Shame surged, and Lily took a deep breath. She was here now. In the middle of a ball with no choice but to find her way.

No sooner had the decision been made than someone arrived to help.

Several someones.

Chapter 8

LONESOME LILY SNATCHED UP BY SCANDALOUS SISTERS; BOLD BEAUTIES BEFRIEND WARNICK'S WARD

"Dear Heaven. That dress should be immediately burned."

"Shush!" another voice admonished. "Perhaps she likes it!"

"Nonsense. No one could possibly like it." Lily turned to face the quartet bearing down upon her. The leader met her eyes without hesitation. "You *don't* like it, do you?"

Lily was so surprised by the direct question that she replied without hesitation, "No."

The dark-haired quartet, each pretty and perfectly turned out, smiled en masse. They were quite striking as a group, if Lily were honest, each in a different brilliant silk, yellow and green and blue and the leader, in red, who said, "That means you're wearing it for a particular *effect*."

"For a man, if I had to guess," Blue said, investigating the line of the bodice, which Lily had lowered and refitted that afternoon. "Amazing," she whispered before leaning in. "Is it for a man?"

"Why would she wear it for a *man*?" Green asked. "To scare him off?"

Yellow spoke this time. "To prove that she doesn't care for his opinion."

"She shouldn't," Red replied as she stopped directly in front of Lily. "Men rarely understand their own opinions. And if you're brave enough to wear this monstrosity, you are smart enough to know that his opinions matter very little in the long run."

Lily shook her head. "He isn't a him. That is, I don't care what he thinks."

Yellow smiled softly, and Lily realized that under other circumstances, she would think that the woman was plain. She wasn't, however. Not when she smiled. "That means there's *absolutely* a him."

"Not in the way you mean it," Lily replied.

"What way is that?" Green asked.

"She says *him* in such a lovely tone," Lily pointed out, feeling rather dizzy speaking to this group. "As though there's some emotion aside from loathing in my feelings for him."

"Loathing isn't the opposite of love, you know," Yellow said.

"Ugh." Red echoed Lily's thoughts. "Don't listen to her. We all rue the day Sophie married for love."

Sophie.

Like that, Lily identified the quartet.

"You're the Dangerous Daughters!" she blurted out before clapping one hand over her mouth, as though she could have kept the observation from flying loose.

Smiles turned to grins. "The very same," Sophie said.

Sophie was Lady Eversley, nee Sophie Talbot, now Marchioness of Eversley and future Duchess of Lyne, married in an utter scandal, six months prior. Which meant . . . Lily turned to Green, the most petite of the three, draped in green. "You're Lady Seleste, soon to be Countess Clare and . . ." She turned to Blue, fairest of the group. "That makes you Mrs. Mark Landry." Rich as a queen, married to a man who, by all accounts, was loud and crass and would be thoroughly unwelcome in the aristocracy if not for his outrageous sums of money.

Mrs. Landry inclined her head. "You may call me Lady Seline."

They were four of the five daughters of the Earl of Wight, a coal miner with a skill for finding valuable stores of the fuel—skill enough to have bought himself, and his daughters, a title. Renowned social climbers, the women had been labeled The Dangerous Daughters by London's scandal sheets. Lily had always thought that much better than the other, less kind name—The Soiled S's.

Of course, now that three of the four had been identified, Lily knew who the fourth was. Her gaze slid to the exceedingly tall woman, beautiful and buxom in her form-fitting red gown, one that would have been utterly scandalous on anyone else if not on Lady Sesily Talbot. On her, it simply looked gorgeous. Beautiful enough to remind Lily that she paled horribly in comparison to the woman.

The woman who had been, only a year prior, linked to Derek Hawkins.

Suddenly, Lily was not so comforted by the appearance and the tacit acceptance of this group of women.

"You know us," Lady Sesily said, "and the rest of the room seems to know you, so who are you?"

"Sesily," Lady Eversley cautioned. "Don't be so rude."

She didn't want to tell them. She didn't want them to dislike her for her past with Derek. She'd heard about what women did to those with whom they felt they competed. And she rather liked this group.

Not that she knew them, really. But she liked them from the scandal sheets. And from the fact that they were speaking to her instead of whispering about her behind their fans.

They didn't even have fans.

Lady Eversley turned to her. "Though, I will say, you are in my home, so it would be very nice to meet you," she said with an amused smile.

"You're right, Sophie. That was far more demure than I was."

Seleste laughed. "As though any one of us has ever been demure."

Sesily clasped Lily's hands. "She is wearing a dress made of dogs. She doesn't care about demureness, obviously. And she has no choice but to tell us who she is so we can protect her from the wolves beyond, who obviously lie in wait." She leaned in close. "Wolves go after dogs."

"As though you'd know a thing about wildlife. When was the last time you left London?" Seline snorted at her sister.

Lily did like them. So, it was time to end it. "I'm Lillian Hargrove."

There was a beat of silence as they all heard her, and Lily waited for Sesily to release her hands and push her away. She did not expect the other woman to clasp them tighter and say, "I've been wanting to meet you for a long time, Lovely Lily."

Confusion flared, followed by a cacophonous mix of suspicion and nerves and disappointment and, at its heart, a kernel of hope.

Lillian blushed. "You wish to know me."

Sesily tilted her head to one side. "Of course I wish to know of you. All of London wishes to know you." She leaned in. "Some more biblically than others, I imagine."

Lily blushed at the words.

"Sesily!"

"Well, really. Look at her. She as beautiful as they say."

"She means you wish to know her *in spite of Hawkins*," Seline pointed out, her husband's notorious bluntness clearly a quality Mrs. Landry boasted as well. She turned to Lily. "Sesily doesn't care about Hawkins."

"Only inasmuch as I care that he lives out his life in deserved misery, the toad," Sesily said before turning to Lily. "Now I understand the dog dress, though. Inspired, really. Though you should know that dress does nothing to mar your beauty."

Before Lily could speak, the Marchioness of Eversley spoke. "Don't mind Sesily, Miss Hargrove; she is unable to keep herself from saying whatever pops into her head."

"Posh. No one has time for circumspection." Sesily waved a hand in the air before adding, "Derek Hawkins bears the two character traits unacceptable in a man: insufferability and a desperation to be admired by all. I might be willing to overlook one of them, but both—" She finished the sentence with an entirely unladylike sound.

"And he's terrible with money," Seleste said.

"The richest poor man in Britain," Sesily agreed. "As though he's a hole in his pocket. The coin spills to the ground as fast as it goes in." She looked to Lily. "It is too bad he is so damn talented, isn't it? We're all blinded by his skill."

Lily was so taken aback by Sesily Talbot's forthrightness that it took her a moment to find words, until Lady Eversley—widely known as the quietest and kindest of the sisters—found them for her. "Sesily, you've shocked her," the marchioness admonished before looking to Lily. "You needn't answer her. She's utterly inappropriate when she wishes to be."

"I didn't wish to be inappropriate!"

"To be fair, Sesily is inappropriate when she *doesn't* wish to be as well," Seline pointed out.

The marchioness laughed and took Lily's hands. "I am very happy you've chosen to join us tonight. When King told me that the duke wanted to launch your season here, I confess, I was more than a little intrigued." Her gaze flickered to the hound and hare in Lily's coif. "Now, even more, because of your particular . . . *flair*."

"Thank you, my lady," Lily said, still rather overwhelmed by the sisters. "But it is not a season. Not really."

The marchioness shook her head. "Call me Sophie. After all, my husband and your duke are too close for *my lady*."

Lily's gaze flew over Sophie's shoulder to the entrance to the ballroom, where Alec and the marquess had materialized, as though summoned by the words. She took in the massive Scot in his ill-fitting coat and trousers, and somehow still more commanding than the rest of the room. Lily's heart pounded—in fury, no doubt, at his utterly inexcusable behavior. "He's not my duke."

"Ding dong," Sesily said softly at her shoulder, her gaze lingering on Alec. "Can he be mine, then? He's in need of a tailor, but I can overlook it for the evening."

No.

Lily had no idea where the instant dislike for the idea of this beautiful, bold woman and Alec together came from, but she didn't like it. Why would she care whom Alec chose to be his duchess?

She didn't.

Not at all.

"He'd be lucky to have you as queen of his drafty Scottish castle," she said, pushing the dislike away.

Sesily's nose wrinkled. "I like the sound of a dukedom and a castle, but who wants to live in Scotland? It is deadly dull."

"That's probably for the best, Ses," Seline teased. "I imagine King would heartily warn his friend away from the likes of you."

"Nonsense," Sesily says. " 'Tis I who should be warned away from him—after all, everyone's heard of the Scottish Brute's conquests." She leaned into Lily, "Not that anyone would ever call him such to his face. But is it true what they say? Is he terribly sexual?"

Lily's eyes went wide. *What?*

Was that what they said about him?

And then the name echoed through her—*The Scottish Brute*—she loathed that moniker. Loathed the idea that it was whispered behind his back. Loathed the idea that he was whispered about, at all.

No wonder he hated London; in that moment, she did, as well.

She couldn't help herself from looking at him, her gaze lingering on his perfect mouth for a long moment, the word *sexual* whirling through her mind, before she remembered that she disliked him. "I wouldn't know," she said.

"Hmm. Probably not, then," Sesily smirked.

"Good God, Sesily. Stop it," Seline said.

"It's important to know a thing like that before one leaps into the fray!"

"Ugh. You should marry him. Polite society would no doubt be thrilled to be rid of you."

Sesily turned to Lily, a twinkle in her eye. "Don't listen to them. Society can't get enough of me."

"No accounting for taste," Seleste teased, and the entire group laughed. Lily couldn't stop her own lips from curving as well—the emotion and energy of the Talbot sisters was undeniable. They were the embodiment of everything Lily had always imagined came with sisters. With family. With friends.

There was such love between them.

Jealousy flared, unbidden and unwelcome, and Lily willed it away. She didn't wish to be jealous. She didn't wish to envy them their close-knit group.

But she did. With every ounce of her being.

And it wasn't just their combined fearlessness in the face of social disdain, as though they'd never in their lives felt shame. Her chest tightened as she listened to their laughter, to the way it echoed with humor and love and trust and a bone-deep loyalty, and she wanted to be one of them. Quite desperately.

The fact that they gossiped publicly and brazenly didn't hurt.

"Too late, Sesily. Look who is after him," Seline said casually, her gaze fixed over Lily's shoulder.

Lily turned to look as a beautiful woman approached Alec and Eversley. She saw him stiffen, even from the distance between them. Saw his gaze trail down, then up the woman's body as she drew close, almost too close, considering where they stood, in full view of Society.

"Who is that?" The question was out before she could stop it.

"Lady Rowley," Sesily said dismissively. "Married to Earl Rowley, devilishly handsome and a thorough cad. He's been after all of us at one point or another. To no avail, obviously, as he very likely has the pox."

"Sesily!" Sophie said.

"Oh, please. It's not as though you haven't thought it yourself."

"Nevertheless, we don't discuss poxes in the ballroom!"

A gentleman passing nearby paused, looking to them with shock, and the sisters burst into laughter. Seline waved a hand and said, "Nothing for you to worry about, my lord," before turning back and saying, "Now Baron Orwell thinks we've the pox!"

"No, no, Lord Orwell," Sesily said too loudly, making Lily blush. "We are discussing Lord Rowley. Do you have an opinion on his probable poxiness?"

"I'm sure I don't," the man said down his nose before hurrying away.

They all laughed, and Lily enjoyed it until her attention was returned to Alec, still in discussion with the Countess Rowley. Sesily followed her gaze and said, "Well. It looks like the earl is not the only one willing to eschew his marriage vows." Lillian couldn't help but agree. They were not touching, but the countess could not be more free with her bosom without stripping bare in front of all London.

Not that Lily cared whose bosom Alec had access to.

"That smile takes years to perfect," Seline said with admiration.

Lillian pressed her lips together and turned away from the couple. "I imagine so."

"Do you think they know each other?" Seleste asked. "I mean, they say he's a wicked catch, but I can't see him with *her*."

Neither could Lily. Not that she wanted to even try.

"If they don't, they will soon enough," Sesily said.

Lily didn't care. Not at all. She forced her shoulder up in a quick, stilted shrug and turned her back to the scene. "She's welcome to him."

"Ooh. Warnick might require a tailor, but he's quite skilled at the cut direct," Sesily narrated.

Lily resisted the urge to turn.

"She looks *furious*," Sophie said in awe before she raised her voice and said, full of unfounded glee, "And here are the gentlemen!"

"This is trouble," the Marquess of Eversley said from behind Lily, and she had no choice but to turn—it was simply good manners. The marquess looked relaxed and jovial, clearly a welcome fifth to the merry Talbot band. Alec, however, looked pale and stiff.

No doubt because he was in Lily's presence once more.

"Don't corrupt Miss Hargrove, ladies," Eversley teased. "Remember, she's new to London's ballrooms."

"We wouldn't dream of it."

"Not on the first night, at least."

"Next time, however, it's a certainty," Sesily replied before turning to Alec and reaching for him. Lily was impressed by the movement, one lithe hand stretched out, leaving him no choice but to accept Sesily's touch. "Your Grace," the woman fairly purred as she lowered herself into a curtsy. "Do tell me something . . ."

Alec seemed to return to the moment and the group. "Yes?"

Sesily peered up through dark lashes and even Lily was drawn to her for a moment. "Are you quite wedded to spending the rest of your days in Scotland?"

"I am, actually," he said without hesitation.

Sesily removed her hand from his. "What a pity." She turned to face the rest of the room. "I shall have to locate another with whom to flirt."

"No one said you couldn't flirt with this one," Seleste pointed out. "It's not as though flirting leads to marriage."

"No," Sesily sighed, distractedly scanning those assembled. "But it's much more fun if it might. And I'm not ending up in *Scotland*. No offense, Your Grace."

"None taken," Alec said. "Should I apologize?"

"It would not be out of line," Sesily replied.

Alec put a hand to his chest. "It is, of course, my loss."

Sesily grinned. "Handsome, rich, titled, and intelligent, to boot. A terrible pity."

The group laughed, and Lily couldn't help herself from joining in, ignoring the thread of envy that coursed through her at Sesily's easy way of bringing out Alec's good humor. Lily wanted that humor for herself.

She stiffened at the thought. No. No she didn't.

She didn't want to like him.

She wanted to leave him behind and start a new life. Far from him.

The orchestra began to play, and like magic, Earl Clare and Mark Landry appeared as if from nowhere to chaperone their respective Talbot sisters to the dance. Eversley bowed elaborately in the direction of his wife. "My love?" he said, the words low and dark like a promise.

Sophie blushed prettily, and took her husband's hand. "You know that, as hostess, I shall have to dance with others as well."

Eversley's brow furrowed. "Then let it be clear that I'm in no way interested in hosting more events. You may dance with Warnick. But that's it."

Sophie laughed and called to Alec over her shoulder as her husband dragged her into the fray. "I'm sorry you'll be saddled with me, Your Grace!"

They were left with Sesily, and Lily sent a little grateful prayer up to the gods for that, as she couldn't bear to be alone with Alec. Not after the way he'd betrayed her. She willed him to ask the unspoken for Talbot sister to dance. But Sesily beat him to it. Turning to face them, she said, "You must dance."

"I—" Lily began over the pounding of her heart, but Alec cut her off.

"No."

Lily ignored the disappointment that came at the curt dismissal. She wasn't disappointed. She didn't want anything to do with the man. And she certainly didn't want to have to dance with him. Touching him was out of the question.

Sesily had other ideas, apparently. "It's not negotiable. This is the first ball of her first season and she's wearing . . . well . . . what she's wearing. You're the highest-ranking man who knows her. So you have to dance with her."

"No one knows who I am," he said.

Sesily smirked. "Your Grace. You're an unmarried duke with a king's fortune. You'd have to be a thorough cabbagehead to believe that no one knows who you are. You may have the worst tailor in Christendom, but you're not a cabbagehead, are you?"

Lily had her own opinions on this particular question, but she stayed quiet.

"I'm her guardian. Surely that's not proper."

Sesily raised a brow. "Half the guardians in London end up marrying their wards. It's an epidemic."

Lily didn't stay quiet then. "Not this guardian. Not this ward."

Warnick cut her a look and said, "I assure you, Lady Sesily, that is not in the cards."

Sesily watched them both for a long moment before saying, "Certainly not. And yet still, you must dance."

At that, the massive Scot sighed and reached for Lily, clearly believing that the inquisition of Sesily Talbot's gaze was less hospitable than a turn about the dance floor with his ward. "Let's get on with it, then."

She snatched her hand back. "No, thank you."

Sesily turned to watch her carefully and then said, "I hadn't picked *you* for the cabbagehead in the scenario."

"I'm not a cabbagehead. I'm simply not interested in dancing with him."

Sesily considered the duke with a long, head-to-toe look, and then said, "Is he rough with you?"

"No. Not unless you count his forcing me to come here tonight."

"I don't," Sesily said before leaning in and saying, quietly, "Lovely Lily, you haven't a choice. Dance with the duke and let London get a good look at you in your dog dress, before they get a good look at you with no dress at all."

Lily froze.

Sesily raised a brow. "The painting is on everyone's lips and you know it. It doesn't help that Derek Hawkins is here this evening, arrived like the unwelcome rat he is on the arm of some ancient widow, one foot in the damn grave. No doubt he thinks she'll leave him a fortune if he plays her dandy, the bastard."

There was no time to be shocked by Sesily's language, Lily's panic flaring, along with frustration. She looked toward Alec in desperation, but his gaze was trained on the far wall of the room. She swallowed around the knot in her throat. "I should like to leave."

"No," Alec said, and she whirled to argue with him.

Sesily spoke first. "Listen to me, Lillian Hargrove. I know better than anyone what Hawkins can make a woman do. If you're to survive this, you must do all you can to make him the villain. The first step is to make London love you. Which begins with dancing with your duke."

He's not my duke.

Surprisingly those were the only words Lily could think as shock and horror coursed through her, so much so that she barely heard Alec's soft, rolling "Come." He was looking at her when she turned to him the second time, his hand outstretched, rich brown eyes holding her gaze.

Holding her.

She settled her hand into his outstretched one even as she resisted the idea. Even as Sesily's words echoed through her. Even as he was pulling her into the dance, pulling her close.

At another time, in another place, she might have realized that Alec Stuart, twenty-first and unwilling Duke of Warnick, was a dancer of the highest caliber. Might have asked why that was the case, considering his eschewing of all things Society. But she didn't. She was too focused on a different man, a man she'd once believed she loved.

A man who had lied to her.

A man who had tempted her with pretty promises. Who'd convinced her to trust him. To pose for his painting without considering the repercussions of the act. Without considering the possibility of what might happen if it were ever discovered.

The woman the world would think her.

And Derek, unblemished.

Lauded, even.

And here.

Alec led her through the steps of the dance for long, silent minutes as she attempted to come to terms with the idea she'd entered the lion's den. That she would likely see him. And that she was dressed as a damn dog. Her gaze flickered to Alec's throat, to the long column that rose above his cravat. To the knot that bobbed there as he swallowed.

She was here, beneath the prying eyes of the aristocracy, because of him.

She let her gaze rise over his straight jaw and his full lips and his long nose to his eyes, which she would have expected to be looking anywhere but at her.

She was wrong.

He was staring right at her, his knowing brown gaze capturing hers with ease, sending a thread of awareness through her. No. Not awareness.

Fury.

"You did this." He remained silent, so she pressed on with her accusation. "You've put me in the same room as him. Fodder for all London, for their censure and gossip. I'm here because of you. Because of your mad plan."

"It's the only way to save your future."

"To underscore my scandal in front of them all? To elaborate upon it?"

"To get you married. The list—they are good men. Eversley's staked his reputation on such."

"The Duke of Chapin has been left at the altar three times. And he's a *duke.* That's a virtual impossibility, unless there's something terribly wrong with him."

"Such as?"

"I don't know, but if three spinsters have deserted him at such a critical time, I'm guessing the answer is akin to scales."

"Well, I'm sure it's not scales, but I said you could cross him off the list."

"He never should have been on the list to begin with."

He sighed. "Then make your own list."

"I don't want a list!" she said, and the words came out frantic and too loud for the room, drawing attention from couples nearby. She lowered her voice. "Why do you care so much? I'm disgraced, anyway, so why not let me go? Why force me to stay for the ceremonial tar and feathering?"

He hesitated, and in that fleeting silence, Lily realized that whatever he was about to say would change everything. Because she could see in his eyes that it would be the truth.

And then he said it.

"Lily, I've seen your wedding dress."

She froze, her breath unwilling to expel. "What did you say?"

He tugged at her waist, at her hand. "Do not stop dancing."

She did not move, finding herself instead frozen to the floor, repeating herself. "What did you say?"

He narrowed his gaze on her. "I found it," he said, softly, like the softest gunshot that had ever been fired for the damage it did in Lily's chest. "And the pile of pretty clothes for your future babe. Those little boots, with the soft red soles. You dream of filling those boots, Lillian Hargrove. And this is your best chance at doing so."

She gaped at him, disbelief crashing through her. She took a step away from him, removing her hand from his clasp. "How dare you go through my things?"

"You were gone. I had to find you," he said, coming close again, his gaze darting around them, attempting to keep them from colliding with other couples twirling by.

As though Lily cared about such a thing. He'd gone through her things.

He'd found the wedding dress. The children's clothing. The things she'd painstakingly crafted for a husband she'd never love. Children she'd never meet. A life she'd never have.

He'd found them—her most private secrets.

And, somehow, it wasn't anger she felt. It was embarrassment.

The dress, the clothes, the tiny socks and boots—they were

all the dreams of a girl younger and more innocent than Lily was now. They were the promises that she imagined whispered in the darkness as she lay beneath the servants' stairs and thought of a future, brighter and more beautiful than the present.

A future she would never have.

They were pretty lies. She knew that now—she'd left them in the trunk for a reason.

And he'd found them.

Shame flooded through her, hotter than any embarrassment she'd ever felt. Hotter than the embarrassment she'd experienced when he'd revealed that he knew about the painting. How was it possible that she was more ashamed of a simple white dress than about no dress at all?

"So you went through my things, like a . . ." She hesitated, looking away from him, now terrified of what he'd seen. Of what he might know about her. ". . . like the great Scottish brute you are. I don't want you here. In my life. Find another woman to manhandle. I hear you're terribly good at it. Your reputation precedes you."

He went stiff as a board at the words, and Lily had the sudden sense that she'd said something terribly wrong.

Not that she should care.

And then he spoke, low and dark, the angry words fairly forced from him. "You forget yourself," he said. "As my ward, your things are *my* things."

Her gaze flew to his. "You beast."

His lips pressed into a long straight line. "And you, the most beautiful woman in London," he said, as though being beautiful was the most ugly thing she could be. "We make a fine match, *Lovely Lily*."

The nickname unstuck her. She pulled away from him and fled the room.

Chapter 9

GUARDIAN? OR GUARD-DOG?

No one in his life had ever frustrated Alec as much as Miss Lillian Hargrove.

He watched her walk away in her ridiculous dress, the bronze and gold and silver fabric flouncing around her with every step, hound and hare bobbing high above her head, and he burned with anger and embarrassment and frustration and a keen desire to leave her there in Eversley House, and return to Scotland.

A desire almost as strong as the one that urged him to chase after her.

He cursed under his breath. He'd hurt her. He shouldn't have told her that he'd seen the dress.

He should have told her he only wanted the best for her. That he only wanted to protect her. That he *would* protect her, dammit. That it was all he'd wanted to do since the moment the damn letter had arrived in Scotland, summoning him to her side. He wasn't a monster, after all. He recognized duty, and he would serve it.

And the more he was with her, the more he wished to serve it.

Perhaps he would have said all that if they hadn't been here, in a packed ballroom, the focus of the aristocracy's attention. If he hadn't been keenly aware of his too-tight clothing, of his own too-big size, of his inability to be genteel or refined in any way.

If he hadn't been blindsided by the arrival of Margaret mere moments earlier. Lady Margaret, now Countess Rowley. More beautiful now than she'd been twenty years earlier, when she'd been Peg, the older sister to his schoolmate, and he'd wanted her beyond reason.

When he'd had her, and believed she'd be his forever.

Marry me.

Alec cursed in the dim light, her long-ago laughter punctuating the memory of her approach tonight, as though she owned him even now, even as she was married to a fancy British earl—just as she'd always desired. The way she'd come too close and reminded him of how close they'd once been.

Of the way she'd left, his heart in her hand, crushed.

Women dream of men like you, darling.

But for a night. Not a lifetime.

King hadn't warned him that she'd be there. Alec supposed he should have expected it. The ball was one of the first of the season, and the first hosted by the future Duke and Duchess of Lyne since the birth of their first child. Even if King weren't brother-in-law to the infamous Talbot sisters, all of London would have been in curious attendance.

But he still could have mentioned Peg would be there.

Alec pushed away the cacophonous memories of a broken heart and a broken spirit, leaving only the memory of Lillian's righteous fury.

He should have been able to manage that fury. To temper it.

And perhaps he would have done, if not for the shock and sting of seeing Peg. Of remembering her. And then Lily had called him a brute and a beast, and he'd remembered the same words on another set of beautiful lips. Another time. Another woman. Another encounter that ended with him left alone, imperfect.

And then, Lily, hurt, lashing out. *Your reputation precedes you.*

Shit.

It wasn't an excuse for his behavior. He should have protected Lily—ironically, protecting her was the only thing he seemed unable to do, despite it being the singular requirement of guardianship.

Perhaps he'd be more successful at it if she weren't so beautiful. If those grey eyes didn't seem to see everything, if she weren't so willing to tell him when he was out of line. When he was behaving abominably. If she weren't so strong and independent and willing to fight for herself.

If she weren't so damn perfect, perhaps he could be a better man when he was with her.

She'd called him a beast, and he was. Somehow, she made him one. Or, perhaps, she simply saw the truth, and left him there, at the center of the ballroom, feeling like one.

The orchestra stopped and the couples around him—doing their best to both stare at and ignore him—began to dissipate as the musicians prepared for the next set. The movement away from the dance unstuck him, and he turned away, committed to a single goal—finding a decent drink.

Crossing the ballroom, Alec ducked through a doorway into a dimly lit corridor that he vaguely remembered led to a series of salons. If he had to guess, he'd imagine there was scotch stored somewhere nearby.

Once he'd found it, he would seek out Lillian, who was no doubt hiding in the ladies' salon, wishing she'd donned an appropriate garment and hopefully regretting the fact that she'd left him in the middle of a ballroom as couples continued to dance around him.

Likely not regretting that at all, as it was his fault that she'd run.

He'd deserved the embarrassment.

And she deserved his apology.

She'd get it. In the form of one of the men on his list. He'd seek one out and deliver him to her—for a waltz and a refreshment. They could take a turn about the room or whatever ridiculous courtship England required.

He wouldn't turn her about the room if he were courting her.

He'd take her into the darkness on the terrace beyond the ballroom—down into the gardens where the light from the ball was gone and the stars above were all they could see, and he'd kiss her until she wanted nothing but to marry him. Until she couldn't remember any words but *Yes.*

Then he'd lay her down on the cool earth, strip her bare, and feast on her with nothing but the sky as witness.

After which, he'd take her to Scotland and marry her. Immediately.

And she would regret it. Forever.

He ran a hand over his face at the thought, the idea of his hands on her—of them soiling her perfection—making him wish he was anywhere but here.

Christ.

He had to get her married. If it killed him, he would do the right thing and get her married.

But first, he needed a drink.

He opened the first door he came to, entering a dark room, leaving the door open to allow some semblance of the already diffused light in. He squinted into the darkness, making out a sideboard at the far end of what he imagined was some kind of study, a decanter beckoning him into the night.

He headed for it, grateful for the quiet, momentary distance from the ball, the aristocracy, and London in general. Both the Marquess and the Marchioness of Eversley had spent their childhood mere miles from the Scottish border, so Alec was confident that whatever the amber liquid in the decanter was, it was whisky as it should be.

He poured two fingers and drank, wrapped in the familiar rich flavor. Satisfaction flooded through him. King was a good friend, stocking the house with Alec's whisky—distilled and bottled on Stuart land. Alec would have to tell Lillian about Scotland's superior whisky at some point—yet another thing her England could not claim.

He leaned back against the sideboard and exhaled, enjoying the shadows that hid him from view. It was so rare that he felt invisible in London, and the moment was warm and welcome and as close to perfect as England could be.

And then she entered the room, and he was reminded of how imperfect England was. Of how it had destroyed him, and threatened to destroy her.

Of how much safer and happier she would be in Scotland, far from this place with its judging eyes and its inane rules. For a moment, he imagined Lily in the wilds of his country. He wanted to see her on the banks of the Oban. On the cliffs high above the Firth of Forth. In fields of heather that spread like purple fire as far as the eye could see.

Scotland would suit her.

The thought came with a longing that ripped him from fantasy and returned him to the moment.

He should have said something immediately. Should have announced himself. And he might have, if she hadn't immediately moved to the window at the opposite end of the room. Whether it was moonlight or the residual glow of the ballroom in the back gardens, she was cast in a light that made her ethereal and so beautiful that his breath caught in his chest.

She raised her hand to the glass window, three long, delicate fingers trailing down the pane, and she let out a long, lush breath, one that filled the room with emotion—frustration. Sadness, and something much more powerful. *Longing.*

Alec's breath returned with force at the last, at the familiarity of it.

Because, in that moment, he longed, too.

The thought shook him. He was her guardian. She was his ward.

She was a grown woman. Ward on a technicality.

It did not matter. She remained his ward. She remained under his protection. And he might have been terrible at protecting her until this moment—he might have failed at protecting her reputation and her emotions—but he could damn well protect her from himself.

And, besides, he did not care for beautiful women. They were pretty promises that too quickly became lies.

The thought returned him to the present, and he made to move, to talk to her and apologize and start anew. To convince her that he would play his role perfectly, and that they would find her the life she wished. A proper man. A loving family. A future that was filled with home and hearth and happiness, as she deserved. Whatever she wished.

But before he could speak up from his place in the darkness, the door to the room closed with a soft snick, startling them both, directing their attention to the shadowy figure just inside the room. "Hello, Lily."

Hawkins.

Alec had an instant desire to destroy the man for risking being found alone with Lillian. For once more tempting the fates of scandal with a dark room and an unmarried woman.

It did not escape him that he'd been alone with her moments earlier, but it was different. There was no time to parse the double standard of the situation, however, as Hawkins was moving toward Lily with a speed Alec did not like. He straightened in the darkness, ready to approach and tear the man limb from limb, but she spoke before he could move.

"Derek." Alec hated Hawkins then, as his given name swirled through the darkness, soft and lovely on her lips. "Why are you here?"

"It's London in season. Of course I am here," Hawkins said. "I am everywhere." He waved a hand. "Like ether."

Alec rolled his eyes.

"Sesily said you're here with a rich widow. For the money."

Good girl. Disdain was precisely what she should be feeling.

"Sesily Talbot is nothing. Cheap as the rest of her family."

What an unmitigated ass the man was.

"I just met her family. They seem quite expensive. And wonderfully honest. Unlike others."

"All that glitters is not gold, sweet Lily."

"It seems to me that Sesily is made of stronger stuff than gold. She's judged harshly by the *ton* in large part due to her brief courtship with you, and yet she remains tall in the face of their scorn. I wish I was as strong as she." The accusation came next. "She refused to be ruined by you."

"I did not ruin you," he said.

"Of course you did. Without care." The accusation was not angry, or hurt. It came on a thread of honesty that Alec at once admired and loathed. She should be hurt. And angry.

At him.

"Poor Lovely Lily . . ." Hawkins said, reaching for her, running a finger down her cheek, down the skin that Alec thought must be impossibly soft. "You . . . you were the mirror that reflected my genius."

Lily closed her eyes at the man's touch. Or perhaps his words. Either way, Alec hated the longing on her face, mixed with pain. He decided then and there to destroy Derek Hawkins. For touching her. For hurting her.

He would leave him broken here, in this dark room. He'd have to apologize to the Marchioness of Eversley, he imagined, and purchase a replacement carpet, but surely she would understand that the world was better off without this loathsome eel in it.

Before Alec could do anything, however, Lily spoke. "You promised me you wouldn't tell anyone about the painting. You told me it was for you and you alone."

"And it was at the start, darling."

"Don't call me that." Lily's words came sharp and steel.

"Whyever not?" Hawkins said with a laugh. "Oh, Lily. Don't be so pedestrian. You were my muse. I am sorry that you misjudged the role. You were the conduit for my art. The vessel through which the world will see the truth of my timeless influence. The portrait is my Madonna and Child. My Creation of Man. For centuries to come, people will see it and they will whisper my name with breathless awe." He paused for effect, then practiced the whisper in question. "*Derek Hawkins.*"

What utter rubbish. If Alec didn't loathe the man already, he certainly would now.

"And what of *my* name?" Lillian asked.

"Don't you see? It doesn't matter what happens to you. This is for *art*. For all time. You are a sacrifice to beauty. To truth. To *eternity*. What would you have me do, Lily? Hide it away?"

"Yes!"

"What purpose would that serve?"

"It would make you decent!" she cried. "Noble! The man I—"

Alec stiffened, hearing the rest of the sentence as clearly as if she'd said it.

The man I love.

"This is the noblest act I could commit, darling."

There was a long silence, during which Alec could virtually feel Lily's disappointment. And when she finally spoke, saying small and soft, "I thought you loved me," Alec thought his heart might explode in his chest.

"Perhaps I did in my own way, sweetheart. But marrying you—impossible. I'm the greatest artist of our time. Of *all* time. And you are beautiful . . . but . . . as I said . . . your beauty exists as a vessel for my talent. The whole world will soon see how much."

He set his hand to her cheek. "Darling, I never pushed you away. I was happy to have you. I would have you still. That is why I followed you here."

The bastard.

Alec stiffened as Lily snapped her gaze to Hawkins's. "Still?"

The artist leaned close, and Alec held back a roar of fury at the nearness, until the pompous prick whispered, "Still. *Now.*" There was no mistaking the sexual promise in the words. "You would like that, would you not?"

That was it. Alec went for him.

Except Lily got there first.

It felt exceedingly good to punch a man in the nose.

She knew she shouldn't do it. She knew it wouldn't solve her problem. Knew, too, that it would do nothing but anger Derek and likely make him more committed to her ruination.

It would only increase her shame—her shame for her feelings, for her behavior, for the consequences of it.

But there was only so much a woman could be expected to take. And once he'd resurrected the shame—along with all the pain and sadness and doubt that he'd settled upon her—she hadn't been able to help herself.

"Ow!" Derek's reached up to check the state of his handsome, exceedingly straight nose. "You hit me!"

"You deserved it," she said, shaking out her hand, doing her best to ignore the sting of it. It was the first time she'd ever punched a thing, and it hurt, frankly. More than she would have imagined.

"You little bitch! You will regret that!"

"Not as much as you will regret using such language with her," came a low Scottish burr from the darkness.

Lily let out a surprised squeak as she spun to find Alec crossing the room, six and a half feet of massive, muscular fury with a single goal—to finish the job that Lily had started.

His fist was significantly larger than hers, and packed an impressive wallop. She should not have enjoyed the sound of bone meeting flesh but, she confessed, it was rather thrilling.

As was the way Hawkins dropped to the floor like a sack of grain.

And the way Alec followed him down to lift him up with the strength of one massive arm and hit him a second time. And a third.

It was when he pulled back for the fourth blow that his coat split in two, right down the back seam. In the sound of the rending, Lily found her voice. "Stop!"

Alec froze, as though she held him on a string. He looked back over his shoulder. "Do ye want him?"

She shook her head, confused by both the question and his brogue, thickened with fury. "What?"

"Do ye. Want him," he repeated. "To husband."

"What?" This time it was Derek who sputtered the reply.

Alec returned his attention to his victim. "I did not give you permission to speak." He looked back to Lily. "If you want him, he is yours."

She believed him. There was no question in her mind that if she announced that she wanted to be Mrs. Derek Hawkins, Alec would make it so. They would be married before sunup. She'd get the man she'd mooned over for months. The one she'd cried herself to sleep for more times than she could count.

Alec would give him to her.

A week ago, perhaps she'd have wanted it.

But now . . .

"No," she whispered.

"With conviction, lass."

"No," she said, more firmly. "You are terribly committed to getting me married, Your Grace, if you think to marry me to *him*."

"I won't marry her!" Derek declared. "You cannot make me!"

Alec glared at him. "Once again, I am nae interested in hearing you speak."

Lily met Derek's gaze. "For the record, as he is the Duke of Warnick, I think he absolutely could make you marry me, *Mr. Hawkins*," she enunciated his lack of title, knowing it made him mad with jealousy, before returning her attention to Alec. "But what His Grace cannot do is make *me* marry *you*. Or anyone, for that matter."

She thought for a moment that she saw his lips twitch at the words. At the way she stood up for herself. She wondered if he was slightly proud of her.

She was rather proud of herself, honestly.

"I would nae dream of forcing you into marriage, Miss Hargrove," he replied.

"We both know that's not true," she retorted. "But I'm not interested in the current option."

"And thank God for that," Alec retorted.

"You'd be lucky to have me," Derek spat.

Alec immediately looked back at him. "It speaks again." He raised his fist and struck Derek once more. "Next time, I'll take out teeth."

A thrill went through her at his unhesitating response. At the way he instantly protected her. She liked it far too much.

If she wasn't careful, Alec would be as dangerous as Derek had been.

More so.

"That's enough, Your Grace," Lillian said. "You've done your damage." Alec stood, bringing Derek to his feet at the same time. When he did not immediately let Derek go, Lily said, "Release him."

Not without a final word. Alec leaned down, terrifying the other man, enjoying the horror on his idiot face. "I told you I would destroy you, did I not? And that was before you touched her. Before you insulted her."

He released his grip, dropping Derek to the ground, sending him scurrying backward like a beetle, reaching for his bloodied nose. "You broke my nose. I am an *actor*!"

Alec reached into his own pocket, withdrawing his handkerchief to wipe the blood from his knuckles. "If you come near her again, I shall do more than break your nose. I shall make it impossible for you to walk the boards of your damn stage. And I shall do so without hesitation. And with exceeding pleasure."

"It won't change anything," Derek sniped. "The moment the world sees my painting, they'll see the truth." He looked at Lily. "No one will have you honorably, and the only companionship you'll be able to find is your brutal duke and a handful of men who want you for just that—*companionship*."

The shame came again. Hot and angry and desperate. And somehow, in all of it, all she wished was that Alec had not heard it.

She wished him to think more of her.

But he did not, of course. Hadn't he said the same to her not an hour earlier in the center of the ballroom?

Sell when you can.

He did not see the similarity, apparently, as he went after Derek again, lifting him by the collar until the man she'd once loved dangled above the floor. Lily's eyes went wide as Hawkins grasped at Alec's wrists ineffectively. "Give me one decent reason not to kill you right now."

Hawkins squeaked his protest.

"Let him go," Lily said.

"Why?" Alec did not look to her.

"Because I am ruined anyway. With or without his murder on my conscience," she said. "And because I asked you to."

He did look at her then, the moon casting the slopes and angles of his handsome face in beautiful light. He was the most handsome man she'd ever seen, even now, his coat in tatters, his eyes flashing fire.

Especially now.

"Because I asked you to," she repeated, her gaze on his.

He put Derek down.

Derek rolled his shoulders back, smoothing his coat sleeves, apparently unaware that his face and cravat were bloodstained. By Alec.

For Lily's honor.

No one had ever cared for her honor before. She wasn't sure if she liked it.

She liked it.

But she had no time to like it. Instead, she turned to Derek. "Remember this when you wake in the morning, and you are able to see the sun. Remember I gave you something you refused me."

"I never threatened your *life*."

She took a deep breath. "That is precisely what you did."

"Lillian," Alec said, and Lily held up a hand at the caution in the word. At his disapproval. He might be her guardian, but she would not allow him to manage her. She stepped around him, coming to face this man she'd once loved, this man who she'd once believed hung the moon beyond.

"I cannot salvage the opinion of those around me, the opinion Society shares. The opinion that will be solidified when you exhibit the portrait." She paused. Took a deep breath. And added, "I cannot ever be rid of the shame I feel for the whole debacle." She looked at Alec then. Acknowledged that he was right. That his plan was the best one. "I cannot ever outrun it."

Understanding flared in his beautiful brown eyes, and she waited for triumph to follow with the realization of what she would do.

She would find a man. And she would marry.

Because there was no other option.

"Get out, Derek."

He insisted the last word. "A lesser man would display the painting tonight to punish you. To punish your brute of a guardian. But I am a greater mind. More evolved than any the world has ever known. And so I bestow upon you my benevolence . . ." He paused in that way that Derek did. The way that he always had when she posed for him. She'd used to hang on those pauses, certain they predicated utter brilliance. Now she knew the truth—all that came out of Derek Hawkins's mouth was sewage. "Consider it a gift, little Lily. For the . . . *inspiration*." The way the word oozed from him made Lily want to retch with regret. "In your week, you might consider making your beast less savage."

Alec stilled, looking down at her hand and then to Derek. "The only thing stopping me from tearing you limb from limb is *her* benevolence, you pompous gnat. Get out."

The words were barely restrained, terrifying enough to send Hawkins running for the door.

Lily watched the door for a long moment after Derek left, eventually speaking to it, unable to look at Alec. "Tell me. If he'd painted a nude man, would London be so scandalized?" When Alec did not speak, Lily answered the question herself. "Of course not."

"Lillian," he whispered, and for a fleeting moment, she regretted refusing him the use of her nickname. After all, if anyone should use it, was it not the man who fought for her without hesitation? Without her deserving it?

She took a deep breath. "My reputation is ruined, because I am a woman, and we are not our own. We belong to the world. Our bodies, our minds."

"You don't belong to anyone. That's the point. If you did, this would not be such a scandal."

She raised a brow. "I belong to you, do I not?"

"No."

Her lips twisted at the instant reply. "Of course not. You never wanted me."

No one ever wants me. Not in any way that matters.

It was his turn to shake his head. "That isnae what I meant."

"That doesn't make it less true."

He watched her for a long moment. "It doesna matter what is true. Only what you believe."

She nodded at her own words on his lips. "Then we are in agreement. I am not interested in laying blame, Your Grace. I am simply interested in leaving this room and deciding which lucky gentleman I must charm into saddling himself with me as wife."

He swore again, and she took it as her cue to leave, turning on her heel and heading to the door where Derek had exited minutes earlier. Once there, she turned back to find Alec still as stone in a wash of moonlight, his coat in tatters, along with a tear in one thigh of his trousers. Set against the dainty furniture in the little sitting room, he looked like something out of a scandalous novel—a criminal, sneaking into a proper home to pillage his spoils.

And, somehow, at the same time, he looked rather perfect.

What if he did want her?

She put the thought away.

"Let me captain this ship, Alec. I might dash it upon the rocks and send myself into the depths, but at least I did it myself."

Before he could reply, she turned away and yanked open the door, coming face-to-face with Countess Rowley, who seemed in no way surprised to discover Lily inside the dark room. Indeed, Lady Rowley simply smiled a secret smile and leaned in. "Is Alec within, darling?"

Lily was set back by the familiarity in the question. "Alec?"

The countess clarified. "Your guardian."

Lily gave a little humorless huff of laughter at the descriptor and opened the door farther, revealing Alec beyond.

Lady Rowley's gaze lit in predatory glee. "I knew it. I just witnessed your former lover exit this corridor looking as though he'd been taken to task by a devastating brute. And I knew it was *my devastating brute*." Lily went stick-straight at the words. She hated the sound of them in the countess's pretty, breathless voice. Hated the possession inherent in them. But most of all, she hated the descriptor, disparaging and sexual, like he was a bear to be tamed rather than a man.

"Alec, you heroic beast," Lady Rowley purred, "I was hoping I'd find you somewhere dark, darling. To resume our *acquaintance*."

There was no question of the meaning of the countess's words.

They were lovers.

Lily ignored the pang of disappointment that surged, telling herself that any disappointment was because she had thought better of his taste in lovers.

It had nothing to do with the idea that he had a lover, full stop.

Lily looked over her shoulder to Alec, who was looking directly at Lady Rowley, with an intensity Lily had never experienced. And she could not stop the emotion that flooded her. Betrayal.

"Darling." The countess sighed. "Look at you, coat in tatters, still as big and broad and strong as ever. My goodness, I've missed you."

Lily closed the door before she could hear the answer. She did not wish to hear the answer. Let him spend the rest of the evening with his paramour. Let her tend to his bruised knuckles and ego. Lily wanted out of this room. Out of this house. Out of this damn world with its rules that meant different things for different people.

And she meant to get out, without him.

This was not the first time she'd been alone, after all. Lillian Hargrove had made a life of being alone. And the arrival of a massive Scotsman would not change that.

By the time she reached the entrance to the ballroom, she was nearly deafened by the cacophonous chatter within. No one was dancing, despite the orchestra playing a perfect quadrille. Instead, all of London stood in little huddled groups, bowed heads and fluttering fans and gleeful sotto voce. Despite the fact that this was an event designed to underscore the social differences between people, gossip remained the great unifier.

Lily was no fool. She knew the subject of the chatter. Knew, too, that she would soon be a part of it.

Even before Sesily Talbot approached, clutched her hands, and spoke, low and quiet. "Good Lord! When I said that you and Warnick should make Hawkins the villain, I did not mean that you should beat him almost to death!"

"It wasn't almost to death," Lily said.

"He crossed the room with a swollen cheek, a split lip, and an eye that would make a fighter wince." Sesily paused. "Not that I didn't enjoy the portrait he made."

Lily couldn't help but smile at that. "I imagine you did."

"He deserved it and more," Sesily agreed before adding, "Was it very exciting to watch Warnick go at him? He's a glorious brute of a man."

Lily was coming to hate the word. "He's not a brute."

"Indeed not," Sesily immediately corrected herself. "He cares for you a great deal, obviously."

She didn't like the way Sesily's words made her feel, full of confusion and something akin to sick. She settled on, "Everyone saw Derek?"

"It was marvelous," Sesily said with glee.

"I suppose I'm at the center of another scandal."

"Pish." Sesily waved the words away. "It's the same scandal. You've nothing on the Talbot sisters. But I shall acknowledge this, you certainly know how to enter a ballroom." Sesily looked to Lily's dress. "And how to dress for it."

Lily didn't find it amusing. Instead, she found it terribly defeating. Regret coursed through her, and she desperately wanted to be anywhere but here. "I don't know what I'm doing."

"Listen to me," Sesily said with firm conviction, squeezing Lily's hands tightly and forcing her to meet her eyes. "You do not let them win. Not ever. There is nothing in the world they like more than tearing a woman down for having too much courage. And there is nothing in the world that makes them angrier than not being able to break her."

Lily looked to the woman, an Amazon set down in the heart of London. Beautiful in her too tight, red dress—a dress that no doubt made other women green with envy. She was everything Lily was not. Confident. Sure of her place. Happy with it, even.

Lily wondered what that might be like.

Perhaps it was all of that confidence that made Lily so willing to talk. Bold enough to say something she probably shouldn't have said. "Derek asked me to be his mistress again."

"Derek is a troll."

Lily laughed, because it was either that or cry. "He is, rather."

"An arrogant, addlepated, pinpricked troll."

Lily's eyes went wide at the creative insult. "One with a great deal of power to ruin me, it seems."

Sesily took her hands again, and there was comfort in the warmth and firmness of her grip. "We shall survive it."

The *we* set Lily back. "We shall?"

"Of course," Sesily said with a shrug. "It is what friends do. Help each other survive."

Friends.

She'd never had a friend. But she'd read about them. She shook her head. "Why would you be so kind to me?"

Shadow passed over Sesily's face, there, then gone. "Because I know what it feels like to have them all loathe you. And I've seen them chase another away. Women like us must stay together, Lovely Lily."

Lily wanted to ask more, but there was no time to do so, as Alec chose that moment to reappear from the hallway beyond, coat shredded, trousers in tatters, gloves stained red with Derek's blood.

"Cor! He looks like a prizefighter. Or worse," Sesily said, her gaze locked on him as he approached and took Lily's elbow in hand. "Oh, the female half of the *ton* wishes to be you, tonight, Lillian Hargrove."

Lily couldn't imagine why, as Alec looked as though he wished to murder someone. As though he had already murdered someone.

"We leave now," Alec growled, ignoring Sesily, and Lily knew better than to argue with the glittering anger in his brown eyes, or the firm set of his square jaw.

Sesily leaned in to kiss Lily on her cheek, and took the moment to whisper, "Be careful. In my experience, men who look like that are ready for one of two things: kissing or killing. And he's already attempted the latter."

Chapter 10

BE STILL MY BEATING SCOT!
DILUTED DUKE DISCIPLINES DEREK

He did not trust himself to speak.

Not when he faced the worst of London in Eversley's ballroom, burning in the heat of their combined not-quite gazes. And not when he guided Lily through the room, and he heard the whispers. *The Diluted Duke . . . Covered in Hawkins's blood . . . The girl is nothing but trouble . . . Poor Hawkins . . .*

Certainly, Alec did not trust himself to speak at the idea that it was Hawkins who deserved the sympathy in this farce.

As if all Lily deserved was judgment.

The Scottish Brute.

He turned at the last, his gaze falling to a woman nearby, her eyes familiar. Knowing. He gritted his teeth, the words echoing through him, his clothes in shreds, the smell of Peg's saccharine perfume still on them. The memory of her hands sliding over his chest, the touch evoking loathing, not of her, but of countless Englishwomen who thought of him as a notch in their collective bedposts—good enough to take to bed, not enough for more.

A conquest. The great Scottish beast.

Come and see me, darling, Peg had whispered, her skilled hands slipping over his chest, as though he belonged to her. As though he would follow like a pup on a lead. She'd slipped a card with her direction in his pocket, reminding him keenly of their past, of the way she'd so easily manipulated him despite thinking him less than her. Unworthy.

How many others had thought the same?

How often had he thought it himself?

He did not belong here, in this place with Lillian, beautiful and English and so thoroughly perfect.

Alec did not speak as he and Lily left the ballroom, passing a shocked King—did not even pause to bid farewell. And he did not speak when he ripped open the door to his carriage and lifted Lily inside.

She did speak, however, punctuating her little squeak of surprise at being hefted into the carriage with an "I'm quite able to climb steps, Your Grace."

Alec didn't reply, instead lifting himself into the carriage behind her, pulling the door closed with a perfunctory click and knocking twice upon the roof, setting the vehicle in motion.

He could not reply, too filled with frustration and shame and embarrassment and a keen sense of unworthiness. Between the state of his clothing and the battle with Hawkins and the arrival of Peg, he'd had enough of this horrible town. He wanted to destroy the entirety of the city, pull it down brick by brick, and return north like the marauding Scots of yore, who had loathed England with every fiber of their being.

He'd bring her with him. A spoil.

He rubbed a hand over his face, wishing himself anywhere but here. He'd never in his life felt so out of place, as though everything he did was wrong. And then there was Lily, who seemed to take every blow delivered and parry with skill beyond her years, a constant reminder that he was an utter failure at doing right.

So it was that Alec was less than thrilled when she spoke again, filling the carriage with her reminders. "Well. I imagine we shall be well received in the best of London houses after tonight."

He bit back the curse he wanted to hurl into the night, choosing silence in its stead.

She, however, did not choose silence. "You cannot honestly believe that anyone will marry Hawkins's muse?"

He speared her with a look. "Don't call yourself such."

"Fine. Hawkins's mistress."

The words set him further on edge. "Were you? His mistress?"

She met his gaze. "Does it matter?"

Only that he did not honor you. Only that he did not deserve you.

"Someone will marry you. Make your list. I'll ensure it."

"Alec," she said, and the tone was one a mother might use with a child to explain why he couldn't make clotted cream from clouds. "Hawkins was covered in bruises. You are covered in blood. If anyone in the world were willing to overlook the initial scandal, this has made it worse."

He looked out the window. "That won't keep you from marrying."

She laughed, the sound without humor. "I haven't spent much time in Society, Your Grace. But I assure you, it will."

"Then we double the dowry. Triple it."

She sighed his name in the darkness, and he heard the resignation in the word. Loathed it. "I wanted to marry," she said, and he stilled, keenly interested in the truth in the words. "I wanted the promise of family and future. And yes, of love. But if I must settle . . ." She trailed off, then returned to the idea, with more conviction. "Alec, I don't wish to settle."

Finally something that they could agree upon. "I won't have you settle. I would never ask you to."

That little laugh came again, so full of disbelief that he found it difficult to listen to. "That's precisely what you're asking me to do." She paused. "Eight days is not enough for a man on that list to not be settling. Eight days is not enough for love."

"Dammit, Lillian, how does this end?" Her head snapped back as though he'd hit her, and perhaps he had, with frustration and anger. "Let's say I give you the funds and you run. Where do you go?"

She opened her mouth. Closed it. Again. And finally, "Away."

He did not want her away.

"Where?"

A pause. Then, "What is Scotland to you?"

"Lillian . . ." he began.

She shook her head. "No. Honestly. Why do you prefer it?"

He shrugged. "It is home."

"And what does that mean?" she prodded.

"It is—" *Safe.* "Comfortable."

"Unlike here."

The difference between Scotland, wild and welcoming, and London, with its rules and its propriety, was so vast it made him laugh. "It is everything here is not. It is entirely different."

She nodded. "And that is what I want. I want away from here. From this world. Why should you have it and not me?"

He wanted to give it to her. Wanted her to know the feeling of standing in a field of heather as the skies opened and rain washed away worry.

But even Scotland could not disappear the past.

"You think this world would not find you? You think you could live as a wealthy widow somewhere? Head to Paris and reign a silken queen? Travel to America and use the money to build an empire? You cannot. This world will return to haunt you. That is what happens to—"

She waited. "To whom?"

"To those who run."

He'd run, had he not? He'd vowed never to let them remind him of the past.

And look at tonight.

Look at his tattered clothes, his bloodstained hands.

He would never outrun it.

But if she found a husband, she might survive it.

She would survive it.

"You stay. Meet the men. See what comes."

She threw up her hands in frustration. "Lord deliver me from meddling guardians. Fine."

Silence fell, and Alec found himself at once grateful and exceedingly unsettled by it. Luckily, it did not last long.

"I told you the coat didn't fit."

He slid his gaze to hers. "What did you say?"

"Your coat. You've split it to shreds. Your trousers, too. You look as though you stepped out of the wilderness and right into the ballroom."

"To be expected from the Scottish Brute," he said.

"No," she said instantly, surprising him. "Not brutish."

It was a lie. He was covered in blood and his clothes were falling from his body. If he'd ever looked the part of a brute, now was it. "How do I look, then?"

She cut him a look. "Are you searching for a compliment, Duke?"

"Just the truth."

She lifted one shoulder and let it fall in an affect he was coming to rather like. Not that he should like this woman. She was too beautiful to be anything but dangerous. "Big."

God knew that was true. "Too big."

"For the coat and trousers, yes," she said, "but not too big."

"The rest of England might disagree."

"I am not the rest of England." She stopped, considering her next words, and added. "I rather like how big you are."

The words sent a thrill through him. She didn't mean it to come out the way it sounded. It was the darkness of the night and the motion of the carriage and the enclosed space.

And it did not matter if he wanted her to say it again and again. Lillian Hargrove was not for wanting.

Now, if only his body would listen.

"I assure you, the rest of England disagrees," he said, shifting on the seat, wondering how much further they had to go.

She smirked. "Not your countess."

Peg. He feigned ignorance. "My countess?"

"Lady Rowley. She doesn't think you are too big."

Peg didn't think that now. Not when he stood before her, the Duke of Warnick, with a higher station than she'd found for herself. But once . . . Peg had valued him much, much less. Even as he'd wanted nothing more than to belong to her.

Alec looked out the window. "She's Lord Rowley's countess, don't you think?"

"I don't, actually," Lily said. "I saw the way she touched at you. Like she owned you. And the way you looked at her. As though . . ." She trailed off.

He told himself not to speak. Not to ask. But somewhere in the silence between them, there was something he wanted quite desperately to understand. "As though?"

She shook her head and looked out the window. "As though you wanted to be owned."

He had wanted it. From the first moment she'd smiled at him when he was a boy, showing him what desire was. Before he'd known what she would make him. What he would make himself for her. He'd have done anything she asked. And he had. He'd trailed after her like a lovesick pup.

Until she'd made it all clear.

Sweet Alec, girls like me don't marry boys like you.

But he wasn't about to tell Lillian Hargrove any of that.

"Peg is not my countess."

"But you were Peg's," Lily said, her silly frock turning her into a dog with a bone.

He sighed, looking out the window of the carriage for a time. "Ages ago. She was sister to a schoolmate."

"And you weren't a duke."

He gave a little huff of laughter at that. "No. If I had been . . ." It was his turn to trail off.

"If you had been?" Lily prompted, and he looked to her, finding her gaze locked on his, waiting. She was still and straight, as though she could wait forever for an answer. She wasn't getting it.

He shook his head.

"You wanted her?"

Like nothing he'd ever wanted before. He'd wanted all the things she'd represented. All the pretty promises she'd never given.

He'd wanted it all. Like a fool.

Lily did not move for a long while, and Alec refused to ask what she was thinking, instead saying, "So, you see, Lillian, I know what it is not to get the match you wanted."

She nodded. "It seems so."

Silence fell between them, and Alec became more and more aware of her in the darkness, of her long legs beneath the silk skirts of her dress, of her graceful hands, wrapped in kidskin, clasped together in her lap.

Those hands began to consume him. He watched them, wishing they were not gloved. Wishing he could see them, bare. Wishing he could touch them.

Wishing they could touch him.

He sat straight at that. She was not for touching.

And he was not for her to touch.

He looked out the window again. How far could they possibly be from the damn dog house? Not close enough, clearly.

And then she said, softly, "I thought he loved me."

The sentence undid him, flooding him with jealousy and fury and a keen desire to stop the carriage, find Hawkins, and finish what he had started earlier. He flexed his right hand, the welcome sting of his knuckles reminding him that he'd done good damage, but not enough.

"Did you love him?" He regretted the words the moment they left his mouth. The answer wasn't for him to know.

And then she answered, slowly destroying him with every word. "My mother died when I was a child. My father never remarried, and when he died, I went to live with the duke. He was kind enough. He settled me. Provided me with rooms and a more than generous allowance." She hesitated, searching for the right words. "He took great pains to be a good guardian. He intended to give me a season, you know. Before he died. But he wasn't a substitute for a family."

"And the staff?" he asked, remembering how little they knew of her.

She smiled, small and sad in the moonlight. "They don't know how to interact with me. I'm neither fish nor fowl. Not an aristocrat. Not a servant. Not family. Not entirely guest. Untouchable. Doubly so, somehow." She paused, wrapping her arms around herself, as though to ward off a chill. Looked away. "I would go months without being touched by another person, beyond a maid helping to button a dress, a gloved hand taking mine to help me into a carriage."

His gaze fell to her hands again, and he loathed the gloves anew. "Your room. Under the stairs."

She lifted one shoulder in that shrug again. "It was nice to hear people. Up and down the stairs. At least I was reminded that there were others in the world. At least I was close to them, physically. Even if I didn't have them in my life.

"I would hear them laugh . . . the girls. They would giggle all the way down the stairs about some silly thing I never knew of. And I would have given anything to trade places with them. To be with them. Instead of where I was—in between worlds."

"Lily," he said, his chest aching with desire to erase all that time alone.

She'd never be alone again. He'd make sure of it.

"I would wonder sometimes—if I'd ever touch another person again. If I'd ever be loved." Looked back to Alec, the truth in her eyes. "He made me feel loved."

The words wrecked him, at once making him want to gather her close and set her far away. And then crush Hawkins into dust for taking advantage of Lily. "And you? Did you love him?"

She looked away again. "Who can say?"

Alec hated the words. The way they did not deny her feelings. He could say. He wanted to put the words in her mouth. The categorical denial. Instead, he said, "He did not deserve you."

One side of her lovely lips rose. "You have a terribly high opinion of me, Your Grace. The rest of the world would say it was I who did not deserve him."

"The rest of the world can hang."

She raised a hand to the glass in the carriage window. Dragged a finger through the condensation there. "I did it, though," she said, softly, lost in memory.

"Why?" He couldn't resist the question.

"A tempting promise. Sometimes . . ." He wondered if she would finish, and she was silent long enough that he thought she wouldn't. And then, "Sometimes, you wait for so long, that it all feels like love."

His chest was suddenly, devastatingly tight. What was she doing to him?

He leaned forward, closing the distance between them and whispering, "I don't wish to hurt you."

"I know that."

"I should never have come." Nothing good ever came from being in London. Especially not when London came with this beautiful woman, who threw everything into chaos.

"There's something rather noble about you coming. For me."

Perhaps it was the way she said it that made it sound nearly magical, as though she'd stood naked beneath the stars like some pagan goddess and conjured him there. Perhaps it was the darkness, the wash of silver moonlight on her porcelain skin that made him reach for her hands even as he knew shouldn't. Knew it was a mistake of the highest possible caliber.

Lily relinquished her hand without hesitation, and he turned it, palm up, revealing a little quartet of buttons on the inside of her wrist. Slowly, he unbuttoned the glove and, tugging on the fingers, slid it from her hand, revealing her smooth, bare skin.

At first, he simply stared at it, feeling as though he existed on a precipice, looking down into a deep abyss from which he would not return. Lily's breath was coming in a quick, staccato rhythm—or perhaps that was his own, filled with desire to touch her.

I wondered if I would ever touch another person again.

The memory of the words whispered around them, and in their silent echo, Alec lifted his own hand to his mouth, pulling at the fingers of his glove with his teeth, removing it with efficiency, before tossing it aside and—before he could regret it—sliding his bare palm over hers.

Her breath caught at the touch, at the slide of their fingers, at the way he captured her small hand in his much larger one.

Her skin was so soft, like silk. Like the sound of the little sigh that came on a lovely exhale. He did not look up at the sound. Refused to, because he knew that if he did, he would not be able to stop himself from what came next.

Instead, he stroked her hand, his palm running over hers, his fingers tracing the dips and valleys of her fingers, until only their fingertips touched, before he once again took her hand, lacing their fingers together tightly.

"Palm to palm," she whispered, and he heard the barely-there teasing in the words. The reference to their earlier discussion of *Romeo and Juliet*.

He should let her go. He meant to.

He didn't mean to say, "The only part of the play that's worth anything."

He didn't mean to look at her, to find her too close and still infernally far away. He willed himself to move. To sit back. To release her.

And then she whispered, "*Let lips do as hands do.*"

"Fucking Shakespeare," he cursed, tightening his grip and pulling her to him, his other hand, still gloved, capturing her, sliding over her jaw, his long fingers curving around her neck and into her hair, scattering pins as he set his lips to hers and kissed her like he was starving and she was a banquet.

She tasted like sin and sex and . . . He didn't know how it was possible, but she tasted like Scotland, wild and free and welcoming.

He stopped, pulling away just enough to put a hairsbreadth

of space between them, and closed his eyes. He should stop. This wasn't the plan. It wasn't possible.

She tasted like home.

Just one more kiss. One more taste. Quickly. Just enough to tide him over until he could get back and breathe again. .

"Alec?" she whispered, and the question in his name was his undoing. Not protest. Not confusion.

Desire.

He knew, because he felt it, too.

Alec groaned and pulled her closer, releasing her bare hand and hauling her across the carriage and onto his lap, where he could get a better taste. He put one arm around her, protecting her should the carriage hit a rut and send her flying, and he returned to her lips, playing over them gently, softly, teasing her with his tongue until she gasped at the sensation and he took full advantage, tasting her silken heat with long, luxurious promise.

She groaned, unexpected and unfiltered, and he went hard as iron beneath her, wanting that sound again and again—that proof of her pleasure. Of her passion.

Her fingers slid into his hair, then, and she held him close, meeting his tongue with hers, matching him with a kiss that threatened to send them both up in flames, along with the carriage.

He growled his pleasure and captured her face between both hands, holding her still as he kissed her, stealing her sighs like a thief.

And he was a thief. Taking without hesitation.

Or perhaps it was she who was the thief.

They stole together.

Marauded together.

Pillaged together.

And it was the most glorious thing he'd ever experienced. Her hands slid inside his shredded jacket as she moved against him, and he lifted her skirts, sliding his hands up her silk-clad thighs, lifting her again, setting her down astride him, scandalous and secret and everything he'd ever wanted.

The carriage bounced again, and she clutched his sides, gasping against his lips at the movement. "Alec," she whispered. "Please." No. She didn't whisper. She begged. And how was he to deny her, especially when she lowered herself to his lap. To him.

He was wickedly hard, too-tight trousers suddenly, brutally uncomfortable.

He groaned her name, stealing her lips again as he pulled her closer, until he could feel the heat of her through his trousers and her pantaloons, and one of her hands slid up, over his chest and shoulders and into his hair again, pulling him close as her tongue met his again and again, and he ached for more of her.

Her free hand clutched one arm, moving it, directing it, sliding it up her bodice to the place where silk met beautiful, pristine skin. "Touch me," she sighed. "Please."

He had to stop. They had to stop. He lifted his lips, gasping for breath. "Lily. We mustn't."

She opened her eyes, desire warring with something far more complicated in them. He could feel her heart racing beneath his fingers, where she held his hand to her, where she burned him with her beauty. "Please, Alec," she said, soft as silk. "Please want me."

She made it sound like it was a choice. As though he did not ache for every inch of her. As though he did not wish to claim her in the most primal way possible and erase the memory of every man she had ever desired.

As though he were worthy of her.

His throat worked as he fought for strength, and he might have found it. Might have, if she did not take matters into her own hands. If she did not take his hand into her own, moving it until it cupped one full, glorious breast. "Please, Alec."

He resisted the urge to move, terrified that if he did, she might continue with this mad temptation. Terrified that if he did, she might stop.

Instead, he extracted his hand from the heat of her skirts and took her face in his hands. He pulled her close, as close as possible without taking her lips, and looked deep in her eyes, the dim light of the lanterns beyond the windows casting wicked shadows across her beautiful face. "Show me," he said.

But what he really meant was *Use me.*

Her eyes widened at the words, and for a moment he thought her shock would stay her. As he watched, however, the surprise turned to desire and, like a gift from God, she did as he asked.

As she was told.

Time slowed in the small space, her hand guiding his, pressing him tight against her. "Touch me here," she said.

He did, feeling her tighten beneath his palm, even through the layers of clothing. She sighed her frustration, pushing into him, eager for more, just as he was. He took pity on her. "Do you intend to wear this dress again?"

She didn't understand. "What?"

"The dress. Are you wedded to it?"

She shook her head. "It is awful."

"Then let's do right by it," he growled, his massive hands coming to the neckline and grasping. Without hesitation, he pulled, and tore the bodice in two, freeing her to his hands and gaze.

She gasped her surprise. "You—"

He had no time for discussion. "Show me, Lily."

And she did, setting his hand to her breast. They groaned their mutual pleasure at the contact before Alec plucked at the tight tip, using thumb and finger to tempt her until he could no longer deny himself, and he set his lips to its twin. She cried out at the touch, her fingers sliding into his hair until he suckled, lightly, just barely, and she needed more, pulling him closer, silently begging him for more.

When he gave it, reveling in the feel and taste of her, certain that if there was a heaven, it was this moment, relived again and again, she moved pressing closer to him, the glorious heat of her cradling him, hard and thick and desperate for release. He growled at the feeling, desperate to release himself, unwilling to do so—unable to trust himself to stop when necessary if he were—

And then she was moving against him, making the most glorious little noises, sighing her pleasure and groaning her desire as he worked her with tongue and lips and made promises to his body that he could never keep.

He would not take her.

He would not soil her.

She deserved better than him.

He lifted his head and looked to her, her eyes closed and frustration clear as she rocked against him, desperate for something she could not find herself. Desperate for something he could easily give her.

For something he *wanted* to give her.

He slid a hand beneath her skirts, the brush of his fingertips on the inside of her knee opening her eyes. Her mouth opened, and he shook his head, staying her words. "Here?" he teased, stroking there at her knee.

She shook her head. "No."

He slid his hand up the outside of her pantaloons, loathing the fabric, the way it blocked her from his touch. But he deserved it, the denial. For what he did. For not being good enough for her. He deserved it, just as she deserved the pleasure he could give her. In this moment. Just once. Without taking his own.

"Here?" he asked again, higher on her thigh, near the crease of it that marked the beginning of her most secret place, where he wanted to be more than he wanted to draw his next breath.

She shook her head again, but this time, the word came out on a little cry. "No."

He found the slit in the pants, and moved deeper, finding the soft curls there, stroking as she panted her desire, imagining their color—a beautiful, secret auburn. "Here, then?"

She was through with the game, and he saw the irritation in her gaze when she found his. And then she spoke, shocking the hell out of him. "Shall I show you?"

She was fucking glorious.

He replied instantly. "Please."

And then her hand was on his, and she was pressing him

deeper, past the curls and into the silken softness of her, hot and gloriously wet. He swore, low and deep in Gaelic.

She gasped a single word as she took what she wanted, her gaze unapologetically on him. "*There.*"

He kissed her then, long and lush, his fingers searching and stroking and tempting her secrets from her until they were without breath. Releasing her lips, he found her eyes closed, as she rocked against him, her hand on his, showing him all the ways she wanted him.

He stopped. Those eyes opened instantly. Furious.

He couldn't help the thread of amusement that coursed through him on a wave of aching desire. "Look at me," he said.

Her brow furrowed in confusion.

"I will give you everything you want, *mo chridhe.* Everything you need," he promised, the words dark and low and filled with the accent he worked so hard to keep at bay with her. "I will show you heaven. But only if you let me watch you find it. That is my price."

The words hung between them, sinful and full of sex, and for a fleeting moment, Alec regretted the last—as though she owed him.

She would never owe him. From this moment on, she would only need beckon and he would come to heel.

He'd never met a woman so dangerous.

But he was already wrecked by her, by her soft skin and her beautiful sighs and her magnificent gaze on his as he teased and touched, as he tested her curves and folds and the glorious dark channel where he wanted to be—beyond reason. Her eyes were locked on his as she rocked against him, begging him for more, narrowing to slits when he offered her slow, wicked strokes, and then widening when he found the spot that would bring her wicked, wonderful pleasure.

He watched those eyes, grey like the North Sea, riveted to him as her breath quickened and her hand clutched his wrist and she panted her desire, and he held that gaze until she called out his name and they lost focus and slid closed and she cried out again and again, branding him. Taking him in the darkness.

Showing him the sun.

When those eyes opened again, they found him immediately, her hands threading into his hair, her lips pressing to his, her tongue sliding into his mouth in a kiss that laid him bare and destroyed him completely, summoning his pleasure, hard and hot and nearly unbearable against her.

He pulled his lips from hers, gasping for breath, somehow still hard and thick as though he hadn't come, wanting to strip her bare and open his trousers and make her his. Here. Now.

Forever.

And then her hands were moving her skirts, and he wondered if he'd spoken aloud. Her fingers played at the falls of his trousers, touching lightly—too damn lightly—and it took him a moment to find the strength to stop her.

Until she whispered, "Oh, my . . ."

And he loathed the reverence in the words.

Women dream of men like you, darling.

But for a night. Not a lifetime.

"No." He lifted his lips instantly, releasing her like she was hot steel, branding him.

Her gaze was wide with confusion. "But . . ."

"No." He lifted her off his lap and set her back on her seat, so quickly that it took her several seconds to understand what had happened.

They were both breathing heavily, and he could not look away from her for a long moment, her bodice in tatters, her legs askew, weak from the pleasure she'd found in his arms. He knew she was weak because he, too, was weak. And aching.

She was so close. He could take her.

She'd let him.

He pressed himself back against the seat, willing himself to turn away. To look out the window. To look down at the floor. Anywhere but at her. But he couldn't, because she was the most beautiful thing he had ever seen.

And then he made the mistake, lifting his hand to his lips, meaning to erase the feel of her there, forgetting that her scent would be on him like a promise. And the desire was more than he could bear. He tasted her, sucking his fingers deep, reveling in her.

Fire came to her eyes as she watched and he saw the truth there. He could have her. She would let him.

Christ, he wanted her.

Even now, even with her hairpins scattered and her long auburn locks falling down around her and the hound and hare, that had been shooting off the top of her head earlier in the evening, now drooping by her left ear.

She looked as though she'd been ravished.

By The Scottish Brute.

This woman wanted marriage and children and love, and those were not things he could ever give her. They weren't things she'd want from him. Too big, too Scottish, too brutish.

Not for marrying.

Not anything like the man she deserved.

What had he done?

He had to get away from her.

He rapped on the ceiling of the carriage, slowing it immediately.

Confusion flashed in Lily's beautiful grey eyes, as he began to strip his tattered coat from his shoulders—she would need it to cover her own shredded clothes. "What are you doing?" She looked out the window. "Where are we?"

"It doesn't matter," he said, tossing the coat to the seat beside her and opening the door before the coach even came to a stop.

"Alec," she said, and he ached at his name on her lips.

He leapt to the ground and turned back. "You didn't ask me the title of the Burns."

She shook her head as though to clear it, the strange change in topic blindsiding her. "I don't care about poetry."

She was frustrated.

Just as he was.

" '*Ae Fond Kiss, and Then We Sever.*' " Before she could respond, he added, "I'm sorry, Lily. For all of it."

And he closed the carriage door.

Chapter 11

FEMALES!
FACE FEARS WITH FLATTERING FROCKS!

Lily did not wear a dog dress the next morning.

Though there were several canine day dresses to choose from, Lily found that she did not require any additional cause of embarrassment for the day. Instead, she wore a dress that she thought was quite flattering—a green silk intended to be worn when receiving callers, but callers where rather thin on the ground at 45 Berkeley Square, and so she'd rarely worn it.

When she'd fled to this place—which she affectionately referred to as Dog House—she'd brought the dress with her in a fit of fancy. Now, however, she was rather grateful that she'd remembered the pretty frock.

After all, it was not every day that one was kissed by a handsome man in a carriage. More than kissed. Far more.

Her cheeks flamed. Not that she wanted it to happen again.

Liar.

It was true. She simply felt that it was only proper to dress nicely with one's kisser. Kissee. She had, after all kissed him back.

More than kissed.

And somehow, despite having been kissed before—despite having kissed before—kissing Alec Stuart, Duke of Warnick, was an experience unlike anything she'd ever experienced.

And so, she put on a pretty dress, and willed it to give her the courage to face him this morning. She entered the breakfast room of Dog House and made herself a plate, noting with a pounding heart that there remained two seats set at the table, which meant that Alec had not yet eaten.

Using the tongs shaped like dachshunds to place a sausage and large piece of toast on her plate, she moved to the far end of the table and sat, doing her best to arrange herself with the casual, effortless elegance that a woman should show when meeting a gentleman with whom she'd shared an interlude like last night's.

Which she did not wish to repeat.

Good Lord. It had been fairly glorious. And then he'd fled. Her gaze narrowed on her plate. Like a coward. After she'd touched him—found him as desperate as she had been.

I'm sorry, Lily. For everything.

What utter rubbish. As though she hadn't been a part of the event. As though she hadn't wanted it.

She'd most definitely wanted it. She simply did not wish to repeat it.

Not at all.

Liar.

She pressed her lips into a flat line at the nagging, repetitive thought. While on the subject of wanting, he had wanted it, too, or so it had seemed when he'd cursed Shakespeare and hauled her across the carriage to set her aflame and show her pleasure she'd never dreamed of finding. And made her want to beg him never to stop.

Cursing Shakespeare seemed unnecessary. And quite wonderful, truthfully.

Luckily, she had not resorted to begging, because she would have been more embarrassed than she was already if she had begged him not to stop and he'd stopped. Summarily. And fled.

The Scottish coward.

It was an embarrassing disaster.

Hence, the frock.

No matter. Lily had other things to think about. Things that had nothing to do with the brawny, handsome Scotsman. Things that were much more relevant to her current situation. To her future writ large.

Things like husbands.

Angus and Hardy punctuated the thought, pushing the door wide with their furry bodies, and setting Lily's heart to racing. Because wherever the dogs were, their master could not be far behind.

Angus immediately went to investigate the contents of the sideboard as Hardy came to greet her, bowing low on his front paws before grinning up at her. Lily reached out and ran her fingers through the big dog's wiry fur, pausing to scratch behind his ear. He tilted his head, his tongue lolling out the side of his mouth, and sighed in adoration.

She couldn't help but smile.

This great beast was nothing but a kitten. A gentle giant.

"You'll be spoiled if you are nae careful, Hardy."

The brogue sounded from the door, rough with morning, setting Lily's heart racing. She looked up to meet Alec's gaze, only to find that he was already headed to the sideboard, head down, kilt swinging about his knees. Had he not spoken, she would have thought perhaps he had not seen her.

His not looking at her made it easy for her to look at him, however, and she did just that, taking in his tartan with far more care than she did the last time she saw him in plaid—when she was too embarrassed to have a good look.

For something so silly, the plaid was tremendously flattering. Though, truthfully, Lily thought that it was possibly likely that a flour sack would be flattering to Alec.

The man had empirically lovely legs.

Not that she'd given much thought to men's legs in her life.

Until Alec. Now, every time she saw him in his plaid, she thought far too much about men's legs.

It was terribly inappropriate.

Lily swallowed, her mouth suddenly quite dry, but did her best to pretend that this morning was perfectly normal. That he hadn't rendered her a speechless puddle of desire the night before.

Don't think of the puddle of desire bit.

"He's a good boy. He deserves to be spoiled."

Alec grunted, placing a forkful of ham on his plate alongside several roasted tomatoes. Lily waited for him to say more, to no avail.

She pushed her food around her plate with her fork, pretending to be deeply invested in the morsels there, as he finished serving himself and came to the table, taking the seat at the far end.

As far from her as possible.

Granted, it was the seat that had been set for his arrival, but still. He could have come closer.

A footman came from nowhere—apparently Dog House had been staffed with speed and efficiency—and filled Alec's cup with steaming tea.

"Thank you," he said, and the poor servant didn't quite know what to say.

Lily wanted to tell the liveried man that he should be grateful the duke spoke to him, as apparently she did not rate conversation. Not even after the previous evening.

Not even after he'd left her senseless in a carriage.

It was no good. She wasn't going to be able to avoid thinking of it. Indeed, every time she looked at him, she could feel his palm against hers, his hands lifting her as though she weighed nothing. His arms around her. His lips on hers. His tongue. His *fingers.*

The room was suddenly uncomfortably warm.

Alec, for his part, seemed utterly comfortable, casually draped into the massive wooden chair at the head of the table, looking like lord of the manor, despite dining off plates adorned with scenes of a fox hunt, using silver etched with canine imagery.

Indeed, he ate like a starving man, his appetite clearly unaffected by her presence.

Lily, on the other hand, felt as though she might cast up her accounts in the heavy silence that fell over the room.

Sensing her distaste for her food, Hardy sighed, setting his head on her lap and looking up at her with forlorn eyes, as though reminding her that he was there, and eager to help. She sneaked him a piece of sausage.

Angus noticed from his place at his master's right hand and immediately came to her opposite side, licking his chops. She found a piece of meat for him, as well.

"They'll never leave you alone now." She looked up to find Alec remained riveted to his food, not looking at her.

Now, Lily found she was irritated. "At least the hounds acknowledge me."

He stilled, fork halfway to his mouth, and Lily was rather proud of herself for speaking up. He looked to her, his brown eyes glittering like whisky in crystal. "What does that mean?"

"Only that their master appears unable to find the decency to say good morning."

He set his fork down and turned to the trio of servants attempting to fade into the wall at the end of the room. "Leave us."

They did not hesitate, closing the door in their wake with a quiet snick that seemed to reverberate through the room, sending Lily's heart into her throat.

Would he kiss her again? Would he do *more*?

It was terribly early for it, wasn't it?

She imagined him crossing the room to pull her from her chair, to set his large, beautiful hands to her face and to take her lips, showing her once more what he showed her last night—that lovemaking could be wild and free and mad and delicious.

Not that she cared if he did. She didn't want it.

He watched her for a long moment in the silence before he said, "Good morning, Lillian." There was nothing teasing or condescending in the words. Just a simple, civilized greeting.

Except something about it made Lily feel entirely uncivilized. And very petulant. "There. It wasn't so difficult, was it?"

"It was not. I apologize. Again."

Again.

I'm sorry, Lily. For everything.

"For what?"

He blinked. "For . . ." He trailed off.

"For forgoing a proper good morning?"

"Among other things."

She stabbed a tomato with her fork, enjoying the way the juice of it oozed out the side. It was gruesome and macabre, if one really thought too much about it, and Lily was finding herself more and more in the mood for the gruesome and macabre.

"What other things?" She shouldn't ask. She knew that. But still she could not resist it.

He did not hesitate to answer. "For my part in this disastrous play."

"Which part is that?" She was rather proud of herself for holding his feet to the fire.

He looked to her, knowing immediately what she was doing. Impressively, he did not back down. "The part that threatened you with more scandal."

"I was in scandal long before you went after him. Derek and I were not exactly clandestine in our friendship. Add you to it, and the gossip pages gave me *nicknames*, for heaven's sake."

"Add me to it?"

She waved a hand. "Lovely Lily when I was out and about with Derek, but when I was seen in Hyde Park, or on Oxford Street, or anywhere else, I was Lonesome Lily—"

He cut her off. "What do I have to do with that?"

"The Woeful Ward."

He muttered beneath his breath, his eyes flashing with anger. "I didn't know—"

"That I existed. I know. I wouldn't worry so much about it, honestly."

"Well, I do worry about it," he grumbled. "More than Hawkins did. More than I did last night. More than you should have."

She narrowed her gaze upon him. "I beg your pardon?"

He did not see how close he was to the precipice. Instead, he explained his words, as though she were a child. "I appreciate that you did not have a mother or a chaperone or whatever it is a woman of your age requires, Lillian, but surely even you knew that if you spent time alone with Hawkins, your reputation would be the victim."

She watched him for a long moment. "And so it is my fault."

He hesitated. "Of course it isn't."

The hesitation was all she heard. "It is, though. I was not forced. I was not drugged. I posed for the nude. For a man whom I thought I loved. For a man I thought loved me." As the words came, so did her anger. "It was for him. *Alone.* Not for you. Not for them. Not for all time. But I did it, Alec. And so the fault lies at my feet."

"No," he fairly barked. "It's Hawkins's fault, dammit. If he hadn't taken such advantage of you—if *I* hadn't—"

She raised a hand to stop him from speaking. "So we get to it. I understand. I am at once responsible enough to be expected to predict my demise and cabbageheaded enough to be victim." She paused. "I suppose you've convinced yourself that I was your victim last evening?"

There were few things more satisfying than seeing the Duke of Warnick, nearly seven feet tall and weighing close to three hundred pounds, blush. But he did, his cheeks awash in color at her casual reference across the breakfast table to the previous evening's interlude. He was clearly displeased by the conversation.

Lily found she didn't care. "There is no need for embarrassment, Your Grace. There is nothing for which to apologize."

"There is e'rything for which tae apologize," he said, loud and urgent, his accent thickening with his frustration. He looked to the door, as though to be certain they were alone before lowering his voice. The brogue lessened. "I should never have done it. Any of it."

The sting of the words, the conviction in them, as though he had awoken this morning to discover he'd done something truly abhorrent, stung. Sharply.

Lily hated it. She pulled herself up straight and played her best British lady, feigning true aristocratic indifference and lying through her teeth. "How very dramatic. It is barely worth mentioning."

He froze. "What do you mean, it is barely worth mentioning?"

Of course it was worth mentioning. It was worth remembering again and again forever. If she had the skill, she would have committed the entire event to paper so she might reread it every night for the rest of her days.

With Derek, it had never felt as though he cared much that she was there. It had always felt as though she was trying to make him see her. But Alec . . . Alec made her feel as though she was the sun, hot and bright at the center of a universe. *His* universe.

At least, she'd felt that way until he had apologized for making her feel that way.

She schooled her features. "I am not entirely without experience."

He stood so quickly his chair tipped back and crashed to the floor, sending the dogs scrambling across the room. He did not seem to notice. "Another guardian would drag the man who gave you that experience to the damn altar."

Good. He was as angry as she was. "Are you a virgin, Your Grace?"

If his eyes grew any wider, they would roll from his head. "What the hell kind of question is that?"

She resisted the urge to shout her glee at setting this enormous, arrogant man back on his heels. "It's only that you remain unmarried, so I wonder how it is that no one ever dragged the woman who gave you your experience to the damn altar."

His eyes narrowed to slits. "You shouldn't curse."

"Ah. Another rule that differs between men and women. No matter," she added, lifting her teacup to her lips. "I politely decline your offer of marriage."

He blinked. "My *what*?"

"Well, you did add to my experience last night and, by such rationale, that should result in a wedding, no?"

He stood there for a long moment, watching her, as though she were an animal behind bars in a traveling show. Finally, he said, "Lily, I'm trying to do right by you. Everything I've done—all of it—has been to protect you. I realize I'm doing a terrible job of it. Last night—in the carriage—it shouldn't have happened." He paused. "I'm your *guardian*, for God's sake."

She did not reply. What was there to say? He regretted the event that had made her feel more alive, more treasured, more desired, than anything in her life ever had. And, sadly, his regret begat hers.

It wasn't as though she expected him to march into the breakfast room and propose. After all it was not as though they'd completed the official act.

But she hadn't expected it to hurt quite so much.

She turned away from him, heading to the windows that lined the far end of the breakfast room. She took a deep breath, trying to ignore the familiar pang—the one that she'd felt all too often. The one that came with being passed over.

She was being silly. She *hated* being silly. And, somehow, that seemed to be all she ever was now.

Hardy seemed to sense her frustration, coming close and pressing his large, warm body against her thigh. There was something very comfortable about the big dog's presence, and she immediately set her hand to his head, stroking his soft ears as she looked out the window, over the gardens of Dog House.

After a long while, she said, "There is a topiary out there in the shape of a poodle."

Alec did not sound amused when he replied. "I would expect nothing less."

"It wasn't my fault," she said, softly.

"Of course it wasn't." And, for a moment, she believed he meant it.

"It wasn't Derek's, either. Not really."

"There, we disagree."

She shook her head, but did not look back to him. "The rules, they are so different for men and women. Why should it matter to the world whom I am seen with? Why should it matter if I have private audience with a man? It shouldn't be their business. It should be just that. *Private*."

There was a long silence as he considered the words, and when he replied, he was closer than he had been. Just over her shoulder. "That's not how it works."

It wasn't fair. Lily had been alone for so long, and finding companionship of any kind had given her such hope. She hadn't even considered her reputation when she'd been with Derek. She'd been too desperate for companionship.

Just as she hadn't considered her reputation last evening in the carriage with Alec. But it hadn't been companionship she'd been desperate for then.

It had been him.

"It's how it should work," she said, looking down at the dog, his soulful brown eyes seeming to understand exactly how she felt.

"It should," he said.

It shouldn't have happened.

His words. Filled with regret. She closed her eyes.

Should was a terrible word.

She squared her shoulders and turned to face him, resolute in her decision to ignore his handsome, angled face and his brown eyes, gleaming the color of whisky. She would not notice any of it. Not his broad shoulders, or the way his hair fell in a haphazard sweep over his brow, or his lips.

She would certainly not notice his lips. They'd done far too much damage as it was.

Sadness and frustration coursed through her, a river of something that could become shame if she allowed it. But she wouldn't. Not again. Not with another man. Not with one who suddenly seemed far more important than the first.

She pushed the emotions away, leaving room for one thing only.

Determination.

She would not feel shame. Not today. Hang the Duke of Warnick and his temptation. If he wanted to get her courted, she would be courted. It was seven days until the painting was revealed, and she wouldn't fall in love in that time.

Couldn't.

She shook her head, resigned to the plan, and hedged her bets. "The Earl of Stanhope," she said, selecting the first name on his idiotic list. "He is my choice."

IT WAS REMARKABLE how quickly one could go from receiving what he desired to questioning why he desired it in the first place.

When Alec had entered the breakfast room, he'd dreaded facing Lily, sure she was planning to accuse him of the worst kind of roguishness and insist that he either send her from London or marry her.

He wasn't certain that he could have done the first, honestly. Not after she'd come apart in his arms the night before, all beauty and perfection and temptation.

And he absolutely would not marry her. She deserved infinitely better than a man who was good for sexual pleasure and little else. Better than a brute beast who, until he inherited the title of Duke of Warnick, was barely worth a second look from fine English roses. And certainly was not worth a second night.

Too coarse. Too unrefined.

Lily was worth a dozen of him. Last night had proved it, and made him resolute in his plan. He would get her married. And when that was done, he would return to Scotland. And he would never return.

He had entered the room, intent on establishing those very clear rules. He hadn't expected her to be so very beautiful, however, clad in the prettiest green silk he'd ever seen, stroking Hardy's massive head as though she'd raised him from a pup.

It shouldn't matter that she liked his dogs.

It didn't matter.

What mattered was getting the girl married.

And so he should have been relieved when she agreed and named her mark, but it wasn't relief that had flooded through him at that. It was something much more dangerous. Something that—if he didn't know better—seemed remarkably like jealousy.

He replied nonetheless, pretending to be unmoved by the announcement. "Stanhope. You know him?"

"Every unmarried woman in London knows of him."

He didn't like the way she said it, as though the man were some kind of prize. "I didn't know of him."

She gave him a little smile. "You do not receive *Pearls & Pelisses.*"

Alec was proud that he even knew what the ladies' magazine was. "As I am a grown man, I do not."

"He's a Lord to Land," Lily said, as if that meant something.

Alec could not hide his ignorance. "What on earth does that mean?"

She sighed, and when she answered, it seemed as though she was irritated with his shocking lack of knowledge. "Lord Stanhope has been at the top of the list of London's Lords to Land for as long as I've been reading the scandal sheets."

"We will return to why you are reading the scandal sheets in short order," Alec said. "But let's begin with why Stanhope is so very"—he grimaced at the idea of saying the idiotic word—"*landable.*"

She counted Stanhope's assets on her fingers. "He's handsome, he's charming, he's titled, and he's unmarried."

Alec supposed women liked those qualities. "Not rich?"

One of Lily's perfect brows rose. "That's where I come in. As you well know. Isn't that the key to your getting me married?"

The words grated. "It's not only the wealth that I expect him to want," he said, before he could stop himself. She was not a fool. She would ask—

"What else is there?"

He likely should not have answered. But there was something about seeing her there, Hardy at her feet, staring adoringly up at her, that made him tell her. "There is your beauty."

Her brows went up in silent question.

It was the truth. She was the most beautiful woman he'd ever seen with her red hair and grey eyes and a face shaped like the most perfect of hearts and a body that had developed in all the best ways.

A body he'd tried desperately not to notice until the prior evening, when it had been pressed against him and he'd had little choice but to notice it. To memorize it.

She was entirely magnificent.

And entirely not for him.

"Marred beauty at best, now that the world knows of the painting."

"That's rubbish," he said, his throat was exceedingly dry. Coughing, he headed for more tea. Drank deep. "The painting doesn't change the fact that you are perfect."

Her words followed him. "And somehow, when you say it, Your Grace, it doesn't sound like a compliment."

"That's because it's not one." He knew he was grumbling, but he could not stop himself. He righted the chair he'd sent crashing to the floor earlier.

When she'd referenced her experience.

As he set the furniture right, he was flooded with visions of what, precisely, that experience might have been. The visions were immediately followed by the kind of experience he might be able to give her.

And that way lay danger.

"With beauty comes trouble," he added, a reminder to himself, more than her.

Lillian Hargrove was nothing if she was not trouble. The worst kind. The kind that made men do idiot things, like kiss her senseless in a carriage until they were both weak from the pleasure.

He ignored the thought, busying himself with drinking his

tea. There would be no weakening from pleasure again. Not with her. Not ever.

She deserved a man legions better than some Scottish oaf who knocked his head on door frames and shredded his clothing while bloodying noses. She deserved a man not nearly so rough. One refined as a prince.

His opposite.

He supposed a Lord to Land—whatever that meant—was precisely such a man. And if Stanhope qualified, then he should be happy for it. Indeed a Lord to Land was what Lily needed. Someone who was so well thought of as a match that their marriage became the news. That it overshadowed the painting.

If anything could overshadow Lily nude.

Which Alec doubted. Because of her beauty.

"Perhaps the Scottish air has addled your brain, Your Grace. Most would say that beauty is a boon."

"I'm not most. I know better. And no beauty like yours is a boon."

Her mouth opened. Closed. Opened again. "I don't think I've ever in my life been so insulted by a compliment."

Good. If she was insulted by him, she'd steer clear of him. "No fear, lass. We're going to capitalize on your assets and get you married."

"My assets."

"Precisely."

"Which are: Beauty." She came toward him. Alec moved to keep the breakfast table between them, sensing her irritation and remembering her right hook from the night before. "And a dowry."

"Correct." At least she understood that bit.

"And what of my brain?"

Alec paused, immediately sensing that the question was a dangerous one. "It's a fine brain."

"Do not tax yourself with such elaborate compliments."

He sighed and looked to the ceiling, exasperated. "My point is that your brain is unnecessary."

She blinked.

It had apparently been the wrong answer. "Well, clearly *I* think your brain is essential to the plan."

"Oh, well, excellent," she said, and he did not miss the sarcasm in the words. "But *you* are Scottish."

"I see you're catching on."

Her gaze narrowed. "Perhaps you should simply install me on the steps from the hours of nine to three for all to come and have a good look at the wares?"

He'd made her angry. Which was fine. Angry Lily was not for kissing. He worked to keep her riled. "While I'm not opposed to such a plan in theory, I'm aware that it might not be appropriate."

"*Might* not be?"

"Definitely not." He shook his head. "I shall send word to Stanhope. You shall meet tomorrow."

Her eyes went wide. "Tomorrow?"

"We haven't time to dally. You've seven days to catch him."

I've seven days to resist you. Alec's teeth clenched at the thought.

"And if he is otherwise occupied?"

"He shan't be."

She raised a perfect auburn brow. "You may not like the title, Duke, but you have most certainly mastered the superior arrogance that comes with it."

He snapped. "You chose the damn man. I'm fetching him for you, am I not?"

Silence stretched between them until he felt like a dozen kinds a beast for yelling. He opened his mouth to say something else. To apologize.

She stopped him. "By all means, then, fetch him."

"Lily," he said, suddenly feeling very much like the morning was getting away from him.

She narrowed her gaze on his. "What did I tell you about calling me Lily?"

The name wasn't for him. She'd made that clear.

"Lillian," he tried again. "Last night—I was—it was—" This

woman turned him into a blathering idiot. How was that possible? He took a breath. "Let's chalk it up to my brutishness."

"Stop calling yourself that. You're not a brute."

"I shredded a topcoat." *And more.* Her bodice.

He would not think on the bodice.

"You need a better tailor."

She was frustrating as hell. "That doesn't make me less of a beast."

Lily was quiet enough that he thought she might not answer. Instead, she said the worst possible thing he could imagine. "Why do you do that?"

"What?"

She moved again, around the table, and he followed suit, keeping his distance. "Call yourself that. A beast. A brute."

The Scottish Brute.

He hesitated. "You've called me that, as well, have you not?"

"In anger. You use it in truth."

Because I will always have it in me. And it will never be good enough for you.

"What do they call me in your ladies' magazines?"

"All sorts of things. The Diluted Duke, the Highland Devil—"

"I'm not a Highland Scot. Not anymore."

"Forgive me, Your Grace, but no one seems to care about truth."

That much, he knew and was grateful for. He did not wish to discuss the truth. "Either way," he said, "it will never happen again." If he vowed it to her, perhaps he would stop wanting it.

After a long moment, she nodded and said, "I shall require a chaperone."

"No. Chaperones get in the way."

"That's the point of chaperones. To get in the way and maintain propriety."

"We don't have time for propriety."

Hardy barked; the dogs were beginning to think that the circling of the breakfast table was a game of sorts.

Lily ignored the dog. "Then why worry about a chaperone at all? My reputation is not exactly gilded."

Because she was every man's dream. And a chaperone was essential. Not just a doddering old lady with poor eyesight and worse hearing. She needed a chaperone who both understood the critical, time-sensitive nature of the situation and was able to—should it be necessary—drop a man into unconsciousness if he were too forward.

There weren't many pugilist chaperones to be had in London on short notice, Alec imagined.

But there was an ideal solution. One he had devised in the dead of night, as he forced himself to think of her as ward and not woman. He was rather proud of his success. "I'm not worried."

She stopped, looking at him with utter disbelief. "You're not."

"Not in the slightest." He rocked back on his heels, crossing his arms over his chest. "I have the ideal chaperone for you."

That auburn brow rose again, threatening to lose itself in her hair. "And who is that?"

He smiled. He had her now. "Me."

She laughed, the sound light and lovely and temptation incarnate. "Honestly."

"I am being quite honest."

Her brow furrowed, and he resisted the urge to soothe the twin wrinkles above her nose. "You are no kind of chaperone."

"Nonsense. I'm the best possible chaperone." He paused, ticking off the reasons on his fingers. "I have a vested interest in your finding a successful match so I can leave London and never return—"

"Something you could do this moment if you'd simply give me the funds to leave."

He ignored the statement and continued. "I am predisposed to loathe all Englishmen, so I will be on my guard more than some aging spinster."

She raised a brow. "You are old and unmarried as well, Your Grace. I would have a care with whom you call an aging spinster."

He ignored the taunt. "And, as a man, I am more than able to predict any compromising situations."

Lily pursed her lips and was silent for a long minute—long enough for Alec to conclude that he had won her over to his argument, particularly when she nodded. "It sounds as though you've planned the whole thing quite perfectly."

"I have, rather."

He'd risen early to do so, committed to getting Lily married soonest. He intended to sign her dowry papers the moment she selected a suitor, and return to Scotland.

And forget about her.

"There is only one problem with your plan."

"What is that?" There was no problem with the plan. He'd considered the plan from all angles.

"It has to do with *compromising situations*."

He did not like the phrase on her lips. Or, perhaps he liked the phrase too much on her lips.

Irrelevant.

There was no problem with the plan.

"You see, Your Grace, since you arrived in London, I've found myself in precisely one compromising situation." She stood straight and leveled him with a cool, grey gaze. "Last night. With you."

It seemed there was a problem with the plan.

Chapter 12

One Duke's Loss Is Another Earl's Gain

When she exited Dog House the next afternoon, dressed for a walk in Hyde Park with a gentleman she did not know, Lily was expecting a simple vehicle. Black. Possibly emblazoned with some kind of canine crest, considering her current residence. What she found, however, was a curricle beyond any conveyance Lily had ever seen.

It was not the sleek two-seated gig that young men rode proudly throughout London. Nor was it the elaborate gilded curricle in which ladies spent their Hyde Park afternoons.

It was unparalleled, and not only because Angus and Hardy sat at the center of the seating block like perfect little canine guards. Enormous and high seated, with great black wheels that reached nearly to her shoulder, the entire vehicle gleamed, pristine in the sunlight, even the wheels—which seemed to have somehow avoided the grime of the city's cobblestone streets.

As if the vehicle and the dogs weren't enough, the horses were remarkable. So black they shone nearly blue in the sun, and perfectly matched—precisely the same height, the same width. They took her breath away.

And all that before the driver appeared, coming around the side of the vehicle, tall and broad and tartan-clad, looking at once exceedingly wealthy and utterly wild with his bronzed legs and his wide shoulders and his eyes that seemed to see everything and his lips . . .

No. *No lips.*

She was not thinking of lips today.

Certainly not lips belonging to the Duke of Warnick.

She lifted her chin in the direction of the curricle as she descended the steps to Dog House. "This is beautiful."

He grinned, turning to admire the curricle. " 'Tis, isn't it?"

She couldn't help but match his smile with a shake of her head. "I've never seen anything like it."

"That's because there isn't anything like it," he said. "It's custom made."

Her brow furrowed. "You've a custom curricle? Whatever for? Do you spend a great deal of time driving about the Scottish countryside, eager to be seen?"

He laughed at the question, the sound warm like the unseasonable day. "It's built for racing. Very light, perfectly balanced, fast as a bullet. It's virtually unbeatable."

She did not care for the image of him careening down a road at high speeds, putting himself in danger, but she ignored the concern. It wasn't as though he were hers to worry about, after all. "Designed by you?"

"By Eversley, as a matter of fact."

Confusion came once more. "So it belongs to the marquess."

"Nae. He traded it to me."

"For what?" She couldn't imagine what a comparable item might have been.

"For a used saddle."

Her mouth fell open. "Why would he do that?"

He smirked, rocking back on his heels. "Because the idiot man fell in love."

She shook her head. "I don't understand."

"Neither do I, but I was not about to turn the offer down." He extended a hand to her. "Shall we go?"

She did not hesitate, letting him hand her up onto the seat—higher than any curricle seat in which she'd ever sat—to take her place next to Hardy, who immediately set his face in her lap for scratching. Lily was happy to oblige.

Alec pulled himself up to sit next to Angus. "You're going to ruin my dog with sausage and adoration."

"Nonsense," she said. "It's not as though I'm dressing him in jeweled crowns."

He smiled at the jest, so quickly she wouldn't have seen it if she hadn't been looking. But she was. He had a beautiful smile. Not that she was noticing for any specific reason. It was simple fact. Like the sky being blue, or dogs having tails.

She was distracted from her line of dunderheaded thought when the vehicle began to move in the calmest ride she'd ever had, the box barely shifting with the motion of the wheels.

It was a glorious curricle. "I should like one of these."

"I shall buy you one. As a wedding gift."

Always with his mind on the goal—to get her married—to make her another's problem. "If it is a wedding gift, it will not be mine. I'd rather it were a—"

He cut her a look. "A what?"

She shook her head. "I was going to say that I'd rather it was a birthday gift."

"And your money is not enough?" he said, dryly.

"My money is my due. A gift, though, I have always thought one would be nice."

"Always thought?" He looked to her. "You've never received a birthday gift?"

She looked away, unwilling to reply with his gaze on her. He saw too much. "When I was a child I did. Trinkets. But once my father . . ." She hesitated, then shook her head. "They are for children, I suppose, gifts. When was the last time you received one?"

"My last birthday."

She blinked.

"Catherine gave me a kitten. She thought I deserved something as arrogant as I was."

Lily laughed. "And?"

"She named the damn thing Aristophanes. Of course it's arrogant."

"And do you love it very much?"

"I tolerate it," he said, but she noticed his lips curving in a small, fond smile. "It gets its fur all about my pillow. And yowls at inopportune times."

"Inopportune?"

"When I am abed."

Lily blushed, imagining the times to which he referred. "I'm sure that is unpleasant for your bedmates."

He did not miss a beat. "You haven't lived until you have been woken by these two beasts chasing a cat up the walls."

Lily laughed, stroking Hardy's lovely, soft head. "Nonsense. I'm sure they are perfect princes."

Without looking, Alec reached to give the dogs a rough scratch, first Angus, and then—his hand fell to hers, on Hardy's head, sending a thrill of awareness through her in the heartbeat before he snatched it away.

"Pardon me," he said. They rode in silence for a long moment, Lily wishing that he would touch her again, until he cleared his throat. "We should discuss the goals of this afternoon."

She looked to him. "The *goals*?"

"Indeed."

She waited for him to continue. When he did not, she said, "I thought the goal was to get me betrothed before the painting is revealed."

"It is."

She looked away, ignoring the pang of displeasure that came with his words. She did not want to be rushed into marriage. That had never been the dream. The dream had been passion and love and something more powerful than a walk in the park. Eyes meeting across a crowded room. She'd settle for eyes meeting across a moderately populated room. Eyes meeting. Period.

Instead, she was about to be shown like cattle.

And all in the hopes that they could trick a man into choosing her before the entire city saw her nude.

It was humiliating, really.

And then he said, "It's important that you appeal."

She whirled to face him. "That I appeal?"

He nodded, the carriage speeding up along the wide street as they sailed toward Hyde Park. "I have some suggestions."

"On how I might appeal."

"Yes."

This was not happening. "These suggestions. Are they as a chaperone?"

"As a man."

It hadn't been at all humiliating before. *Now* it was humiliating. Perhaps she would topple off this remarkable conveyance. Perhaps its uncommon speed would blow her into the Thames and she would sink into the muck.

If only they were nearer to the Thames. No such luck. "Go on."

"Men like to talk about themselves," Alec said.

"You think I don't know that?"

"I suppose you should, considering your friendship with Hawkins," he offered, the wind strangling the words.

"We were never friends," she snapped.

"I'm not surprised by that, either," he allowed. "It's difficult to imagine anyone wishing for his friendship."

She'd wished for far more than friendship from Derek Hawkins, but that was irrelevant. She watched him for a long moment and said, "You don't."

"You're damn right I don't. I don't want that man breathing the same air as me. Ever again."

"I mean, you don't like to talk about yourself."

Except to call himself a brute. A beast. What had happened to him to believe that? To think himself coarse? If she allowed herself to think on him, he was all grace and glory. Muscle and sinew and features that were the envy of grown men everywhere, she imagined. And his kisses—

No.

Thank heavens, he stopped the wayward, dangerous thoughts. "I'm Scottish," he said, as though it explained everything.

"Scottish," she repeated.

"We're less arrogant than the English."

"The English, who are worse at everything in the world than the Scots."

He shrugged one shoulder. "That's not arrogance. That's fact. The point is, you should ask him questions. About himself. And let him blather at you."

She blinked. "Blathering. How very romantic."

He smirked, but went on. "Ask him about things Englishmen like. Horses. Hats. Umbrellas."

She raised a brow. "Umbrellas."

"Titled Englishmen seem to be exceedingly concerned with the weather."

"It does not rain in Scotland?"

"It rains, lass. But we are grown men and so we do not weep with the wet."

"Oh, no. I imagine you frolic in it," she said, wryly. "For what better scent than that of wet woolen tartan?"

He raised a brow. "Second suggestion. You should do your best not to disagree."

"With you?" she retorted.

"As a matter of fact, that would be helpful in the long run, but I meant with Stanhope. Men like women who are agreeable."

"Biddable."

"Exactly." Alec seemed happy that she had caught on so well.

"Well, I've sat for a legendary nude portrait. If that isn't biddable, then what is?"

He cut her a look. "I wouldn't bring up the portrait."

"You're taxing my small female brain with all these rules, Your Grace."

He sighed. "Do you want to marry or not?"

"Oh, yes," she retorted. "I dream of a husband who will blather on at me."

He sighed. "You're being deliberately obtuse."

"Are you certain it's deliberate? After all, you encouraged me to leave my brain at home, did you not?"

"That brings me to the last suggestion."

"Do my best to sound like a cabbagehead?" His lips twitched. He was amused. "It must be remarkable to be able to find this conversation amusing, Your Grace. Do go on and tell me your last brilliant suggestion."

"Put your best features forward."

She gaped at him. "What on earth does that mean?"

"Only that if he's so very landable, you likely have a great deal of competition."

They turned into Hyde Park, Rotten Row looming ahead of them. The carriage slowed to a stop, and a well-dressed man noticed them from several yards away. He smiled a warm greeting, and it occurred to Lily that, if that was indeed, Frederick, Lord Stanhope, then he was precisely what *Pearls & Pelisses* claimed him to be. Tall, sandy-haired, and handsome, with a wide, winning smile and kind eyes.

"Well. He's most definitely a Lord to Land," she said.

If only Lily could work up excitement about him, the afternoon would be off to a tremendous start. But, instead, she was taking courtship advice from a Scotsman. About her best features.

It did not bode well for the afternoon.

"If you like that sort of thing."

She turned to him. "Handsome, titled, and unmarried? You're right. It's a very strange preference."

Alec grunted, and Lily took the irritated sound as a sign that she had won their little battle. As Lord Stanhope approached, she turned to face Alec, noting his large leather-clad hands still holding the reins. "I suppose you're going to offer an opinion as to which of my features are best enough to be put forward?"

"No," he said.

Lily could not hide her surprise. "No?"

He shook his head. "Lead with whatever you like." He leapt down from his seat and she watched him come around the curricle to help her to the ground.

As he clasped her waist in his hands, the touch sizzled through her, unsettling. More so when he said, softly, so only she could hear, "All your features are best."

ALEC INSTANTLY DISLIKED the Earl of Stanhope.

It was obvious why women *did* like him, of course, despite his being a pauper. Lily had enumerated his positive qualities multiple times over the course of the day, had she not? Handsome, titled, and unmarried.

Charming, too. That much was clear the moment the dandy sauntered up, silver-tipped walking stick in one hand, in his perfectly tailored, somehow unwrinkled trousers and coat, bowed low over Lily's hand and said, in perfect English boarding school inflection, "Miss Hargrove, thank you for joining me."

Too charming.

And then the bastard kissed her.

Granted, the earl kissed her gloved knuckles, which Alec might have found a perfectly reasonable—if somewhat ridiculous—greeting when one was meeting a woman one might one day marry. Might have, of course, if he hadn't been occupied with wanting to rip the man's far too handsome head right from his body for putting his lips where they didn't belong.

Instead, Alec saw to the horses, ignoring the blush on Lily's cheeks and trying his best to forget the feel of her as he'd lifted her to the ground mere seconds earlier.

"It's a great pleasure, Lord Stanhope," she said, her voice lilting and lovely. "Unconventional circumstances aside."

Alec looked to Stanhope, who was staring right into her eyes, the rude bastard. "Unconventional?" the earl prompted.

"We've never met," Lily said.

"I saw you at the Eversley ball, but did not have the opportunity to ask for an introduction before you left," Stanhope said, leaning in far too close. "Society will be terribly scandalized."

Alec nearly groaned. She couldn't possibly think the man amusing. He was so . . . *English*.

"I did not see you," she said.

"Well, you are easy to find in a crowd."

She laughed. "Dressed as I was, I believe you."

The earl joined her in the laugh, bright and rumbling, and Alec wanted to hit something. "Were you dressed strangely? I did not notice."

She grinned wide, setting Alec's heart pounding in his chest. "You are an excellent liar, my lord."

This had been a mistake.

She liked the idiot aristocrat. And he liked her, Alec wagered, his gaze falling to the way Stanhope held Lily's hand—as though he owned her.

Alec did not like that.

No one owned her. She owned herself, dammit.

"Keep your distance, Stanhope," he growled.

The moment Alec spoke, Angus and Hardy leapt down to give the earl full inspection. The fop released her hand to crouch low and greet the dogs. "What glorious hounds," he said as Angus licked his jaw. "What a very good dog."

First Hardy fell for Lily, and now Angus liked this peacock. England was destroying his dogs. That was perhaps the most pressing reason why he had to get Lily matched and return to Scotland.

But she wasn't matching with this man, that was damn certain.

"Angus. Enough," Alec commanded from where he was hitching the horses.

Angus stopped with a little whine of protest and the earl stood.

Alec noticed that he sneaked in a final little scratch behind the dog's ear before coming to his full height. He supposed that the man wasn't *all* bad.

"Warnick," Stanhope said with a wide, friendly smile. "It's rare to see you in London, let alone here. At the fashionable hour." His gaze slid over the skirt of Alec's tartan, glittering with humor. "I see you dressed for the occasion."

Alec raised one black brow. "I'm wearing a coat, am I not?"

Lily smiled over Stanhope's shoulder, and Alec ignored the thread of pleasure that came with making her smile. He'd donned a coat for her, as a nod to her presentation on Rotten Row—Rotten indeed. But he'd kept the plaid. On principle. To remind himself that he did not belong here.

With her.

She did a fine job of reminding him herself, however. "You can take the Scot from Scotland . . ."

Stanhope grinned an idiot grin at the words. "But not the Scotland from the Scot, I see."

They were already finishing each other's ridiculous sentences.

Alec growled and turned away.

The earl wouldn't stop blathering. "It shan't be the *coat* that will attract attention from the ladies of London."

"It's you who should worry about attracting ladies," Alec shot over his shoulder. "That's what you're here for."

An uncomfortable silence fell among them, the only sounds the rustle of wind through the trees above and the chatter on the road beyond, far enough away to sound like a low hum.

Or perhaps the low hum was inside his ears.

He shouldn't have said it. Shouldn't have pointed out that this entire afternoon was fabricated to get Stanhope and Lily together. Courting.

Fabricated by Alec.

He turned back to find Lily's cheeks blazing red, her gaze fixed on the ground between her and the earl. Alec wanted to go to her and apologize for his crassness. For everything. It seemed that was all he did these days—apologize to Lillian Hargrove. For being a damn brute.

He did not have a chance to apologize, however, as Stanhope leapt to rescue her with impressive speed, extending one arm as though Alec had never spoken. "I would be incredibly honored if you would turn down the Row with me, Miss Hargrove."

Lily's gaze lifted, and she smiled at the earl. "I would enjoy that very much."

Alec's heart began to pound with irritation and frustration and something else he was not interested in investigating. Instead, he directed his attention to Angus and Hardy, now sitting beside him on the ground, staring up at him in superior canine judgment.

He scowled at the dogs.

Stanhope looked to the open, empty curricle. "Is there a chaperone who might join us?"

Alec crossed his arms over his chest. "Aye, there is."

Stanhope looked to Lily.

She set her hand to the earl's proffered arm and turned her back to Alec. "My chaperone situation is also somewhat unconventional."

Stanhope took the situation in stride, his gaze settling on the dogs. "An impressive ménage." He leaned in and whispered, "Never fear. I am very good with animals."

A beast joke. How droll. The ass deserved to have his head handed to him.

She laughed. "I do hope so, my lord."

Was she flirting? Was that a flirt?

Alec did not care for that.

They set off down the dusty Rotten Row, which Alec assumed Lily and the rest of London would refer to as "nature." Of course, it was nothing even resembling nature. It teemed with people, clusters of women in fine dresses, flanked on both sides by swifter forms of travel—couples in curricles and men on horseback. It was most definitely the fashionable hour; it seemed as though there was barely enough room to walk on the footpath, one was simply carried along by the stream of people.

He knew that chaperones were supposed to keep a proper distance from a couple in situations like this, but if he did, he might lose track of them. Stanhope might be so consumed with talking about himself that someone might take the opportunity to ferret Lily away. Or, worse, Stanhope could ferret her away.

Anything could happen to her.

It was best that Alec stay close. Angus and Hardy clearly agreed, as they were just ahead, flanking the couple.

"Is it always this crowded?" Lily asked the earl, her voice curling up and around Alec, who bit his tongue to keep from answering her.

"Not usually," the earl replied. "I assume the day's popularity is for one of two reasons. It could be the beautiful weather . . ."

He trailed off and smiled down at Lily until she looked up. "Or they all heard you would be here."

Lily was far too smart to fall for such treacle.

He couldn't see her face over the brim of her pretty pink bonnet, but he did see a flash of white teeth before she dipped her head and looked away.

She liked it.

Good Lord. "Don't embarrass the girl, Stanhope."

Lily's head snapped up and she looked over her shoulder at him, her eyes going slightly wide—at his proximity no doubt. She was blushing, her cheeks red as though they'd been in the sun for an afternoon instead of a quarter of an hour.

He raised his brows, waiting for her to speak.

She turned back to Stanhope. "You are an expert in flattery."

Alec huffed. Of course he was an expert in flattery. He was a poncey Brit. Trained to charm and seduce women.

Stanhope set one gloved hand upon hers, where it clutched his arm. "I do my best, of course, but it's quite easy to flatter someone so lovely."

The huff became a growl.

"Tell me, my lord, do you walk the Row often?"

"I do. I quite like it." He looked down to her, his brown eyes twinkling. "Particularly when the company is of such caliber."

Alec snorted, and Lily cut him a look over her shoulder before increasing her pace, no doubt to get away from him. The earl easily adjusted to the new speed, as did Alec. After a pause, Lily said, "I imagine you are in high demand as an escort."

The little minx. She *was* flirting.

"Not nearly as much as I'd like you to think, I'm afraid," the earl said. "I'm aging out of interest, unfortunately."

She shook her head with a laugh. "Your humility is unnecessary, my lord. I'm certain London's ladies are nothing but grateful that you remain eligible."

He smiled. "And you, Miss Hargrove? Are you grateful for it?"

She damn well wasn't, Alec wanted to roar. There was nothing about the Englishman that was worthy of her gratitude. And certainly nothing that she would be attracted to.

Certainly nothing she'd be interested in marrying.

"I am grateful for the company," she said, and Alec's breath caught at the words that reminded him of their conversation in the carriage two nights earlier.

I wondered if I would ever touch another person again.

He'd never in his life wanted to touch another person so much as he had in that moment, as she'd confessed her fears and her doubts and the reasons she'd turned to Hawkins. And then he had, kissing her, adoring her until he couldn't think of anything but why he should not be touching her. Of why she deserved a better man.

A good man. A man with grace and gentility who would not defile her with coarseness and size and past. One infinitely better suited to her than he was.

One like the Earl of damn Stanhope.

Assuming that the Earl of damn Stanhope was well-suited to her. They didn't know that he was suited to anyone. After all, he was seven and thirty, and unmarried. If that was not proof of a problem, Alec did not know what was.

The path twisted slightly, and the afternoon sun cast his shadow over Lily and Stanhope. "Why aren't you married, Stanhope?"

Lily gasped and whirled around to Alec. "You can't simply ask that!"

"Why not?"

Her mouth opened and closed as though she were a fish. "Because it isn't done!"

"How do you know what is and isn't done?" he asked. "You've never had a season."

She looked to the sky in exasperation. "Because the entire universe knows this isn't done." She turned back to the earl. "My apologies, my lord. My *chaperone*"—she tossed the word over her shoulder with a glare—"is *Scottish*."

Stanhope looked from Lily to Alec and back again, one sandy brown brow arched as though he had myriad questions but held them back. Finally, he chuckled. "No need to apologize. The duke simply asked a question half of London wishes they had the courage to. I imagine I remain unmarried for the same reason many do." He paused, then added, "I am not the best of catches."

"Or you're a damn scoundrel," Alec grumbled under his breath, and Lily stopped short. Releasing the earl's arm, she smiled up at him through gritted teeth and said, "Would you excuse us, my lord?"

Stanhope's brows shot up. "Of course."

"Excuse who?" Alec asked.

"Us," Lily said. "You. And me."

"Me?" he said, pressing one hand to his chest. What on earth had he done?

She glared at him. "You."

With that, she turned her back on the two men and made her way through the throngs to the edge of the path.

He looked to Stanhope, who grinned up at him as though he were nothing but exceedingly entertained by the afternoon. Resisting the urge to put his fist into the earl's face, he followed Lily.

He caught up with her as she hurried through a space between horses trotting down the path and reached the green grass that edged the Row. He ignored the way his heart leapt when she turned, grey eyes flashing with anger. She was close enough to touch, and he found he wanted to do just that.

Which was very unchaperonelike.

He took a step back.

"What are you playing at?" she asked.

"I don't know what you mean."

"You think we cannot hear your grunts and grumbles? And your inappropriate questions?"

He spread his hands wide. "I'm merely doing my job."

"Your job as what, exactly? Insulting babe on a leading string?" She pointed to the dogs, who had joined them. "Hardy has better manners than you do."

He looked to the dog, whose tongue lolled at his name, a length of drool several inches long gleaming in the sun as though to prove Lily's point. Comparing him to the hound was rather unfair, he thought.

"My job as chaperone. I'm keeping him honest."

She scoffed at that. "If the goal is to get me married, Your Grace, honesty is the last thing that we want to trade in."

She looked over his shoulder, and he followed the direction of her gaze, finding Lord Stanhope now holding court at the center of the throngs on the Row, chatting with a couple seated high on a curricle, laughing and enjoying himself.

Looking the perfect candidate for marriage.

She continued, "You are, without doubt, the worst chaperone in the long, venerable history of chaperones. Spinsters the world over are wringing their lace caps."

He knew she was right, but he had no intention of admitting *that*. "I suppose you are an expert in the behavior of chaperones."

"I know they are not supposed to loom," she snapped.

"I am not looming."

"You are nearly seven feet tall. All you do is loom."

"What would you have me do? Shrink to the size of your fairy suitor?"

She rolled her eyes. "He's taller than most men in London!"

He smirked. "Not taller than me."

"Well, of course not. You're virtually a tree with legs." She sighed. "Don't loom. Follow behind at a decent distance."

"And what if he is inappropriate?"

She spread her hands wide. "There are ten thousand people in screaming distance. You think he is going to be inappropriate? You're mad. I thought the goal was to get me betrothed."

"There's no need for hyperbole. It's not ten thousand. And that *is* the goal."

"Well then, you worry about your own business. Select one of the myriad ladies who can't keep their eyes from your scandalous legs."

The words took him aback. "I beg your pardon?"

She huffed a great sigh of exasperation, put her hands to her hips, and looked down the Row. "They're all looking at your legs. Which I can only assume you like, or you'd be wearing some kind of respectable attire."

He turned to look in the direction of her gaze, noting several women immediately redirecting their gazes from him. "It's perfectly respectable."

"In *Scotland*," she said. "In England, we don't show our knees."

"That's ridiculous."

She moved her hands to clutch her skirts. "Oh." She made to lift the dress. "Then I should simply show mine?"

His brows shot together. "You wouldn't."

"Whyever not? They are no doubt some of my best features. The rest of London will see them soon enough, and Lord Stanhope would certainly enjoy them."

He had no doubt of that. Indeed, the very discussion of her knees made Alec want to drop to *his* knees, lift her skirts, and inspect the hell out of them.

He'd murder Stanhope on the spot if he saw Lily's knees.

He pushed away the thought. "What would you have me do, Lillian?"

"Wear trousers."

"Why?" He smirked, making a show of smiling at a nearby group of women trying to look as though they weren't looking at him. They blushed and tittered and turned away, and Lily groaned in disgust. He raised a brow. "Are ye jealous, lass?"

She looked as though she wished to do him serious bodily harm. "Why would I be? If you went with one of these ogling women, you would be less trouble for me." She waved at the masses beyond. "You've your pick of all London, Your Grace. Have at it."

I pick you.

No. No he didn't.

He looked down at her. "It's you who is here for the picking, Lillian."

"I would be infinitely more pickable if I lacked my Scottish shadow." She paused, then added, "I am returning to Stanhope."

Every part of him resisted the idea. "That's fine."

"I don't wish you to follow me."

"I have better things to do than follow you."

She nodded. "Excellent. Good-bye then."

He nodded, growing more and more irritated by the second. "Good-bye."

And she turned and sauntered away, the pretty pink muslin of her walking dress teased him, the play of light over the skirts making him think about all the pretty pink things that they covered. Ankles and calves and thighs and . . .

Knees.

He swore roundly in Gaelic, deliberately looking away from her as she approached the Row. Resisting the urge to watch her. To follow her. To guard her.

It worked, until Alec heard the loud "Oy!" coming from her direction.

He turned to see a massive horse, manned by a young rider. A rider who had obviously lost control of the high-strung beast, now headed in panicked terror straight for Lily.

Alec was instantly at a dead run.

Chapter 13

ABSENCE MAKES THE SCOT GROW FONDER

He was the most maddening man in Christendom.

One moment, he was making love to her, the next he was recommending she draw attention to her best features to attract another man, and the third, he was doing all he could to drive that man—who seemed to be a perfectly decent, rather excellent catch, it should be added—away.

Did he want her married? Or not?

And what of what she wanted?

She lifted her gaze to the throngs of people on the footpath, her eyes meeting those of Lord Stanhope, a half-dozen yards away. Empirically, he was perfect. He was titled and charming, handsome and mannered and—even better—seemed to enjoy her company.

He would make her a sound husband.

If only she could muster enthusiasm at the idea.

She might have been able to, Lily was certain, if not for the horrid Duke of Warnick making it so very impossible to think of any other man but him. Not that she was thinking very flattering thoughts of him at this point. She was thinking deeply unflattering thoughts, as a matter of fact.

As though to prove it to herself, she began to tick said thoughts off in her head.

First, he was far too large. Modern men had no reason to be the size of prehistoric hunters.

Second, from what she could tell, he did not own even a single pair of trousers that fit him. What kind of a man didn't own trousers?

Third, he seemed only able to socialize with dogs. Lovely dogs, she acknowledged, but dogs nonetheless. She had yet to hear him have a sustained conversation with a human that did not end in anger or bloodshed.

Except with her.

With her, they sometimes ended in glorious carriage rides filled with remarkable pleasure.

She shook her head, stepping over the bounds of the green and into the Row. *Unflattering thoughts only.*

Fourth—

"Oy!" The call came loud and somewhat panicked from somewhere to her right, and Lily turned to look, only to see a furious chestnut bearing down on her. She froze, suddenly, horribly unable to move. She closed her eyes, expecting to be fully trampled.

And then it was upon her, knocking her backward, sending the breath from her lungs, cursing in furious Gaelic among a chorus of feminine screams and masculine shouts and several excited barks.

No. Wait.

She wasn't being trampled.

And the horse wasn't cursing in Gaelic.

She opened her eyes to find him leaning over her, his gaze searching her face as she struggled for breath.

"Lillian," he said, and she heard the relief in his tone. "Breathe."

She tried. Failed. Shook her head.

"Lillian."

She couldn't breathe.

"Lillian." He sat her up.

She couldn't breathe. *She couldn't breathe.*

"LILY." She looked to him, met his firm brown gaze, inches from her. "You will breathe. We've knocked the air from your lungs." He ran his hands down her arms and back up as she opened her mouth to pull in air. Failed. "Stay calm." His warm hands came to her face. Cradled it like crystal. His thumbs stroked her cheeks. "Listen to me." She nodded. "Now. *Breathe.*"

Air came like he'd willed it.

She gulped it in in deep gasps, and he nodded, guiding her through it. "Good, lass. Again." Tears came, unbidden, on a wave of relief. He pulled her tight against him, and she clung to the lapels of his coat as he spoke. "Again. *Breathe, mo chridhe.*"

For long moments, it seemed as though it was just the two of them, sitting in the dirt of Rotten Row, the entirety of London disappeared. She clutched him, breathing him in in great gasps, the scent of crisp linen and tobacco flower bringing strength and calm. And then London returned with a cacophony of noise. Lily looked up to find a wall of people staring down at them, watching as she regained her breath. The sea of prying eyes had her blushing her embarrassment and releasing Alec's coat. "I am—" She took another breath. "I am—" She did not know what one said in such a situation as this. So, she settled upon, "Hello."

No one moved.

No one, that was, but Lord Stanhope, who stepped through the crowd and came to her side. "Miss Hargrove! Are you hurt?"

She shook her head. "Only my pride."

He smiled and picked a leaf from her hair before reaching down to lift her soiled bonnet from the ground. "Nonsense. It could have been anyone. That horse was quite out of control."

"Lily!" She looked toward the cry to find several women at the front protesting as Sesily, Seline, and Seleste Talbot pushed through the crowd. "My goodness, Lily!" Without hesitating, the three collapsed in pools of silk to protect her on all sides. "You could have died!"

Sesily was nothing if not dramatic.

"I did not die, thankfully," Lily said. "I was very fortunate that the duke appeared in the nick of time." She turned to meet Alec's gaze, secretly wanting to reassure herself of his presence.

Except he wasn't there.

She looked up and down the Row, searching for his familiar red plaid. His comforting height. His strong hands and firm Scots jaw.

He was nowhere to be seen. In fact, the only evidence that he'd ever been there to begin with was Angus and Hardy, sitting sentry just behind her, as though they had been left there by their master.

Left, along with her.

I have better things to do than follow you.

Her chest constricted at the memory, and she struggled to catch her breath again.

"He's gone," she said, softly.

"He rushed off like a bat from hell," Sesily said, and a titter came from the crowd. She turned to face them. "Oh, please. We are not even able to speak the word *hell*? It's a location, is it not? I'm allowed to say Hyde Park or Knightsbridge or . . ."

"Cockington," Seline interjected, sending a ripple of affronted gasps over the assembly.

Lily coughed to cover her laugh.

Lord Stanhope crouched to help her to stand, and when he spoke, she heard the amusement in his tone. "Well. That will disperse the crowd more quickly than anything else."

She smiled. "Is there even such a place?"

His lips twitched. "It's in Devonshire."

"Well, then," she said matter-of-factly, "she has a point."

"It seems that having the Talbot sisters in one's corner is quite helpful in redirecting attention."

"You'd best remember that, Lord Stanhope," Sesily said, "as you would not like us if we were not in your corner."

"Bubble bubble, boil and trouble," Seleste said.

Lily and Stanhope looked to each other.

"It's double double, toil and trouble," Seline corrected.

"It is?" She turned to Lily.

Lily nodded.

Seleste looked to Stanhope. "Well, that doesn't make sense. It's a cauldron, isn't it? With witches?"

Stanhope nodded. "It is."

"Shouldn't it bubble?"

"It bubbles in the next line," Lily offered.

Seline rolled her eyes. "This isn't really relevant."

"I'm just asking," Seleste said.

Stanhope's eyes filled with laughter. "Either way, my lady, I wouldn't dream of crossing you."

"There, then. Goal achieved."

Lily laughed, the sound quickly becoming a cough.

"For heaven's sake, Seleste. Lily nearly died," Sesily said. "Stop making her laugh."

Stanhope offered her an arm. "My carriage is not far, Miss Hargrove. I'll happily escort you home." He looked to the other women. "Perhaps the ladies will join us?"

The trio did not hesitate to agree.

"Excellent," he said, turning back to Lily. "Allow me to see you settled on the green, and I shall fetch it."

Lily let him escort her away from the dirt path, Hardy and Angus following silently, watching her carefully, seeming to sense her myriad feelings about the afternoon. Once she reached the grass, she stroked the dogs' wide, handsome heads and spoke, raising her voice for the benefit of all assembled. "My lord, I am feeling better by the moment—"

At least, the parts of her that were not wondering where Alec went were feeling better by the moment.

She had trouble believing that he'd left her alone. Yes, it had happened after they'd argued and agreed—for the best, was it not?—that they were better off separated than together when it came to her possible courtship.

But she'd nearly been run down. She could have been seriously hurt.

He'd been there to save her.

And then he'd left her alone. With Stanhope. Who hadn't left. Stanhope had stayed, as a decent man should. And so Lily would, as well.

She pointed to a rise in the green nearby, where a large tree stump beckoned. "Perhaps we might sit for a bit." She turned to look at her companions. "And talk?"

In moments, she was seated on the stump, the warm May sun beating down upon her as her companions encircled her, as though protecting her. Hardy came forward and set his head in her lap, and Angus arranged himself at her feet.

Realizing the strangeness of the situation, Lily felt more than a little guilty about forcing the earl to join them, and offered him a release. "My lord, you really have been more than kind. But I am loath to prey upon that kindness. I'm certain my friends will be willing to see me home."

He smiled down at her. "Nonsense. This is certainly the most exciting day I've had in months, and might well continue to be. You have no idea how deadly dull parliamentary sessions can be."

"Wait," Seleste said.

"Are you—" Seline added.

"*Courting?*" Sesily finished the thought.

Lily blushed, as Stanhope smiled. "As a matter of fact, Miss Hargrove and I met not an hour ago. We were just taking a turn up the Row."

"Oh!" the sisters said in unison, before sharing a look that indicated their collective understanding that a walk in the park was a precursor to something much more important.

"Well, we wouldn't like to interrupt," Seleste said.

Her sisters were already moving. "No!" Seline said. "That sounds very important."

It was amazing how the presence of these three was somehow able to make one feel both exceedingly pleased and harrowingly embarrassed.

And then Sesily spoke, her blue gaze on Lily, seeming to see far more than Lily would like. "What was Warnick doing here, then?"

Being a hero.

Lily ignored the thought. "He thought he would play the chaperone."

"He's done a terrible job of that," Seline blurted. "He left you in a ditch!"

He'd left her.

"It wasn't a ditch, precisely," the earl pointed out, his serious gaze on Lily.

"It might as well have been," she said.

"No matter," Sesily said. "*We* shall play the chaperone."

Oh, dear. "That's very kind, but—"

"It's an excellent idea, don't you think?"

She looked to Stanhope, who appeared to be taking the entire event in stride, but it occurred to Lily that if she had been asked to imagine a more disastrous first meeting with an eligible lord, she would be unable to do so.

The only way it would be more of a disaster was if she were interested in marrying him. Which she wasn't. Not that he wasn't a fine man. In every way. Indeed, he made her feel perfectly pleasant.

Shouldn't pleasantness be the goal? Shouldn't a marriage be based on kindness and good humor, and if one's husband was handsome, all the better, no? Except it seemed that one should find one's husband's handsomeness tempting. Desirable. One should have trouble ignoring his square jaw and unruly hair and his fine knees.

Not knees, specifically.

Knees, for example.

She didn't care about any particular pair of knees.

Particularly not about the pair that had just left her to the aristocratic wolves on Rotten Row. Alone.

Solitude was not unfamiliar to Lily, however. And she was more comfortable with it than most. Comfortable enough to speak the truth in a situation that had no need to be drawn out longer than necessary. One hand stroking Hardy's ears, she returned her attention to the earl, and decided to speak what they both no doubt felt. "My lord, you needn't pretend this was a successful afternoon. I appreciate your gentlemanliness, but I do not wish to keep you when I am certain you have an infinite number of other activities that might better entertain."

The entire group grew silent in the wake of her honesty, until Lord Stanhope nodded and said, "You think we are not suited."

"I think you require a woman far less troublesome than me."

He smiled. "I think troublesome might be precisely what I require."

She shook her head. "Not my kind of troublesome."

He watched her for a long moment and said, "I don't think you're as troublesome as you think."

She laughed, humorlessly. "On the contrary, my lord. I am exactly as troublesome as I think."

The words were freeing, somehow, perhaps because the painting would be revealed soon enough—the scandalous truth would ruin her eventually. There was something powerful and relieving about taking ownership of it. If she was to be revealed, why not speak of it? It was her truth, was it not? Hers to share.

She looked into his handsome face and clarified. "The painting."

Her companions went still as stone, and the only sound that followed her confession was the low din of chatter from the Row, two dozen yards away. It occurred to her that the silence might be worse than the whispers. Silence was so lonely.

She did not wish to be lonely any longer. Tears threatened, and she forced herself to take deep breaths, refusing to allow them access.

She would not cry.

Not ever in front of people. No one would ever see how much she ached with loneliness. With fear of it.

Just as she was about to stand, the earl crouched, making a show of petting Angus, but Lily had the sudden impression that he had assumed the position to be able to look directly into her eyes. "It's none of their business, you know. Society's."

She laughed at the words, so honest and so thoroughly irrelevant. "I don't think Society would agree with you, my lord. Indeed, I think they would say it's very much their business. Very much yours as well, considering this afternoon."

One side of his mouth rose in a small, knowing smile. "I am nearly forty years old, Miss Hargrove, and I am on the hunt for a wife with a fortune. I know about mistakes."

She believed him, but still. "It's easier for you to live with yours, *Lord Stanhope*." She gently emphasized his title to prove her point.

He tilted his head. "Perhaps for Society. But I must look at myself in the mirror just as you do."

She watched him for a long moment, then said, "You should not court me, my lord."

One of the Talbot sisters gasped her surprise as Stanhope raised a brow. "And if I wish to?"

Lily shook her head. "London practically brims with pristine, good-natured heiresses. You're too kind to settle for such an utter scandal."

He waited a long moment and said, "Too kind? Or too English?"

"I told you!" Sesily blurted out, turning to her sisters with a triumphant smile before looking to the earl. "You saw it, too!"

Lord Stanhope stood, offering Sesily a wide smile. "One would have to be blind not to see it."

A thread of unease coursed through her, her hand stilling mid-stroke on Hardy's large, grey head as she looked from one to the other. "I don't know what you mean."

"And did you see the look on his face when he saved her?" Seleste interjected with a sigh. "I'm not sure I've ever seen anyone so obviously out of his mind with emotion."

Seline smirked. "I was so distracted by it that I entirely forgot to see what he was wearing beneath his skirts."

Sesily pointed to her sister. "Oh, bollocks. I did, as well." Lord Stanhope coughed. "Apologies, my lord. But, curiosity and all that."

Stanhope's brows rose. "Naturally."

Lily was stuck on the tale of Alec's concern. Her brow furrowed. "What nonsense. He left me. With you lot." She paused. "No offense."

"None taken," the quartet said in unison.

Breathe, mo chridhe. She didn't understand the words, but she'd heard the concern in them, even the promise in them. That he was with her. That he would take care of her. That she was not alone.

And then he'd left her.

"Not that I care he left me," Lily said, feeling as though she needed to underscore the point.

"Of course not," Stanhope said, and she had the distinct impression that, though he'd said the gentlemanly thing, he did not believe her.

Sesily was decidedly less gentlemanly, instead cutting Lily a disbelieving look. "Please. When Warnick disappeared, you looked as crestfallen as a babe without her sweets."

Lily stood at that, irrationally irritated. "Nonsense," she repeated again. "He doesn't give a whit about me. He only wants me married so he can return to his life in Scotland. He doesn't even care to whom." She turned to the earl. "No offense, my lord."

Stanhope smirked. "None taken."

Lily nodded. "I only agreed to the ruddy plan because of the ruddy painting. It's going to be revealed, and my ruin will be final, and Alec won't give me the funds to leave because he's convinced I must be married. That I wish to be married."

"Do you?" Sesily asked. "Wish to be married?"

Yes. But to another.

"No. Not like this." She looked to the earl. "Again, no offense, my lord."

Stanhope grinned, seeming to be enjoying himself immensely. "Again, none taken."

The afternoon had apparently unlocked Lily, and she could

not stop speaking her thoughts aloud. "The point is, I don't wish to saddle some nice man with a betrothal that will end in disgrace, or to . . ." She paused. "Or to . . ."

She stopped, mind whirling.

"Or to?" Sesily prodded.

The solution crystallized.

She looked to Sesily, then to Stanhope. "I must go."

THAT EVENING, LILY did not attend supper at Dog House.

Alec arrived on time and took his place at the head of the table, waiting for minutes that stretched into half an hour. As the time passed, he prepared himself for the confrontation that was sure to come—the explanation of his deserting her in the center of Hyde Park in the wake of her peril, all of London looking on. Of what he'd been thinking.

The truth was, he'd been thinking of nothing but chasing down the imbecile who'd entered Hyde Park on a horse he could not control. The moment Alec had made certain that Lily was alive, breathing, and would be well, he'd headed for the nearest horse, pulled some pompous aristocrat down, and, with barely a word, headed off in the direction of the runaway steed, leaving the baron he'd upended sputtering in anger.

It hadn't made him feel any better about the situation, which had sent his heart straight to his throat as he'd watched the horse bear down upon her, running at full tilt, desperate to get to her and terrified that he might not reach her in time. And then he'd had her in his arms and it hadn't mattered where they were or who was watching; all he'd cared was that she was safe.

He'd loathed the panic in her eyes when she'd struggled to regain her breath, he'd wanted to chase it away, and then do serious damage to the man who'd been responsible for it.

He'd caught up with the rider—a young man barely out of school who was as frightened as he was unskilled, even before Alec arrived to frighten him more. When he'd returned to find

Lily, she'd been gone, returned home by the ladies Talbot, he'd been told when he burst through the front door of the Dog House. Returned, along with both hounds.

Angus had been there to meet him, but Hardy, the four-legged traitor, had obviously cloistered himself with Lily.

Alec had assumed he'd be reunited with his missing housemates at the evening meal, but as thirty minutes had turned into forty-five and then a full hour, he'd realized that, once again, Lillian Hargrove had left him alone for a meal.

If he wished to speak to her, he was going to have to go looking for her.

Also, to retrieve his errant hound.

Exiting the dining room, Angus on his heels, he nearly ran down the aging, curious housekeeper.

"Your Grace!" she announced, as though she hadn't been loitering in the hallway beyond, no doubt wondering what he was doing, alone, in the dining room.

He had no patience for pleasantries. "Where is she?"

Mrs. Thrushwill's eyes went wide. "Your Grace?"

He looked to the ceiling and begged for patience. "Miss Hargrove. Where is she?"

"She asked for a tray earlier this evening. I think she is ill."

Was she hurt?

It was possible that she'd been hurt more than he thought. She might have cracked a rib. Or struck her head when he'd pulled her to the ground. He took a large step toward the housekeeper, until he was close enough to tower over her. "Did she call for a doctor?"

The housekeeper shook her head. "No, my lord."

Shit.

He was already on the way to her. "Call a damn doctor."

He headed to the upper floor that housed the bedchambers, immediately bypassing the larger rooms for the smaller ones, reserved for guest use. He opened several doors before Hardy came from around a corner and stopped short with a little bark.

Alec looked to the dog. "Where is she?"

As if he understood, Hardy turned tail and disappeared around the corner once more. When Alec followed, he found the dog standing at attention, face to a mahogany door, tail wagging and sighing little, urgent cries.

"Good boy." Alec pet him absently. "I'll deal with you later. We're going to discuss your shifting loyalty."

But first, he set his hand to the door handle and turned.

Inside, the room was pitch black.

"Lily?" he said, moving quickly toward the bed, heart pounding. It was early and she was already dead asleep—perhaps she was hurt.

Or worse.

He said her name again in the darkness, concern flooding him. "Lily."

No answer. No movement from the bed.

He fumbled for a flint on the table and felt to reach the candlestick there, dropping the little box from his hand as the flame burst into being, and turning to the bed.

Lily wasn't there.

Neither were the bedsheets.

That was when he noticed the open window, and the string of sheets running over the sill and across the floor to the leg of the oak bed.

She had escaped.

Absconded in the night.

If, of course, she'd made it the three stories without killing herself in the process. He rushed to the window and leaned out into the dark garden beyond, looking down to the ground with no small amount of terror that he'd find her broken body below.

All he found was a dangling rope of bedclothes, swaying in the wind.

Cursing, he surveyed the rest of the grounds, hoping to find that she was practicing some kind of military maneuver instead of actually escaping Dog House in the dead of night to go God knew where with God knew whom.

The thought gave him pause.

Had she enjoyed Stanhope's company so much that she'd decided to leave?

Was it possible they were eloping?

It was preposterous, of course. Alec wanted her married. He wouldn't withhold his consent. But still, he couldn't stop himself from conjuring the image of the largely nefarious things she and the perfect aristocrat might do once absconded into the night.

If Stanhope kissed her, Alec would remove teeth.

And that's when he saw her.

The back of her, barely there in the darkness, scaling the garden wall as though she'd been stone climbing for all her life.

In men's clothing.

"Where is she going?" he said aloud to the dark and still and dogs.

None of the trio answered, not even when Alec tested the strength of her handmade rope and, without hesitation, followed her into the night.

He was down the surprisingly well-constructed rope, across the garden, and over the wall in three minutes—quickly enough for him to see her, hair tucked up into a men's cap and breeches revealing far more than they should, duck into a nearby alley.

He nearly got her.

But as he came out on the far end of the pathway, it was to find the door to a hack a dozen yards away closing with a perfunctory click. He'd missed her by seconds.

Turning, he hailed a hack of his own, climbing up onto the block with the driver instead of into the carriage behind.

"Oy! Don' care who y'are, sir. Ya ride in the carriage."

Alec ignored the words. "Follow that hack."

The driver was not green, thankfully, and he snapped the reins without hesitation, even as he said, "Followin' costs ya double."

"I'll pay you triple. But don't you dare lose them."

He would not lose her. He would keep her safe if it killed him.

The driver continued with renewed vigor, trailing Lily's hack as they wove through Mayfair, south and east, the streets becoming narrower and grittier.

Where in hell was she headed?

Stanhope held a venerable title, with an ancient row house in Mayfair. He was also a gentleman. There was no way he would have summoned Lily in this direction on her own.

Perhaps she wasn't on her own.

Perhaps he was inside the carriage with her, doing God knew what.

Alec knew, as well. Knew the feel of her. The taste of her. Remembered every moment he'd spent with her in his own carriage two nights before.

If Stanhope was doing anything like that, he'd murder him.

He growled aloud at the thought, knowing he had no right to think it.

This carriage was far too slow. "Give me the reins."

The driver shot him a look. "No, sir."

"I'll pay you five times what you're asking."

"I'm not lettin' you drive, mi'lord."

"Fifty pounds." The reins went slack. The horses slowed. Madness threatened. "I'll give you fifty pounds if you let me drive."

It was enough to buy another gig. A nicer one than this hack.

"Who are we followin'?" The coachman asked in shock.

Alec took the reins and with a mighty, "Hyah!" they were off, the horses seeming to understand that they were driven by a man with power, skill, and a desperate desire.

They careened through the streets, wheels rattling on the cobblestones, cool wind on Alec's face, easing the frustration that had lurked—grown—since he arrived in London days earlier. He wanted a race. He wanted his curricle and matched horses and the wild roads of Scotland in the dead of night, terrifying and freeing and his alone.

Instead, he had the tight turns of London, chasing after a woman he wanted more than anything to keep safe.

He loathed London.

"Who are we followin'?" The coachman shouted above the clatter of wheels, clutching the driving box in panic.

Alec flicked the reins again. "No one important."

"Beg pardon, sir," the man asked with a laugh, "but fifty quid ain't no one important."

Alec ignored the words. Of course she was important.

She was slowly becoming everything.

The coach crossed into Soho, storefronts suddenly ablaze with lights, prostitutes and their clients spilling onto the streets, pubs and gaming hells tempting passersby.

"Where the hell is she going?" he said as he tempered the horses, his frustration threatening once more.

"Looks like Covent Garden, if I 'ad to say, sir."

And, like that, he knew what she was doing.

It wasn't Stanhope she was going after. It was Hawkins.

Derek made me feel loved.

The memory of her story, of the way the pompous ass had manipulated her with his pretty promises, sent a thread of rage through him. The rage was followed by fear, which came with a second, possibly worse memory. A memory of Hawkins offering to take her to mistress. Of Alec leaning over the pompous git in the dimly lit back room at Eversley House, looking over his shoulder at a wide-eyed Lily and asking her if she wanted him.

No.

She'd said the word, but Alec hadn't believed her. He'd heard the doubt in it. The uncertainty. He'd asked her to say it again.

Pushed her to do it.

She had, but perhaps she hadn't meant it. Perhaps she did want him. Why else would she be here at—

"They've stopped, m'lord."

He pulled up on the reins, gaze focusing on the carriage several dozen yards ahead in front of a nondescript row house tucked behind Bow Street. The door to the hack opened and Lily descended in her ridiculous outfit—trousers and shirt that billowed around her, clearly lifted from a wardrobe belonging to a much larger man—hat pulled low over her eyes, hair tucked up beneath.

She tossed a coin up to the driver and the hack moved, heading quickly out of sight in search of a new fare. She hadn't asked him to wait. Which meant she was planning for a long stay.

Did she not think she would be missed at home?

Home.

The word unsettled him. It wasn't as though the damn Dog House was his home. It certainly didn't feel anything like his home in Scotland. And somehow, he wanted Lily to feel it was home. He wanted her to feel safe there. To believe that there was something good there for her.

Something a damn sight better than whatever was inside the building she was skulking around.

He passed the driver an exorbitant amount of coin. "The rest when I return. Wait for me."

The driver did not hesitate, leaning back on the block and tipping the brim of his cap down over his eyes. "Yes, sir."

Alec was in the shadows within seconds, moving toward her as she paused outside the door and extracted something from her pocket. A key? She had a key to this place, quiet and dark and close enough to the Hawkins Theater for Alec to be certain of what was inside. Of *who* was inside.

She slipped through the door, letting it swing shut behind her. The lock clicked as he drew close, and he cursed in the darkness.

He was going to have to break in.

CHAPTER 14

A PICTURE IS WORTH A THOUSAND WARDS

As a man with a powerful sense of self-worth and a minuscule amount of actual worth, Derek Hawkins spent the majority of his time in full view of Society, trying to convince the aristocracy that the former was as well-founded as the latter was a travesty.

Consequently, he was never at home in the evenings.

No doubt, on that particular evening, he was at a club, or a dinner, or revealing his outrageous pomposity to a group of simpering women, each more desperate than the last to win the attention of the great Derek Hawkins, if for only a moment.

Not that Lily did not understand that desperation.

She had, after all, basked in its glow for long enough to be summarily ruined.

Lily had no doubt that if he weren't so obsessed with the world's perception of him and his genius, he wouldn't have so summarily ruined her. Certainly, he wouldn't have paraded the woman in his already famed painting in front of all the world, without hesitation.

Without consent.

But no one had ever been important enough to Derek Hawkins to inspire him to act with honor. She knew that now. Was grateful for it, even, as she found she had no qualms entering his home, uninvited, when she knew he was not home.

If he did not want her there, he should have asked her to return her key, no?

Locking the door carefully behind her, she turned, ready to climb the stairs to her destination quickly, eager to avoid the housekeeper, who doubled as cook, and the butler, who doubled as valet.

She had not expected to find the house so dark, however, and eerily quiet. She'd hoped for fires in the hearths along the way, some dim light to reveal her path, but there was nothing. She found a candle on the table near the door, and scrambled to light it.

When that was done, she should have immediately headed for her destination—but something about the emptiness of light and sound made her curious. She ducked into the front room, which had, when she had played the role of Derek's muse, been filled with elaborate gilded furniture.

It stood empty now.

The discovery sent her further into the bowels of the house, toward the kitchens, where a fire was always lit. The two aging servants were rarely far from the warmth of the room. Tonight, however, they were nowhere to be found. The hearth was dark. And there was a pile of dishware next to the large sink that was unexpected.

Someone was living here. Alone.

Returning to the front of the house, she peeked into other rooms, finding each one empty of its contents. A stray chair here and there, but no room ready to receive. Her heart in her throat, she crept up the stairs. Was it possible he no longer lived here? The thought spurred her forward, fast and full of nerves.

What if it wasn't here?

She opened the door to his bedchamber, immediately grateful for the sweet scent of his preferred perfume assaulting her. He lived here. Which meant the painting was here. She crossed the room, putting her hand to the door that adjoined his most precious space, the room he called his Room of Genius. She tried the handle, only to find it locked.

Of course.

Setting the candle on the low table between the bed and the door to his studio, Lily opened a drawer to search for the key. It had to be there. She'd come too far for it not to be there.

And that's when she heard the sound, soft and nearly silent from beyond the room itself. There was someone there.

Heart threatening to beat from her chest, Lily turned left and right, desperately seeking an exit. She was on the third floor of the house, so escaping via the window was not an option. There was a massive cupboard on the other side of the room, large enough for two people, if she had to guess, but far too close to the door to the hallways beyond to consider it as a hiding place.

The noise came again, and her gaze flew to the door, convinced that she could hear the handle turning.

Derek was here.

She was under the bed in seconds, with a little prayer of thanks to her maker for men's clothing. She'd never have fit with skirts and crinoline.

She held her breath as the door opened, and she squeezed her eyes shut, holding her breath and trying with every ounce of her energy to resist the urge to move. To turn her head. To flee.

The door closed, and he was in the room with her.

It was only then that she realized she'd left the candle burning. He would know instantly that someone had been there. That someone *was* there.

This had been a terrible mistake.

Footsteps sounded, quiet and firm as he moved through the room.

The door to the armoire opened quickly. Closed.

She willed her breath to come easily, desperate to keep quiet.

He made his way slowly around the foot of the bed, black boots coming into view as he crossed to the table where the candle burned. The light shifted, and though she could not see, she assumed he had lifted the candle.

And then the bed shifted above her. Just barely, and her eyes widened as the boots moved. And a bare leg came into view.

Followed by a knee, and a fall of tartan.

And the candle, held by a massive bronzed hand.

And, finally, Alec's face.

She squeaked her surprise, her heart seeming to pound worse with the reveal of his identity than it had done when she thought he was Derek. "What are you doing here?"

"You have two options," he said, the words low and rumbling with brogue. "You may come out from under there, or I will come in and fetch you."

She narrowed her gaze. "Now you wish to keep my company?"

His features matched her own. "What does that mean?"

You left me, she wanted to say. *Alone. Wishing for you*. Instead, she settled on, "I cannot come out until you move, Duke." He raised a brow, but moved, and she followed him out, coming to her feet, already fighting. "What are you doing here?"

"Making sure you don't get yourself caught or killed."

"Killed," she scoffed. "No one is going to kill me."

"You could have fallen from the window—how were you even able to make a bedsheet rope?"

"Sesily taught me."

He looked to the ceiling. "Of course she did. The scandalous leading the scandalous."

"She is my friend," she said, "And I did not fall. As you see, I am quite alive."

"Remarkably," he replied. "You took a hack here, dressed in . . ." He paused, and fury flashed in his eyes, "Whatever this is."

She looked down at the ill-fitting trousers and the too-large shirt and coat. "It's men's clothing!"

"You look ridiculous! No one in his right mind would think you male. At best he'd think you an urchin playing fancy dress."

"The driver didn't seem to notice."

"The driver also didn't notice you were being followed, so I would not laud his powers of observation."

Her brow furrowed. "You cannot simply follow a woman wherever she goes, you know. You nearly scared me half to death."

"You broke into a man's house and hid beneath his bed!" he said. "What if it had been him and not me?"

"It was not him!" she whispered, irritated. "It was you! And you shouldn't be here!"

"Oh, but you belong here?"

"More than you!"

"I forgot," he said, "you have a damn key! I assume this is Hawkins's bedchamber?"

"Not that it is any of your business," she replied, "but he never reclaimed the key."

"That is absolutely no reason to use it," he snapped. "Are you lying in wait for him? Planning to tempt him back to you?"

He was horrible.

Lily narrowed her gaze. "How did you guess," she responded, unable to keep the sarcasm from her voice. "This is my special brand of seduction: ill-fitting men's clothing and hiding beneath beds for men who have no qualms ruining me."

His brows rose. "I do not pretend to understand the female mind."

She snatched the candle from his hand. "Go away. You're not welcome here."

"And you are?"

"I've business to attend to. I shan't take long."

He paused, watching her for a long moment before he narrowed his gaze on her and said, "Why are you here?"

"Does it matter?"

"It does if you still love him."

The words rendered her speechless. "Love him?"

It seemed impossible to imagine now, two months later, with all that had happened. The painting. The exhibition.

Alec.

Not that Alec impacted her heart. At all.

Liar.

She cleared her throat at the thought. "Why not speak your mind, Your Grace?"

He scowled at the honorific. "Do you love him? Still?"

"No," she said, unable to keep the shock from her voice. "Of course not. He is nothing of what I thought he was. Especially not now. Especially now that I—" *Especially now that I am able to compare him to you.*

Alec remained scowling. "Then why are you here?"

She sighed, looking past him to the door to Derek's studio. "If you must know, I'm here to take matters into my own hands."

"What does that mean?"

"Only that I am tired of waiting for salvation to find me. I've had guardians and suitors and men who made more pretty promises than I can count. And I am tired of believing those promises. It's time for me to make my own promise. To myself."

He did not move. "And what promise is that?"

"The promise to save myself." She pointed to the door. "That's his studio. Two months ago, that's where he painted the portrait."

He inhaled sharply. "And?"

"And, as the subject of the painting in question, I intend to take what's mine."

There was a long silence as the words settled between them, before he nodded once. "Let's do it, then."

She shook her head. "I just told you that I don't require a savior. I shall save myself this time."

He turned toward the door to the studio. "I heard you. But I am here and this door is locked."

"I was about to look for a key when you terrified me into hiding," she snapped.

He looked back at her. "Under the bed, by the way, is a terrible place to hide. What if he'd been heading for sleep? You'd have been stuck under there all night."

She raised a brow. "You're simply jealous that you wouldn't have fit under the bed."

A smile flashed at the irritated insult, and Lily loathed the warmth that coursed through her at the knowledge that she'd made him laugh.

She didn't care about making him laugh.

He'd turned away, at any rate. With a firm tug, he tore the door from the jamb, as though the lock were made of paper and glue, and the warmth was replaced with shock as she stared at the demolished doorway. "Tell me, Your Grace, do houses in Scotland have doors?"

He did not hesitate. "Rarely."

She should not find him amusing. "Now Derek will realize we were here."

"You do not think he will notice when the painting is gone?" Alec said, as though it were that simple.

It occurred to Lily that it probably should be that simple. That she'd been willing to enter the room and take the painting, and Derek would have known when he returned that someone had done it. But for some reason, the splintered wood, the proof that it had been Alec who was here—it struck her. He'd followed her from the house, all the way here, and inside to ensure her safety, and once he'd heard her plans for the evening, he hadn't forced her to leave them. Instead, he'd offered to help. In his own way.

By removing the door that had been her final barrier to success.

Somehow, despite being an enormous, overbearing, entirely difficult man, he'd also been tremendously kind.

He set the door to the side and retrieved the candle from the bedside table, lifting it into the darkness of the studio beyond.

Which was when the candle became a glowing reminder of what he would find within.

"Wait!" Lily cried as she tore past him into the darkness, putting her back to the room, placing herself squarely between his light and the paintings beyond. "No." She extended her hand. "Give it to me."

He clearly thought she was mad. "We don't have time for this, Lillian."

She shook her head. "You're not coming in."

"Why the hell not?"

"Because I won't have you seeing it."

"Seeing what?" She cut him a look. "Oh."

"Precisely," she said. "Oh."

"I won't look," he said, advancing, pressing her back into the room.

"You're correct," she replied, forcing herself to stop moving. To stand her ground. "You won't look. Because you won't see it."

He looked to the ceiling. "Lillian. We haven't any time for this."

She beckoned to the candle. "Then give me the candle."

He relinquished the light. "There. Can you find the damn thing and let's go?"

"First, promise you won't look."

"You're being ridiculous."

"That may well be the case. But it's my reputation that requires protecting."

"I've been trying to protect you! From the start!" he argued.

"And you may finish by promising to avert your eyes from anything you see that might be scandalous."

"It's a *painting*, Lillian. It was made to be seen."

Sadness flared, along with frustration and the shame that she loathed so much. He was not wrong. How could she not have expected it to be seen? But somehow, the idea that he might see it . . . it changed everything. "I didn't intend it to be seen."

He was silent for a long time, and she wished for more light, so she could see his eyes when he said, finally, "Fine."

"Promise."

"I promise."

"The rest."

He sighed. "I promise I won't look."

"Turn your back."

"*Lillian.*"

She held her ground. "You wish to be my guardian? Guard. Watch the door."

He hesitated for the barest of moments before releasing a long breath of exasperated air and turning from her. "Just get the damn thing."

She nodded. "Excellent," she said, turning to begin her search.

There was only one problem, she realized as she lifted the candle and redirected her attention to the room she'd known so well.

It, too, was empty.

Everything was gone. The paintings that had lined the walls, the low settee where she'd posed for days, the easel Derek had furiously, painstakingly worked over as the sun flooded the room, making dust dance in the air between them. It was all gone.

She supposed she shouldn't be surprised. After all, everything that had to do with Derek Hawkins was fleeting, as though he only existed when in the presence of others.

Perhaps that was true of the painting, as well.

Perhaps it only existed when viewed by all London.

She laughed, high-pitched and panicked, and Alec turned. "What?" That's when he noticed the room. "Where is everything?"

She shook her head. "Gone."

"Gone where?"

She turned to him. "I don't know. It was here." She pointed to the wall where windows received brilliant southern light throughout the day. "The painting was right there."

He scowled. "You posed here?"

She ignored the question, instead repeating one of his earlier ones. "Where is everything?" She giggled, the sound high and unsettling and panicked. "Where did it go?"

Alec crossed to her. "Lily," he said quietly, "we'll find it. There are a finite amount of places where he could have hidden it."

"There are a hundred places," she said. "A thousand." Frustration grew, tightening in her chest. "This is not a Scottish keep, Alec. It is *London*." She paused. Looked at him. "Do you believe in fate?"

"No."

She smiled, small and sad. "I do. This was my only chance. My opportunity to save myself. Perhaps, though . . . perhaps my disgrace is fated."

"It's not."

She didn't reply, turning back to the room to whisper to the empty walls, "I wanted to find it."

For the first time in three weeks, one day, she'd had hope that her life might be hers once more. That she might survive.

She looked to him. "I begged you to let me run. To let me end it my way. And then you gave me hope and I thought this was the answer."

"It is," he said, his gaze firm and full of something akin to pride. "Clever girl. It is. We will find it. Anywhere in London. Running is not the answer. This is."

And, God save her, she almost believed him. His sure certainty, as though all he had to do was will it so and it was done.

She *almost* believed him. "I thought it would be here."

"And if it were mine, I would keep it here." The reply came without hesitation.

She looked up, meeting his eyes, whisky in the golden candlelight. "What does that mean?"

He looked away, as though he'd been caught confessing something he should not have. "Only that I would keep it close."

"If it were your best hope of a legacy, you mean."

"No," he said softly. "That's not what I mean."

She caught her breath at the words, at the way they thickened the air around them. "What then?"

He was so close, now, close enough to touch, and Lily was consumed with the keen memory of two nights prior, in the carriage. Of touching him. Of him touching her.

She shouldn't do it.

Not here. Not ever.

And still, she lifted a hand, feeling the tremors in it as she set it to his chest, feeling his heart beating strong and fast beneath the swath of tartan that crossed his shoulder. Time stopped. They both stared at that place, where her pale hand rested against the red of his plaid.

He was so strong.

So warm.

Her gaze lifted to find his gaze on hers, waiting for her. Quiet and strong and patient, as though it were his whole purpose. To wait for her. To be with her.

To be hers.

Her lips parted at the thought, and his attention flickered to the movement, the dark and silence cloaking them in each other.

She lifted her chin, offering herself to him. He dipped his head, closing the distance between them. *Yes. Please.*

She would give anything for him.

Her eyes slid shut.

"Lily," he whispered, the word a kiss of breath against her lips, filled with devastation and desire.

Yes.

And then he released her. Cleared his throat. "We should leave before he returns."

Like that, it was over, and the room spun with the speed of his departure.

She pressed her fingers to her lips, wishing she could will away the ache there—the wanting. He wanted to kiss her. She'd seen it.

Why hadn't he done it?

Was it Derek? Was it her past? Was he too reminded of what she had done here?

Of who she had become here?

Regret came, harsh and painful, and Lily stiffened, hating it. Hating all of it. Every minute that had led her to this moment, in the room where she'd laid herself bare for one man, and ached for another.

With no choice, she followed Alec back into the bedchamber, attempting to appear as unmoved by the moment as he was. "What if he's left? Absconded with it?"

Alec ripped open the doors to the massive wardrobe in the

corner, revealing a sea of clothing in silks and satins and wools and linens—every color imaginable. "I assume he is not gone."

She shook her head, drawing nearer. "Derek would never leave his clothes behind."

He looked to her. "He's a peacock, you know."

"I know," she said, reaching for a turquoise vest, brocaded in gold thread. "But peacocks can be very compelling."

A low rumble sounded from his chest, followed by a distinctly grumpy, "Compelling is not the same as worthwhile."

Her fingers stilled on the shimmering blue fabric. "Scotsmen are the latter, I suppose?" Later, she would wonder why on earth she thought the words appropriate. Where on earth the words had come from.

But in the moment, as they stood in the dark, her past and future colliding in disappointment and frustration and doom, she didn't care.

He looked at her, the silence of the house cacophonous between them. He cleared his throat, and Lily heard the nervous catch there. "More worthwhile than he is."

More compelling, as well.

She closed the wardrobe doors and turned, pressing her back to them, staring up at Alec towering above her. "Why did you leave me?"

His brow furrowed. "I'm here."

You left me here, as well.

She shook her head. "This afternoon. With Stanhope."

"You told me to leave you."

Had she? She supposed she had. But then—she shook her head. "But you didn't leave me. You saved me. And then you left me."

He was silent for a long moment, and she would have given anything to know what he was thinking. Finally, he said, "You were well. And Stanhope was there."

It was what she had expected—a quick, perfunctory answer. But it wasn't true. And she knew it. She shook her head. "But why did you leave me?"

"Because . . ." He trailed off, and silence stretched between them for an eternity before he added, "Because you deserve someone like him."

"I don't want someone like him," she said.

"Why the hell not? Stanhope is a damn prince among men."

"He's very kind," she said.

"Is that a problem?" he sputtered. "Kind, handsome, titled, and charming. The holy trinity of qualities."

She smiled. "That's four qualities."

He narrowed his gaze on her. "What is wrong with you, Lily? You could have him. He knows about the painting and doesn't mind. Indeed, he seemed only to enjoy your company."

She should want Frederick, Lord Stanhope. She should sink to her knees and thank the stars that he was willing to have her. And yet . . . she didn't.

She was too busy wanting another. Impossibly so.

Not that she could tell him that. "We've known each other for two hours. He couldn't possibly desire me."

"Any man in his right mind would desire you after two minutes."

She blinked.

He shut his mouth.

"What did you say?"

"Nothing. We must go."

"I'm a scandal."

"You're the very best kind of scandal," he grumbled as he headed for the door to the room.

At least, that's what she thought he said. "I didn't hear you."

"You're the very worst kind of scandal," he said, louder.

That wasn't what he had said. She couldn't keep her smile from her face. "What does that mean?"

"You're the kind of scandal a man wants to claim for his own."

She gaped at him. She'd never in her life heard something so romantic. And she certainly hadn't expected it to come from the mouth of this massive, moody Scot.

"That's very kind," she said.

"There's nothing kind about it," he said.

"There is, though," she said. "Derek didn't want me at all. And that was before I was a scandal."

"Hawkins was an idiot," he said, more sound than words. He was stopped now, at the closed door to the room, one hand splayed wide against the mahogany.

She was transfixed by that hand. By its ridges and valleys. By the scar that ran an inch below his first knuckle, stark white against the brown of his skin. "What happened to your hand?"

He did not move. "I met with the jagged end of a broken bottle."

"How?"

"My father was an angry drunk."

Lily winced, wanting to go to him. Instead she said, "I'm sorry."

Still he did not look at her. "Don't be. I left the day after he did this."

"I'm sorry no one was there to care for you."

The fingers flexed against the wood—the only indication that he heard her. "We should leave."

"Do you think someone will want me?" she asked that hand, knowing she shouldn't. Knowing that the question revealed far too much of what she wanted.

He pressed his forehead to the door and spoke in low, growling Gaelic before switching to English. "Yes, Lillian. I think someone will want you."

"Do—" She stopped herself.

She couldn't ask him.

No matter how much she liked the idea.

"Don't ask me," he whispered, and the sound made her ache.

He couldn't. He didn't like her. He never seemed to like her, that was. He seemed to view her as nothing but trouble.

Didn't he?

She could not bear it. "Do you? Want me?"

He did not swear in Gaelic that time. He swore in fast, wicked English.

"Don't answer," she said, immediately, at once terrified he might and desperate for him to.

He did not lift his head from its place against the door. "I'm to protect you. I'm to protect you." He said it like a litany, for himself. For God. Not for her. "I'm to protect you."

"Don't answer," she repeated, ignoring the pang of rich desire coursing through her. It was simply that in the moment, she'd wished him to. Quite desperately.

Because, if Alec wanted her, she might have a chance at the life of which she'd once dreamed. With a man far more noble than she'd ever imagined.

I'm to protect you.

And perhaps it was that she had spent so much of her life alone, but the idea of being protected, of being partnered with someone who wished for her safety as she wished for his, was the most tempting thing she'd ever experienced.

But he'd left her, after all. Ridden away, as though they were nothing to each other.

And perhaps they weren't.

She'd never been very good at understanding what she was to others. Or what they were to her, for that matter.

She nodded once, desperate to put the whole conversation behind her. "I understand. The answer is no. I should never have asked."

There was a long moment, when she thought he might reply. Thought he might turn his head, look at her.

Tell me you want me, she willed him. *Tell me this . . . us . . . it could be.*

He didn't. Instead, he let out a long, ragged breath and that hand that transfixed her balled into a fist. He pressed it against the door, his knuckles going stark white, the tendons in his arms straining. And then he spoke.

"No," he said. "You shouldn't have."

He opened the door with a force that would have ripped it from the hinge if it were locked, as the studio door had been.

And he disappeared into the darkness.

Chapter 15

DILUTED DUKE DESERTS WOEFUL WARD

He deserved a medal.

For saying no. For not turning to her, taking her, making love to her until his hands stopped shaking with need. For not ruining her, thoroughly, there in the darkness, on the floor of Derek Hawkins's bare bedroom.

Do you want me?

He wanted her like the Highlands wanted mist.

But he would be damned if he was going to take what he wanted and destroy the possibility of her getting what she deserved. A life with a man who was worthy of her. He'd thought it before he'd discovered her plans to steal the painting back, but once he'd committed to helping her, to finding the portrait and destroying it before it could be brought to light, his conviction was redoubled.

He would find the thing.

And he would protect her, dammit.

I'm to protect you.

How had he gathered the strength to leave her, not to turn to her. He'd heard it in her breath—the truth—the fact that she would give in to him. That she wished to. That she wanted him again. That she wanted more.

More. He'd thought he'd known what wanting felt like. What longing meant. And then he'd met Lillian Hargrove, and he'd realized the truth—that everything for which he'd ever hungered was nothing compared to her. There was nothing he would not pay. Nothing he would not do for another taste of her.

And that he was unworthy of her.

And as she'd stood in that empty house, in that empty room, where she'd once been nude for another man, he'd been willing to pay. To do. And he'd resisted.

To protect her. To give her a chance at the life she desired.

Because now, she had a chance for more than a marriage of convenience. Now, if they could find the painting, if they could steal it, she might still be ruined in the eyes of London, but she could avoid ruination in the eyes of the world.

Clever girl.

He should have thought of it himself. Would have, if he wasn't so blinded by her beauty. By her strength. By everything about her. But he'd been too busy protecting her. From London. From her future. From her past.

From himself.

Yes. He deserved a damn medal.

When they'd left, it had begun to rain in earnest, and he'd continued to do the best thing for her, stuffing her into a hack and climbing onto the block next to the driver, for her own safety.

Or for his.

He wasn't certain what he would do if he ended up inside the carriage with her, next to her. Sharing her space. Breathing her air. Smelling her, somehow like heather and Highlands.

The rain stung his face as the carriage careened around corners, returning her to the safety of Grosvenor Square, where they would lie in their beds, separated by walls adorned with dogs, and he would pretend to sleep, aching to go to her. To strip her bare and worship her with his hands and lips and tongue—

The thought had him growling in the cold May rain, recalling her taste. Recalling the peaks and valleys of her body and imagining how her most secret places would feel against his tongue.

"Problem, m'lord?"

Of course there was a problem.

He wanted Lily with a raging intensity. And she was not his to want.

"Stop the carriage up here," he said, digging deep in his pocket to pay the driver. "Where are we?"

"Hanover Square."

"I shall walk from here."

"Sir. It rains."

As though he hadn't noticed. "Take your passenger to Grosvenor Square."

His fingers brushed a piece of ecru in his coat pocket, and he extracted it, along with his purse. Looked down at it in the light bouncing about from the hack lantern. *Countess Rowley.* Peg's calling card. His unknown valet must have transferred it from his shredded coat to this one.

He paid the driver his exorbitant sum, received his obsequious accolades, and climbed down from the carriage as the door opened from the inside.

Don't let me see you, he willed her. He didn't know that he would be able to resist her again. And, at the same time, *Let me see you.*

"Alec?" His name on her lips a gift in the rain.

"Close the door," he said, refusing to look. Not trusting himself to see.

A pause. Then, "It is raining. You should ride inside."

Near her. Touching her. He could not help the huff of frustration that came at the words. He should not ride inside. He should not be near her. He had a single task. To protect her. And he was the most dangerous thing in her world right now.

"The hack will return you home."

"What of you? Who shall return you home?" The soft question threatened to slay him. The idea of a home they shared. The impossibility of it.

"I shall walk."

"Alec—" she began, stopping herself. "Please."

At the word—the one she had whispered so much while in his arms, the one that promised so much and asked for so much more than he was able to give—his hands began to shake again, just as they had in Hawkins's house. He clenched them, willing away his desire.

Would he ever not want her?

"Close the door, Lily." She had no choice but to follow the order when he looked up to the driver. "Drive on."

The carriage was instantly in motion.

He rubbed a hand over his face, loathing London. Wishing he were anywhere but here.

England will be your ruin.

Removing his hand, he looked down at the card. At the direction beneath the name. *Hanover Square.*

Come and see me, Peg had whispered when she'd slipped the card into his coat pocket.

Earlier, Lily had asked him if he believed in fate, and he'd answered truthfully. Fate did not put him here, in Hanover Square, with Peg's calling card. A too-skilled valet and a too-frustrating ward had done it. And, as he watched the carriage disappear into the darkness, the sound of horses' hooves and clattering wheels masked by the rain, it was not fate that sent him to the door of number 12 Hanover Square.

Come and see me.

It was his own shame.

He waited for no time before a maid arrived in the foyer to escort him into the depths of the house, up a back stairway and to a room that he identified before the door even opened.

Peg's bedchamber.

And she, within, standing by the fireplace, blond hair glittering gold in the light—as gold as the silk nightgown she wore, low and clinging to the curves he had worshipped a lifetime ago, thinking they would be the first and last he would ever worship, thinking she would wish him to worship them forever.

"I knew you would come," she whispered, low and secret, as though the maid weren't there. And then the girl wasn't there, disappeared into the hallway and closing the door behind her with a soft snick.

"I did not," he said.

She smiled, that knowing smile from two decades earlier—the one that made promises she would never keep. "You underestimated my irresistibility. And you wore your kilt, you glorious thing." She moved to the bed, lying back against the pillows, arranging herself in a way so casual that it could only have been practiced.

And it was. He had, after all, seen her in just such a position before. In a different place, in a different world, when he'd been young and green and desperate for her beauty. For her perfection.

And it had ended differently than tonight would.

Because then, he had been even more desperate for what she represented. For a future he would never have. For acceptance by her world. For England.

Now, he wanted none of those things. Now, all he wanted was Lily.

And he was here to remind himself that she was not for him. That every time he touched her, he soiled her with his past. And his shame.

"I am not here for you," he said coolly.

A sleek blond brow arched. "Are you sure?"

"Thoroughly."

She sighed and leaned back, unmoved by the pronouncement. "You waste my time then, darling. Why *are* you here?"

Why indeed? What did he want from this moment? When had Peg ever given him what he wanted?

She did not wait for him to arrive at his answer, instead saying, "If you are not here to play, then you should return home to your little scandal."

He snapped his attention to her. "What does that mean?"

"Only that you made it quite clear at Eversley's ball that you were willing to do anything for the girl. Even make a scene. And I know you learned your lesson about scene making years ago." She paused, then said, "I confess, had I known that Alec Stuart—without family or funds—was to be a duke with a king's fortune, I might have reconsidered your very sweet offer."

They all would have. And he would have had a different life. One that had not included a long line of women who thought him worthy of play but not pride.

Peg smiled, cold and ugly. It occurred to him that she might imagine herself beautiful—that he had once imagined her so. Now, however, he knew what beauty could be. How it might come, with strength and pride and purpose and eyes the color of the Scottish sea.

She spoke again. "Would it help to hear that yours was my prettiest proposal? I still recall it. *I shall do right by you. We shall spend the rest of our days happy.*" She tutted. "Young and green and utterly unknowing of women and the world."

For a heartbeat, he was fifteen again, an idiot boy. "I learned my lessons of women years ago." There were those whom he deserved and those he did not. And of course, the one he wanted more than anything fell into the latter category.

Peg underscored the thought. "And we ladies learned our lessons about you, did we not?"

This was it. The reason he'd come. The reminder of his station. Of the life he could never have. And still, he resisted it. "You know nothing about me."

One side of Peg's mouth raised in a wry, knowing smile. "I know more than she does, I'd wager." A pause. "Or has she already ridden the Scottish Brute?"

He narrowed his gaze before he could stop himself, unable to deny the shame and fury coursing through him. Unable to hide the truth from Peg.

Peg's lips formed a perfect pout. "Oh, darling, still as sweet as ever. You care for the girl."

"No," he said.

Liar.

The tut again, followed by movement as she came off the bed, toward him, the gold silk slithering against her like skin. "You forget, Alec Stuart, I was the first woman you loved."

"I never loved you," he said, refusing to move as she came close, refusing to flinch as she reached up and put her cool hand to his face, erasing the lingering memory of Lily's.

He supposed he deserved it.

"That's not what you said then," she said quietly. "Sweet-faced Scottish Alec, big as a house, like nothing I'd ever seen. Like nothing I'd ever *felt*." She pressed herself to him and he resisted the urge to push her away, wanting the lesson. Wanting the reminder of who he'd been. Of what he'd been. She lowered her voice to a whisper, her hand reaching to the hem of his kilt, fingertips grazing his thigh, making him cringe. "Let the girl have it, darling. Let her feel it. You shan't be her first, but neither will she be yours. Think on it. You are well-suited."

He wanted to roar his fury at the way she said it, as though he were anything close to Lily. And then Peg added, "And when she's had enough of you, come back to me. I would dearly love another go."

"Never."

She pressed close. "Not even if I remind you of my tremendous performance?"

"Odd that you describe it as such, as I find I lack interest in an encore."

Peg's hand flew, sharp and angry, the crack sounding an alarm in the quiet room. He did lift his hand to ease the sting of the blow, instead reveling in the sensation. In the message of it. In the reminder it delivered.

"Do not get above yourself, Alec Stuart. You may be the

Diluted Duke now," she said, "but there was a time when you existed because of my benevolence. You would not like it if the world knew the truth."

"I don't give a horse's ass if this world knows the truth," he said. "Remember, Lady Rowley—my secrets belong to you as well. Be sure to tell your friends. No lady likes her underthings aired."

She scowled. "You *are* an underthing."

He had her. "At some point, our past had to be a boon, no?"

There was a long silence, and then she said, "My secrets or not, you would not like it if your Lovely Lily knew the truth about you. I would watch my tongue if I were you."

Peg was wrong. He would be grateful for Lily to know the truth. It would make wanting her easier, because it would make having her impossible.

Nevertheless, he should not have come. Outside the house, he had wondered why he was calling on Peg, why he allowed her calling card to summon him. Now, he knew the truth.

He wanted her. The reminder she served.

The proof that Lily's perfection was not for him.

He left the house resolved to two things: first, Lily would have happiness in the hands of the best man they could find; and second, that man would never be him.

DESPITE HAVING STARED into the ribbon case inside Madame Hebert's modiste shop on Bond Street for the last quarter of an hour, Lily could not have named a single color inside. She was too consumed with the admonition that had repeated itself again and again for the nearly three days since she had last seen Alec.

She should not have asked him if he wanted her.

She should not have betrayed the insidious thought that had taken root in her mind, the product of protective actions and provocative kisses and a thread of hope that she should have known better than to allow access to her thoughts. To her heart.

And still, like a simpering imbecile, she had asked him.

Do you want me?

Her cheeks flamed at the memory. How could she have possibly imagined it would result in anything but embarrassment? She had seen him struggle with the answer, as though he hadn't wanted to hurt her. To tell her the truth.

Despite that, he'd told her. Because he was nobler than other men. Better and nobler. *He'd said no.* Better and nobler and not for her. Not even as she wanted him quite desperately.

And then, as if telling her the truth had not been enough, he'd disappeared.

She'd waited for his return three nights earlier, ultimately falling asleep in the receiving room at Dog House, not wishing to miss him. He had not returned. Nor had he returned the day after. Nor the day after that.

He'd even taken the dogs which she had to believe meant he had no intention of returning, no matter how much she wished for it.

And so, this morning, Lily had taken matters into her own hands, and called in reinforcements.

"Aren't you happy that we decided to take on the mantle of chaperone?" She looked up from the ribbon case to find Lady Sesily Talbot on the opposite side, grinning widely. "We're near to fairy godmothers with all of our hard work and dedication."

In the corner, Seleste and Seline lingered over a collection of hairpins and accessories that some would call de rigueur and others would call de trop. They giggled at something in the pile, and Lily wondered what it must be like to have such little about which to worry. They were married—or nearly so—to men who were rumored to adore them. And so they lived without hesitation. Without loneliness. Always part of an *us.*

Lily felt a keen spear of jealousy as she watched them, imagining how her life might have been different, if only. If only her father hadn't died. The duke followed suit and the others, like little toy soldiers, all in a row. Perhaps she would not have been alone on Michaelmas. Perhaps she never would have met Derek. Never sat for the painting.

Never met Alec.

She inhaled sharply at the thought, rejecting it instantly. She would not trade meeting Alec. Not even if she had driven him away. Not even if she never saw him again.

"Dear Lily," Sesily said, breaking into her thoughts, more than welcome to do so. "Would you like to tell us why we are here?"

> *I have found it.*
> *We attend Hawkins's performance tomorrow.*
> *With Stanhope.*
> *You require a gown. No dogs.*

The missive had arrived along with directions to a modiste shop on Bond Street that morning, unsigned. It had not required signing. And still she wished for it, some kind of personal acknowledgment. What would he have chosen? Alec? His initials? His title?

Not the last, certainly.

Ugh. She was disgusting herself. He'd invited another man to join them. If that weren't enough to prove her simpering was cabbageheaded, she did not know what was. She looked to Sesily, trying for brightness. "I require a gown."

Sesily raised a brow. "And the bit where you look as though you are a lad missing his favorite pup?"

She shook her head. "I don't know what you mean."

"Because we are friends, I shall be patient and wait for you to tell me."

Friends. The unexpected word, one that Sesily used so quickly, as though friendship were natural and honest for her. As though it could be for Lily.

The ache in Lily's chest grew more insistent.

"My ladies." Madame Hebert, widely believed to be the best dressmaker in all of London—the scandal sheets claimed that she was rescued from Josephine's court at the height of the wars—stepped through a nearby set of curtains. "It is a pleasure to see my favorite sisters again—" She looked to Lily. "*Non!* Not only sisters! Three and a new face." She drew closer, setting a hand to Lily's jaw, turning it left, then right. "You might be the most beautiful woman I've ever had in my shop."

It was not a compliment, but instead stated as fact. Lily blinked. "Thank you?"

"This is Lillian Hargrove," Sesily interjected. "Ward to the Duke of Warnick."

One perfect black brow rose, the only indication that the modiste heard the words.

"Or simply Lily," Lily replied.

The dressmaker nodded. "You are here for Warnick."

If wishing made it so. She pushed the thought aside. "No."

"For another," Seleste interjected with glee. "Earl Stanhope."

Except she wasn't. Not really.

Madame Hebert did not look away from Lily. "I heard you wore a dog dress to the Eversley ball."

"You did?"

The Frenchwoman narrowed her gaze. "It is true?"

"I was trying to prove a point," Lily said, suddenly even more embarrassed than she was the night of the ball.

"To Stanhope?"

She straightened her shoulders. "To Warnick."

There was a long moment while the dressmaker considered the words. And then, "*Oui.* I shall dress you."

"Oh, excellent!" The trio of sisters clapped their hands excitedly. "She's obviously going to need *everything.*"

"Not everything," Lily corrected, "Only a dress for—"

Madame Hebert was already moving, pushing through the curtains as though Lily would simply follow. And she did, the Talbot sisters nearly carrying her along. "She does not dress just anyone," Seline whispered. "She's very particular."

"You'd think if she were particular, she'd avoid the scandal,"

Lily whispered back. "Do you think she knows about me?" They entered the workspace and fitting rooms of the dress shop, revealing several seamstresses sewing beneath windows along the far wall, along with a woman poised on a raised platform, back to the door, young woman at her feet, pinning the hem of a lush amethyst silk.

"I never avoid the scandal," Hebert replied, as though she'd been a part of the conversation all along. "It's scandals who are seen. And I like my clothing to be seen." She turned to face Lily, indicating a platform nearby. "I would have avoided you before you were a scandal, Lovely Lily. When you were Lonely Lily."

"I do adore Hebert." Sesily sank onto a nearby chaise and repeated herself to the older woman. "She's going to need *everything*."

The dressmaker tilted her head, considering Lily for a long moment before she said, "*Oui*."

"*Non*," Lily said. "I only need a dress for the theater."

"Valerie," Hebert was already turning away, summoning a younger woman nearby. "Bring me the blues." Turning back, she said, "I've a handful of dresses that shall work for you, and require minimal adjustments before tomorrow night. But as I told your duke, the rest of the trousseau will have to come in time."

"He's not my—" she began the denial before the Frenchwoman's entire sentence settled. "Trousseau?"

"One of my very favorite words." Seline sighed from her place next to her sisters on the settee nearby. "The best part of marriage."

"Well, the second best part," Seleste said dryly, sending her sisters into giggles.

"Lily will learn about that bit," Seline replied. "And with Stanhope—what a treat."

"He is terribly handsome," Seleste agreed.

Sesily, however, remained quiet, watching Lily carefully, through eyes that seemed far too knowing.

"The Earl of Stanhope is not going to marry me," Lily said, turning away to the modiste, who was busy sifting through Valerie's armful of gowns, finally extracting a stunning cerulean gown. When she held it up for viewing, Lily nearly gasped at the rich color. "It is beautiful," she said, unable to stop herself from reaching for it.

Madame Hebert nodded. "*Oui*. And you shall be beautiful in it." She thrust it into Lily's hands and pointed to a dressing room. Lily did as she was told and returned within minutes, the gown a shockingly near-perfect fit for her.

"Oh, my," Seleste sighed.

"That is it," from Seline.

Sesily smiled broadly. "He shan't know what's hit him."

For a fleeting moment, the words summoned a vision of Alec, eyes narrowed to slits, hands reaching for her, just as he had in the carriage on the way home from the Eversley ball. What would she do to capture his attention again? To summon his touch? His kiss?

She'd wear this dress every day for the rest of time.

And then she remembered it was not for Alec. It was for another man. One she must catch. In three days' time.

The dressmaker pointed to the unattended platform, her staff swarming like beetles, immediately fussing about her, barking orders in French, pinning with wicked speed, as though she had been born with a pincushion attached to one wrist. Lily did not speak French well enough to know what was being discussed, and so she did her best to remain still as they moved about, letting only her eyes move, from the Talbot sisters on the nearby settee to the others in the shop, seamstresses, a woman in the corner who appeared to be calculating the accounts, and the other customer who had apparently completed her fitting and was, in that moment, exiting a dressing room.

Lily's gaze widened.

Countess Rowley's gaze trailed the blue gown to the floor, taking in the cut, the fall of the fabric, the hemline, before rising again to meet Lily's eyes, a knowing, unsettling glint in her own. And when she spoke, it was with all the calm of a queen. "He shall adore that."

The room quieted in the wake of the pronouncement, the only movement the subtle straightening of the trio on the chaise.

Lily did not speak. Too afraid to do so.

The countess did not feel similarly. "He always liked blue."

She would not rise to the bait.

"Thank you," she said, deliberately returning the countess's appraisal. "I rather like blue myself."

One blond brow arched. "You know he came to see me three evenings ago."

"Who does she—" Seleste began.

"Has she been with—" Seline chimed in.

Sesily raised a hand, stopping them from speaking even as she rose to her feet, as though she might save Lily from this moment.

As though anyone could save Lily from this moment.

Three evenings ago, she'd asked Alec if he wanted her. Three evenings ago, he'd said no.

"I don't believe you," she said.

It was a lie. She did believe it. Three evenings ago, he'd gone to this woman, this cool, unmoving, *unmoved* woman. The opposite of Lily. Thoroughly aristocratic and filled with London perfection. And his past.

And Lily had returned home, and waited for him.

And he had not come.

The countess saw the lie for what it was. She smiled and approached, looking every inch as though she was made for this place, this moment. Looking like the kind of woman any man would want. Beyond scandal.

Beyond shame.

Jealousy shot through Lily as the countess neared, a small, knowing smile on her lips. "He came to me, because he wanted the reminder that you are not for him."

The words stung like a blow, hard and wicked.

Lily refused to show it.

She straightened, willing herself strong. "If he came to you, *Peg*, then I assure you, I am not for him."

"Good girl," she thought she heard one of the Talbot sisters say.

Surprise warred with anger on the countess's face, there, then gone, disappeared by that cool mask. "Poor Lovely Lily. Don't you see? Alec is not built for a lifetime, but instead best used for one night."

Even without full understanding, the words whipped their punishment, and Lily did all she could do, turning to the modiste. "Are you through, Madame?"

"Not quite," the Frenchwoman said from her place at the hem of the gown. "But the countess is." Lady Rowley was not given an opportunity to respond before the dressmaker was snapping her fingers and a collection of young women arrived to move her into the front room.

Seline and Seleste released twin breaths from the settee as Sesily rushed forward. "That woman is a termagant." She drew close. "You handled her beautifully. I was particularly impressed by the use of her given name."

The name Alec used with her.

The name he'd used with her for God knew how long.

He had gone to her. And he'd left Lily.

"I . . ." She trailed off, unable to find words. She looked down at her hands to discover them shaking. She looked up to Sesily. "I don't know what to do."

Sesily met her gaze and took her hands, holding them tightly, keeping them still. "You remain strong. And you never, ever let her see you tremble."

"Agreed," Seleste joined them, along with Seline. "Nor him."

Lily shook her head. "I don't know to whom you refer."

Sesily smiled at the proper words. "Of course not. But if you did . . ." She paused. ". . . know to whom we refer, that is . . . if you did . . . I assume you'd choose him over the other?"

Tears threatened, and Lily looked to the ceiling, willing them away. Willing herself away from here. As Madame Hebert stood from her place at Lily's feet, crossing the room to a cabinet full of fabric, Lily reminded herself that Alec was not an option. He was never an option. And two nights past, he had made it more than clear.

She looked to her friend. "He does not want me."

"Bollocks," Sesily said.

Lily shook her head. "It is true. He left me alone in the house. I have not seen him in three days. Apparently he left me to seek comfort in the arms of . . ." She trailed off, and waved an arm in the direction of the front room of the shop. After a long moment, she added, soft and sad, "Yes. Yes of course, I choose him."

It was the first time she'd admitted it aloud, and the words were terrifying and heartbreaking all at once. She wanted him. More than she'd ever wanted anything. "But he doesn't want me."

"Oh, Lily," Sesily said, climbing up onto the platform and wrapping her in an embrace. Lily had always heard that friends' embraces made one feel better, but this did not. This made her feel worse. It made her want to give herself up to the other woman, to cry and wail and leave all her sadness, all her hopelessness, at Sesily's feet.

But somehow, in that wanting, she discovered the truth.

That it also made her feel like she was not alone.

"We've another sister, did you know that?" Sesily said, and it took Lily a moment to catch up to the change in topic. "Seraphina."

Lily nodded. "Duchess of Haven." The fifth of the Soiled S's, accused of trapping a duke into marriage, disappeared from London months earlier.

A shadow crossed Sesily's face. "Sera couldn't win her duke. Not in the end."

Sometimes, love was impossible. Lily understood that.

Except it did not seem that she understood the Talbot sisters, who looked to her with new resolve. "But *your* duke. You shall get him. We shall help."

It wasn't possible of course, but it was a wonderful fantasy.

Lily removed herself from the embrace, dashing away tears to discover Seleste and Seline had joined them. That she was not alone. That she was not one, but four.

Five.

For behind the Talbot sisters stood the French modiste, London's most revered dressmaker, holding a length of fabric and watching her with a keen, knowing eye. "If you choose him," she extended her arms, revealing the fabric. "You find him. And you wear this."

Lily's eyes went wide as she took the offering, the movement punctuated by little excited gasps from her friends. Holding the fabric in her hands, she admitted it again, her single, undeniable truth. "I want him."

"Then he is yours," Sesily replied, her words dry and full of knowledge. "Truthfully, if that does not win him, the man cannot be won."

Chapter 16

TARTAN: TEMPTING TEXTILE? OR TERRIBLE TREND?

Alec didn't think it possible, but the Kensington town house once owned by the aging Number Nine and his wife was even worse than the dog house.

Evidently, Lady Nine had been a collector. Of everything.

In the three days he had been living in the deserted town house off Regent Street—Settlesworth had mentioned something about a boating accident in the North Country that took Duke and Duchess Nine tragically together—Alec had been overwhelmed by tables full of miniature animals, shelves laden with porcelain statues, and glass-doored cabinets chock full of tea sets. It occurred to him that when this particular house had been downsized to a skeleton staff, several maids had likely been kept on for the purpose of dusting the mad collection of useless items.

It also occurred to him, as he entered the house in the dead of night, greeted by Angus, the dog's wild tail wagging, barely missing a low-lying table filled with little china bells, that he should have selected a different house. This was not a place for beasts—of the four- or two-legged variety.

He crouched to give the dog a proper greeting, "Good evening, friend." Angus leaned in for a scratch, sighing his pleasure at Alec's touch. "We've each other, at least." He looked up, surveying the foyer. "Where is Hardy?"

He was not entirely surprised that the second dog was missing—Hardy had spent the last three days sighing and wandering the house aimlessly, as though he longed for his lost love.

As though she had not imprinted herself on every part of him in the week he'd known her, she'd also ruined his dogs.

It had been the most difficult thing he'd ever done, returning to the Dog House that night, resigned to find a new home, where he would not threaten her future. From which he could guard her from a distance.

She'd been asleep in the receiving room when he entered, the dogs at the hearth nearby.

If not for the lingering scent of Peg's perfume on his plaid, he might not have been able to leave her. But he had. And now he had a miserable dog to show for it.

With a sigh of his own, he stood, making his way up the central staircase to the bedroom that had been prepared for him, Angus trailing him in the darkness. Hardy would survive. He would resume his ordinary life, and return to his ordinary character when they returned to Scotland.

Alec could only hope he would do the same.

Time grew short and Scotland loomed like a promise. A place where he would have no memory of Lily. Of her beauty. Of her smile. Of her strength. Of all the ways he wished to—

Love her.

He shook his head at the thought, insidious and unwavering. He did not love her. He would not love her.

He could not love her.

He simply had to stay away from her for three days.

Three days.

Three days to find the painting, to destroy it. To give Lily the life she deserved. He would return her life to her. And she would choose one of her infinite futures, and live her life, strong and beautiful and brilliant beyond measure.

Without him.

He'd spent the day with West and King, devising the most likely location for the painting prior to the exhibition. Planning his movements for the following evening, when Hawkins would take the stage for all of Society, and Alec would search the rear rooms of the theater.

And while he did it, while he protected her, Lily would remain in a box high above the stage, and fall in love with Stanhope.

He gritted his teeth at the thought.

It was what was best for her. It was the way she would survive everything—the gossip, the rumors, the truth. The earl was obviously keen on her, and willing to overlook her past. The money helped, no doubt. But he seemed a decent fellow.

One Lily deserved. One who might one day be worthy of her love.

Unlike Alec.

He exhaled harshly, turning down the hallway to what was kindly referred to as the master's suite, ignoring the long shelves of figurines and collected useless rubbish, aching for sleep. For a night unconsumed by fits of self-loathing and the nearly unbearable desire to rise and go to Lily. And fall into her arms and make love to her until the past had fallen away and the present was all there was.

And she was all there was.

He shook his head, reaching for the handle to his rooms, desperate to put her away from his thoughts even as he knew he would not be able to. Even as he knew he would enter the room and strip himself bare and take to the bed, hard with the memories of her hands and mouth and mind.

He pressed his forehead to the great mahogany door, shame and desire flooding him, making him desperate to turn around and head for Grosvenor Square, and take her. Make her his. Revel in her, and damn the consequences.

He willed his breath calm, his hands still.

Three days. He could stay away from her for three days.

He opened the door, already dreading the room's cluttered decor and the small, spindly-legged bed with its flimsy canopy. Inside, candlelight spilled across the floor, warm and golden. Hardy lifted his head from his spot at the foot of the bed, tail thumping on the heavy coverlet.

But Alec wasn't looking at the dog.

He was looking at Lily, fast asleep at the center of the bed, in a pool of golden candlelight.

Wearing nothing but his plaid.

A better man would leave her. Close the door and find another bed. Another house. Another country.

A better man would have the strength to protect her from himself, the greatest danger she would ever face. The man who would claim her, keep her . . . despite being desperately, wholly unworthy of her.

He was not a better man.

His hand tightened on the door handle. He had tried to be. He had wanted to be. But now, here, bearing witness to her utter perfection, he no longer had the strength for it.

He ached for her. He wanted her. He wished for her.

It had only ever been her.

And in that moment, everything he was, everything he would ever be, was hers. And tonight, perhaps, he could fool himself into believing that she was his.

He looked to Hardy, pointed to the hallway. "Out."

The dog followed the order instantly.

Alec closed the door, already heading for her. He stopped at the bedside, looking down at her as she slept, her hair a pool of auburn fire against the crisp linen. The bed was not too small. It was the perfect size for her—a fairy queen in her bower. She moved, one bare shoulder peeking out from the red tartan—pink and perfect and calling to him. He could not help himself. He groaned.

She opened her eyes at the sound, immediately finding his, as though the universe had connected them with a string. She did not start at his presence, as one might expect, finding a man of his size at one's bedside. Instead, she smiled, soft and full of sleep, and Alec warmed with wicked pleasure. "You are home."

She waited for him.

"How did you find me?"

The smile widened. "You are not the only one with access to Settlesworth, Your Grace." She looked to the table several feet away, hosting a porcelain animal tea party. "I would not have thought this would be quite your aesthetic, though."

He might have laughed if he did not want her so much. If he were not so broken by her presence. "Why are you here, Lily?"

She blinked, and he loathed himself for the doubt that flashed in her gaze. "I—" She stopped. Took a deep breath. Met his gaze with renewed certainty. "I came for you."

His knees weakened, but he resisted the urge to go to her. To touch her. To give in to his desire. Somehow. Instead, he said, "My mother was English."

A pause. Then, "As was mine."

He ignored the reply, edged with humor, her eyes glittering and making him want her more than ever before as she threatened to laugh. As she tempted him more than he'd ever dreamed possible. "She was beautiful. My father was wild over her. Allegedly."

"Allegedly?"

"By the time I arrived, neither cared for the other. They lived in Scotland—in the Highlands—and he worked the family distillery. She thought he was wealthy and landed, and he was, but the business—the estate that came with it—it was not run by another. It was run by Stuarts, had been for generations. He was a man who harvested wheat and sheared sheep and tarred roofs and mucked stalls. And she loathed it."

She sat up as he spoke, the Stuart plaid wrapped about her, auburn hair down around her shoulders, and he resisted the urge to drink her in. Focused on the tale—once cautionary, now prophetic. "She was not made for Scotland, my father would say. She was too perfect. Slender like a reed, but unbendable. She could not bear the cold, the wet, the wild. We moved south, to the border, to another estate owned by the family. And my father thought the proximity to England would change her. Would return the girl he'd once loved."

"That is not how it works." She clutched the plaid to her breast, the fabric tempting him with little glimpses of shadow.

"You told me once that love is a powerful promise." And it was. "My father learned that firsthand. As did I."

Her eyes widened and he loathed the sadness there. "What happened?"

"She left us."

Lily's lips opened in a little, silent inhale. "When?"

He wanted to touch her more than he wanted to breathe, but this story, this prophetic tale, required telling. "When I consider it, she left our hearts long before she left us in truth. I cannot remember a time when she was happy."

She did not look away from him. "Not even with you?"

"Especially not with me. I was all Scots. Too big. Too coarse. I would come in from the fields and she would shake her head in disappointment and say, to herself as much as to me, *Nothing about you fits.*"

Her brows were stitched together. "What does that mean? Fits where?"

"Here," he whispered, the word harsh with memory. "The afternoon at the park. When you told me that you hadn't received a birthday gift since you were a child?" She tilted her head in silent question. "I think you had the best of the possible scenarios. I doubt my mother ever even knew it was my birthday."

What a ridiculous thing to remember. He was a grown man, four and thirty, and thinking on his childhood birthdays as though they mattered. He cleared his throat. Tried for calm. "She ran, eventually. She'd been sick for months—consumption—and she was convinced that it was Scotland that was doing it. Killing her." He looked away. "I often wonder if she thought it was me."

"She didn't," Lily said, and he could not help himself from

looking at her. From meeting her grey eyes and drinking in the certainty in them. "It was not you."

And for a fleeting moment, he wondered what might have become of him if he'd had Lily then, when his whole world had crashed down around him.

She might have saved him. Might have loved him.

Might have borne him a line of beautiful little girls, red-haired and perfect, who would have worn the little clothes she'd sewn and mended his heart.

Instead . . . "She died not two weeks after she returned to England."

Lily gasped his name and reached for him, but he stepped out of her reach, not trusting himself in the wake of her touch. "You did not kill her."

"I know," he said. "But neither did I save her."

She shook her head. "You cannot save us all."

"The moment I was old enough, I fled as well. For England. For school. My father—" He stopped.

"What of him?" she asked, her gaze falling to his hand, where the scar reminded him of his father every day.

And then she was watching him. More beautiful than a woman should be. "When I was in school, they made us learn the myths." Her brow furrowed in beautiful confusion, but he did not give her time to reply. "We were required to translate them from the Greek, and every boy in the course loathed the project. King did all he could to get out of it. He paid me to do the work for him on more than one occasion."

She smiled, turning on her side, sending the plaid sliding against her, a whisper of wool on skin. "You did not attempt to escape your studies?"

"I did not have the luxury of it."

She nodded. "Not yet a duke."

The Scottish Brute.

He shook his head, watching as the fabric clung to the swell of her hip, to the curve of her breast. "Do you know about Selene?"

She smiled, small and sweet. "She was goddess of the moon."

He nodded. "She was also sister to the sun and the dawn, the daughter of Titans and a beauty beyond words. She was the scandalous child—the one who was changeable and unsettling. She could move the tides and light the heavens and provide cover for the nefarious deeds of the world if she wished. The sun came every day, as did the dusk, but the moon, it was like joy. Purposeful and inconstant. She was queen of the night."

Lily watched him with rapt attention, and his fingers itched to touch her, but still he kept himself from her.

"One night, as she moved across the sky, her light touched on a sleeping shepherd."

"Endymion," Lily said, the name a rapt whisper.

He nodded. "He was the most beautiful thing she had ever seen—peaceful and good, and everything she'd ever wanted. Selene fell immediately in love, despite keen awareness of the impossibility of their match. She could not be with him, not every day. Not all day. Her time with him was limited. Ephemeral."

She sat up then, clutching the fabric to her, covering all the beautiful, secret parts of her—all the parts he would give everything to see. "Alec—" she said, as though if she could stop the myth, she might be able to stop the course of their tale.

"He woke as she stood over him and, witnessing her unbearable beauty, fell instantly in love as well. But he could not bear to be without her, not even for a day. Not even for a moment. Not even for a breath. And so he begged the gods to grant him eternal sleep, so that he might never know what it was to live without her." Alec lifted one hand, finally, lifting a long auburn curl from the place it draped over her shoulder, watching it slide through his fingers, tempting him with silken promise, making him want to bind his wrists in the stunning stuff and remain her prisoner forever.

"He would take even the smallest part of her if it meant having any of her at all," he said.

Her lips parted on a little intake of breath, and Alec ached to kiss her. "What happened?"

"Zeus gave him his wish. Endymion slept forever, ageless and deathless. And she came to him at night and watched over him with her beauty."

"No," she said, her grey eyes suddenly glistening. "They were never together?"

Alec's hand moved to her cheek, his thumb capturing the single tear that escaped before it could mar her perfect skin. "They were together for eternity," he answered, the words coming low and thick with longing. "He dreamed forever . . . always of holding the moon in his arms."

Silence stretched between them, their gazes tangled, Alec willing himself to learn the lesson he was trying to give her. That love was not always happiness. That it was too often sorrow.

And then she lifted her hand to his, holding his palm to her cheek. "I don't wish to hold the moon in my arms, Alec," she whispered, grey eyes unwavering. "I wish to hold you."

She dropped the plaid and it pooled at her hips, baring her to him, all perfection in the golden candlelight. Alec followed the fabric, sinking to his knees at the side of the bed, desire rendering him unable to stand. He bowed his head and whispered her name, a sacrifice at her temple.

She touched him gloriously, her fingers sliding into his hair. "Alec," she whispered, "Please. Please choose me."

As though he could choose anything else.

He lifted his head, reaching for her, taking her in hand, holding her steady. "Be certain, Lily," he whispered. "Be certain you want me. I am coarse and unrefined and I shall never be worthy of you. But I lack the strength to deny your will."

Her eyes went wide for a moment before she spoke, the words hot and clear as the sun, "I am not a child. I know my mind. I know the consequences to my thoughts. To my actions. I know myself. I know what is to come. I wish it, Alec." If the words had not broken him, the movement would have—the way she leaned toward him, her lips a breath away from his.

"*I will it.*"

And he was hers. For one night. For eternity.

Chapter 17

DILUTED DUKE DAMNED BY DESIRE!

He kissed her like she was air.

Like she was all he'd ever wanted. Like she was temptation and sin and he could not stop himself.

And she reveled in it, running her hands through his hair, then down his shoulders and over his massive arms, aching for him to be closer. To be on the bed with her. She pulled back to tell him that, to beg him nearer, only to find him already watching her, brown eyes turned nearly black, lips stung with the kiss she had happily returned.

"Alec," she whispered.

"Anything," he said. "I am yours."

Mine.

How long had she wanted this? How long had she ached for it? How many nights had she lain awake wishing that someone like this—strong and kind and heroic beyond measure—would find her? Would claim her?

Would love her?

She closed her eyes at the thought, knowing she asked for too much. He might not love her. But tonight, for as long as he was here, with her, she could love him. And it might be enough. "Mine?" she whispered.

He watched her carefully, his gaze lingering over her face, as though he was trying to memorize her, and she did the same, taking in his strong, unbearable beauty and wishing his words true. Forever. "Yours," he whispered.

He made the word sound filthy. And she wanted it all the more.

She shook her head. "But it is I who is wrapped in your colors."

His gaze slid down, over her bared breasts, to the fabric pooled at her waist. He reached for it, his fingers running over it for the barest breath before he looked to her, brow furrowed. "This isn't my plaid. It's the Stuart tartan, but it is too soft."

She nodded. "It is cashmere. The dressmaker gave it to me before I left this morning . . ." She paused, not wanting to think of the dressmaker. Of the reason she had been there. For a dress for the theater. For a trousseau.

Not wanting to think of the other woman who had been there. His woman.

Alec would not let her think of those things, however. His beautiful brown gaze captured her. "You knew it would slay me."

Lily smiled. "I hoped it would."

He pressed a kiss to her shoulder. "Here," he whispered to the skin there. "This is what I saw when I entered the room. This shoulder, bare and perfect against my plaid. And you . . ." His lips moved down, over her collarbone, down the slope of her breast. "You . . . beautiful enough to be a Scottish queen."

He took the tip of her breast in his mouth, teasing until it was hard and begging for everything he would give her, for the licks and pulls at her flesh, even as she knew she should resist. Knew she should be ashamed. But with Alec, nothing felt shameful. Nothing felt wrong. It felt as though this moment—it was her purpose. He was her destiny. She cried out at the sensation and he gentled, worrying the straining flesh with the light graze of his teeth, making her pant his name and beg for more.

He lifted his head. "Is that how you like it, *mo chridhe*?"

She caressed his shoulders, her hands sliding up to cup his face, to tilt him to her for a kiss. She whispered against his lips, "I like it however you wish to give it."

He took control of the caress, sliding his tongue deep and claiming her for his own. Marking her. Ensuring that she would never be able to think of kissing without thinking of him. Of now. Of this night.

He kissed her in long, lingering caresses, addling her mind with soft, sinful pleasure until she nearly didn't notice that he had peeled away the tartan on her lap. And then his fingers were caressing, delving deeper in long, lingering strokes, and she noticed. Clearly.

She writhed beneath his touch, sighing her pleasure into his mouth.

"You taste of peppermint," he said after a long, lingering lick at her lips. "How is that possible?"

"Sesily." She sighed, desperate to find thought as his fingers played and tempted, making promises of what was to come.

He raised a brow, humor in his gaze. "Another Talbot trick?"

"I wanted to taste good," she said, a blush running over her cheeks.

He held her gaze for a long moment as he slid his fingers deep, and she gasped once, twice, before he removed them, bringing them to his mouth as he had in the carriage days ago. She blazed like the sun as she watched him slide them deep into his mouth, as he tasted her secrets, the visual making her ache. "You taste wonderful. No peppermint required." He leaned in again, licking along her jaw to her ear. "I should like to eat you up."

Her cheeks flamed at the words, and she thought she might perish from embarrassment when his fingers resumed their movement, dipping, swirling, and then disappearing again, rising to lazily paint the tip of one breast in slow, wet circles. "Shall I eat you up, lass?"

Before she could answer, he moved again, sliding down her

body, licking and sucking until she sighed her pleasure and held him to her, aching for more. He repeated the action on the other breast, leaving her awash in need, aching for something she could not name.

She lifted his face to hers. "Alec," she whispered, squirming on the creaky bed. "Please. Come to me."

He shook his head then. "I am not done tasting you, love."

Love.

The endearment was enough to set her squirming again, even more so as he moved her, pulling her legs to the edge of the bed, and—she closed her eyes—spreading her thighs wide. "Lie back," he said, the words rough and deep and outrageous.

She blinked. "Aren't you going to . . . ?"

"Taste you," he said, his massive hands sliding up her legs, over the soft skin of the inside of her thighs, setting her heart to pounding as his fingers moved higher and higher, until they were a wicked promise at the junction of her thighs. He stared at her for a long moment, until she closed her eyes from the heat of his gaze.

Finally, he pressed a kiss against the soft skin of one thigh and said, "You are perfect here—not that I should be surprised. Slick and wet and desperate for me, aren't you?"

"I don't know," she said, suddenly afraid of what he was about to do, of what he was about to make her feel.

He growled at that. "You are. You are the most perfect thing I've ever touched." He pressed a kiss to the soft skin of her thigh. "You humble me with your body."

Unable to stop herself, she lifted herself to him, aching for his touch. "It is yours," she whispered. "All of me. I am yours."

He growled at the words, turning to nip the inside of her knee before lifting her leg and settling it, shockingly, wonderfully, on his shoulder. "You have it wrong, love. It is not I who owns, but you." He pressed a kiss to the curls that hid the heat of her. "Your lips taste like Scotland," he whispered at the core of her. "But here, you taste like heaven."

And then he was kissing her in that glorious, secret place, and she was gasping her shock and pleasure, and doing as she was told, lying back as he licked and sucked and reveled in her. She sighed his name, her hands moving to his head, fingers sliding into his hair. "Alec," she whispered. "I am yours. Forever."

The words seemed to unlock him, to make him wild and desperate and wicked and wonderful; a growl came deep, the vibration against her core making her just as wild. Just as desperate. Her fingers clenched in his dark curls, and she did not hesitate to hold him to her, to move against him.

His hands slid beneath her, lifting her, holding her to him like a banquet, and she cried out as he licked, finding all her secrets, giving her everything she'd ever desired. "Yours," she whispered again and again, and finally, as he drove her higher and higher, he ripped the word from her on a wild, loud scream.

He lifted his head at the sound, leaving her there on the precipice of something glorious. He pressed a soft kiss to her thigh, licking in little circles until she looked to him, meeting his magnificent gaze as he stared up the length of her. "You stopped."

He did not move for a long moment, and then he leaned forward and blew a soft stream of air through her dark curls. She writhed. Called to him.

"How shall I prove it?" he said, lazily, his gaze locked on the heart of her.

"Prove what?"

" 'Tis I who is yours."

She did not have time for it. "Alec. Please."

He licked the center of her, long and lush and outrageously, and she cried out before he smiled, wide and beautiful, and said, " 'Tis I who is yours, *mo chridhe*. What shall I do to prove it?" He laughed, low and deep and liquid against her. "There. Tell me the thought that turned your whole body pink in the candlelight."

"You know," she sighed, the words nearly a whine.

"I do," he said, as though they had all the time in the world. "But I wish you to command me, love. I wish you to be my goddess. And I, your servant. I wish you to know your beauty.

Your pride. Your perfection. I wish to honor it. With every part of me."

His words set her aflame.

It did not matter that they were mad.

She looked to him, desperate for his mouth once more. "Then do so."

He raised a brow in question. "Say it." He licked her again, and she went tight as a bow. "Honor me, Alec."

The words flooded her with pleasure. "Honor me, Alec."

"Worship me, Alec."

She closed her eyes. "Worship me, Alec."

"Kiss me, Alec."

"Kiss me, Alec."

And he did, driving her wild, making love to her with slow, savoring strokes, his hands lifting her to him like a feast. She pressed her hips to him, continuing the litany, repeating it again and again, until she found the precipice once more, and this time he did not stop, not even as she tumbled over the edge, his hands and mouth and tongue the only discernible thing in the riot of pleasure.

And as she clutched him and cried out the commands he had given her, she added another. "Love me, Alec."

Love me.

And he did. In that moment, even if it never happened again, he loved her. She knew it.

As she came down from her pleasure, she reached for him, pulling him to her, aching for more of him, for all of him. He came to her, climbing up over her, the bed—at once too small and also perfectly sized because it kept him close enough to touch—creaking at the movement, as he pushed her back and leaned down, pressing warm, wonderful kisses to her jaw to her ear.

Her hand reached for the hem of his kilt, finding warm, muscled skin there, beneath the wool. She stroked up his long, muscled thigh, higher and higher, finding only warm bare skin. She could not hide her shock. "You wear nothing beneath."

He lifted his head, meeting her gaze. "Nae."

"Sesily wondered."

He kissed her deep. "Sesily can find her own Scot to make the discovery. I am claimed."

Hers.

The words emboldened her, and she tracked the bare skin to the front of him, to where he strained for her, hard and hot and—

He hissed his pleasure at her touch. "Lily."

"You are magnificent," she whispered.

"I am too big. A beast."

She stroked him, long and lush. "You are too perfect. A man."

He closed his eyes and put his forehead to hers. "Thank you."

There was something in the words. An ache she did not like. A doubt she did not wish. She stilled. "Alec?"

He shook his head. "Do not stop. Christ, Lily. Do not stop."

She did not, stroking again and again, reveling in the size and strength of him. "There is a small thing I should like to discuss."

He hissed a laugh. "The word *small* is a bit unsettling when you are just there, lass."

She stroked him, long and loving, until he groaned his pleasure, the sound sending a similar feeling through her. "I like that," she whispered.

"I assure you, not half as much as I like it." He stilled, then kissed her, stealing thought for a moment. "What is it you would like to discuss?"

She had difficulty recalling. "You remain clothed."

His gaze found hers. "And?"

It was her turn to kiss, to caress, to steal breath and thought. And, finally, to whisper, "And I *will* you . . . not clothed."

He closed his eyes. "I think I should not—"

"Are you mine?" she whispered. "Truly?"

They flew open. "Forever."

The word opened her up. Brought the light in. "Then prove it, Alec. Honor me. Worship me. Kiss me." This time, she stopped at the last.

He did not. "Love me," he whispered.

And she told the truth. "I do."

He closed his eyes again, and she saw the pain flash over his features, as though the words had been a curse instead of a gift. Doubt flared deep inside her. "I am sorry," she whispered, summoning his gaze to her with her own fear. "I cannot stop the truth. I love you."

He did not reply except to move, giving her precisely what she wanted. He stood up, shed his clothes, revealing his magnificence, the hard expanse of his chest and the tight, rippling muscles of his stomach, ending in a remarkable cut of flesh above his hips, angling down to the part of him that appeared to ache for her as much as she ached for him.

He returned to her, the bed creaking beneath his weight as she reached for him, her legs opening as he moved between them, coming down over her, his arms holding his weight off her, his size protecting her. "Never apologize for that. I shall treasure it. Forever. Even when you discover how unworthy I am of it."

Her brow furrowed, but she was unable to ask him to explain it, because he was kissing her, stroking her, guiding her, *protecting her.* He slid into her in a perfect, glorious movement, making her sigh and gasp and cling to him as he moved in a perfect rhythm, watching her responses, finding the places she most desired him, giving her everything she wanted, and eventually—once he found their rhythm—rocking against her, pressing and rolling and driving her higher and higher, until she was crying his name and clinging to him, begging him with words she should never have used.

Harder. Faster. Deeper.

And he gave it to her without question. Without quarter.

"Open your eyes, Lily," he whispered, his lips at her ear, his tongue stroking there and making her mad with desire. She did, and he watched her, lids heavy with desire. "Don't stop looking at me, love."

"Never," she whispered. "I will never stop."

"I need you," he replied. "I need this. I don't know how I will live without it."

"Never. You will never have to," she whispered. "I love you."

He kissed her again, and she realized that he'd stolen more than her heart. More than her breath. He'd taken away her shame.

She was his. And in that knowledge, she found herself. She found her strength.

And it was glorious.

They careened toward pleasure together, hard and fast and finally, finally there, like heaven had opened up and spilled down upon them, pleasure coursing through them, their names on each other's lips, the ground falling away.

No. Not the ground.

The bed.

One thin leg had collapsed beneath their combined weight, beneath the force of their pleasure, and the whole thing tipped, sending them sliding off, Lily letting out a little shriek as Alec turned to bear the brunt of the fall, clutching her to him as he landed, hard on the floor, with a deep grunt.

A moment passed while Lily attempted to take stock of the situation—one moment, on the bed in the most magnificent experience of her life and the next, spread across Alec's chest on the floor of the bedchamber.

Just as she came to terms with the event, a crack sounded and Alec cursed, immediately turning them, putting her back to the floor and covering her with his body as the canopy came down with a mighty crash atop them, a large piece of wood striking him across the shoulders and knocking the nearby table, from which a porcelain squirrel, complete with teacup, smashed to the ground.

Remarkably, it was only then that the dogs barked.

Lily began to laugh. She had never in her life been so happy as she was in that cacophonous disaster of a room, where she finally, finally felt whole. Naked and cold and on the floor . . . in the protective embrace of the man she loved. Not ashamed. Not used.

Not at all lonely, for the first time in forever.

Relief and joy and emotion drove the laughter for long minutes, until Alec moved off her, lifting the canopy from where it had fallen and sitting up, and she realized that she was alone in her amusement. That Alec, instead, was stone-faced.

She stopped laughing and sat up, immediately. "Alec?"

"This was a mistake."

Cold dread threaded through her, but she did her best to ignore it. To pretend it was something else. "Well, it might be best if we stock sturdier furniture, if we are to have such lovely—"

"Not the bed."

She did not pretend to misunderstand. She shook her head. "It wasn't a mistake."

It could not have been. Nothing that felt so perfect, so right, could be a mistake.

He was not a mistake.

But she . . .

Doubt whispered as he turned away, putting his wide, muscled back to her. He did not look back when he said, "I assure you, it was."

He stood, magnificent and muscled like a Greek god, and she recalled the story he'd told, suddenly understanding why Endymion might choose endless dreams of his love over the possibility of losing her for even a moment. If given the choice, Lily would sleep now, forever, if it meant having a taste of him.

"We shall have to marry."

The words came so softly that she nearly didn't hear them. Or, rather, nearly didn't believe he'd said them. There had never been words she had wished to hear more. And yet, they destroyed her; the emotion in them—keen, clear regret—was undeniable.

Shall have to.

As though it would be a trial. As though he did not wish it. Of course he wouldn't wish it.

She was a public scandal. And he, a duke.

She reached for the plaid she'd been wearing, extracting it from beneath the fallen canopy. Wrapping herself in it, wanting to shield herself from the truth.

He cursed, his gaze trailing over the tartan and the bed, destroyed with their lovemaking. "What have I done?" he whispered.

She stood at the shaming, stinging words, refusing to allow them to slay her.

"There is no need for you to marry me," she said, trying for calm. For cool. Trying to show strength even as the words made her weak.

His brows knit together, the angles of his face sharp in the shadows, and for the first time since he'd broken down her door, she saw the beast in him, wild and frustrated. He replied, but it seemed as though she had not spoken. "We marry. It is the only choice."

In her dreams, she had imagined this moment. Alec proposing marriage. But in those dreams, he proposed from passion. From love. Never from duty. And certainly never with regret.

Marriage to Alec Stuart, Duke of Warnick, might have been Lily's greatest desire . . . but she did not want it like this.

She had given him all she had—her love. And it was not enough for him. And so she gave him the only other thing she could.

His freedom.

"You forget, Your Grace, that you cannot force me into marriage."

His eyes went wide with recognition as she invoked the most important clause in her guardianship agreement. "Lily," he said, warning in the word.

She turned toward the door, unable to meet his gaze any longer. "I shan't marry a man who regrets me. I may not deserve better, but I owe myself that."

She did not expect him to reply. And she certainly did not expect him to reply with such anger. "Goddammit, Lily," he thundered, deep and low and thick with brogue. She turned back to find the muscles of his broad, bare chest rippling with barely contained fury. "You think I would be the one who regrets? You think it would be me who was shamed?"

"I do," she said, the words coming on a wave of confusion. "Of course it would be. Marrying Lovely Lily? The ruined Miss Muse? What worse a choice for a duke?"

He came toward her, and she thought he might take her in hand before he stopped short, crossing his arms across his magnificent broad chest. "Lily," he said, the words no longer angry. Now, exhausted. Resigned. "I promise you. I would not regret you for a moment. You, on the other hand . . . you would regret every minute we've ever shared."

Impossible.

"I would never regret it." She stopped. "Alec. What I said—I love you."

He turned away from her, reaching for his coat. "I shall take you home."

This is my home. Wherever you are is home.

Tears threatened, and she resisted the words. Instead, settling on a single question. "Why?"

For a moment, she thought he might answer, his throat working, his gaze the only thing in the room. She willed him to answer. To reveal whatever demons loomed for him. When he spoke, it was not a reply, but a declaration.

"Not me. Another. Someone worthy." And then he said, "We shall find the painting. And we shall set you free."

Chapter 18

SOMETHING WICKED INDEED: SCOTTISH BRUTE SPIED AT SCOTTISH PLAY

England shall be your ruin.

As a child, Alec had heard the words dozens of times. Hundreds of them. Every time he had begged his father to send him to England. To follow his mother. To honor her. To find the place she loved—a world that had promised more for her than the Scottish borderlands ever could.

England shall be your ruin, the old man would say. *Just as it was mine.*

And now it was true.

Like his father, he loved an Englishwoman of whom he was unworthy. Unlike his father, he was willing to do anything to save her from a future replete with disappointment.

I love you.

He should never have made her say it. Should never have allowed himself to bask in it.

But even now, those words rioted through him, making him ache. It would make everything to come that much more difficult—knowing that she would stay with him if he asked. That she would lower herself to be with him.

He had one way of protecting her from that life. One final chance that would give her the life of which she dreamed. And so he stood alone in the largest box at the Hawkins Theater—belonging to Mr. and Mrs. Duncan West, the newspaper magnate and his legendary aristocratic wife—waiting for the show to begin. He wore a coat and trousers that ostensibly fit him, but nevertheless felt as though they would strangle him, slowly, throughout the evening.

"You look terrifying," King said as he stepped through the curtain and into the box, his charming wife on his arm.

Alec bowed low over the marchioness's hand before standing straight and saying, "My lady, I am ever amazed by your patience and tolerance with such a fully tactless husband."

Sophie laughed at the words. "It is a great trial, as you can imagine, Your Grace." She paused. "For what it is worth, I do not think you terrifying in the least. I think you quite dashing."

"Not as dashing as I, though, correct?" her husband interjected.

She made a show of rolling her eyes, even as King pulled her tight to his side, color high on her cheeks as he pressed a kiss to her temple. "The poor Marquess of Eversley. Ever maligned by the world around him."

King's kiss moved adoringly to her bare shoulder in a display of affection that no doubt scandalized women peering through opera glasses throughout the theater. "I'm terribly wounded, love. You shall have to do something to make it all better later this evening." Alec attempted not to hear the marchioness's sharp intake of breath at the caress, before King turned to him and said, "Dashing indeed, Warnick. I see you saw my tailor."

"I did," he said, deliberately turning from the couple to survey the floor of the hall.

"For the theater?" King asked, innocently enough for Alec to know that danger approached. "Or for something else, entirely?"

"King," his wife warned softly.

"It's a reasonable question. One hears things about beautiful wards and their taciturn guardians."

Alec cut him a look. "Why would I dress for her?"

"Why indeed," King said, and Alec resisted the urge to wipe the smug look off his friend's face.

"The goal is to get her married to another."

Not entirely, any longer. He didn't want her married. He wanted her free. He wanted her with a world of choices spread out before her. He wanted to give her the future she wished—whatever it might be.

I love you.

Whatever it might be, beyond him.

"I understand the stated goal," King said. "I simply don't understand its inception."

Alec's gaze narrowed on his friend. "What is that to mean?"

"Only that I do not understand forcing the girl to woo another. When she has a possibility so very close at hand."

"King," the marchioness said again.

King turned to his wife. "Look at him. I've haven't seen Alec Stuart in a properly fitting English suit since school. It's obvious for whom he dresses, so why not marry the . . ." He trailed off, and Alec gritted his teeth.

No. Don't see it.

Understanding flared in King's gaze. "You won't marry her."

"I will not."

Pity chased understanding away, and Alec wanted to leap from the balcony to save himself from King's approach. From his soft words, unable to be heard by any but the two of them. "Alec," he said. "School was a long time ago."

"I know that," Alec replied curtly.

"Do you, though?" King paused. "You are a different man. A man, full stop. She would have you. All of you. She would be lucky to—"

Alec moved, stopping the words on his friend's lips. "Don't you dare. Don't even suggest that she is the one who would be lucky in such a scenario."

King's eyes went wide, and his voice grew louder. "You're a *duke*. She's the scandalous daughter of a—"

Alec's gaze narrowed. "Call her scandalous one more time."

His friend was intelligent enough to remain silent.

"I am barely a duke. I was *seventeenth* in line. Like the setup to a goddamn farce. And so far beneath her it is obscene." He looked away. "It does not matter. I am not her future."

He had a chance to have her unruined. A chance for her to remain without him. To survive however she liked. To not regret. And he intended to take that chance.

And leave her with a better man than he could ever be.

He knew that in most circumstances, the most noble act would be to marry her. But in his case, nobility came with making a place for Lily to be happy and well provided for with a better man. One without shame behind him.

The previous evening had been a disastrous mistake.

He was racked with guilt over his inability to resist her. To ruin her again, with his body and his past. And his desire.

Guilt. Not regret.

He would never regret touching her.

And that would be his punishment.

A vision flashed, Lily barely clothed, surrounded by the proof of his coarseness. The broken bed, the canopy in shambles, the porcelain figurines smashed to the ground, she remained perfection incarnate. A goddess among ruins.

The ruins of his hand.

Of his touch.

In that keen awareness, he could not help but tell her the truth.

You will regret me.

But she would not regret what he did for her. Of that, he was certain. And so he was here, tonight, in a supremely uncomfortable suit, waiting for the rest of London to arrive, so he might commit a crime.

And give the woman he loved the life she deserved.

The curtain moved and West entered, his highborn wife on his arm, the two looking like royalty. And they were in this new age, where the news could elevate or destroy, and the ground shifted beneath the feet of the aristocracy. In a matter of years, women would survive Lily's scandal as long as the news was on their side. The world would see the truth of her—that she was glorious and worthy only of their adoration.

Not so now, however.

Now, he required West for more than the papers.

The other man met his gaze, nodding a greeting from across the box so that he could dispense with the formality when he reached Alec, his wife firmly on his arm. The lady's presence made it impossible for Alec to do the same. He bowed, greeting her with the title to which she was entitled, despite her marrying a commoner. "Lady Georgiana."

She smiled, broad and beautiful. "Your Grace," she said, setting her hand in his with a curtsy that would put a duchess to shame. "I do not use the title. I am Mrs. West." She turned to her husband. "Proud beyond measure to be so."

The love in the words was unmistakable, and Alec found himself, for the first time in a long while, believing in the emotion here, surrounded by couples who seemed to have touched it despite its ephemera.

Perhaps the box would bless Lily. Bring her the love of which she'd once dreamed.

The thought ached, even as he forced himself to complete it. Pushing aside the knot in his throat, he looked to West. "Tell me you have it."

West reached into the pocket of his top coat and extracted a sheaf of paper. "That you must ask is an insult of the highest caliber. I should call you out."

"I would choose broadswords. And you would not enjoy the outcome," Alec said, taking the paper.

"Christ," West said. "The Scots really are a prehistoric people."

"I rather like the idea of broadswords," Mrs. West said, dryly. "I should like to see you with one, husband."

He turned to her, his voice going low and dark. "It can be arranged."

Alec rolled his eyes and opened the document, not caring that the rest of London watched. He stared at the map for a long moment, committing it to memory before depositing it into his own pocket. "I shan't ask you how you procured it. But I am grateful for it."

West's gaze lingered on his wife. "I have excellent connections. Ones that extend far beyond my reach." He returned his attention to Alec. "And there is another thing you should know. Hawkins is evicted from his home in Covent Garden. If gossip is to be believed, he is bedding down here."

Alec nodded once. "As the home is emptied of its contents, I am unsurprised."

One of West's golden brows rose. "And how do you know it is empty?"

"Would you believe connections beyond my reach?"

"No." He paused. "But if those connections were worth their salt, they would tell you to offer to buy the painting tomorrow if you cannot steal it tonight."

Alarmed by the frankness of the newspaperman's words, Alec's gaze flickered to West's wife, who he knew was on the Selection Committee of the Royal Academy. The lady inclined her head. "As far as I am concerned, you play the role of Robin Hood here, Your Grace. If I had my way, the thing would have been banned from exhibition the moment Miss Hargrove was made mockery."

Alec bowed again. "My lady." Turning to West, he added, "Thank you."

With their mutual support, he was prepared to do whatever he could to get the painting. Now, all that was left was for Hawkins to take the stage, so he could destroy the man and win Lily's future.

As though he had summoned her with the thought, she entered the box on the arm of Lord Stanhope, who had collected her from Berkeley Square, where Alec had deposited her the evening before, after they'd destroyed both his sanity and the home of Duke and Duchess Number Nine.

Lily had begged him to let her stay, and he'd turned her away, praying that her anger would consume the other, more dangerous emotion that tempted him so thoroughly.

He was rather proud of himself, honestly, for orchestrating this particular scenario. As sending her away was, perhaps, the most difficult thing he had ever done.

Lady Sesily Talbot trailed behind them—a perfect chaperone considering her sister and brother-in-law stood mere feet away. If one was willing to ignore the fact that Sesily Talbot had taught Lily to escape a home from the third floor and also to wonder what was beneath a man's kilt.

Not that he had not enjoyed her discovery immensely.

He cleared his throat, shifting his weight and longing for the concealing folds of his plaid.

No. Sesily was the best available choice, as viable chaperones for Lily were somewhat thin on the ground and he had learned his lesson at Hyde Park.

Lily laughed up at the earl as they entered, and though she was obscured from view, Alec was instantly drawn to the sound, to her glittering eyes, to the wide, open smile she offered the gentleman. Memory flashed from the preceding night, a keen reminder of what it had been to hold her in his arms as she'd laughed without hesitation, free and honest, like breath.

Alec's hands fisted at his side, itching to lay the perfect earl low.

And then Lily was looking at him, and he was the one laid low. She stopped laughing instantly, unable to keep her emotions from her gaze. He identified them immediately: Disappointment. Betrayal. Anger. And behind it, shame.

What in hell was *she* ashamed of?

He could not ask her, despite a keen desire to do so.

Stanhope released her to greet the others in the box, and Lady Sesily put a hand to Lily's shoulder, drawing her attention. Leaning in, the other woman whispered something and Lily straightened beneath the words, calm settling over her. Alec made a mental note to destroy any man who disparaged Sesily Talbot ever again, for she played marvelous sentry for Lily.

When he was too weak to do it himself.

The Marchioness of Eversley and Mrs. West extricated themselves from their husbands' dotage to greet Lily, and gratitude flooded Alec, the two aristocratic ladies lending the full force of their combined power to Lily's reputation. With their support, she would survive the gossip that would linger after he found the painting and destroyed it.

The ladies moved, clearing a path and indicating Lily should take a seat at the front of the box, in front of all London, bold and proud and unafraid of being seen in Hawkins's theater. It was then that he saw her for the first time, head to toe. Saw what it was she wore.

The air was suddenly gone from the room.

The dress was the most stunning blue he'd ever seen, silk and perfectly suited to her, with a low neck that made him want to blindfold every man in the room and press wild, lingering kisses along the expanse of skin it revealed. But it was not the dress that destroyed him. It was the sash, tied tight around her waist, falling to the floor in a wide red swath.

It was his plaid. Again.

It should not have moved him. After all, had he not seen her wrapped in the tartan the night before, alone and nude on his bed? Had that not been the worst of all prospects? The one most likely to shred his patience and his nobility?

How was it possible this was infinitely worse?

The evening prior had felt like a gift. Tonight felt like a declaration of war. Like an invasion. A claiming. As though she stood in front of all London and claimed Scotland for her own.

Claimed *him* for her own.

And he was expected to resist.

As she approached, Alec found himself backing away, until he came up against the edge of the balcony and she said, low and without emotion. "Have a care, Your Grace, or you shall topple into the seats below."

The prospect was not unpleasant when confronted with the alternative—facing her, looking like a queen. "You wear my tartan."

She raised a brow. "Is it yours? I did not notice."

Bollocks.

He wanted to pull her to him and kiss her senseless at the lie. Instead, he narrowed his gaze and lowered his voice to a whisper. "What is this game you play, Lily?"

She tilted her head and matched his volume. "Nothing but the game you insist upon. We neither of us are very good at truth, are we?"

Ironically, he replied with it. "No, we are not."

She nodded, her lips pressing into a thin line. "The item you seek?"

"I am told it is here."

"And what am I to do whilst you play the role of swashbuckling hero?"

He wanted it to be true. But the role was not for him. "Not hero," he said. "Guardian."

"Ah, yes. My hero is to be another."

No. Never.

He was saved from answering by the dimming of the lights, footmen around the theater dousing candles, marking the start of the performance and summoning Stanhope, who placed a hand at Lily's elbow, making Alec want to commit murder. "Shall we sit, Miss Hargrove?"

If a duke killed an earl, did the hierarchy of the aristocracy come into play? Did it matter? Newgate seemed a reasonable sacrifice for destroying a man who touched Lily while she wore the Stuart plaid.

Luckily for Stanhope, Sesily approached Alec. "Your Grace, it seems you are landed with me, as we are surrounded by turtledoves."

It took a moment for him to find his tongue. "It is my pleasure, my lady."

She raised a brow. "Obviously."

They sat, and Sesily leaned in. "The wolves watch her, Duke. I suggest you refrain from making it any harder than it already is."

"I don't know what you mean."

"I think you know precisely what I mean. They do not watch the stage. They watch her."

He did not look at Lady Sesily, too focused on the back of Lily's head, on the curl of her hair, on the line of her neck. He inhaled, meaning to calm his rioting emotions, but instead catching her scent—Scotland and sanity.

He looked across the theater, desperate for something other that Lily, and found the whole world watching them—opera glasses trained on the box. On Lovely Lily, once Derek Hawkins's muse, now his disgraced mistress, surrounded by champions who were not enough—who would not be enough if Alec did not succeed in his task.

"He knows his role," Sesily said quietly, returning Alec's attention to the earl, seated in front of him. Stanhope leaned in as the box darkened and the curtain opened, whispering in Lily's ear, making her laugh.

Playing her savior in front of her judge and jury.

The role Alec would have done anything to play.

"I cannot—" The words came unbidden, unwelcome, and he stopped them before they betrayed too much.

Unfortunately, Sesily Talbot saw everything. "Then you should not be here," she whispered. "If you are unable to be the man she requires, then it is only fair that you remove yourself from the playing field."

His hands fisted on his thighs. "You overstep yourself, Lady Sesily."

"It would not be the first time," she said. "But what sort of friend would I be if I did not name you for the coward you are?"

If she were a man, he would call her out.

But she was a woman. And so he was forced to acknowledge that she was right.

Far below, Hawkins took the stage, and the theater erupted into applause. The bastard preened beneath the accolade before he spoke his first line. "*So foul and fair a day I have not seen.*"

Alec was out of the box like a shot.

HE'D LEFT HER again.

She stared blindly at the stage, as the man with whom she'd once imagined herself in love wooed all of London with a magnificent performance. Not that she noticed a bit of it. She was too busy seething.

How dare he leave her again? How dare he make her feel as he had the night before, make her confess her love, make her love him all the more, and then summon her here, tonight, on the arm of another?

And then leave her?

I love you. How many times had she said it? How many times had he demanded it from her?

And then he'd spoken his words, full of regret and shame, words that had echoed through her since he'd deposited her like an unwanted parcel on the steps of the Berkeley Square house.

We shall find the painting and we shall set you free.

And tonight, he passed her off to another man. Infinitely better. Infinitely kinder as he sat beside her before London. In front of the instrument of her ruin.

And somehow, infinitely less.

Why did he not want her for himself?

He'd made his pretty promises last evening—rendered her breathless with his powerful words, vowing desire and desperation. Made love to her as though she was the only woman in the world, and he the only man. And then he'd refused her. Regretted her.

Why?

And, worse, why did Lily want him just the same?

Love was a hateful, horrible thing, somehow made worse in

the darkness of this damn theater, this place that had brought her nothing but shame—shame she would gladly wear if she could have Alec along with it.

But she couldn't have him. Even as he offered her choice, he refused her the only choice she wished to make.

And so she would take the rest of what he offered. *Freedom.*

She stood, turning for the back of the box. Sesily met her gaze, understanding, and raised a brow. Lily did not pause, making her way through the box blindly, not caring who saw. Not caring who knew where she was going.

Caring only about finding him and telling him precisely how much she loathed him. She pushed through the thick curtains and into the brightly lit hallway beyond, empty of people—all of whom were no doubt watching Derek, odious and compelling in equal measures.

There was no sign of Alec, which meant he was already headed into the bowels of the playhouse, searching for the painting. Her heart began to pound at the thought of him setting eyes upon it. Somehow, the idea of his finding it, touching it, claiming it, was worse than the idea of all of London seeing it.

She headed for the back stairwell, the one that twisted down to the wing of the stage, resolved to be there when he found it. To claim it before he could.

"Miss Hargrove." The words stopped her and she turned back to find Lord Stanhope at the entrance to the West box.

"My lord—" she began, not knowing what to say.

He found the words for her, approaching. "Take care."

Sesily entered the hallway as well, hanging back when Stanhope looked over her shoulder. "Do not mind me, my lord. In this play, I am merely the unskilled chaperone. Imagine me in need of spectacles and terribly hard of hearing."

Lily could not help but smile at her friend.

Stanhope approached again, his own smile near-blinding. "You are lucky to have such friends, Miss Hargrove."

"I am, my lord." She hesitated, then added, "It is something of a new experience for me. As is having such a kind gentleman who sides with me."

"I think you would not find me kind if you knew me long."

She wondered at the words from this man who seemed so very perfect. "You are wrong," she said. "You forget I have had my share of unkind men. And you are not one. I would wager well that you are good."

"Heiress chasing is not the most honorable of activities."

"I hope you will chase more worthy ones in the future, my lord."

He shrugged one shoulder, a lock of hair falling over his brow, making him look effortlessly charming. "It shall be terribly boring, don't you think? I find I enjoy playing the part of the other gentleman."

"You should not be the other, you know. You should be the gentleman."

"And would you have me, Miss Hargrove? As gentleman?"

She would be lucky to have him. And yet, "No, my lord. I would not saddle you with my scandal."

"And if I would have it? If I would bear it?"

She smiled. "Then you most certainly do not deserve it."

"It has nothing to do with the scandal, though, does it? It has to do with the gentleman."

Tears threatened at the kind words. "It does. I am afraid I have chosen poorly."

He raised a brow. "You know, I think you are wrong. I think you have chosen the best gentleman of all."

She thought it, too. But for some reason, he would not have her.

You will regret it. You will regret me.

He was the best gentleman. If only he would see it.

"Thank you, my lord." And she was off, rushing down the stairs to her scandal. And to the man she would claim, if only he would allow it.

Chapter 19

THE ART OF WARNICK

It wasn't there.

Alec stood at the center of Derek Hawkins's offices, turning in a slow circle, seething in fury and frustration.

The painting wasn't there.

The rest of the empty studio from Covent Garden was there, lining the walls, six canvases deep, a collection of artwork that would make the docents of the British Museum squeal with excitement. It seemed that, in addition to being a superior bastard, Hawkins was, in fact, a superior talent. Which meant Lily's portrait was as beautiful as they said.

Allegedly.

As it was not there.

What next? How would he save her?

There was no time. He had two days to find the painting. Two days before it was revealed to the world and Lily had no choice but to marry him. And it wasn't there, goddammit.

He resisted the urge to lower the candle to the nearest canvas and set the entire theater ablaze. Hawkins would deserve it. For threatening her. For using her. For *touching* her.

Alec cursed, long and wicked in the darkness.

"What does that mean?" She spoke from the doorway.

He hadn't heard the door open. He whirled to face her, the candle in his hand casting her face into flickering golden relief as she stepped inside and closed the door behind her. "You should be upstairs."

She approached, and he moved backward, until his trousers brushed against a large still-life of pears and he had no choice but to stop. She, however, did not stop.

Why didn't she stop?

"Upstairs," she said. "With Stanhope."

"Yes."

"Instead of down here. With you."

"Yes." Couldn't she see it?

"While you risk all to save me."

Why didn't she understand? He would give up everything he had, everything he was, if it would keep her safe. "Yes."

A long silence stretched between them, muffled shouts from the stage beyond somehow making the room seem smaller. More intimate. Alec wanted to climb the walls to escape it. To escape her.

And somehow, she seemed perfectly calm. "It is not here, is it?"

He exhaled. "Nae."

"I gathered as much when I heard you cursing." How was it that she was so calm? "And so my demise approaches." She smirked, indicating the theater beyond the door. "Like Birnam Wood."

"What have I told you about Shakespeare?" he snapped.

She smiled. "Last I heard, you were cursing him quite thoroughly."

"It is my right as a Scot." He tried not to look at her. She was so close now, close enough to smell. To touch. To ache for. And they were alone.

She whispered his name like a sin. "Alec?"

He swallowed. "Yes?"

"What does the curse mean?"

He shook his head. "It does not translate."

She waited for a long moment before he lifted his gaze to hers, her grey eyes silver in the candlelight. "And what does *mo chridhe* mean?"

He shook his head. "It does not translate."

One side of her mouth rose in a little, knowing smile. "Is it better or worse than the curse?"

She was killing him. He was trying to be noble. To protect her. And—

"Why do you not want me, Alec?"

He wanted her with every ounce of his being. How did she not see that? He closed his eyes. "Lily. Now is not the time."

"What better time than this?" she asked. "What better time than now, on the eve of my destruction?"

"We've tomorrow to find it—"

"We shan't find it. That has never been our prophecy."

"Stop referring to the damn play like it's relevant. Everyone dies at the end."

"Not everyone. From the ash comes a line of kings." She paused, then said quietly, "Scottish ones."

"Cursed ones. There are no kings in Scotland now."

"Aren't there?"

He ran a hand through his hair, frustration coursing through him, setting him aflame. "Get out, Lily. We've another day, and I shall find the damn painting if I turn London inside out. Go to Stanhope. And see if he might be your happiness."

"He shan't be," she said.

"You don't know that."

"I do, though," she said. "How could one man make me happy when I love another so well?"

He turned for the door. "You know not of what you speak."

They had to leave this place, before they were caught. And he had to find air—she'd thieved it from the room with her beauty, like a fairy. And now hear him—thinking Scots madness like the damned king beyond.

He'd reached the door when she spoke, "I know you are a coward."

He looked back at the words to find her unmoved from her place at the center of the room, surrounded by the work of the man who had ruined her, straight and strong and proud as Boadicea. And wearing his plaid like a banner.

She was perfect.

He turned away without speaking, and she threw her next spear. "I know that I tremble from wanting you."

He bowed his head, pressing his forehead to the door.

The stage beyond went quiet, as though all of London had hushed to let her be heard. And then, quiet and longing, "I know that last night, you trembled as well."

The words broke him. He was moving before he could think, and she was in his arms, wrapped about him, and her lips were on his, and she was sighing into his mouth like he was the greatest gift she'd ever received. He kissed her, reveling in the feel of her lips on his, of the way she softened instantly against him, as though she had been waiting for this moment—for him—for a lifetime.

Just as he had waited for her.

He lifted her, carrying her to the desk at the far end of the room, setting her down and taking her face in his hands, aligning their lips so he might taste her again and again, memorize the softness of her lips and the pretty little moans she sighed when he slid his tongue over her lips, stole into her softness, thieved from her like a beggar at a banquet.

He kissed her until they were both gasping for breath, until he lifted his lips from hers and removed his hands from her, holding them up, wide and weak between them. "I still tremble, Lily."

Her gaze flickered to them, eyes going dark and devastating when she noted their shaking. When she reached for one, bringing it to her lips, kissing each fingertip before turning his hand palm up and pressing a warm, wet kiss to the center of his palm.

And when her tongue slipped out and swirled a circle there, branding him with her mark, he growled and took her again, licking deep and slow, until she writhed against him, sighing for more. He broke the kiss, trailing his lips over her cheek to the lobe of her ear, where he whispered, "I will ever tremble. There will never be a time when I do not ache for you. When I do not want you with every thread of my being."

"Then have me," she said, her breath hot at his ear. "Take me. Claim me. I am yours." The words roared through him, nearly deafening him with desire.

But he did not deserve her.

He stepped back. Releasing her. "I am not the hero of the play, Lily. You must choose a better one. One more worthy of you. That is the point of this entire exercise."

A beat. And then she came to her feet like an avenging queen and pushed him away from her with enough strength to set him off balance. "I choose you, you lummox."

Good. If she was angry, she might leave him alone.

"I am not an option," he said.

"Yesterday, you offered to marry me," she replied.

And he would have done it. Would do it still. If only . . . "I am not enough."

The sound she made bordered on a scream, full of frustration and anger. "You are a *duke*, Alec. And I am the orphaned daughter of a land steward who has been ruined in front of all London."

"Not *has been*. Not yet."

"You were not there. I assure you, it is roundly done."

"It is not done until the painting is made real. And it shan't be. Not if I can stop it."

She shook her head and spread her arms wide, indicating the room. "You cannot stop it! He will win this battle. He won it the moment he marched up to me in Hyde Park and convinced me that attention was akin to love." She gave a little, humorless laugh. "Ironically, I seem to be caught in a similar web now."

He froze. "It is not the same."

She cut him a look. "You are right. It is not the same. Derek never made me feel ashamed of myself."

What in hell? "All of this—every bit of it—has been to keep you from shame. To keep you from regret."

"How many times must I tell you that I do not regret it?"

He lost his temper. "Goddammit, Lily! Can you not simply trust that I know? That the hero you spoke of abovestairs—he is not me? You think I do not wish to marry you and protect you and love you as you deserve? You think I do not wish my past erased and this dukedom mine in truth so I might get down on my knees and beg you to be with me? So that I may make you a duchess? You think I do not wish for those children? The ones you planned to dress in pretty little embroidered clothes? The ones who would fit those silly red boots?"

Her eyes were wide, and he did not care. Still, he raged. "You think I do not wish to take you to our marriage bed and make love to you until we no longer shake? Until we no longer *move*, for the pleasure of it? You think I do not love you? How can you not understand it? *I love you beyond reason.* I think I might have loved you from the moment you closed the damn door in my face in Berkeley Square. *But I am not the man you deserve.*"

He stopped, breath coming fast and angry, self-loathing coursing through him, and he forced himself to look at her. Tears glistened in her eyes, and he hated himself for what he'd done. "I am not he. Not for a lifetime. Not even for the one night we had." He thrust his hands through his hair. "We must go before we are found."

She did not move from her place. "What did you say?"

He looked to her, "What?"

"You are not for a lifetime. You are for one night."

The words were a wicked blow, unexpectedly cruel on her lips. Recovering from the sting, he nodded. At least she understood. Perhaps she would leave him in peace now.

He would never be at peace again.

"We must go," he said, wanting to claw at his cravat, tight about his neck.

Lily was not through, however. "What did she do to you?"

He stilled. "Who?"

"Countess Rowley."

Memories of the past raced through him. *How did she know?* It did not matter. He should have told her before then. The truth would drive her away as surely as he ever could.

And that was the goal, was it not?

No.

Yes. It was the goal.

He turned for the door. "We must go."

"Alec."

"Not here, Lily. Not while all of London waits beyond this room." And he tore the door open, without hesitation.

All of London was not beyond, it turned out.

Only one of London was there.

Derek Hawkins stood on the other side, dressed in Renaissance garb, broadsword dangling from his hand. He raised the blade, setting it to Alec's chest, just above his heart. "I do not know the law in Scotland, *Duke*, but in England, we are within our rights to kill intruders."

OF COURSE DEREK was here to muck everything up.

Right now, she would give everything she had to disappear him from his place at the door, making a mountain of a molehill, threatening to kill them, if she'd heard correctly. Lord deliver her from men with a flair for the dramatic. She checked the clock on the desk.

It was half-nine and the theater was in intermission. It occurred to Lily, vaguely, that she hoped Sesily was as good at being a poor chaperone as she was at being a scandal, because Lily and Alec were going to require an excellent excuse for their absence as the entire box realized that they were missing.

Something better than *Oh, they are likely breaking into Hawkins's office, stealing Lily's nude, and having an amorous encounter upon his desk.*

In this particular case, the truth was not an appropriate excuse.

Especially now, as it seemed they would be waylaid further.

Certainly, they should not be here, in this inner sanctum. But neither should Derek be. She approached, refusing to cow to this man who had so thoroughly used her. Remarkably, because two weeks past, she would have cowed. Two weeks past, she'd been a different woman.

Two weeks past, she had not had Alec.

Alec, her massive Scot, whose broad shoulders and superior height dwarfed Derek, blocking her view as she advanced, having had enough of Derek Hawkins. "Should you not be on stage, Derek?"

That's when she saw the sword, poised high and dangerous, the tip of it at Alec's heart. Alec, who looked calmer than any man should be in that position.

Lily froze, terror threading through her at the image. "What do you think you do, you madman?"

Derek did not look at her. "I protect what is mine. My theater. My art. And I am willing to do anything for it." He paused, looking down at Alec's empty hands. "You are wise to have avoided taking anything from within."

When Alec spoke, it was with utter, complete disdain. "You think I want your artwork? To what end? To grace my walls with your child's play?"

The words were rife with insult, and Lily's jaw dropped. How could he taunt a man with a broadsword pressed to his chest?

Derek sneered. "I think you want at least one piece of it, Diluted Duke."

"There you are right. But I've no intention of looking at it."

Derek laughed. "I suppose you think that having seen the real thing, you do not require it."

While Lily gasped at the insinuation, Alec did not move, except to raise his hand and clutch the blade of the broadsword in one massive fist. Her gaze fell to his fingers, expecting them to bleed with the cut from the blade. Her stomach flipped at the idea that he hurt himself for her. "Let us go, Derek. You must return to the stage. And we've taken nothing."

Derek raised a brow. "How do I know that is true?"

She cut him a look, spreading her arms wide. "You think I hide canvas beneath my skirts?"

Alec did not let Derek finish. "Let's get to it, shall we, Hawkins? You've a play to return to . . . and I've anywhere else to be than to watch it."

Derek scowled. "You're no longer welcome here."

Alec's reply was dry as sand. "You wound me. Truly." If there were not a sword between them, Lily might have laughed. Instead, she held her breath until Alec said, "How much?"

Derek did not move. "How much for what?"

"You're impoverished. You've lost the house in Covent Garden, the studio. Your paintings line the walls here because, no doubt, you've nowhere else to sit them. From what I am told, the theater breaks even, but you cannot stop losing money at the tables. So I ask again—and you will not insult me by pretending not to understand—how much for the painting."

Derek shook his head. "It is priceless."

"I do not believe you."

"Believe me. It is the greatest artwork since the Creation of Man." His gaze moved to Lily. "Look at her, Warnick. You see her beauty, no doubt. Imagine what it looks like when portrayed by a *genius*."

Lily could only see one side of Alec's face—enough to see the muscle in his jaw clench and tic with anger and frustration. "Name the price."

Derek shook his head. "There is no price. My version of Lily is not for sale." His gaze flickered to Lily, "You see, darling? Perhaps I am the hero of the play, after all. Your duke has no trouble selling *you* to the highest bidder." He paused then, like a rude child. "Oh, wait. No. He isn't selling you. He's giving you away. With a fortune as a bonus payment."

Alec's hand tightened around the sword, his knuckles going white, and Lily stepped in to ensure his fingers were not severed. She did not shift her gaze from him. "I think you ought to reconsider, Derek."

"For you?"

"Would it make a difference if I asked?"

"No. That painting will sell all the others. That painting will make me a name for the ages."

"And the fact that it is a painting of me? That I never intended for it to be seen?"

He gave her a long, pitiful look. "Then you should not have sat for it, darling. I shall revel in the wealth that comes from it, earned from you. As though you'd worked for it yourself, flat on your back."

Lily gasped at the coarse words as Alec moved, fast as a cat, the broadsword turning in the air like magic, in his grasp in an instant. He took Derek by the lapels of his ancient costume and virtually carried him to the wall in the hallway beyond, setting the blade of the wicked-looking sword to his cheek. "For one so renowned on the stage, I find it difficult to believe you tempt fate so well as to exhibit such hubris while in this particular costume. You would do well to remember what happened to Macbeth."

Derek's gaze found Lily's over Alec's shoulder, and she saw it there, the expectation that she would rescue him. That she would reenact the last time they had been together as a trio. The last time Alec had threatened Derek.

She would rescue him no longer.

He must have seen it in her eyes, as he looked back to Alec and spat, "I play a brutish Scot with a whore wife. And lo, I discover a similar pair skulking about the playhouse."

Alec pressed the sword deeper into his cheek, his words going soft and terrifying. "What did you call her?"

Derek narrowed his gaze. "You heard me. And remember, I am qualified to identify the characteristic." He paused. "I was there *before you*."

Lily paled at the words. At the scathing insult in them. Shame flooded her, and she wished to do the man serious damage for everything he'd ever done. For everything he'd ever said. And for that, spoken to Alec. Reminding him of her past. Of the things she'd done that she could not take back. "Today, like a fool, you have handed me a weapon that you toy with while prancing about your stage. A weapon I have trained with for decades."

He pressed the blade deeper, and Derek inhaled, sharply. "What do you think your patrons would say if you were found here, in this dark hallway, gutted by Macbeth's blade? Do you think they would believe you summoned him here, to this playhouse? What is it they call it? The Scottish Curse?" Derek's eyes closed and Alec leaned in close. "I am your Scottish Curse, peacock. More terrifying than any ghost story you could imagine. But take heart. I've no intention of killing you.

"I promised you once that I would destroy you," Alec said, his words barely there and somehow shaking the walls. "Make no mistake—I will ruin you just as you ruined her. And when you are old and withered and no one in the world can remember your name, you will quake with the memory of mine."

Derek inhaled quickly and then released a little cry of pain, and Lily started at the sound, which was punctuated by a wild clatter of the sword as Alec flung it down the dark hallway. "Fetch, dog. 'Tis your cue."

And Derek did, running after the sword, collecting it without looking back.

Lily watched Alec for a long moment, his breath coming in and out on waves of fury, his hands clenched and that tic in his jaw becoming more pronounced. He looked as though he were on springs—as though at any moment he might launch himself down the hall and onto the stage to finish what he had started.

She ached to go to him, and then she did, moving to his side. Taking his big, beautiful arm in hand, feeling the muscles ripple beneath her touch. "You did not have to defend me."

Alec looked to her. "What?"

"To Derek. He is not wrong."

"What?" His brow furrowed, and for a moment Lily wondered if it was possible that she was speaking a language other than English.

"It is my mistake, is it not? I sat for the painting. I trusted him. I . . ." She hesitated. "I thought. . . ."

He came at her, taking her shoulders in his hands. Holding her with a firmness she would later dream of. Ache for. "Hear me, Lillian Hargrove. You did nothing wrong. It was not your mistake. You loved him."

"I did not, though. I see that now." She gave a little huff of humorless laughter. "I suppose I should be grateful for the realization."

"How?" he asked.

Her brow furrowed. "How?"

"How do you see it now?"

She smiled. Told the truth. "Now, I know what love is. How it feels. And what I would do for it in earnest."

He closed his eyes at the words. Turned his head away. "We must return above. I've work to do. We've one day to find that painting."

She released him at the words. At the hope in them. At their meaning. He still hoped to find it. To remove it from exhibition. To set her free.

It was ironic, was it not, that she had once fairly begged him for her freedom. She'd asked for money. For independence. She'd begged him to leave her and return to Scotland and let her make her own choices. Carve her own path. Face her own fortune.

And now, as he offered it to her, all she wished was to be trapped. By him.

I love you beyond reason.

"Alec." She did not know what she would say next. How she would keep him. How she would win him.

So, she was unable to do either, as he was ignoring her, already moving, headed for the stairs, taking them two at a time, and she hurried to keep up with his long strides. She was tall, but he was Herculean, and by the time they reached the hallway that abutted the boxes, he was yards ahead of her, striding purposefully past the West box even as Sesily poked her head out to find Lily.

"You've something on your gown." Her friend's eyes went wide. "Good Lord. Is it *blood*?"

Lily looked down, taking in the mark at the shoulder of the beautiful blue dress, where Alec had held her firmly and told her that the past was not hers to bear.

As he bled for her.

"Is it Hawkins's?" Sesily asked. "He's back on the stage, but with a gash in his cheek that I'm not certain is called for in the play. Though, to be honest, I haven't been paying much attention. I confess I like a witch now and then, but not near as much as I like the idea of Alec putting a gash in Hawkins's cheek."

"It is not Hawkins's blood. It's Alec's."

"Good God," Sesily whispered.

"You shouldn't curse so much, you know."

Sesily cut her a look. "Are you about to tell me it is not ladylike?"

Lily shook her head. "I am not exactly a paragon of respectability."

"Excellent. Then hang anyone who prefers I not curse. Sometimes, the words simply suit."

Lily nodded. Then, after a long silence, she said, barely loud enough to be heard, "Shit."

Sesily's gaze was instantly on hers, and Lily saw the pity there. "What has happened?"

And there, in the hallway of the Hawkins Theater—the only place in London she should be stoic—Lily began to cry. She'd made a hash of it all. The painting was to be made public. And there was nothing to be done. And still, that was not her sadness. "He loves me beyond reason."

Sesily tilted her head. "That does not sound so bad."

"And still he refuses me. Claims he is unworthy of me for some ridiculous reason."

"What reason?"

"I don't know. If he would tell me, perhaps . . ." Lily dashed away a tear. "He won't tell me."

Sesily nodded. "Then you must force it from him."

"Does he seem the kind of man who is easily forced?"

Sesily did not miss a beat. "He seems the kind of man who would throw himself into the Thames if you asked him to."

The tears came again. "I asked him to want me—and he refused."

"Because all men are addlepated imbeciles who deserve to be strung up by their thumbs in St. James Park and set upon by bees."

Lily blinked. "That's terribly creative."

Sesily smirked. "I may fantasize now and then."

They laughed together, until the curtains moved and Mrs. West poked her head out from behind the curtain. "Ah. I see Miss Hargrove has returned." She looked up and down the hallway before exiting the box. "And your duke?"

"He is not my duke," Lily said flatly.

"They never are, dear, until they are," the newspaperman's wife said dryly before adding, "I assume that you were unsuccessful in your quest?"

"For Alec?" Lily said.

One golden brow rose at the words. "I was referring to the painting."

Lily blushed, hot and horrified. "Of course. The painting. Yes. We were unsuccessful."

The woman hesitated, then said, "First, you may call me Georgiana. Mrs. West makes me sound the taciturn patroness of a North Country finishing school. Second, I am sorry that the duke is an idiot. But in my experience, all men are until they find reason. And the best of them do find reason." She paused, then added, "And third, you might like to know that the painting is scheduled to be hung tomorrow afternoon, when the exhibition has closed for the night. It will remain covered until the reveal the following morning."

Lily did not understand the point of the information, and she remained silent until the beautiful young woman smiled and said,

"I have it on excellent authority that there will be a window open at the back of the hall tomorrow night. At half-past twelve."

Lily blinked. "Are you—?"

Georgiana nodded like a queen. "If I'd had my way, that lout would have been eliminated from the exhibition the moment it became clear that he'd taken advantage of you. I don't care how beautiful the painting is. He's a bastard."

Lily could not find words amid her surprise.

Sesily had no trouble finding words. "Well. Isn't that lovely?"

"I find I do not like it when men take advantage of women," Georgiana said, boredom in her tone. "And so, my dear, I hope very much that you will take advantage in return. Now, I think I shall return to the play, as I assume from the gash on Hawkins's face and the blood on your gown that this might well be my last time watching this particular lout tread the boards."

She turned back to the box. "My lady—"

Georgiana turned back.

"How are you able to ensure—"

That knowing smile returned. "My husband is not the only one with far-reaching connections." She lowered her voice, so only Lily could hear. "Wives of remarkable men must stay together. I hope you will remember me when you are duchess."

And then she was gone, the words hanging in the corridor like a promise.

Lily took a deep breath, unable to look away from the curtains, still swinging with the force of the woman's entry. All those years without friends. How many times had she longed for them? And now, they came from the woodwork. Enough of them to make her feel real. Like a whole person.

Nearly whole.

She would never be whole without Alec.

He wanted to give her choices? To give her freedom?

Then she would take that freedom. And she would make her choice. It was the easiest choice she had ever made.

Chapter 20

ACTIONS SPEAK LOUDER THAN WARDS

Alec spent the entirety of the next day—the final day before the exhibition—tearing London apart. He'd called in every favor there was, desperate to find the damn painting. To save Lily from what was bound to be her future.

And, finally, he'd summoned Stanhope to him.

The earl came, his curiosity clear when Alec met him in the main sitting room of Number Nine's town house. Stanhope looked about him, taking in the shelves and curio cabinets filled to bursting with figurines. Running a finger along the trunk of a porcelain elephant on a low table nearby, he said, "I did not take you for a collector, Your Grace."

Alec was unamused. "I cannot find the painting."

"I assume it will be easily found tomorrow."

Frustration flared. Did no one in the entire city understand that this was Lily's only chance to survive the scandal?

Not only.

That was why Stanhope was here, and why Alec's heart was in his throat. "I need you to take her away."

The earl blinked. "I beg your pardon?"

"Do not make me say it again." He did not think he could.

Stanhope turned for the sideboard without asking. "Scotch? Or, whatever this is?"

Alec had never in his life needed a drink so much. "Please."

The earl poured two glasses and delivered one to Alec before sitting on a low settee covered in hideous fringe. "Where do you wish me to take her?"

Nowhere. "Scotland."

Stanhope raised a brow. "You do not think yourself better suited to that particular task?"

The words threatened to destroy him.

He wanted to show her Scotland. He wanted to watch her feel the spray of the Firth of Forth on her skin for the first time. He wanted to stand with her in the wilds of the Highlands and breathe her in until the scents of heather and myrtle and Lily were forever intertwined.

He wanted to lay her down on his plaid in a patch of golden sunlight and make love to her beneath mountains and sky and heaven, until she cried out his name. He wanted to grow old with her there, filling the corners of his keep with their happy babes, and their babes' babes, wearing those little red boots she'd kept secreted away from the world.

But he was not for her. "She needs someone better than I."

"And you think that man is me."

"I have seen you together. You make her . . ." He paused, loathing the words. "You make her smile."

I want her to smile forever. With a man who deserves her.

"Making women smile is a particular talent." Stanhope drank, then coughed wickedly. "I suppose I should not be surprised that this house contains only swill."

Alec did not laugh. He could not find the energy. "You are a good man, Stanhope. And you do not grow younger. And you require an heir. And a fortune. And Lily is . . ." Alec drank, deserving the burn of the terrible liquor.

"She is perfect," Stanhope said. "With or without the painting."

Alec closed his eyes at the words, simultaneously grateful for the earl's understanding, and loathing it. He did not wish her to be perfect for anyone but him. He nodded nevertheless. "She is."

"The problem is—she is also very much in love with you." Alec's gaze snapped to the earl's. "I make the chit smile, Warnick, but that is the easy bit. You could make her happy, if you decided to do so." He set the glass on a low table next to the settee and stood. "I'm afraid I must decline your offer of an anvil marriage. Tempting though it is."

Alec stood as well, desperation and fear and elation coursing through him. And still he said, "And what of the dowry?"

Stanhope did not hesitate, releasing a long, disinterested breath. "Is not worth it. Not if I've a tragic love story on my conscience. There are other dowries. I hear there is a rash of American heiresses this season." He paused then, before saying, "If I may?"

"All you have said so far, and now you hesitate?"

"This is London, 1834. All is able to be overcome with a single act. You have it right, and at the same time entirely wrong."

Alec's heart began to pound. "And what is that act?"

"You don't make the girl a countess, married for money; you make her a duchess, married for love. The world enjoys nothing more than a Cinderella story." He opened the door to the room, revealing an aging butler.

Stanhope moved past the servant, turning back from the foyer to find Alec's gaze. "I hope you will be the prince, Your Grace. She deserves all good things."

And so it all fell apart. Alec had come to London nine days earlier to play the role of unwilling guardian and noble savior. To restore her reputation and get her married and get back to Scotland to a life that did not include her. A life that had satisfied him.

Until he'd met her, and all of it had gone to hell.

And he'd failed her on all levels.

And to make it all worse, fallen in love with her.

He yanked the paper from the butler's ridiculous silver tray and opened it, dread pooling deep, certain this day could only get worse.

> *I require your assistance.*
> *Meet me tonight. Half-twelve.*
> *-L*

Below, a line of direction, the mews behind the Royal Academy of Arts. It was then that Alec knew her plan—pride flooding through him at the realization. She was beautiful and brilliant and brave as a damn warrior.

Of course, she was the instrument of her own saving.

She was magnificent enough to save herself and the world in the balance.

If only she could save him, as well.

Several hours later, he drove his curricle into the mews that ran behind the Royal Academy, the night casting deep, dark shadows across the empty space. He was deliberately early, wanting to be there before her, to assess the danger of this particular mission.

He stepped down from the driver's box, his attention already on the building ahead of him. He had half a mind to do it himself, without her.

But he should have known better.

She was already there, stepping out of the shadows as though she'd been in the darkness forever, a queen of the night.

A queen in trousers, cap pulled low over her brow.

How long had she been here? Anything could have happened to her. And he would have been too late to save her. A failure again.

Never enough.

He headed for her, frustration and desire warring within him. "What is this?" he said, pressing her back into the darkness, shielding her from prying eyes.

She reached for him. Took his hand in hers. Slaying him with the simple touch as she opened it and ran her hand over the bandage at his palm. "You bled last night."

"What of it?"

"You bled for me." She pressed a kiss to the bandage, and an ache began, high and tight in his chest. She looked up at him, her eyes shielded by the brim of her cap. He would have done anything to see those eyes. But they were not for him. "I wish to make him a laughingstock for that alone."

Not for herself? Not for all things Hawkins had done to her?

He swallowed around the knot in his throat. The desire. The need. He pushed himself to remain aloof when all he wished to do was pull her into his arms. "You summon me with two lines on a scrap of paper? You come alone? In the darkness? To commit a crime?"

She stood her ground. "It is not the first time I have attempted this particular crime, Your Grace. Nor is it the first time you have." She smiled, white teeth flashing in the shadows. "But it will be the first time we succeed."

Christ. He loved her.

"Be careful, or you shall curse us."

She grew serious then. "No. The universe could not possibly deny me this, as well."

Before he could ask her to elaborate, she moved to the window. His gaze slid to her backside, where the trousers she wore fit indecently. Perfectly. His mouth went dry as he watched her stand on her toes, unsuccessfully attempting to look inside.

"Trousers again," he said.

She turned to him, making a show of looking to his plaid. "Well one of us should wear them, do you not think?"

He raised a brow at the smart words. "You think I cannot do all required in a kilt?"

She watched him for a long moment, until he thought she might not reply, and then she said, "I think you can do anything you like, wearing anything you wish."

The words were tempting beyond reason, and made him want to press her to the wall and show her all the things he would like to do.

He was prevented from doing so, however, by the task at hand. "I require a boost."

He blinked. "A what?"

"That is why you are here." She smiled, as though it were a perfectly ordinary request. "You shall boost me up. And I shall come around and open the door. And we shall get it done."

"You are not going inside alone."

She turned to him. "What do you think will happen? I shall be mauled by a sculpture?" He narrowed his gaze and she sighed. "I do not think I could boost you, Alec."

He reached up and clasped the window, which opened wide without any hesitation. "How did you know this would be open?"

She grinned. "I made a friend."

He loved the pleasure in the words. The thrill in them. He wanted her to have a hundred friends. A thousand of them. Whatever made her happy. For the rest of time.

You could make her happy.

He pushed the earl's voice away. "A friend."

She nodded. "Quite a good one, it seems."

"Well, any friend who encourages a life of crime is a good one, I find," he said dryly.

"The boost, Alec. We haven't all night."

He pushed her aside, and gripped the sill. "You meet me at the door."

When she replied, he heard the disbelief in the words. "Alec. That ledge is six feet from the ground and you are wearing a kilt. You couldn't possibly—"

He lifted himself up and onto the ledge and through the open window. He turned back to find her gaping at him, and he could not resist. "What was it that you were saying?"

She scowled. "My friend also thinks you're an idiot."

He couldn't help himself. He laughed. "She is right about that." And then, "Meet me at the door." She did, not two minutes later, stepping into the building before immediately turning back for outside. "One moment. I nearly forgot."

She returned, large, fabric-wrapped painting in her hands. "My final gift to Derek," she said, when Alec raised a brow at the parcel.

He took it from her. "Lead the way." She extracted a candle and flint from her trouser pocket. "You are, once more, impressively prepared." Before she could reply, he said, "Let me guess. Sesily."

She smiled. "You wound me, sir. I am successfully indoctrinated in scandal. This bit is me."

Of course it was. He watched her light the candle, the flame casting her beautiful face in a warm, golden glow. And then he followed her through the exhibition, the walls covered from floor-to-ceiling in thousands of paintings—too many for any one to be appreciated.

"This is madness," he whispered. "How is it that anyone would care about a single painting in this sea of paint? Enough to make you a scandal?"

She did not look back as they entered the main gallery, long and impressive, with a dais at one end, a curtained spot beyond. "You think it a love of art that makes them clamor for the scandal? They can have art anywhere. But gossip—that is far more interesting." She pointed to one wall. "That is the other great painting of the exhibition. Constable."

He stopped, considering the landscape, small and barely visible in the darkness. He looked down at the parcel in his hand, larger than the watercolor by ten times. "I suppose I cannot hope that the painting we seek is this size?"

"It is not."

"Of course not." He grumbled. "Hawkins does nothing in half measures."

"Perhaps it is my beauty that cannot be contained in such small proportions," she said.

He snapped his gaze to her. "The darkness has brought out your sharp wit."

She tilted her head, then turned away, moving toward the dais. "Perhaps it is my own panic that has done it."

Whatever it was, he did not wish it gone.

She came to the foot of the stage, and hesitated. Approached, coming to her elbow. "Lily?"

"This is where I disgraced myself," she said. He watched as she put her fingers to the edge of the platform and huffed a little laugh. "I disgraced myself before this, I suppose. But here, it was where it all became clear, as though someone had illuminated a room I thought was a ballroom, and turned out to be a privy."

"You did not disgrace yourself. He disgraced you. That is a different thing, entirely."

"It is. But it is not the case. I am not a child, Alec. I knew what it was I did. I knew what might come of it. I knew that I might one day be a scandal." She paused. "And I did not care. I did not wish to be anything but Derek's."

The words came like a blow, jealousy raging through him at the thought of her with Hawkins, the man who had utterly eschewed responsibility for her. The man who would never be good enough for her. Hero enough for her.

She continued. "The world harbors impressive hatred for women who make the mistakes I did. Beauty, used for anything but the holiest of acts, is a sin." She looked up to the dais, to the place where the curtain hung, thick and still, hiding her shame from view. "And not one person was willing to question his role in the play. He was to be lauded for his acts. Tell me, what did I do that was so different than him?"

"Nothing," he said, wishing only to assuage the pain he heard, keen and unsettling, in her voice. "You did nothing wrong."

She smiled. "Society thinks differently."

"Hang Society."

She raised a brow. "What did you do wrong, Alec?"

That question again. Astute and direct. The question he would have to answer eventually.

But not here. Not now.

He shook his head.

She watched him carefully, candlelight flickering over her

beautiful face. "If I were to tell you what you told me—that you did nothing wrong—what would you say?"

He looked away from her, unable to meet her eyes. "I would say you are wrong."

"Because you are a man and she is a woman?"

"Because what I did is far worse than what you did."

"You believe that."

"I do."

"And yet here we are, committing a crime for me. And not for you."

He was not going to tell her. Not then. "Let us commit the crime, then. And be done with it."

For a moment, he thought she might argue. Might push him. And for a moment, he worried that if she did, he would tell her everything there, in front of thousands of paintings, on the damn dais of the Royal Exhibition.

But she did not. Instead, she set her candle down and removed the parcel from his hands before ascending the platform and saying, "Turn away, please."

He did, without hesitation. He had made her a promise, and he would honor it, even as he knew that this was his only chance to see the painting. To know just how beautiful it was. Not that he required a look at the art to know its beauty. It was a painting of Lily; of course it was glorious.

But it would pale in comparison to her in truth.

And so he stood in the silence, listening to her move—to the soft scrape of woolen trousers over her skin, to the whisper of linen as she crouched low and unwrapped the painting he had carried. To the little catch of breath that came as she lifted the painting from the wall. As she replaced it with another. And then, as she crouched again and wrapped the nude for removal.

By the time she stood, he was rabid with jealousy, wishing that he was one of the paintings—a length of canvas, the recipient of her soft, determined touch. "You may look," she said, quietly, and he turned, drawn to her voice—which should have been filled with relief but was, instead, filled with humor. Her back was to him, arms akimbo, and she stared at the prime location on the wall where—

He laughed.

Jewel. She'd hung Jewel in her place.

He moved up the steps to get a better look at the brilliant, utterly perfect punishment for Derek Hawkins. The dog in glorious repose on her red satin pillow, the light gleaming along her spindly grey legs, her bejeweled crown tilted just so on her head.

Lily turned to him, her grey eyes gleaming silver with laughter. "I think he should be more than pleased that we have credited him with such a beloved piece."

Alec nodded. "I think it exceedingly generous. To both Hawkins and the world at large. He will no doubt be supportive of the choice—what with his desire to bring masterworks to Society."

"For all to see," she said.

"We really have done the world a service."

"This particular birthday gift might make up for all the birthday gifts I have missed over the years." She grinned at him. "Thank you."

He moved toward her, unable to resist her in her reckless beauty, the excitement and anticipation of the evening—of their actions—summoning him to her like a hound on a leash. As he drew close, towering over her, her laughter faded, and she tilted her face up to him, even as he put his hands to her cheeks, running his thumbs over her high, perfect cheekbones.

"I love your laugh," he said, unable to keep the soft confession from her.

She pressed his bandaged palm to her cheek. "And I, yours. I wish I could make you laugh every day." He closed his eyes, his own wishes echoing hers. She threaded her free hand into his hair and added on a barely-there whisper, "I could try, Alec. You could let me try."

For a moment, he let himself imagine it, her hand wrapped in his, her teasing smile, her raucous laughter, her remarkable strength. He imagined standing beside her. Honoring her. Adoring her. *Kissing her.*

And then his lips were on hers, and it was not imaginary.

There was nothing wild about it, and that was likely why it threatened his sanity. It was soft and without urgency, as though they had a lifetime to explore each other. As though it had come on the heels of laughter in the garden at their home, children surrounding them, like a hint of a promise for the future—for a time when they had more time.

It was perfection.

And it slayed him, especially when she clenched her fingers, pulling his head back just enough to sigh, her lips parting on his name, a magnificent breath that could have sustained him for a lifetime. "Let me try," she whispered again, her lips against his, teasing and tempting.

Yes.

Please. Yes.

But it wasn't a viable answer. The answer was no.

And he was going to have to tell her everything to prove it to them both.

With a final, lingering caress, he pulled away and lifted the painting she'd carefully wrapped in cloth. Tucking it under his arm, he extended his hand to her, reveling in the way she came to him, in the ease with which she slid her hand—ungloved—into his, their palms pressing together as though it was the most natural thing in the word.

Without releasing her, he led her from the gallery in silence, pausing to allow her to collect her candle. Outside, he lifted her up into the curricle, sliding the painting against the block. When he took his place beside her and set the horses in motion, he could not resist taking her hand again, loving the feel of it, warm and strong in his grip.

Halfway to Berkeley Square, she laced her fingers through his, and he wondered how he would ever let her go. He didn't then—not when they pulled into the mews and he climbed down from the block, not when he lifted her down, not even when he collected the painting. He released her only when the boy came out of the stables to collect the curricle, not wanting to draw attention to the figure that had returned with him.

They entered the house through the back entrance, Angus and Hardy greeting them in the quiet, dark kitchens with wagging tails and lolling tongues, Hardy happier than he'd been in recent days to have them together.

Alec understood the dog's response. He, too, was happier when they were together. After they'd given the dogs proper attention, he took her hand again and led her to her chamber—the tiny room beneath the stairs that remained just as she'd left it, filled with books and papers and silk stockings draped over the bedpost.

He set the painting down, leaned it against her trunk as she watched, confusion in her eyes. "Here?"

He nodded. "It is the only place in the house—in all the houses—that is full of you."

"Too full of me," she said. "There is barely room for us both."

Precisely the point. Because once he had told her all his truths, she would not wish him there any longer. And he would have no choice but to leave, because there would be no room to stay.

She seemed to understand the reasoning without his speaking it aloud, her brow furrowing as she reached for his other hand, as though she could keep him if she held on very tightly.

But she could not keep him. Not when he—

"Tell me," she said softly. "Whatever it is—"

He took a deep breath, knowing what the truth would do. Hating what it would do. And then he released her hands and did as she asked.

He told her everything.

Chapter 21

ALL'S FAIR IN LOVE AND WARD

"I left Scotland when I was twelve."

Lily did not know what she expected him to say, but she did not expect that. And then, "I should say, I ran from Scotland when I was twelve."

She desperately wished to touch him, to make sure he understood that whatever he said to her, whatever had happened in his past, she was with him. But she had learned enough about Alec Stuart in the past ten days to know that touching him would do nothing but remind him of the burden he carried. And so, instead, she clasped her hands together and sat, perched on the edge of her little bed, as though it were perfectly normal to be here.

"My mother left when I was eight." He looked down at his hands, large and strong and perfect. "I remember very little of her, but I remember how my father responded to her leaving. He was angry and full of regret. And when she died mere months later—"

It took all Lily's strength not to push him.

He regrouped. "The messenger came and my father read the news in front of me. He showed no emotion. And he would not countenance mine."

Lily closed her eyes at the words. He'd been a child. And no matter who she was, or what kind of mother she had been, she'd been just that. His mother.

"Alec," she said, wanting him close. He started at the words and met her eyes. "You shall hit your head if you are not careful. Sit? Please?"

She would have done anything for him to sit with her. But, instead, he chose the little chair at the desk, pulling it out and dwarfing it with his size. With his glory. She drank him in, aware of their knees, inches apart in the little space. "Go on."

"All I remember of her was that she spoke of England. Of how it suited her. Of how she loved it. Of how much better it was than Scotland."

She smiled. "I suppose she could have come up with three things superior to those of Scotland."

One side of his mouth kicked up. "Likely more than three." He grew serious. "I missed her, oddly. It did not matter that she was not the best of mothers. And so, as she had, I, too, longed for England." He laughed, small and quiet. "I know that must be difficult to believe."

"Self-proclaimed reviler of all things English as you are."

"Not *all* things English. I find I have warmed to one thing." The words shot through her. *He meant her.* And still, he did not let them linger. "I wanted to go to England. To follow her. To see the country she loved. The place she longed for with such intensity that she left her child to find it."

He stopped, lost in the story, his hands coming together, the fingers of one hand finding the scar on the other. The one his father had given him. She watched those hands for a long moment, wishing she could soothe them. Finally, she said, "And?"

"My father wouldn't have it. He vowed to disown me. To cut me off if I left." Lily's heart began to pound. "And I did not care. I wrote to everyone I could find. Distant relatives—my father was vaguely English, as well, you'll not be surprised to discover, considering I was seventeenth in line for a dukedom."

She smiled. "I imagine he would have been equally thrilled to inherit."

"Likely less thrilled," Alec allowed.

"And so?" she asked.

"A distant relative sent a letter. Called in a chit. Whatever it was, it worked. And I had a spot at a school. My father did as he'd promised—told me I could never come home. But I did not care. My tuition was paid in full. A generous relative." He smiled, rubbing his scarred hand over the back of his neck and suddenly looking very much like the boy he must have been. "Perhaps one of the sixteen. That would be ironic."

Lily envisioned him, king of the schoolboys, handsome and tall and better at every sport there was. "I imagine you were terribly popular."

His head snapped up, his brown eyes meeting hers. "They hated me."

Impossible. "How is that—"

"I was tall like a reed, all bones and Scots braggadocio. And they were born of venerable titles and ancient lands and more money than I could ever imagine. I was an imposter, and they knew it. They judged it. And they beat the arrogance from me."

She felt the words like the blows they described. And still, she shook her head. "They were children. They could not have—"

"Children are the worst of all," he said. "At least adults judge quietly."

"And so?"

"For the first three years, I had no choice. I was poor, forced to clean floors and wash windows in the time I did not study in order to pay for the bits that tuition did not cover, and they could smell it on me, the need for funds." He smiled, lost in the memory, and she could see young Alec there, the little boy alone and desperate for companionship. It was something Lily understood keenly.

Something she would never wish upon another.

"King was the only boy who wasn't cruel."

The words made her wish the Marquess of Eversley were there, so she could thank him for his long-ago kindness. But she had a feeling the story did not end with the two boys as happy companions.

Alec was leaning forward, his elbows on his knees, his head bowed, as though he were in confession. And Lily's heart pounded with fear for the boy he once was.

She could not stop herself. "What happened after three years?"

He gave a little huff of humorless laughter. "I grew." Confusion flared as he shook his head and elaborated without looking at her. Telling the story to his hands, large and warm and clasped tightly together. "More than a foot in a few months. Taller than any of them. Broader, too." He paused, then looked up at her. "It hurts, did you know that? Growing."

She shook her head. "How?"

That smile again, the one that made her want to hold him until they were old. "Physically. You ache. Like your bones cannot keep up with themselves. But now that you ask, I suppose it hurts in every other way, as well—there's a keen sense that where you have been is no longer where you are. And certainly nothing like where you are going." He stopped, then whispered, "Nothing like where I was going."

"Alec—"

He continued as though she had not spoken, as though, if he stopped, he might not be able to start again. Lily pressed her lips together and willed herself to listen. "They went from judging me, from teasing me, from mocking my very existence . . . to loathing it. Because they could no longer dominate me. Now, I was the one who dominated. I was the—"

She reached for him then. She knew the words that were coming. Had heard them on his lips a dozen times. Her hands clasped his tightly. "Don't say it. I hate it."

He met her gaze then, and she saw how much he hated it, as well. "That's why I have to say it, Lily," he said softly. "Because it's apt. Because I am the Scottish Brute."

She shook her head. "You aren't, though. I've never met a man less so."

"I broke down a door the first time we met."

A thrill shot through her at the memory, at the sheer force of his will. "Because you wished to get to me. To protect me."

For a moment, she thought he would deny it. But instead, he looked deep into her eyes, all honesty. "I did wish to protect you."

"And you have."

He looked away, his gaze settling on the stockings draped over the end of her bed, left there before she fled days ago. "I haven't, though. I've never once been able to."

She threaded her fingers into his, aching for him. "You're wrong."

"You've had to do it all yourself."

"No," she said, forcing him to meet her gaze. "Don't you see? You've given me the power to do it. You've given me the strength for it. You wanted to give me freedom? Choice? You have. Again and again. Without you—"

He shook his head, stopping her. "I was a brute, Lily."

"You weren't," she said. "They hurt you. You fought back."

"Indeed, I fought. Like a damn demon. I wanted them all to know that I was not for their play any longer. That if they came for me, they would risk losing everything."

She nodded, proud of the boy he had been. Knowing that she should not wish pain upon a group of children, but grateful that he had found a way to win with them. "Good."

He laughed again, low and humorless, and shook his head. "You won't think so when you hear the rest."

He tried to pull his hands from hers, but she wasn't having it. She clutched him tighter. "No." He looked up, surprise and something much more unsettling in his eyes. Something like fear. She shook her head. "You are here. And I am with you."

She saw the words hit him. Saw the deep breath he took in their wake.

Saw him resolve to strike back.

"The boys could not fight me and win," he said quietly. "And so their sisters finished the work."

SHE WAS THE most beautiful thing he'd ever seen, and he could sit there until the end of time, watching her. But he loved her too much to keep her, and so he told her the truth, knowing it would drive her away. Knowing it would prove that he was not for her. That she could find another, infinitely better.

You could make her happy, if you decide to do so.

Stanhope's words were the worst kind of falsehood. The pretty one. The one that tempted enough to ruin a man, and the woman he had vowed to protect. And so, when her brow furrowed in her confusion at his words, he gave them to her again, clearer.

"My school was paid for, but everything else cost money. Food. Drink. Linens. The wash. And the work I had done for it—it was suddenly unavailable; no doubt the cooks and cleaners at the school had been paid well to forget I existed. I could not survive without funds." The memory of those months, desperate and hungry and angry, lying in the dark, wondering what would come next. "King would sneak me food and put my shirts in his laundry now and then, but I was proud and it felt like—"

"Friendship," she whispered. "It was friendship."

It had been. King had always watched for him. But—"It felt like charity."

She nodded, and he saw the understanding alongside the sadness in her eyes. Alongside the pity. "It is hard to believe we deserve better."

Did she not see? "Don't compare us. You were never—"

"What?"

The frustration in the question unlocked him. He stood, forcing her touch from him, unwilling to bear it. Being here, in Lily's little room, was the worst of it. Every word was wrapped in her, and even as he paced, he was barely able to move—his size reducing the space to a step. Two.

Finally, he stopped, thrusting his hands through his hair. He let out a long breath and said, "Peg came to me when I was fifteen." He felt her still at the name. At the words. "It was Michaelmas holiday."

"It is always Michaelmas," she said, softly, and he did not understand. She did not give him a chance to ask. "Go on."

"She was the older, very beautiful sister of another boy. I was hiding from the families who had come to visit, telling myself I required study."

"But you were simply trying to ignore what you did not have yourself."

He looked to her. "Yes."

She smiled, small and sad. "I know that well."

He ignored the comparison. Pressing forward. "She followed me. No one was in the library . . . and then she was."

Lily's gaze narrowed. "How old was she?"

"Old enough to have had a season. Old enough to know what marriage would be for her." He thought of Lord Rowley, debauched and rich as a king. "She came to me and offered me . . ."

"I can imagine."

"You can't, though." This was the bit he had to say aloud. It was the bit that would convince her that they were not for each other. That he would never be worthy of her. "When it was over, I did what was expected to be done. I told her I would seek out her father. That I would marry her."

Lily's attention was rapt, and he loathed it, the way she saw into him. The way she understood him more than anyone ever had. "She refused."

He turned away. Looked out the window, over the dark London rooftops. "She laughed." He paused, his own humorless laugh coming on the heels of the words. "Of course she laughed." He put a hand to his neck, wishing he were anywhere but there, reliving the sordid past. "She was daughter to a viscount. Set to marry an earl. And I was poor and untitled and Scottish. And a fucking fool."

"No," Lily whispered.

He did not turn. Could not. Instead, he spoke to the city beyond. "Not poor any longer." He was lost in the memory. "She paid me ten pounds. It was enough for a month of food."

"Alec." She was behind him now. She'd come off the bed, and he could hear the desperation in her voice. He had to turn to her. To look at her. To show her the truth.

And so he did, seeing the tears in her eyes, hating them. Loving them. What a life it would have been if it had been Lily who had found him in the library all those years ago. And instead . . .

"She sent her friends after that. Aristocratic girls who wished for an opportunity to play in the gutter. To quench their thirst for mud. To ride the Scottish Brute."

He saw the words strike her. Hated himself for doing it even as he forced himself to finish. "They paid my way through school. And I played the whore. I suppose I should be grateful that, as a man, it was never the shame it would have been if I were a woman. I was revered. They whispered my name like I was their favorite toy. A fleeting fancy. Peg used to say that I was the perfect first and the worst possible last."

"I do not care for her," Lily said.

Peg was not the point. He pointed to the trunk on the wall. Made the point again. "When I tell you that I am unworthy of you, it is not a game. It is not a falsehood. Those pristine white clothes, the hems you've embroidered with love and dedication, the damn boots with their little leather soles . . . they are for another man's children. The dress. It is for another man to strip from you. A man infinitely better than I."

He begged her to understand. "Don't you see, Lily? I am not the man you marry. I am the *other.* The beast you regret. But now—you can have another. A man you deserve." He pointed to the painting. "That *thing* . . . the painting they would have used to destroy you—it is no longer your albatross. And now, you may choose a different path, far from the scandal. Whatever one you wish. Don't you see? Choice is the only thing I can give to you."

She opened her mouth to answer and he slashed a hand through the air, begging her to be silent. "Do not. Do not choose me. How are you not able to see the truth? I will never be for you. I could not even—I arrived in London with a single task—to protect you. And I couldn't. I could not keep you from them. From the gossips. From Hawkins. Dear God, you were nearly run down on Rotten Row. And that's before I took advantage of you. I should never have touched you."

He waited for the agreement to come. For the judgment.

He waited for her to leave.

And when she moved, he braced himself to watch her go. Except she did not leave. Instead, she came to him. He stepped back, desperate to avoid her, too broken to touch her. But the room was too small and she was a superior opponent.

She did not touch him.

Worse. She reached up and removed the pins from her hair, letting it fall around her shoulders like auburn silk. His mouth went dry and his gaze narrowed before she said, "I've something to say now, if I might."

As though he could stop her, this warrior princess, dressed like a pickpocket about to thieve his damn heart.

"It is a great fallacy, you know. The idea that *first* is most meaningful. That *second* is. That any that follow are. That the circumstances of those early encounters somehow mean more than the one we choose forever. It is the lie the world tells us, but you have taught me to know better."

She looked to him, the love in her eyes stealing his breath. "I have heard your tale. And now it is time for you to hear mine. When I am old, Alec, and I look back on the faded memories of my life, shall I tell you of what I will think? It will not be him. And when I think on my scandal, I shall be grateful for it, as it will have brought me you. But I will not think much on it, because I will be too busy thinking of you. Of the days we sparred and the nights I wished we might. Of the hours I spent wrapped in your plaid. Wrapped in you. Of the way you look at me, as though there has never been another woman in the world."

And there hadn't been. Not for him. She put her hand to his chest, where his heart threatened to beat from it. "Of the way you have held me. And the way I have loved you.

"So tell me, Alec Stuart, self-made man turned duke, strong and kind and brilliant beyond measure." She was going to destroy him with her words and her gaze. "When you are old, of whom will you think?"

And suddenly, it was the only question that mattered.

"You," he said, reaching for her. Or perhaps she reached for him. It did not matter, as she was in his arms.

And it was true. He would remember her.

"Always you. Forever you."

Even if this night was all he had.

"None of it matters," she said, the words strong against his lips, "Not the past, not the women, not the scandal. None of it matters when we are here, and we have each other." And then she was kissing him, and he was lifting her in his arms and her legs were wrapped about him as though she belonged there.

And she did.

Without breaking the caress, he returned her to the bed, lowering her to sit on the edge of it, coming to his knees at the bedside. She released his lips and pulled away. "No," she said. "I do not wish you on your knees."

"You shall like it when I show you all the things I intend to do to you from this particular position," he said, his lips finding purchase at the soft, warm skin of her neck before opening and giving him access to the line of her jaw and the lobe of her ear. "Leave me here to worship you, love. And I shall make it worth your while."

He took her lips again, loving the little sigh she released, the way she went limp at the touch, as though he she could not resist him.

As though he was as irresistible as she was.

The caress lingered until her hands fell to his shoulders and she pushed him back, again, putting space between them. "I don't want you on your knees, Alec," she repeated. "I want you."

His hands threaded into her hair, "I am with you, love. I couldn't be anywhere else."

She shook her head. "You don't understand." She leaned back. "I don't want you with me. I want us with each other."

When he finally understood the words, they were like a blow to the side of the head. He sat back on his heels there, on the floor of her tiny room under the stairs, and watched her for a long moment, as color rose in her cheeks and she said, "Do you see, love? I want us together."

She wanted them equal.

Not a guardian and his ward.

Not a duke and a miss.

And not the other.

He swallowed, unable to find any other words but "I see."

She had once more ruined him.

She saw the truth in him and smiled, wide and gleeful, before she went to her knees on the bed, shucking the coat and shirt she'd worn as a disguise that evening—as though she'd removed men's clothing from her person a dozen times—revealing her high, lovely breasts, soft and perfect as peaches and fresh cream.

His mouth watered, and he raised his attention to her auburn hair, cascading around her shoulders. And then she reached for the fall of her trousers.

He watched her for a long moment his eyelids growing heavy with desire before he could not help himself. "Stop," he growled, his gaze riveted to those long, lovely fingers where they lingered at the fastening of her trousers.

She stopped.

He rubbed the back of one hand across his mouth, aching for her. Afraid of her.

"Are you going to do it?" she whispered.

With effort, he rose his gaze to her. "Do what?"

She smiled at him—not the coquettish smile he'd seen on women before in this particular situation, but something far more dangerous—she looked happy. Gleeful. Eager.

You could make her happy if you decide to do so.

He pushed the thought away. He didn't want Stanhope here. And then she replied, and the earl was the farthest thing from his mind. "Are you going to tell me what you want me to do?"

He was assaulted with images—with hundreds of ideas of what he'd like her to do for him. To him. To herself. He returned his attention to the trousers, a half-dozen buttons in the way of what he wanted. And he did as he was asked.

"Take them off."

Her smile turned utterly satisfied. "With pleasure."

The trousers were gone before he had time to appreciate her skill with the fastenings, shucked across the room, revealing bare legs that promised sin and salvation all at once. She lay back on the tiny bed, one long arm covering her breasts, and the other cutting a swath across her beautiful, rounded stomach, the hand covering the place he wanted more than anything in the world.

"Go on, Your Grace," she teased, knowing that with every breath, with every movement, with every stunning smile, she made him mad with desire. "What can I give you next?"

"Open for me." The command shocked him even as her lips fell open in a stunning, surprised inhale. For a moment, he thought he'd gone too far. And then she did, spreading her beautiful thighs wide on the narrow bed. She did not, however, move her hand.

He raised a brow. "Minx."

She smiled. "You will have to be more specific about your desires, Your Grace."

She was magnificent.

"I desire you," he said.

The smile widened, but the hand did not move. "Much more specific."

He unclasped the pin on his shoulder, holding his plaid in place, and her eyes widened, her fingers tightening so barely that one might not even notice. One might not notice, that was, if one were not fully riveted to the woman in question, hard and hot and desperate for her.

He was naked in seconds, his cock hard and aching for her.

Her eyes widened, and she—dammit—she licked her lips, her gaze trained on him. "More specific, even, than that."

"I desire that you move your hand, lass," he said, approaching the bed and staring down at her, reveling in her glorious nudity. "So that I might have a closer look at you."

She raised a brow. "Only a look? Is that some kind of Scottish half measure?"

His lips twitched at her teasing and he let his burr take over. "Once I've seen ye, lass, if yer lucky, I might touch ye, and once I've touched ye, ye can wager I'll be tastin'."

She laughed then, wild and free, like the Highlands. "I think, Mr. Stuart," she whispered, moving her hand, revealing a thatch of secret, stunning auburn hair, "that if ye'll be touchin' me, it'll be you who is lucky."

And she was right. He was the luckiest man alive. For the night.

To honor that good fortune, he laid himself down next to her, and proceeded to do all he'd promised, whispering to her the whole time, revealing her secrets in the little room as he made love to her. "So soft," he said at her ear, his lips lingering over the soft skin of her neck. "So wet." He licked, worrying the lobe between his teeth as he slipped a finger through her folds, drenched with her desire. "So warm," he said, that finger sliding deep and returning again and again, swirling and petting and stroking until she was writhing beneath him and he moved to her breast.

He licked, long and slow, before taking the straining tip between his lips and sucking, soft and rhythmic, in time to the movements of his hand, and she came off the bed like she was pulled on a string, one hand threading into his hair, the other finding his, strong and sure below, slowing it as she rode her climax to its glorious end.

And it was glorious. She turned pink with pleasure, with excess. And when she settled, sighing his name and opening those eyes to meet his, he could see that her thoughts had scrambled.

She dragged his mouth to hers once more, kissing him slow and deep and thorough.

And when she released him, he said, "I desire it again."

Her eyes went wide and her lips curved into a little O. He moved, this time spreading her thighs apart with his shoulders and lifting her to his mouth with one arm, turning her into his banquet. Loving her with his hands and mouth until she came apart in his arms, his name first a whisper and then a scream on her lips.

And when she'd collapsed once more in a heap on the bed, he pressed soft kisses to her stomach and whispered, "You, Lily. It will always be you. Everything. Always. You," until her breathing returned to normal and he growled, "Again," before pressing his mouth to the center of her, where she glistened, warm and pink and sated.

"Alec," she sighed, barely able to find the words. "Please. Love. What of you?"

As though there were anything in the word that would give him more pleasure than the taste of her on his lips and the sound of her in his ears and the feel of her in his hands.

One last time.

"Once more," he said. "Once more." And he made love to her with slow, slick strokes, gentle and slow, honoring her. Worshipping her. Pleasuring her until she found her rhythm once more, moving in time to his strokes, to her own desire. Until she came again, hard and long and magnificent, her hands in his hair and his name on her lips.

This.

This was what he would think of when he was old.

HE HAD DESTROYED her with pleasure.

She was in pieces on the bed, without ability to move or even think, when he came up to lie beside her, to hold her as she trembled, weak from his hands and mouth and words. She turned into him, his large, warm arms coming around her.

"You betrayed me," she said to his broad chest, rubbing her cheek across the crisp hair there, unable to summon the energy to say it with more conviction. "We were to be with each other."

"And we were."

She shook her head. "You did not take your pleasure."

He pressed a kiss to her forehead. "That was the most pleasurable experience of my life, love. Sleep." The words rumbled beneath her ear.

As though she could sleep with him there, with the hard length of him against her thigh like a promise. She was not going to sleep. Not until he had received his pleasure as openly and as thoroughly as she had.

Not until she had given it to him.

"No," she whispered, sending her hand over the planes of his chest, enjoying the way the muscles of his torso tightened beneath her touch, and he hissed his desire. "I've other plans."

"Lily," he spoke her name in the flickering candlelight, his hand coming to hers, halting it on its path, just as her fingers found the place where soft hair grew thicker. "You don't have to . . ."

She turned her face into the warmth of him, pressing a soft kiss to the skin on his chest. And another. And another, until his breath was coming harsher and she could feel the deep pulse of his heart beneath her lips. Only then did she slide her tongue out in a little circle, honoring him, adoring the way he drew tight like a bowstring at the touch.

She moved, her lips sliding down his body, over his torso, his free hand coming to her hair as he spoke her name low and dark and wonderful. She imagined he intended to stop her, but then she was licking over the planes of his stomach, breathing him in, and he was trembling at the touch, and—thank Heaven—forgot to stop her.

Not even when she moved her hand, sliding his away, clearing a path to the place she desperately wanted to reach. She leaned back, reveling in the size and strength of him—glorying in the fact that he was hers in that moment, as her mouth watered and her fingers itched to claim him.

And then ran her lips up the hard, straining length of him, breathing his name as he arched off the bed with a wicked curse, and she gloried in the power he had given her. The strength. The pride that this man was not only hers, but that she was about to give him all he desired.

She licked over the tip of him, the salt and sweet of him tempting her even as he groaned her name, his hands coming to her, fingers sliding into her hair—not pulling to or pushing away, but cradling her with near-unbearable gentleness.

"Once more," she whispered his words back to him, and the groan deepened, his fingers flexing against her as she parted her lips and took him slow and deep, adoring the feel of him. The steel of him. The desire that rioted through him.

And through her, as well, as he gasped his pleasure in a wicked, tempting echo of what she had experienced only minutes earlier.

She'd never in her life wanted anything more than Alec's pleasure, and that desire drove her further, licking and sucking and drawing him as deep as she could, playing with speed and sensation, finding the places that seemed to drive him wild and trying—desperately—to send him over the edge.

His hands tightened in her hair. "I can't . . . Lily . . . Please . . . If you don't . . . I won't be able to . . ." The words were a growl, deep and fierce. "*Lily.*"

"I don't want you to stop," she whispered to the pulsing, beautiful head of him. "I don't want you to hold back. I want you to give it to me. All of it. Let me revel in you."

He whispered her name, dark and sinful in the little room, and Lily thrummed with power. With passion. With her own desire as she sucked deeper, licked, found a rhythm that brought them both to the edge, a string of Gaelic on his lips as he gave himself up to her, to passion, and finally, finally, with her name on his lips, to release.

She stayed with him, adoring him as he basked in his pleasure before ultimately lifting her to lay with him, pulling her into his arms, running his hands over her naked skin, whispering long strings of his lovely, lyric language against her hair, interspersing the words with soft, lingering kisses until she shivered and he pulled a blanket over them both.

"That was—"

The words were barely there—a rumble beneath her ear as much as anything else—trailing off, his thought incomplete. She smiled, kissing his chest. "I agree."

"Lily," he whispered, those massive hands still moving, cloaking her in warmth and love and security. "My Lily."

She closed her eyes and sighed. "Yours."

His hands stilled at the word, just barely, just enough for her to shift at the change, and he began anew, long, languid glides that tempted her with comfort she had never before experienced.

"Sleep," he said, and there was something in the soft, rough word that sent a thread of unease whispering through her, but she was too exhausted to consider it. Too consumed with him to be able to think of a time he might not be with her. Touching her. A part of her.

His hands stroked over and over, until avoiding sleep became an impossibility. Lily closed her eyes and pressed closer to him with a final, soft plea. "Be here in the morning. We shall start anew." And then, from the edge of sleep, "Do not leave me. Be here."

Be mine.

Not two hours later, she woke in the darkness, cold and alone beneath the covers of her Berkeley Square bed. The curtains were open, but the London night beyond was dark as soot—the darkness that came when it was nearly dawn.

She sat up to light the candle on the bedside table, knowing even before the spark turned to flame what she would find.

He was gone.

Tears came, desperate and unavoidable as she looked around the room, this room that she'd chosen because she'd once been so lonely, and now fairly breathed with the memory of him. Of his touch. Of his kiss. Of his past and the way it destroyed him even as it made him the man he was.

He'd left her.

She threw her feet over the edge of the bed and Hardy sprang awake, a yelp of surprise waking Angus, who slept at the threshold of the room.

Hope slammed through her. The dogs were here. He had not left.

And still, the thread of certainty remained.

She set one hand to Hardy's big head, staring down into the dog's soulful eyes. "Where is he?"

Hardy sighed longingly, and Lily understood the pathetic sound better than any she'd heard in her life.

He had left. No doubt thinking she should be without him.

No doubt thinking she could be without him.

That was when she saw the letter. On the desk, propped up next to the still-covered painting, was an envelope in familiar ecru. He'd left her a note, drafted on her own paper. Propped on a pair of baby boots—the ones with red leather soles.

He had left her.

Dreading the truth, Lily reached for the envelope, her name in bold, black scrawl across the face.

Opened it.

> *The dowry is yours. The money due to you today, as well. And, of course, the painting, to do with what you wish.*
>
> *I am leaving you Angus and Hardy—they have loved you from the start, and will be able to protect you better than I ever could. Not that you need them. You have always been strong enough to keep yourself safe.*
>
> *You are the most glorious woman I have ever known, beautiful and passionate and powerful beyond measure, and no man will ever be worthy of you, especially not me. You asked me once for freedom, Lily, and though I have been a terrible guardian, today, I can give you that. Freedom to leave this place or stay in it. To be a queen of London and the world. To have the life you wanted. The life you*

dreamed of. The children, the marriage, the little feet that fit these silly red boots.

Whatever you choose.

Never doubt I will think of you, Lily. Then, and now.

Happy birthday, mo chridhe.

—Alec

The words swam with tears.

He'd left her.

Lillian Hargrove had been alone for the lion's share of her existence. Since the moment she'd lost her father, she had lived beneath the servants' stairs of a ducal mansion, between the glittering world of the aristocracy and the more ordinary common one. She'd learned to be alone here, in this room, in this house, living a quiet half life that lacked the promise of her dreams, and then a scandal that threatened even that.

And then Alec Stuart had broken down her door and vowed to protect her.

And her life had changed. And her dreams had changed. Now, they were of him alone. And he thought himself unworthy of them.

Her whole life, she'd been terrified of loneliness. Of living out her years with no one to share them with. And now, here, she knew the truth—that she'd trade a lifetime of the loneliness that had once so threatened her for a single day with Alec. Without hesitation.

For an intelligent man, the Duke of Warnick was a proper fool.

He'd left her. Like Endymion, choosing an eternity of dreams over a lifetime with the goddess he loved. There had been a time when Lily had thought she understood the choice. After all, dreams could feel terribly real.

But now—now that she had held him in her arms, laughed with him, loved him—dreams were nothing compared to the reality of him.

Her gaze settled on the painting, wrapped in cloth, leaning against the chest where she had once kept her dreams—dreams she'd thought destroyed by scandal.

Scandal that had brought him to her.

Scandal that he had taught her to bear, unashamed.

He could not leave her. Not when she needed him so much. Not when she loved him so well.

Not when he had so thoroughly become her dreams.

If he wanted her to put those little boots to use, he could damn well fill them himself.

Chapter 22

LILY LAID BARE!
MISS MUSE OR MISUSED?

All of London had chosen to attend the final morning of the Royal Exhibition, and why would they not? The legend of Derek Hawkins's masterwork had been broadcast throughout the city's rags, shouted by newsboys and whispered in ballrooms.

It was not the artwork London came to see, however; it was the scandal.

Lovely Lily, revealed.

"It's horrible, really, what he did," Alec heard at his elbow as he pressed through the crowd. "No girl deserves that." On the surface, the words were sympathetic, but they were injected with such salacious glee that he gritted his teeth.

"She should not have sat for it if she did not wish for it to be made public," came an utterly disdainful reply, and he realized that attending the exhibition might have been a poor idea, for he wanted to murder every person who spoke ill of Lily.

It was easy to throw stones at scandal when one's own tales were still secret.

He pushed himself through the throngs, into the exhibition hall.

"And there," a woman nearby said loudly enough to be heard, but softly enough to pretend it wasn't for his benefit. "The guardian."

"A terrible one, it seems," another said on a gleeful giggle. "And am I surprised? Look at the man. Clothed as a barbarian. There are ladies present. We can see his *knees*."

"And what lovely knees they are," the first replied, her words thick with innuendo.

It was not the most ladylike sentiment he'd ever heard expressed, considering these two were so angry at his mere presence, but Alec let the comment pass. He could not murder all the gossips in London, no matter how well he would like to. In less than an hour, he'd be high atop his curricle, going hell-for-leather up the Great North Road, headed home.

Not home.

He would never be home again. Not as long as Lily was elsewhere.

He cleared his throat at the thought. *Yes, home.* England had always been his ruin, and today was no different. Indeed, if the last ten days had done nothing else, they had shown him the truth of his father's curse.

It did not matter that he left the woman he loved.

Everyone I have ever loved has left.

She'd said the words to him at the start of all this, when he'd convinced her to stay. To face London. To marry another. When he'd convinced her that he'd save her. And he'd vowed to find her a man whom she could love. A man who would not soil her with his past, and who would give her everything she'd ever dreamed.

Yes. Alec had left her. But, to a better life. One that would let her open that damn trunk and use all the things inside, if she wished it. One that would give her a perfect, gentlemanly hero and a beloved family and a happily-ever-after that he—

He stopped.

That he would give everything to be a part of.

When he'd arrived in London ten days earlier, she'd asked him for freedom. For choice. And last night, he gave it to her.

The hall was packed wall to wall like a tin of fish, everyone straining to see the dais at the front of the long, massive room, and Alec had never been more grateful for his size. He did not have to strain. He was tall enough to see Hawkins's decimation play out from his place. And though he wished to push to the front and set his fist in the man's face, he knew better—he would watch the reveal of Jewel and leave amid the shock and awe that would ensue.

And he would go back to Scotland. In peace.

And forget this place.

Liar.

He shifted on his feet at the thought and crossed his arms.

"Do you think he's here to call Hawkins out?" a man said from nearby.

"For Hawkins's sake, I hope not. Look at the man."

"There's a reason they call him the Scottish Brute."

"Perhaps he *will* call him out." The last was spoken on a breath of anticipation.

Alec set his jaw. Duels were for hotheaded children. He had other plans for Hawkins. As he stood there, waiting for the pompous scoundrel to arrive, Hawkins was receiving notice that his membership to The Fallen Angel had been rescinded—Duncan West most certainly had friends in powerful places.

Similarly, an announcement would soon be made that several exceedingly wealthy aristocrats—the Duke of Warnick included—were funding a new theatrical venture. It would go head to head with the Hawkins Theater, and make it very difficult for him to find patrons of his own.

But this morning would be the worst of all Hawkins's punishments. It would strike him hard and fast, in his pompous, arrogant face. And so Alec was here to watch.

Because he might not be able to have Lily, but he could have this—her honor.

And then smug-faced Hawkins was taking the stage along with some other Englishman, and the crowd quieted, until the only sound was Alec's beating heart.

"As you know," the older man began, "the Royal Academy of Arts selects a single piece to be revealed on the final day of the annual exhibition—a piece that we believe is so indicative of the quality of British artistry that it moves directly from here to the entryway of the British Museum, and then tours the country. This year, the artist selected for this great honor is Derek Hawkins."

No mention of the fact that Hawkins destroyed a reputation in the balance.

No mention of the fact that Hawkins was an ass, either.

Hawkins preened beneath the rapt attention of the crowd, and it occurred to Alec that there was never in history a man who deserved what was coming to him more.

And then Hawkins began to talk. Something about genius. About his gift to the world. About his exceeding talent. And then he said, "I only wish the model were here, so you might all compare the two and know that my talent has turned brass into gold beyond value."

Paupering the man was not enough.

He deserved to die of something slow and painful.

"And so, adoring fans, I shall not keep you from it any longer!" He stepped back and, with a flourish, "I present, *Beauty Bestowed*!"

With the utterly arrogant title echoing through the exhibition hall, Alec actually found something to enjoy about that morning. Because when the curtain fell and Jewel was revealed, that smug smile would fall and Derek Hawkins would be ruined.

The curtain fell, and a dropped pin might have echoed thought the silent hall, thousands of people within so thoroughly captivated.

Not by Jewel.

By Lily.

She'd returned the painting. And it was a masterpiece.

She was draped across a settee in a dark room, light playing off her beautiful skin, the curves and peaks and valleys of her glorious body highlighted by skilled brushwork and color that seemed at once impossible and utterly perfect. But it was not her body that drew Alec's attention. It was her face, the way she looked directly at the viewer, without timidness or shame. Without hesitation. As though the moment depicted involved two people alone—Lily and the viewer.

It was a painting that lacked regret. And it was hers, more than it would ever be Hawkins's.

She'd returned the painting.

Of course she had. It was the act of a woman who would not be shamed. Who would not be made a scandal without her permission. And though it was stunning, the painting paled in comparison to the woman herself, magnificent and unparalleled.

He was struck deep with pride.

He would never let her go. Not after this. Not after seeing this act of supreme courage—one that would forever inspire him to match it. He wanted to spend his life by her side, attempting to be the man that this woman—this brave, strong, beautiful woman—deserved. He was too selfish to let another have her.

He wasn't going home to Scotland. He was going home to her.

And once he was through telling her precisely what he thought of her skulking about in the London night, he was going to win her back.

Because, if the reveal of this portrait meant anything, it meant this: his Lily was exceedingly unhappy with him for leaving her.

Which made perfect sense, of course, as it had been an act of supreme stupidity.

He would make it up to her. He would convince her to choose him, as well, and he was going to marry her, and spend the rest of his life making it up to her. With pleasure.

It was only then, transfixed by the stunning painting and the keen knowledge that it paled in comparison to the woman he loved, that he remembered his vow to Lily. The promise he'd made never to look at the painting.

She was right, of course. It was not for him.

Just as she was not for the world.

The instant the realization came, Alec turned his back to the portrait.

He was already moving—headed to her. To find her. To marry her. To love her.

He did not have far to go, as she was there. Waiting for him.

Wearing his plaid.

She stood tall and proud like a goddess, uncaring that they stood a stone's throw from her nude. But Lily did not look to the room. Not to the dais. Not anywhere but at him, and he wanted to roar his pleasure at her unwavering attention.

Twin desires shot through him—making him at once wish to lift her into his arms and carry her far from London's prying eyes and also to grab her to him and kiss her until neither of them could think. And then get her to the nearest vicar.

He didn't have a special license. Another reason to loathe England. Bollocks banns. He wasn't waiting for them.

It seemed they were headed to Scotland after all.

He resisted the urge to carry her, immediately, to his curricle, however, because of the other emotion flashing in her beautiful grey eyes.

Lily was furious.

"I don't want your money," she said, arms akimbo, as though they were anywhere but there, in front of all London. As though half a dozen heads hadn't turned their way the moment she'd spoken. "I don't want my money, either."

She was angry, but there was something else there. Something like fear.

He hated it—wanted to chase it away. He stepped toward her and she held up a hand, stopping him with nothing but a look, like a queen. "And I most definitely don't want your dogs."

He stepped closer at the lie—close enough that he could touch her. That he could catch her if she ran. "You've ruined my dogs with your table scraps and your scratches," he said, softly. "They belong to you, now, my love."

That's when the tears came. "Don't call me that." He ached at the words, instantly reaching for her. She took a step backward. "No. Don't you dare touch me. I've things to say."

"Then I'm afraid you're going to have to stop crying, because I don't think I can watch it without touching you."

She dashed an errant tear from her cheek. "I don't want any of your silly gifts. And I don't want you to send me off into the world to choose a different life. I choose *this* life."

He nodded.

"Don't you dare nod at me, as though you've known it the whole time." Her voice rose, and he heard the strength there. "He didn't destroy my dreams with that painting, Alec."

He knew that now. He hadn't understood before.

"That painting isn't me. It's oil and canvass. He can have it. *They* can have it," she said, waving one long arm to the assembly. "They can send it all over the world, and it will never be me. But you . . ." She paused, the words suddenly softer. His breath caught, hearing the accusation in her words. "You *did* destroy my dreams."

The words sent cold fear rioting through him.

He reached for her.

"No." He stopped, and she said, "You *left* me. How many times did you tell me my shame was misplaced? That I deserved more? Better? A man worthy of me? You were right. I do deserve all those things. More than *this*."

Fear became terror. Dear God. She was going to be rid of him.

The air had left the room. Alec struggled to breathe.

And then she said, "Do you know why I put it back? I put it back because it was wrong to deny it—this thing that is a part of me. That I refuse to be ashamed of. That you *taught me* not to be ashamed of. I am not ashamed of my passion. Of my choices. I am not ashamed of my past, Alec."

She should not be.

He opened her mouth to tell her so, but she added, "And I am certainly not ashamed of you."

Breath returned.

"You want me to choose? *Let me choose.*"

He nodded. Found his voice. "Do it. Choose."

She came to him, then, close enough for him to see the silver in her beautiful grey eyes. "I choose all of it, dammit. The scandal. The Scotland. The dogs. The drafty castle. I want Burns instead of Shakespeare. But most of all, I choose you, Alec Stuart, lummox, idiot, coward, cabbageheaded duke." She paused, then added, "Against my better judgment."

She chose him.

The glorious madwoman chose him. Somehow.

He was the luckiest bastard in Christendom.

He reached for her then, unable to resist the urge to touch her. Cradling her face in his palms, he tilted her face up to meet his, unable to find words in the flood of joy that coursed through him. "Lily."

Her hands came to rest on his. "You left me."

The words, soft and wounded, threatened to slay him. "Love—"

She shook her head. "Alone. Again. Only this time it was worse. This time, I knew what it was not to be alone. I knew what it was to love."

He did not know how to reply. And so he did the only thing he could think to do, not wanting to chase her away.

He released her and sank to his knees.

Her eyes went wide. "What are you—"

It was his turn to speak. "I thought I was saving you," he said quietly, staring up at her, adoring every inch of her, wanting her with a desperation that clawed at him—that he wondered if he would ever slake. "When I came here, I thought I was to protect you. To play the part of guardian. Of savior."

"I did not need a savior," she said.

"No, *mo chridhe*. You didn't. But I did. And it was you who did the saving. Lily . . . you have saved me."

She reached for him. "Alec—"

He bowed his head, aching for her touch. "I am yours, my love, body and soul. When I am old, I do not wish to think of you. I wish to *be* with you. I wish to love you."

"Stand up, my love," she said, her hands in his hair, and when he looked up, her tears were in earnest. "Please, Alec. Stand."

He did, coming to his full height, his hands returning to her face and tilting it up to him so he could see her reply, whispered so softly he could barely hear it. "You," she said. "You."

"Always," he replied. "Forever."

He kissed her then, long and deep, lifting her high in his arms until her arms were wrapped about his neck and he held her off the floor for the caress, which lasted at once for an eternity and a heartbeat. They separated only when they had both lost the ability to breathe, but Alec did not put her down, instead clutching her close and burying his face in the warm curve of her neck, breathing deep, willing his heart to slow.

She laughed and he lifted his head. "What is it?"

"We have an audience, it seems."

He shook his head. "No. They're too distracted by the painting." He growled. "How did you do it?"

She grinned. "Guess."

He groaned. "Sesily."

"I needed a boost," she said simply. "But—"

He cut her off. "The two of you, together. You are trouble. You realize I'm going to have to murder half of London, now, for having seen you nude?"

She tilted her head. "Perhaps not, though, considering no one is looking at the painting."

He turned to the room, massive and packed to the gills, come to see the legendary masterpiece of Derek Hawkins. Not one observer was turned to the front of the room, however. They all—to a person—had their backs to the painting.

Facing far more interesting gossip.

He raised a brow. "They still look at you. I don't care for it."

"At least this way I am clothed." She grinned. "Still a scandal, but clothed."

"Nonsense." He kissed her again, long and slow and deep, until the women around them gasped their shock. "Duchesses cannot be scandals."

"Not even if we try very hard?"

"Well," he replied, "if anyone can do it, my love, 'tis you."

"I shall require a partner."

"No doubt a grueling task, but one I see no way of avoiding," he teased.

She pressed her lips to his, soft and lingering. And then she said, "When can we marry?"

"We can be in Scotland in four days if we leave now."

She smiled, and he caught his breath. "Then I think it is time you take me home."

BEAUTY BESTOWED TRAVELED throughout Britain and across the Continent, making it as far east as St. Petersburg and as far west as New York City, exhibited in the greatest homes and museums in the world, lauded as a singular masterpiece, rivaling the *Mona Lisa*.

But *Beauty Bestowed* was different from other portraits. It was not a painting of a nameless muse. It was the portrait of Lillian Stuart, née Hargrove, twenty-first Duchess of Warnick, and the Scandal of 1834.

And whenever it was exhibited, wherever, her story was told. *Their* story was told. The story of Lovely Lily, and the duke who so adored her that he tossed her over his shoulder and carried her off to Scotland on the last morning of the Royal Art Exhibition, under the watchful, envious eye of all London.

It is no wonder that none can remember the name of the artist.

Epilogue

CITY CELEBRATES!
DEPARTED DUKE & DUCHESS DESCEND

Ten months later

The door to the sitting room between the master and mistress's chambers at 45 Berkeley Square flew open, ricocheting off the wall as the Duke of Warnick pulled his duchess inside.

"Alec," she whispered with a mix of glee and horror. "Someone will hear!"

"Don't care," he growled, closing the door behind them and pressing her against it. "You should be grateful I did not break it down to get you inside. Come here, wife."

Lily wrapped her arms around his neck, loving the feel of his hands on the bodice of her dress. Wishing the dress gone. "What's happened to you?"

"You danced with too many men tonight," he said against her lips. "They all wanted a look at the queen of the season. I didn't like it. Poncey Englishmen. Stanhope was the last straw."

She laughed at that. The Earl of Stanhope was the least threatening man in England now that he'd found himself a lovely young widow who was purported to be quite wealthy. Considering the way the Earl and Countess lingered together at the edge of the ballroom, seemingly unaware of their surroundings, Lily thought he'd made a very good match, indeed.

As had she.

She pulled back to look at her husband, moonlight streaking through their bedchamber. "You once wanted me married to one of those Englishmen."

"An error in judgment."

"Indeed," she said, and he kissed her, deep and thorough, pulling away only to run his lips over her jaw until she sighed her pleasure. "I needed that."

A low laugh rumbled from him. "Am I neglecting you, love?" His hands moved to her skirts, and Lily ached for his touch as the silk rose higher and higher. "It's only been a few hours, but I am happy to redouble my efforts."

"You do your very best, Your Grace," she said, gasping as his strong hands found the skin of her thighs above her stockings. "But sometimes, a woman surrounded by England needs a taste of Scotland."

He stilled at that, his head coming up, whisky-colored eyes finding hers in the darkness. "What did you say?"

She smiled. "I know we've only been here a week, but I miss home." In the ten months since they'd left London, Lily had made a home for herself at Dunworthy, learning the nuances of the estate's distillery, glorying in the warm, Scottish summer, wrapping herself in wool from the castle's sheep in the winter—when her husband was not keeping her warm, which was rare. She went back for another kiss before adding, "And you . . . you taste of it."

"You like it?" he asked, and the doubt in the question surprised her. It had been months since she'd heard it last, on late nights when it would creep into his thoughts and he would offer to bring her back to England if it would make her happy.

But England did not make her happy. Not the way he did.

She kissed him again, deliberately misunderstanding. "Yes, husband. I like the way you taste. A great deal."

Doubt was replaced with desire. "I meant Scotland, minx."

She matched his look. "Aye, *mo chridhe*. I like it very much."

He growled at the words in perfect Scottish brogue, and let out a long sigh of his own. "Well then, why in hell are we here?"

"Because you have a sister who begged for a season."

Cate had been thrilled to receive Lily at Dunworthy when they had returned from London, excited beyond measure to have a sister, just as Lily had been. The two became fast friends and, within weeks, Alec had agreed that Cate could have the season of which she'd dreamed.

It had not occurred to him that the season would require months in London. "Let's leave her here and go home."

"No. Did you see her tonight? Her happiness?"

"No," he lied. "Between the two of you, I spent the entirety of the evening wanting to beat off London's male population with a large stick." He kissed her again, deep and lovely. "Let's go home, lass. I want to make love to you in the mist."

She shivered at the words. "They have mist in London."

"Not Scottish mist."

Her laugh was replaced by a long groan when his hands moved again, sliding higher, toward the place where she wanted him quite desperately.

He cursed soft and wicked. "Duchess?"

"Mmm?"

"Why aren't you wearing underthings?"

She sighed. "For this precise reason."

"And you did not tell me so at the ball? Do you realize what I could have done with that information? We could have defiled several of the Eversley House sitting rooms."

"I intended it," she said, willing him higher. Aching for him to give her what she desired. "But I was waylaid." She stopped. "Between ensuring that Cate received the proper introductions and the Duke of Montcliff—"

"What about Montcliff?"

"I'm feeling quite proud of myself, honestly. The Duke of Montcliff added one hundred thousand pounds to the scholarship fund tonight."

Inspired by her own childhood and Alec's past, Lily had thrown herself into the work of ensuring that children who lacked funds or connection had the means to secure the futures they desired. The ones they deserved. She wished to give possibility to as many children as she could. And the stoic Duke of Montcliff's surprising donation had made that goal even more real this evening.

Her announcement garnered Alec's attention. "One hundred thousand? Honestly?"

She reached for him, her fingers feathering through the hair at his temple. "Remarkable, no? Think of the choices they'll make. Think of the freedom they'll have."

He bowed his head, leaning into her touch, before he took her in his arms once more. "You, my love, are remarkable."

She blushed at the praise, even as she basked in it. "Apparently he liked the idea of being in partnership with us. Did you know that we are society darlings? It's a disappointment, really. I had thought scandal had more stick."

"Mmmm. Disappointing indeed," he said, distracted again, turning her to face the door, working at the buttons down the back of her gown. "I am happy to scandalize you now, if you like."

"If you do not mind very much, Your Grace."

"Not at all," he teased at her ear. "I want a look at these missing undergarments." He began to work at the buttons. "Must there be so many of these?"

She laughed. "You need a button hook."

"I beg your pardon," he said with affront. "I need no such thing." His hands went to the top of the dress and Lily gasped as he gave the dress a mighty tug, sending buttons flying across the room.

"You ruined my dress." She gasped, not caring in the slightest.

"I shall buy you a dozen more," he said as the dress fell in a pool of silk at their feet. "It was worth it. Turn around."

She did, proud and fearless, eager for his gaze. For his touch. For him.

"You are glorious."

She smiled, heat coming high on her cheeks. "I've something for you."

He raised a brow. "I see that."

The smile became a grin. "Something else." She took his hand then, leading him to the entrance to the duchess's bedchamber, which served as a wardrobe and private office rather than sleeping quarters, which was best, as the bed was currently occupied by dogs.

Two massive grey tails thumped at their appearance, and Alec went to greet the hounds as Lily crossed to the little desk in the corner of the room.

She lit a candle, revealing the box she had left for just this moment. Lifting the parcel and turning back to face her husband, she said, "I had a conversation earlier this week with Bernard."

"Love, I have to say, your invoking the name of our solicitor standing in the nude, candlelight flickering across your stunning skin, is not precisely how I wished the evening to proceed."

"It turns out, husband, that tomorrow is your birthday."

He quickly calculated the date. "It is, as a matter of fact."

"And we shall have a serious conversation about you keeping such information from me, I assure you. As I intend to do with your sister. I shouldn't need a solicitor to apprise me of such a thing. But thank goodness for Bernard."

"Yes. I've always found him a great asset." She laughed at the dry words, and he came closer, pointing to the box. "Is that my present?"

"It is, as a matter of fact."

"May I have it?"

"Do you deserve it?" she teased. He did, of course. She'd never known a man so deserving.

His gaze darkened. "Only tell me what I might do to earn it, my love, and I shall do it with pleasure."

The words sent a thrum of desire through her as she imagined all the things he might do for her. To her. The things she might do in return. Her breath quickened, and he drew nearer still, his fingers coming to the box, removing it from her hands as he said, soft and low and liquid, "I do not require a present. I only require you."

She shook her head to clear it of her own desire. "No," she said. "Open it."

He did, sliding the top from the small, square parcel and peered inside. Lily was riveted to his handsome face, made even more beautiful in the flickering golden candlelight, his perfect, tempting lips already curving in anticipation.

And then anticipation was gone, replaced with confusion.

And then surprise.

And then joy, as he reached into the box and extracted the pair of little white boots, complete with red leather soles.

Joy turned to adoration when he looked at her. "Your boots."

Lily smiled. "No longer mine."

Alec was on his knees, then, pulling her to him, pressing kisses across the soft, bare skin of her stomach, whispering in Gaelic to the child who grew within. "You have given me so much," he said, finally, to Lily. "And now . . ."

Lily's hands came to his head, reveling in her proud, strong Scot—the man who had given her everything she had ever dreamed. Holding him. Loving him.

They stayed like that for a long time, until the Duke of Warnick stood, lifted his duchess into his arms, carried her to their very sturdy bed, and loved her, quite thoroughly, in return.

Author's Note

The inspiration for this and all Scandal & Scoundrel books is modern celebrity gossip, something that readers who—like me—have a secret love for *US Weekly*, *TMZ*, and *Tatler* will notice right away. While *Scandal & Scoundrel* is my creation, scandal sheets are not new. Nude paintings seem innocuous enough now, but one need only think of hacked cell phones and secret tapes from recent years to see that the more the world changes, the more it stays the same. I am indebted to the inspiring women who have stood tall in the face of reveals like Lily's in recent years.

The *Scandal & Scoundrel* series could not be written without the vast, fascinating collections of the New York Public Library and the British Library—the gossip columns of newspapers long defunct remain in their archives. For this book, I am also grateful for the archives of the Royal Academy of Arts, now in its 248th year—which continues to exhibit contemporary British art to the public at large during its annual summer exhibition. It should be said that, while Exhibition-related people and paintings in the book are historically correct, the idea of a final, touring piece to be revealed on the last day of the exhibition is all mine.

As with all my books, this one would be a pale version of itself without Carrie Feron (who is always right), Nicole Fischer, Leora

Bernstein, and the outstanding team at Avon Books, including Liate Stehlik, Shawn Nicholls, Pam Jaffee, Caroline Perny, Tobly McSmith, Carla Parker, Brian Grogan, Frank Albanese, Eileen DeWald, and Eleanor Mikucki. Special shout-out to Lucia Macro for wonderful conversations about all the best bits of romance. And, of course, many thanks to the remarkable Steve Axelrod.

Thanks to Lily Everett for extensive celebrity "research," to Carrie Ryan and Sophie Jordan for always answering the phone, to my sister Chiara for an early read, and to Ally Carter for a late one.

To Eric, thank you for being the best of men. To V, may you always face scandal with strength, and be better for it. And to my amazing readers, thank you for always taking the journey with me—nothing without you.

As *A Scot in the Dark* goes to the printer, I'm hard at work on book three in the Scandal & Scoundrel series—the story of Sesily's disappeared sister, Seraphina, and the duke she did not win. Join me (and the rest of the motley Scandal & Scoundrel crew!) in 2017 for *The Day of the Duchess*!